To my wonderful son, Henrik; and his wife, Martine, in Hong Kong.

Kirsten Refsing is a professor emerita in Japanese Studies and has published many academic works about the languages of Japan and about British missionaries in Japan from 1860 to 1900.

This is her second novel. She lives in Copenhagen and has four children and seven grandchildren.

Kirsten Refsing

CHANGES IN THE SHADOWS

AUSTIN MACAULEY PUBLISHERS™

LONDON • CAMBRIDGE • NEW YORK • SHARJAH

A CIP catalogue record for this title is available from the British Library.

ISBN 9781528919852 (Paperback)
ISBN 9781528962865 (ePub e-book)

www.austinmacauley.com

First Published (2020)
Austin Macauley Publishers Ltd
25 Canada Square
Canary Wharf
London
E14 5LQ

Part One
Childhood

Prologue

At the age of ninety-two, Miss Eva Hope Maundrell was getting rather forgetful of many things. She had lived in the nursing home in Caversham for seven years. She could not always remember the names of the young staff members or her fellow pensioners. She did not really care to try to remember anything much from one day to another anymore. Instead, she spent her time reliving her memories from her childhood and youth in her head. She was going to die soon, she knew, but that did not worry her. In fact, she felt that she would like to die sooner rather than later. She felt that she had finished with her life now and wanted to know whether there really—contrary to her belief—was an afterlife, as the church claimed.

She had been born in 1887 in Nagasaki in Japan, where her father had been an Anglican missionary. He had been a rather old and grumpy man when she was a child and he had died when she was nine. She had moved to England with him and her siblings three years before his death in 1896, and she only remembered bits and pieces of her early childhood. She had been cared for by Sarah whom she had believed for a long time was her mother, until one day when she was ten years old. Sarah had come to her and explained that her real mummy had gone to heaven when Hope was only a few weeks old and that Sarah was just her big sister. She had read a letter which her real mother had written to her shortly before she died. She still had the letter, and now she reread it in her mind for the thousandth time:

My dearest Hope,

When you are old enough to read this, you will never really have known your mother, so I want you to have this letter to remember me by. I gave birth to you, my last child, but my body was not strong enough to be there for you when you grew up. I was called home to the loving Lord in heaven, but I will always watch over you from above. You will grow up to be a fine young woman, I know. Your father and your sister Sarah will give you the love and guidance you need to grow. Goodbye and much love from your mother, Eliza.

Hope knew its contents by heart, but she had kept the letter all this time because her mother had written it herself, and the old letter was the only tangible evidence that she had ever had a mother named Eliza.

School

Hope was six years old when her father and Sarah took what was left of their family back to England for her father's retirement. Besides Sarah and her father, she had also lived with her sister Eleanor, who was four years older than her, and her brother Arthur, a year younger than Eleanor. Besides, as she had learned then, she had several older sisters and brothers in England, where they had been in boarding schools. Over the first six months, she had got to meet all of them, four big brothers, all grown-ups, and three big sisters from fourteen to eighteen years old.

Hope had only vague memories of her life in Japan. She remembered that her father had remarried when she was four years old. Alice had come into their life, first as a lay helper in the mission and later as their father's wife. Alice was an orphan, adopted by her grandparents and brought up in Brighton. When her grandparents had both died in 1889, she was all alone in the world, but through the good offices of friends Alice had come into contact with Mrs Goodall, who wanted her to come to Japan to work with her in taking care of the Japanese children in her school. Here, Hope's father had got acquainted with Alice, and since he felt that he needed to marry for his young children's sake, they got married in 1891. However, Alice was not strong, and Hope remembered her mostly as a shadowy figure who had to lie down several times during the day because of headaches and exhaustion from coughing. In February 1892, Alice had passed away, only twenty-nine years old.

Hope remembered a few other things from Japan. When she was two years old, there had been a large earthquake in Kumamoto, which was also felt in Nagasaki. Hope thought that she remembered the sudden feeling of the ground shaking under her feet, and Sarah had told her afterwards that she had cried and been rather upset for days after that. Then there had been another earthquake two years later, a much stronger one, but far away in Nagoya. This was when she had learned the word 'earthquake'. She even remembered the Japanese word for it, *jishin*, but after they had moved to England, it no longer held the same fear for her. She had other memories that she thought might be from Japan, but they were less clear now, partly removed by the passing of time, partly by what she had later read about the country.

When they had come to England, they had moved to her father's old hometown, the village of Calne in Wiltshire, where they had bought a small house on Curzon Street close to the centre of town and the river Marden. It was soon decided that Arthur and Hope should be enrolled in the local school together with Eleanor. Since 1881, the Gladstone government had made elementary schooling compulsive, so this was no longer a choice. The Maundrell's had relatively little money, so they sent the three youngest children to a local school set up in Calne under the British and Foreign Society. The school was run by an elected school board and financed by charity and small fees from those students who were able to pay them. It was a mixed school for boys and girls, and it was non-denominational. The Christian religion was taught without reference to any particular sect. Teachers were required to attend a place of worship every Sunday, but they were free to choose where.

When Hope was nine years old, her father had died suddenly from a heart attack. Sarah said that his heart had broken when he had lost his wife nine years before, and it had never healed completely. They were allowed to inherit the house, and their older brothers chipped in to pay for their expenses. Eleanor, who was now thirteen years old and had left school, helped Sarah earn a little money by washing and sewing for other people.

***

The school was in a small house in Church Street next to the church, and it had started out with thirty-eight students in 1868. The schoolmaster was John Edward Wood. The number of pupils had increased rapidly, and when Arthur and Hope entered in 1894, there were about one hundred and fifty of them. They were taught reading, writing, spelling, arithmetic, grammar and scripture. Also, the children were kept in physical form by marching and by exercising indoors on cold or wet days. Ladies from the town came now and again to inspect the girls' needlework. A great deal of time was spent on teaching the children a variety of songs and how the musical notes should sound.

Their work was graded, and the headmaster gave prizes to those who had achieved the highest marks. But some of the children were required to help at home, and their attendance was low at times. The Rev. Wheeler presented the children with magic lantern shows every winter when the ground was covered in heavy snow. In spring and summer, there were occasional outings to tell the pupils about the nature which surrounded them. There were also 'object lessons' in which the children would learn about minerals, animals and birds, and about ethics and good behaviour. Arthur left the school when he was twelve to serve at one of the farms in the neighbourhood, while Hope stayed with Sarah and Eleanor in the house in Curzon Street.

***

In 1897, when sixty years had passed since her coronation, the country celebrated Queen Victoria's diamond jubilee. Hope was ten years old, and the school closed for three days for the celebrations. Sarah and Eleanor took Hope along to London to see the parades, but first, they went to Reigate in Surrey where their oldest brother Henry had recently started in St David's School as an assistant teacher. He had promised to accompany them to London. They all set out for London on the train and arrived at Victoria Station in the early evening. Well in advance, Henry had used the school's telephone to book some relatively cheap rooms in a guesthouse close to Victoria Station, only a walking distance from the station. The crowds, the noise and the smells in the London streets overwhelmed Sarah and Eleanor. Hope was amazed and a little frightened. She had never seen so many people in one place before, so she clung to Sarah's hand as they walked. Their rooms at the guesthouse turned out to be two small rooms at the top of a narrow house, but they were clean, and the widow who received them was kind and welcoming. She would serve them breakfast downstairs every morning from seven to eight, but the rest of the meals would be their own responsibility.

They went to buy some supper nearby and strolled around Belgravia for some time. On Grosvenor Place, they passed behind the garden of Buckingham Palace where the preparations for the next day were in full swing. When it was getting dark, they walked back to the hotel and went to bed.

In 1897, Great Britain was the most powerful country in the world. More than a quarter of the population on Earth was under its dominion. Queen Victoria ruled over it all as the only sovereign holding the throne for so many years. She had been the queen even before Hope's father had been born, all through her mother's life, and there she was, still the Queen of Britain and the Empress of India. Indeed, she could say that the sun never set on the British Empire. Only a large earthquake in Calcutta on June 12 put a slight damper on the preparations for the jubilee.

The colonial secretary, Joseph Chamberlain, had proposed that the diamond jubilee should also be celebrated as a festival of the British Empire, and so it was. All the heads and representatives of the countries in the British Empire were invited to take part in the celebrations.

On the twenty-first of June, the otherwise grey and drab London had turned very colourful. The Union Jack was draped from balconies on all the main streets, festoons of flowers were hung, and coloured ribbons in blue, red and white were also hung from windows and roofs as well as decorating people's clothes. Everywhere, crowds of boisterous and laughing people thronged and cheered.

Thousands of people turned out to watch the royal procession to St Paul's Church. Henry and his sisters had come early and found standing places along the route. The day was overcast, but that kept very few people back, and the sidewalks were very crowded. There were vendors trying to sell souvenir jubilee flags, mugs and programs. Henry bought a program for himself and told his sisters what they could expect and when. To keep people in place, there were soldiers with bayonets forming a wall of bodies to hold people back. Queen Victoria telegraphed a message of thanks to the whole of her empire, and a cannon was fired to signal that the procession was ready to leave the palace. Finally, the seventeen-carriage convoy drove out of the gates of Buckingham Palace and began the parade. At this time, the clouds had dispersed, and the sun's rays began to warm the air.

The queen rode in an open carriage drawn by eight cream-coloured horses. The queen herself was dressed in black as she had been since Prince Albert had died thirty-six years earlier. In contrast, the colonial forces, which represented all the nations under the empire, wore their most colourful uniforms. The crowds cheered and here and there small groups were singing 'God Save the Queen'.

The queen herself suffered from arthritis and found it too hard to climb the cathedral's stairs, so the service was held by the Archbishop of Canterbury outside at the foot of the west steps. The queen remained in her carriage, and after the service, she continued her circuit through London before she returned to Buckingham Palace.

When evening came, there were bonfires on the hills all through Britain, and the cheering and singing went on through most of the night. Free meals for the poor were served in the streets of London and Manchester. The pubs were kept open till 2:30 am and served free ale and tobacco because of the celebration. Long before that, however, Henry and his sisters had found their way back to the guesthouse and into their beds. Hope was excited and found it hard to sleep. When she came down for breakfast the next morning, she chattered about all the things she had seen and heard the day before.

After breakfast, they packed their things and Henry took them to the train station and helped them on the return train. He was staying in London till evening, because he had a few errands to take care of before he returned to his school. Sarah, Eleanor and Hope went back to Calne and couldn't stop talking about the latest fashions they had seen and about what the fat old queen had looked like in her carriage.

***

After the jubilee, Hope went back to school and duly did her schoolwork and played with her friends. She did well in all her subjects and when she reluctantly left the school in 1899, she had to find some kind of employment. She would have wanted to study more, but their financial circumstances would not allow that. She would have to go into domestic service, and her sisters started to look for an opening for her. In the meantime, she stayed with Sarah and Eleanor and practised cooking, cleaning, sewing and other domestic tasks.

Domestic Service

After a little over a year, there was an opening for her from April 1st with a family in Manchester, where she would have to look after three children and to help the maid and cook in between. The children were two, four and ten years old—a boy and two small girls. The boy would be away at boarding school most of the time.

Sarah was a little worried that Hope would be moving so far away, but the family that would employ her was a missionary family, back in England on a long furlough. She could stay with them for almost two years until they had to go back to Africa, and after that time, she would have a good chance of finding a new employer in Manchester with a reference from them. The missionary family Hope had been born and raised in seemed to her new employer to be a guarantee that she would have some understanding of their children's difficulties in adapting to a new lifestyle in England. Sarah also gave her permission because of the family's missionary background, which might ensure that they were nice people like her own father and mother had been. She hoped that they would see Hope as a member of their family, like her parents had looked upon Chiyo, their Japanese maid, who had stayed with them all through Sarah's childhood.

***

The new year of the new century had begun on a Monday, and Hope became busy, getting ready for the move to Manchester. Sarah would go with her and stay the last few days of March in the city with Hope. The old queen had died at the age of eighty-one in January and been succeeded by her elderly playboy son, Edward VII, and his Danish queen, Alexandra.

The train ride to Manchester would take most of the day, and Sarah and Hope would arrive in the late afternoon. They would find a guesthouse to stay in, and two days later, Sarah would accompany Hope to the family's house and meet the people her little sister would be working for. Manchester was a large and dirty industrial city with a growing population, which had by then reached almost 700,000. It was the third-largest city in the United Kingdom after Glasgow and London. The main reason for its rapid growth had been the cotton factories, where even children were employed. These factories had to be built and maintained, and the growing population needed a variety of services, which provided new opportunities for work. For some, it meant better wages and more freedom, but for others, it meant squalor and abject poverty. The city's infrastructure was slowly beginning to catch up so that clean water and sewage systems were improving citizen's lives, at least for the higher and middle classes. The streets were bustling with pedestrians, horse-drawn wagons, trams and an occasional motorcar.

Many Irish people had moved to Manchester to find work. They were actively fighting for home rule, and besides them, unions and other organisations were beginning to fight for better working and living conditions. Manchester had become a hotbed of radical movements, among them the Manchester Women's Suffrage Committee. They were working with the Independent Labour Party, which was also working to extend the franchise for working men. As several bills to introduce women's rights were introduced in Parliament and defeated, the women's movement was growing increasingly impatient.

Sarah and Hope saw many posters around the city as they walked around to see the sights.

"Sarah, what do you think about women's vote?" asked Hope as they were sitting down for a rest on a bench in Victoria Park.

"Well," Sarah began, "I do not really know what to think. When I think of our mother's life, I think that she bore child after child, and in the end, it killed her at too early an age. I, therefore, think the liberals are right when they say that birth control is necessary for women's health and to limit the awful poverty that blights so many families. But I do not think many men care about these problems. So, I guess I am in favour of more women in positions where they can speak for the rights of women and children. I hope they will succeed, but it may take a very long time."

"I think I would like to know more about such matters, and I hope that moving to Manchester may give me a chance to educate myself on social and political topics, now that I live in such an interesting city. I would like to hear Mrs Pankhurst and others like her speak," Hope said excitedly.

"Be careful in what you say and do," said Sarah. "There are many who think such thoughts are sinful and unnatural, and they might react very harshly if they hear you talking about it."

Hope nodded her assent and promised Sarah that she would be very discreet and do everything that was expected of her as well as she could.

***

The following morning, they walked to the house near Liverpool Road and met the Rev. White and Mrs White for the first time. John White was attached to St Matthews Church, but he spent much of his time travelling to different parishes to raise money for his mission in Africa. Mrs White was a tall, gaunt figure dressed in black, but she had a kind face as she welcomed them into the drawing room. The maid served them tea while the mistress asked Sarah and Hope about their background. Sarah replied politely to all her questions, and in the end, Mrs White asked Hope about her plans for the future. Hesitantly, Hope replied that she would be in domestic service for now, but eventually, she might want to train as a nurse when she was older.

"Do you not wish to find a husband and be married?" Mrs White asked.

"I do not think so," said Hope. "Maybe at some time, but first, I want to train for a professional skill, so I can help people who need me."

Mrs White looked a little surprised hearing such words from a girl who was barely fourteen years old.

"Maybe you eventually want to go somewhere overseas? God in heaven knows that there are many sick people in need of good and dedicated nurses in Africa."

"I think there are many here in England as well," said Hope, "but it is too early for me to have any specific plans."

While they were talking, two small pretty girls with curly blond hair had entered the room, and the youngest had climbed to her mother's knees.

"This is Hope who will look after you while we are in England," said Mrs White. And to Hope she said, pointing to the girls, "This is Fanny, and here is her little sister, Polly. Say hello to Hope now!"

Both girls said a cautious "Hello", and Hope got down to sit on her knees on the floor and said: "Hello, Fanny and hello, Polly. Let us be friends."

"Will you play with us?" asked Fanny.

"Yes, I will," said Hope. "Will you show me your rooms?"

Fanny nodded, and Hope got up from her kneeling position and asked Mrs White if it would be OK for her to go with the children. Fanny grabbed her hand and looked to her mother for permission. When Mrs White nodded, Fanny held out her hand to Polly and said: "You come, too, Polly."

***

Polly climbed down from her mother's knee and took Fanny's hand, and all three girls left the room. At the stairs, Hope offered to carry Polly, and Polly let herself be carried up the stairway.

"Where now?" asked Hope, and the girls pointed to a door on the right.

"This is our playroom," Fanny said, "and we sleep in another room."

Hope opened the door to a large room, where the winter sun streamed in through the windows. "How nice," Hope said. "Will you show me your favourite toys now?"

Meanwhile, in the drawing room, Sarah told Mrs White about their childhood in Japan and her mother's death shortly after Hope was born. She also told her that their father had died in November five years ago, so that Sarah and her brother, Henry, were now helping their younger siblings along in the world as best they could but on very little money. Mrs White nodded thoughtfully at this. "The missionary's life is hard," she said, "but sometimes his family's life can be even harder, especially if they are left to fend for themselves when he is no longer there to be the breadwinner."

They discussed the terms of Hope's employment. She would be paid 12 shillings per month for the duration of the time she was to be employed, and she would have one day off per month. In return, she would look after the children, wash and mend their clothes, play with them and clean their room and tidy up after them. When the children were napping, and in the evenings, she was expected to help with cleaning the dishes and in general, do what she was asked. Mrs White was often out in the evenings, so she would expect Hope to be on hand to bathe the children and put them to bed. Hope would share a room with the other girl who was employed as a maid of all work, Annie.

***

Sarah called for Hope and asked her to come down, and while Fanny and Polly talked to their mother and Sarah, Annie was asked to show Hope to their room in the attic, which they were going to share. They went up the back stairs to the attic where there was one small room with two beds and a dresser. The room had a window, which looked out on the back garden. There was no fireplace, and when Hope asked how they would keep warm in the winter, Annie just shrugged and said, "We make ourselves a hot water bottle and sleep with our overcoats on, but we will not stay in here much, anyway. We shall be working around the house and sometimes in the kitchen. It is only for a couple of years, anyway."

"What will you do afterwards, Annie?" Hope asked.

"I think I shall try to find work in a factory or perhaps in a shop," Annie answered. "What about you?"

Hope hesitated, but then she blurted out that she would like to train to be a professional nurse if she could get admitted to one of the nursing schools when she had reached the required age of eighteen. Until then, she wanted to do whatever work she could get.

They returned to the hall where Sarah was waiting to say goodbye. Hope gave her sister a big hug and said, "Do not worry about me, Sarah. I shall be fine here." She did her best not to show any tears, but Sarah was sure her little sister's eyes were wet.

***

Hope settled into the White family's house and spent a lot of her time with the children. Sometimes she helped Annie clean and polish the silverware, and when there was extra work to be done because of guests coming to the house, but most of her time was spent with the children and the work around them. She got along very well with Annie, who was almost fifteen years old, and she grew to love the two little girls. When their brother was home from school, she tried to draw him into games with his sisters, but he was a rather sullen boy who preferred to be on his own. Hope tidied up after him and washed his clothes, but he completely ignored her and only spoke to her if he had to. Hope was almost relieved when he left for school again.

When she had been with the White family for a year and eight months, the time had come when she would have to look for new employment. Mrs White had a friend on the hospital committee for the Manchester Southern Hospital for Diseases of Women and Children, so she asked Hope if she should speak to her friend about Hope. "Oh yes, please," said Hope.

Training to Be a Nurse

And so it happened that after she had said fond goodbyes to the White family, who were setting out on their long voyage to Africa, she found herself in the Manchester Southern Hospital for Diseases of Women and Children as a skivvy. If she did well and showed character, they might take her on as a nurse probationer and then for the three-year's training as a registered nurse after she had reached the age of eighteen. Hope was now almost sixteen years old, and in the beginning, she was only asked to scrub floors and rinse bedpans. But she paid attention to what was going on around her, and she occasionally talked to the patients when there were no nurses around to tell her to hurry up and finish her work. On her days off, she went to the library and read books by Florence Nightingale and others about how best to nurse sick patients. Early on, she understood the importance of hygiene, and it made her less resentful of the hard and repetitive work that was required of her. It also made her very careful about doing her very best, and occasionally, her work would be praised by the matron in passing. She longed for the day when she could start training.

Hope soon found out that she had a special gift to soothe frightened children in pain, and after a while, she was permitted to stay with recalcitrant child patients when they were going to have any painful procedure done. She would hold their hand and whisper into their ear, distracting them from whatever was going on around them. She was heartbroken when one of her small friends passed away from a disease that could not be cured.

She also cleaned in the women's ward where she felt slightly intimidated by some of the recovering women and their frank talk about their ailments or about their families. When she had worked at the hospital for two years, she got taken on as a nurse practitioner in the maternity and the children's wards. In the maternity wards, the talk among the women was also sometimes rough, but she loved the way the new mothers talked about their babies. The relief and happiness on their faces when both mother and baby had turned out to be healthy and unscathed after their traumatic birth experience was so sweet. Hope felt a strong longing for her own mother who had died after giving birth to her.

Hope liked the life in the hospital and its unpredictability, but she also despaired when patients died and the doctors could do nothing. It was even worse when the patient was a dying child. In time, their desperate helplessness got to her, and she began to have difficulty sleeping at night. She developed black rings around her eyes and lost weight, and one day, when she had just keeled over from exhaustion, her supervisor finally asked one of the doctors to take a look at her. The doctor diagnosed her with nervous exhaustion and advised her to take leave and go back to stay with her family and regain her strength.

Student Teacher and Suffragette

When Hope returned to Calne in 1907, she was warmly welcomed by Sarah and Eleanor, who nursed her and made sure she got lots of rest and fresh air every day. They had taken in a boarder since Hope had gone to Manchester, and Eleanor had begun to sew for some of the wealthier women in town. They brought her pictures of what they wanted made, and Eleanor tried to make as good a copy as she could. She had turned out to have a real talent for fashion, and since her sewing was also of very good quality, she had a small but reasonably stable income from that. Their boarder was a young woman from Guernsey who was working as a teacher in St Mary's School, where she taught history and English at the elementary level. Her name was Mary, and she was 24 years old, a rather plain woman with long blonde hair, which she wore in a tight bun. For work, she dressed in a long black skirt and a white high-necked blouse buttoned in front and a warm jacket or shawl for cooler days. Her best traits were her eyes and her smile. Every day at supper, she would tell amusing stories of the children's behaviour and make all the sisters laugh, including Hope.

Mary would also speak of the importance of education for women and how they would need to better themselves so as to be able to take a role in society and politics. She told them over dinner that she had been to a meeting held by the new society formed by Mrs Pankhurst. It was only for women, and their slogan was 'Deeds, not Words'.

As Mary spoke of the meeting, Hope's eyes shone. She had realised that she might not be cut out for nursing, and in consequence, she had written to the hospital that she would not be back. Could she become a teacher instead? She had already been back in Calne for several months, and she needed to find something to do so that she could contribute to the household finances. Even though Sarah and Eleanor were better off than they had been when she left them four years ago, she wanted to make something of herself and become self-supporting in the future. She helped out with sewing, washing and ironing as she got better, but in her heart, she knew that she wanted to have a different life. Maybe teaching was really what she wanted to do?

Hope applied to St Mary's for a free place in the secondary school with a view to qualify for a teacher's training course later and becoming an elementary school teacher. With a recommendation from Mary, she succeeded in getting a free place in the secondary school in return for helping out a few days a week supervising the youngest pupils. Sarah and Eleanor were very supportive, and although they did not have enough money to pay for her education, they could now at least manage without any contributions from Hope for a few years.

**

The Second Boer War had ended in 1902, and Arthur Balfour had become prime minister and introduced the Balfour Education Act to promote better schooling in the UK. In 1903, Emmeline Pankhurst and her daughter Cristobel had started their own organisation to fight for votes for women, the 'Women's Social and Political Union'.

Hope started her high school education in 1907 and took to book learning with a passion. She soon began to thrive and gain weight again. One day in the autumn of 1907, she asked Mary whether she could come with her the next time there was a meeting of women, and Mary nodded and said that she would be glad to go with her. Then Eleanor said she would like to come, too, if Sarah did not mind.

They decided to go up to London for the National Union of Women's Suffrage Societies protest march arranged with the WSPU to show that the two organisations were equally committed to the women's franchise in spite of having different views on the methods needed. It was held on the 9th of February, so they took the train up to London early in the morning. About three thousand women from all backgrounds had gathered at the Hyde Park Corner to march to the Strand. Unfortunately, the weather was miserable with heavy rain falling, and the streets became muddy, but spirits were high. Crowds had gathered by the sides of the route, and the marching women's banners showed the broad participation from all walks of life. It was a demonstration of how serious the women were, and a grudging recognition could be seen in the following day's press reports. Mary, Eleanor and Hope returned by train to Calne in the late afternoon, wet, dirty and happy.

Franchise for women had been included in New Zealand laws in 1893 and in Australia, 1894, so it seemed that the bill introduced in Parliament might be successful this time, although similar bills had been rejected by Parliament since 1867. But again, Parliament kept stalling.

When they met over dinner later that week, they discussed the frustrating fight.

"Men do not really want to relinquish any control to women," Eleanor said. "I am very surprised and frightened by the hatred we sometimes see. Maybe we really are trying to tinker with the natural order of things, like they say?"

Both Hope and Mary protested. Mary said: "Of course men want to protect their power and authority, and naturally, they are frightened when women show themselves to be both capable and intelligent. They are just hanging on to their privileges. But these courageous women will not let them do that forever."

Eleanor protested, "This time was peaceful, but at other occasions, we have seen how some of the more militant women have tried to strike the policemen with their handbags. They also destroy property now and then."

"The women are only violent when policemen are trying to break up their meetings or try to arrest women who interrupt a speaker who spouts nonsense," said Hope. "They are being such bullies, and I do not blame the women for defending themselves!" Sarah tended to agree with Eleanor that violence was deplorable, especially in women. She recommended patience and persuasion as the solution to what they all agreed was wrong, namely that women did not have any power and influence on how society was run. But Mary said, "Women have tried persuasion and patience for almost forty years now, and they have not gained an inch. Not an inch! These past two years, women have been imprisoned for small infringements, and they are not even held as political prisoners in Section A, where they might wear their own clothes and have access to writing apparel. Instead, they have been put in Section B with the thieves and murderers like ordinary criminals."

Such unfair treatment of ladies of some standing woke up the press who had not paid much attention to the women's cause in the beginning, and it gave a great deal of welcome publicity to the WSPU.

***

Hope continued her education, and in 1910, she graduated from secondary school and took up a post in Guernsey as a student teacher for a year. With practical experience under the guidance of a trained teacher, she felt ready to gain more experience. The year after, she taught in Derby, and finally, after passing an examination, she was ready to enter a teacher's training college in April 1912.

Her last year as a student teacher had been an eventful one. In April, something happened that, for a while, grabbed everyone's attention. A very large ship had been built for the transatlantic trip to America and was accordingly named the 'Titanic'. It had been built to the newest specifications in Ireland and was thought to be unsinkable, but one night, it collided with an iceberg in the North Atlantic Ocean and sank. It was carrying 2,224 passengers and crew, and more than 1,500 of them died. The ship did not carry enough lifeboats, maybe because it was thought to be unsinkable, so many people died in the icy waters. Besides many wealthy and famous passengers in first class, it also carried second- and third-class passengers, many of the latter poor emigrants from England, Ireland and Scandinavia. The survivors were picked up by another ship and arrived in New York three days later, but it took still another four days before there was a full list of those who had survived and those who had been lost. There was a great deal of confusion about who had been lost, because some people had travelled under aliases or perhaps had not boarded the ship after all. Hope knew nobody who had travelled on the ship, but the tragedy of the disaster and the stories from the survivors touched her deeply as she read everything about the catastrophe that she could lay her hands on.

***

The same year saw the Festival of Empire open on May 11 at the Crystal Palace in Hyde Park to celebrate the coronation of George V. It was a very hot day in May, and Hope went with some friends from Derby to see the exhibitions of the colonial wares inside the three-quarter models of the parliamentary buildings of Canada, South Africa, New Zealand, Australia and Newfoundland. A miniature railway called the 'All-Red' was constructed with stations at each building. All the buildings in the grounds had been constructed with timber and plaster so that they could be taken down again later. The tour also included a South African diamond mine, an Indian tea plantation and a Canadian logging camp. There were reconstructed farm villages with live farm stock, poultry and bees.

Inside the Crystal Palace itself were exhibitions of British arts and industries. And, of course, the park included an amusement park with rides. Over the following weeks, there was a great pageant called the Pageant of London and the Empire, and Hope went in June to see the part that dealt with the Viking invasions of England, which she was studying at the time. The festivities continued all through the exceptionally hot summer, and they generated a joyous mood around the city.

On March the first, 1912, the suffragettes had smashed store windows around Oxford Street, and although Hope was not in London, she cheered for them in her heart. *It cannot be long before Parliament gives in*, she thought. *This cannot go on for much longer. When some of the finest women in this land have found themselves desperate enough to do such deeds, then the men in Parliament must realise that continued suppression of their voices will only make matters worse.* However, the more violent the protests became, the more forcefully the anti-suffragists and the police resisted.

Education and New Friends

Hope had applied to The London Day Training College which had been established under London University. She wanted to live in London to see how the women's movement was progressing. With her good exam results, she was accepted and received a maintenance grant, so she could afford a place to board in London. She would also look for an extra job as an uncertified teacher for the duration of her time in the teacher's training college to pay for the rest of her expenses.

Hope arrived in London at the end of March 1912 and the college recommended a room in the apartment of a single lady, Mrs Bloom, in Southampton Row near the training college in the Bloomsbury area of London. It was a small but rather nice room with a bed and a writing desk. She installed some bookshelves using bricks and planks and put her books and papers on them. The room also had a small wardrobe for her clothes, shoes and other things. The window looked out on Southampton Row where horse carriages and pedestrians were passing by all the time in the daytime. Hope felt safe and empowered by having this place which was truly hers as long as she paid the rent. Her landlady was the widow of an Irish gentleman who had been employed in a large bank until he fell ill and died. Mrs Bloom had two sons who had both moved away in order to work, one in a Birmingham trading office and the other in administrative work overseas in India. The widow was about fifty and mainly lived on money sent to her by her two sons. She had many friends who came to see her or whom she went out with, and she did not interfere much with Hope's comings and goings.

The London Day Training College was run by the principal, John Adams, a Scottish educationalist who gave the new students a rousing welcome on the day they started. He was passionate about schooling, and he made a deep impression on Hope. He talked about how they had to excel in both the subjects and the methods of teaching. He introduced the master and mistress of method, who would supervise their actual teaching for the duration of their time in the college.

"I am aware that many of you may be quite experienced in teaching," he said, "but there is no doubt that with careful and intelligent appreciation of methods, together with occasional supervision, most of you will improve your teaching dramatically. We bear a heavy responsibility towards the young minds that have been and will be placed in our care—we must not do anything to destroy them!"

When Hope left the school after her first day, she felt convinced that she had chosen the best possible future for herself. She went to the library, got a membership card and borrowed the books she had to read for her first course. The library had a reading room, and since its atmosphere was very nice and its chairs relatively comfortable, she decided to do much of her studying there. She went to the bursar's office to make sure her registration was completed with her new address, and then she strolled along Southampton Row to buy some bread and milk for her breakfast the next morning. She had been invited by Mrs Bloom to take her evening meal with her and a few friends in the apartment. Like herself, both Mrs Bloom and her friends were passionate about the cause of women's movement, and Hope spent an enjoyable evening in the company of the older, but like-minded women.

***

The next days and weeks passed in a blur. She went to school and studied in the library. She took most of her meals in the student hall, and when she had a day off, she walked around Bloomsbury and visited the shops and bookstores. Sometimes she went with some girl friends from school, and if they could afford it, they went for tea in one of the cheaper places. Hope soon found several good friends, and she got particularly close to one girl, Emily Browne, who shared her interest in the women's movement. Emily had long dark hair which she wore in a braid on top of her head. She had brown eyes and the most charming smile Hope could ever remember having seen. Emily had grown up in Chelsea as the youngest of three daughters of a merchant. She was better off financially than Hope, since she came from a relatively well-off family, where her younger brother would one day take over their father's business. Emily's two older sisters had married, but Emily had insisted that she did not want to marry. Exasperated, her parents had agreed to let her move in with a London relative and train as a teacher until she came to her senses. Emily laughed as she told Hope all this, and in the end, she said, "My family will never understand, but I would rather die than have to serve a man and bear his children. I like the suffragettes, and I would like to fight with them for women's right to vote and be part of the people who make the decisions in this country. And I want to be a teacher so that I can support and encourage young girls in thinking for themselves."

25

Hope applauded Emily's self-confidence and immediately declared her agreement with her sentiments. She had chosen the teacher's training school to be able to make an independent living for herself. She had no wish to marry either, and she told Emily all about her life so far.

"I was born in Japan where my father was a missionary and my mother died when I was born. She had ten children before me. I was raised by my sister, Sarah, who has been like a mother to me. We moved back to England when I was six, and my father died a few years later. So, I have always known that I had to find a way to live on my own. I tried to work in a hospital, since I wanted to be a nurse, but I had to stop when I got ill myself. At home, we had a boarder, Mary, and she was the one to inspire me to turn to teaching. I worked as a student teacher for a few years before I was able to apply for the college, and here I am. Mary also got me interested in the women's question, and she took me to the demonstration in front of Parliament two years ago. We left when scuffles broke out between the police and some of the women."

"I read a little about that, and I would very much have liked to be there," said Emily. "Now there have been more arrests, and I have heard that in prison, the women are put together with thieves and murderers." They both shuddered at the thought.

"Let us find out more about what those women are doing," said Emily, and Hope nodded in agreement.

Before long, the two were inseparable friends and began to study together in the library. Emily's parents had placed her with an aunt in Gordon Square where she was under supervision at night, but in the daytime, she was free to come and go as she liked.

In the spring of 1913, they both had to sit for their first-year exams, and they both studied hard. When the examination was over, and the results were published, they had both passed and were eligible for their second year of training. Hope, who had been teaching in an evening school for the past year, got a raise in her salary, which she sent to Sarah and Eleanor in Calne. At the same time, she asked her sisters if she could bring Emily home with her for a few days of rest before their second year started. Sarah immediately wrote back and invited Emily to stay with them in Calne for as long as she liked.

***

One morning in late March, the two young women boarded the train for Calne. Hope had warned Emily not to speak too much about the women's cause, since Sarah and Eleanor might not be very interested in the topic. But in this, she was mistaken.

When they sat down for tea, Sarah and Eleanor wanted to hear all about what they were doing in school and in their free time. Hope and Emily told them about the school and the exam which they had both just passed. They talked about the Bloomsbury area where many students lived and the almost village-like atmosphere around Russell Square and the streets that border it. They talked about their principal whom they both admired very much. After a while, Eleanor asked whether they had heard anything about how the women's movement was going.

"Do you and Sarah still think that they are a bunch of troublemakers?" asked Hope.

Sarah said that they used to think so, but in the past couple of years, they had gradually come to think differently. They had discussed the topic many times with Mary, who still lived with them, and little by little, she had convinced them of the necessity of the cause. "The solution to the plight of poor women and children, who get left behind by the men who were supposed to take care of them, so they end up in a poor-house, must be for women to get an equal say in law-making. Girls must be educated and learn a trade, so that they can earn a living if they have to," declared Sarah, and Eleanor chimed in, "I think the suffragettes are courageous women who will even go to prison for their convictions."

Hope and Emily laughed.

"There we were on the train, thinking that we had better stay off the topic for your sakes," said Emily. "Hope, you tell them what we have been doing."

Hope lifted up her skirts to reveal her garters in the suffragette colours.

"We have to be inconspicuous because of the school and our scholarships, but in our free time, we go to as many meetings and rallies as we can. We have even heard Emmeline Pankhurst speak once, and we read about the WSPU in the papers. We both want to be more active when we have gotten our certificates two years from now."

"Yes," said Emily, "and we plan to do everything we can to guide our future female pupils towards independence."

"I applaud that," said Sarah, "but do be careful and do not get arrested, please, both of you."

Mary came home from work while they had tea, and Sarah invited her into the drawing room to join them. The five women had an enjoyable talk and agreed to meet in London the following year when Mary planned to move back to Guernsey.

***

In the evening, Hope asked Sarah for news of her siblings. "Well," said Sarah, "I do not hear from them very often, except for Henry who writes regularly and visits once in a while. He is still doing well and still teaching at Reigate. Sophia has moved to Ireland, and we usually get a Christmas card from her and her husband. They have no children yet. William is becoming a professional cricketer and seems to be getting on well. Henry tells us that he is very popular with women and has fathered an illegitimate child. That is all we know. Bertha and Edith are both well, and Edith is thinking of emigrating to New Zealand while Bertha has begun seeing someone that she might want to marry. His name is Frank, apparently. Ernest is stationed in Brunei as an administrator. Arthur is with the navy in India and doing very well. He writes occasionally, but he does not tell us much about what he is doing. I suppose a lot of it is secret."

Hope nodded. She did want to know about her sisters and brothers although she hardly knew any of them, except for Sarah, Eleanor, Arthur and Henry. Actually, Henry had written her an encouraging letter when he found out that she had chosen to train as a teacher, and she had kept him regularly informed of her progress. Her other siblings seemed to have their own separate lives. She doubted that the fact that they had a baby sister called Hope had ever made much of an impression on them. Some of them might even blame her for having been the cause of their mother's death. She asked Sarah, "Do you think they blame me for causing mother's death?"

"No, definitely not!" Sarah protested. "And if any of them should even think such a thought, I would never speak to them again!" She continued, "Our mother loved our father more than everything. I think she loved him more than her own life. She had been told by a doctor to have no more children because of her health, but she could not bear to cut off their marital relationship, so she did not tell him of the danger for several years. So, she became with child one more time. There is no way you or anyone else can blame the child that resulted. I saw how she loved you and how sad she was to leave you. You are simply the result of a love so strong that it defied common sense. I am sorry you never got to know her…"

Hope felt comforted by Sarah's words. "You have been like a mother to me, Sarah. I could not have wished for any better mother."

They both sat quietly for a little while, and Hope held Sarah's hand in hers. The following days, Hope and Emily explored the landscape around Calne on long walks. They had packed a basket of bread, cheese and milk or apple cider, and after lunch, they took out a book each and would sit on a blanket, leaning against each other's backs to read for a while.

***

One day after they were back in London, Emily brought a small weekly newspaper to the library where she and Emily met to study for their classes. It was called *Votes for Women* and was published by a married couple, Mr Frederick and Mrs Emmeline Pethick-Lawrence. Emily had bought it from a woman selling it in the street. It was funded by the Lawrence's and helped by volunteers to distribute it at the price of 1d. It had a drawing on the front page, and inside, there were several in-depth articles on social problems. It also covered meetings and protests, and it was seen as the official organ of the Women's Social and Political Union.

Both Emily and Hope wanted to help with selling it, but as both were studying on public scholarships, they felt they had to keep a low profile. Besides, they did not really have a lot of free time. The curriculum in the college was really heavy, and frequent inspections from the Local Education Committee kept them on their feet. They did, however, attend some meetings in their spare time and heard many eminent women speak on the unfair distribution of power and wealth in society.

The suffragette movement was getting on relatively well, but in June 1913, tragedy struck. A prominent and passionate member of the movement since 1906, Emily Wilding Davison, died for the cause at the age of thirty-nine. She was well known for the many times she had been in prison and force-fed for her beliefs and actions as well as for the articles she wrote in *The Suffragette.* On the fourth of June, she had taken the train to the Epsom racecourse and stood among the spectators with a suffragette banner. Apparently, her plan was to throw the banner around the neck of the king's horse, but when she stepped out in the middle of the racecourse, the king's horse galloped into her and threw her through the air. Both the horse and the jockey fell down, too, but sustained only minor injuries. Miss Davison was wounded so badly that she died four days later, never regaining consciousness.

On the ninth, when Emily and Hope learned about their fellow suffragette's desperate act from the newspaper, they cried in each other's arms. They had heard Emily Davison speak on several occasions, and now that she was dying it just seemed too sad. They joined the memorial service at St George's Church on the fourteenth of June and swore to each other that her death would only make them more determined.

***

On July 26, a women's pilgrimage gathered in Hyde Park. Women from as far away as Carlisle had, since June, been making their way by foot, bicycle or carriages towards London to join. On their way, they lectured and passed out pamphlets, but several times, they were exposed to loud booing and threatening behaviour from male crowds, so that they had needed police protection to get through some of the cities. Ultimately, when everyone had reached London, there were 50.000 women gathered. It was all organised months in advance by the National Union of Women's Suffrage Societies, who wanted to show that they were fighting for the same things as the suffragettes but using peaceful means. Emily and Hope were there as well even though they sympathised more with the militant movement. It was a peaceful day, and the sun was shining, and they could not help but admire the many women who had walked so far to get there.

"Parliament must take notice now," Hope said on their way home.

"I am sure they take notice," Emily said, "but the question is, when they will take action!"

The militant suffragist continued to use tactics similar to before, among others slashing valuable paintings in the National Gallery with knives and cleavers and marching in the streets of London.

***

Both Hope and Emily were doing well at school in their second year, and by careful saving and a little help from their families, they had been able to have enough for a week's holiday in the summer of 1914.

Hope had spent the winter of 1913 with Sarah and Eleanor in Calne, and the day after Christmas, Emily had suddenly shown up. "I hope you will take me in for a few days," she said. "I cannot get along with my family. They still keep trying to marry me off in the most unsubtle ways, and I just cannot stand it anymore."

Hope had given her a warm hug, and Sarah and Eleanor had also been happy to see her. They said she was, of course, welcome to stay with them for as long as she wanted. She could sleep in Hope's room while she was there, and they could go back up to London as soon as New Year was over.

On Boxing Day, they prepared a few boxes of delicacies to give to the poor people in the parish, and they went around with some of the other ladies from the church to distribute them. The rest of their holidays, Hope and Emily helped Sarah and Eleanor with the work around the house or went arm in arm on long walks in Calne and its vicinity. They passed by the Harris pork-processing factory, which employed so many of the villagers. They noticed the sweetish smell that got stronger the closer they got to the factory, and Emily wrinkled her nose a little. They were both very happy to have escaped that kind of hard and unpleasant work.

They went past The Green and St Mary's Church, where they visited Hope's father's grave. Hope could hardly remember him now, but she had heard from some of her siblings what a wonderful man he had been when her mother was alive, so she put some holly on his grave and prayed for his soul. Hope was not really a believer in God anymore, but she liked the small rituals that belonged to the faith. She mentioned this to Emily, but not before they were well out of the cemetery again.

"I did not have a very religious upbringing," said Emily. "What I know about Christianity today is mostly what I have learned in school. The teacher in my primary school told us about Jesus as if it was a set of facts, and I naturally accepted it as such. It wasn't until I began training as a teacher that I even began to question it. Now I do not know whether I am a believer or not, but I do not want to teach the school children anything I do not know or feel for sure."

"Me neither," said Hope. There was a lot more to be said on the topic, but it felt like dangerous ground and neither felt inclined to talk further about it for now. Instead, Hope began to talk about the summer holiday they were planning the coming summer.

"What do you think about Sarah's suggestion?" she asked. When they had discussed their plans with Sarah and Eleanor the day before, Sarah had said, "You should go to Cornwall and visit the school your older sisters went to. I went there some years ago, and it is such a beautiful landscape, with great and impressive beaches."

"Tell us more," Emily had said.

"It has a beautiful seaside and mountains as well. It is a long train ride, I know, but it may be less crowded than the usual places," Sarah had said.

"I have never been anywhere near that part of England," Emily said, "so why not? We had better read up on it and find the best place to stay." And then it was decided.

They spent New Year's Eve much like any other evening, and when the church bells rang at midnight, they hugged each other, and Sarah had prepared a punch, so they drank to each other's health and happiness in the new year of 1914.

First Trip with Emily

Finally, the summer holidays came around, and Hope and Emily were ready for their trip to Cornwall. A few days before they left London, they learned from the newspapers that the Austro-Hungarian Archduke Franz Ferdinand and his wife had been assassinated by a Bosnian Serb in Sarajevo. It was quite shocking, but they did not pay too much attention to it at the time.

They had decided to start in Truro where they would visit Sophia, Bertha and Edith's old school. The headmistress, Miss Amy Key had married in 1889 and died in 1906 from cancer, so there was a different headmistress, but they just wanted to look at the school and the town where Hope's sisters had spent their childhood. Afterwards, they would go down to Penzance to spend a week in a hotel and take long walks along the beaches and in the mountains.

The next day, in the early afternoon, they arrived in Penzance station. They had decided to stay at the Riviera Palace Hotel in Alverton Road and had written ahead. They walked from the station but had their luggage delivered later, and at the hotel, they were heartily welcomed and shown to their room. It was a very nice room with running water and a view of the sea, and they decided to go for a walk on the promenade while they waited for their luggage to arrive. It was a lovely summer day, and the fresh, salty breeze was a welcome change from London, which had been very hot and muggy since May. From the coast, they could see St Michael's Mount and decided to walk there the next day.

When they returned to the hotel, their luggage had arrived and after a quick change into summer dresses and lighter shoes, they grabbed their hats and went for tea in the hotel's tearoom. They asked their hosts whether there would be anything going on in the early evening and were told that a band would be playing on the promenade bandstand. They went down to the quay and found the bandstand and a rickety bench to sit on, where they could listen to the music, before going back for supper. The next day, they asked for a picnic basket to take along for their expedition to St Michael's Mount. They walked leisurely along the coast and enjoyed the view and the fresh air.

"Did you know that people in Cornwall used to think that the land was populated by giants a long time ago?" asked Emily.

"No, I did not," said Hope. "How do you know?"

"Well," said Emily, "I found an old book yesterday when we returned from our late afternoon walk. It was on the shelves in the tearoom. It was written by a man who collected old tales from Cornish people in the middle of the last century. William Bottrell, who heard the tales from his grandmother and later from some tin miners, published it in 1870. I started reading it last night, and I wanted to read aloud to you, but you had already fallen asleep."

"I am sorry I missed that," said Emily. "Maybe I can read aloud for you tonight. Would you like that?"

"Only if you do not fall asleep while reading," laughed Emily and gave her a light push.

"I do not fall asleep in the middle of reading," said Hope indignantly and pushed back. They both laughed as they walked on towards St Michael's Mount. After a while, they reached Marzion, a small town on the coast from where one could gain access to the mount. It was still low tide, so they decided to walk along the causeway across to the mount and the small village of the island. There they found a place to have lunch and tea, and afterwards, they set out to climb the rough stone steps to the castle. They walked slowly and took the time to look at the gardens, which in spite of the inhospitable cliffs were surprisingly colourful and lush. But most impressive was the old castle which had formerly been a target for pilgrims' travels to the monastery that lay on top. When the reformation came, the monastery was abandoned and turned into a well-fortified prison. It closed in 1863 and was subsequently turned into a historical monument. It contained several beautiful rooms, a chapel, a library, and the former refectory.

Hope and Emily sat for a long time on some big stones to rest before undertaking the long walk back to their hotel in Penzance. They both loved history and tried to imagine how life had been for the people of the various ages. The monks trundling over the causeway in mediaeval times, the prisoners who were kept isolated there until just decades ago… They agreed that things were much better now and wondered what the future would hold and expected it to be even better. They wondered how long it would take before women became equal citizens with men. Not long, they were sure.

Then they set out for the long walk back. They were tired, and they longed for supper and a rest with their feet soaked in a long, hot footbath.

***

They woke up the following morning quite refreshed and agreed to walk around Penzance to see what the town had to offer. First, they walked along Market Jew Street and down to the beachfront. Then they went to see the impressive St Mary's Church, which was rebuilt in 1836 when the original church had become too small. It was a lovely day, and they had both brought a book to read, so they sat down at the market place on the step of the market house to read and relax. Before they had to return to London, they also visited Morrab Gardens and looked at the various plants that were imported from warmer regions and did not grow outdoors in any other place in England. Inside the garden was a fine library, and Emily spent some time studying the books with a view to using some of the material in her future classes on botany. In the garden, she also sketched some of the leaves and wrote their characteristics down. In the meantime, Hope had found a nice place in the shadow of a tree where she sat reading. When Emily joined her, they ate some of the food they had brought, and Emily asked Hope what she was reading.

"I am reading this book by E.M. Forster called *Howard's End*. Have you read it?" Emily had heard about the book which had come out the previous year, but she had not read it yet.

"I have about fifty pages left," Emily said. "Then I will pass it on to you. It is really fascinating, and Mr Forster writes so well."

"Fine," said Hope. "I finished my book yesterday, so I really would like to start another. Do you want to read mine? It is by P.G. Wodehouse."

"I would like that, but first I want to read the other book, I brought. Gertrude Bell's *Syria, the Desert and the Sown,* which is about her travels in Syria and Palestine. She is really a remarkable woman. Did you know that she speaks Persian and Arabic, and she has travelled all over those countries in the Near East? She has climbed mountains, and she is also interested in archaeology. She is really an adventurous woman, and you cannot help admiring her."

"That sounds incredibly interesting," said Emily. "I will read it after you, if I may. What else did she do?"

"The book is from 1907, so I do not know so much about her more recent achievements, but she must be a formidable woman. And, of course, you may read it after me."

"There are a few women who travel quite intrepidly around the world," said Hope. "I once read a book by Isabella Bird, who went to Japan. I wonder how they manage doing that. Maybe they are simply rich, but I cannot help thinking that they also travelled to get away from their oppressive life prospects in England, where they were expected to obey a man and do nothing on their own."

"I am sure you are right," said Emily. "You and I are somewhat like them, although not as courageous. But maybe we could work on that? How about going to Paris next summer?"

"Yes," said Hope, "why not? Let us go next summer. We both speak French, so it cannot be that hard to make our way around."

On their last full day in Penzance, they took a carriage to Land's End, the most westerly point in England. They got off and walked the last of the way along the top of the cliffs. The view over the sea and the rocks below was wild and beautiful and when they finally reached the promontory, they were stunned at the thought that from here there was nothing but sea until one reached North America. The lonely Longships Lighthouse erected on a tiny rock island in the sea just off the coast only seemed to underline the vastness of the ocean.

When the two young women got back to the hotel that evening, they agreed that it had been the best holiday ever. They had enjoyed each other's company and had no doubt that the future would bring many opportunities for exciting holidays together.

***

Back in London, the heat hit them, and everyone agreed that it was the longest and hottest summer ever. The fresh sea air in Cornwall had been cooling, but in London, the air seemed to have come to a standstill. Hope and Emily went to Calne for a couple of days. It was only a little bit cooler than London, and the farmers worried about drought. Mary had left in April to return to Guernsey to teach and look after her old parents, but Sarah and Eleanor were well. They had looked forward to hearing Emily and Hope tell them about their trip to the south, and they were not disappointed.

World War One

When Hope and Emily got back to London from Calne, they realised that black clouds might be gathering over Europe that could be more serious than they had first thought. After the assassination in Sarajevo, Austria-Hungary had issued a number of demands to Serbia, some of which had been rejected. Then, Austria-Hungary declared war on Serbia in late July, and a crisis followed as the countries in Europe began to call on their allies to join them. Hope and Emily followed this in the newspapers from one day to the next.

Russia mobilised to support Serbia, and Germany decided to invade Belgium and Luxembourg before going on to France. This made England declare war on the Germans on the fourth of August, just before Hope and Emily were starting their third year in the teacher training college.

People in England thought that it would be a brief war, probably over by Christmas, but after the Germans were stopped from advancing into France, the soldiers on both sides dug long trenches to protect themselves and to carry out occasional attacks. On the eastern side, the Russian army had successfully fought the Austro-Hungarians but were stopped by Germany before they could take East Prussia. When the Ottoman Empire entered the war in November on the side of the Central Powers, fronts were opened in the Balkans and the Middle East. Italy then joined the Alliance, and Bulgaria joined the Central Powers.

In England, many young men signed up for combat against the Germans in Belgium and France, and many women also got engaged in work for the war, driving ambulances, working in factories or at least knitting socks and scarves for the soldiers. The war would in time be called 'The Great War' because it involved so many countries and cost so many people their lives.

The suffragettes had decided to pause their movement to help their country during the war, hoping that such a gesture would be appreciated by the government and seen as an argument for women's votes after the war.

All their thoughts about a European holiday were gone, and instead, Hope and Emily discussed what they could do for the war effort. Many women had taken jobs in the munitions industry and a number of other areas of society to replace the men who had gone to fight, but Hope and Emily felt that they had to finish their education and start working, so that was not an option. Instead, they rolled bandages and knitted woollen stockings, scarves and other equipment for the soldiers. They both signed up for the Women's Auxiliary Army Corps and were put on neighbourhood watch patrol two evenings a week.

The school exhorted them to keep studying as normally as possible, but it was impossible to ignore the mood change that had come over everybody. Every now and then, they would see people wearing a black armband to signify that one of their family had been lost on the battlefield. Mostly people talked about the war in terms of good and evil: the Germans were evil people who tried to kill all the good people who were British. She discussed it with Emily, and they often ended up agreeing that it had to be something in the nature of men's inborn characteristics that made it so hard for them to settle conflicts in any other way than through violence. Both women were patriots and wanted their own side to win as quickly as possible, but they were not completely blind to the fact that there might be women on the other side feeling exactly the same.

After the initial optimism, the war dragged on in Belgium and Northern France for two years, while both parties tried to come up with new ideas or technology that might push their advantage. In April 1915, the Germans used chlorine gas for the first time on the Western front. After that, both sides used various poison gasses on each other, and it became one of the biggest horrors of the war. Gas masks were kept close at hand at all times, even by civilians, to put on as soon as any suspicious smells were detected. Gas masks also became a necessary part of the children's daily lives, dangling from school bags and bicycles, to and from school.

Both sides developed tanks for use in advances, and both sides suffered heavy losses. In 1916, Britain introduced general conscription, and a summer offensive by the French and British troops was one of the most murderous ever. In one day, almost 20,000 British soldiers were killed, and many more wounded. The entire Somme offensive from July to November cost more than one million casualties. Besides the trench warfare, there were great naval battles. Mines were dropped along coastlines, and submarines were deployed to attack and sink each other's merchant ships and cut off supply lines. The newly invented aeroplanes were soon converted to use in the war, and terror bombing of cities became another weapon. The Germans also used Zeppelin airships to carry bombs to drop on London, and blimps were used for observations of enemy troop positions and movements. The French built a false model of Paris to confuse the Germans, and abstract painters were hired to hide the tanks behind camouflage netting…

Emily and Hope followed as much as they could through the newspapers and whatever chains of communications they could. When they graduated in the spring of 1915, after a year very much centred on practical pedagogic, they had qualified for the third and highest class of the teacher's certificate. Often, they would be given a class to teach under the supervision of the mistress of methods who would take notes during the class and talk about them with the students afterwards. They read books by Friedrich Froebel, Maria Montessori and other well-known educationalists, and they discussed in class how they could use these theories in practice as schoolteachers. Hope did slightly better than Emily in the practical subjects, since she had more experience, but otherwise they were very equal in other subjects, and they both passed the final year with good grades.

Part Two
Beginning of Adulthood

During the last months of their education, Hope and Emily had begun to look for work. If possible, they would prefer to work in schools for lower middle-class or middle-class children. They wanted to avoid the 'ragged schools' for the poor because they did not want to spend all their time keeping discipline in a class. They both wanted to educate girls they could impress with ambitions and independence of mind and who might have a chance to better their position in society with a solid education. There was a shortage of male teachers because of the war, so they both managed to find positions at the Highbury Hill High School for Girls in Islington. They decided to move to an apartment not too far away from Bloomsbury but closer to the school, so that they could commute on bicycles every day. They each bought a so-called safety bicycle and spent the summer practicing in a park before they braved the roads. They eventually found a relatively cheap apartment on the top floor of a house in Clerkenwell. It had a small bedroom with two beds and a drawing room and kitchen plus a water closet out on the stairs. It would do for the first few years, and they moved in as soon as they could before they were going to start teaching in April.

For their first night in the new apartment, they pushed the two beds together so that they could enjoy each other's closeness. The year before, when they had been in Cornwall together, Emily had kissed Hope full on her lips and declared that she loved her, and Hope had reciprocated. But so far, their mutual love had been chaste. Now that they lay so close and had the privacy of their own apartment, they went further and cautiously began to explore each other's breasts while they kissed. Hope was the one to stop the caresses to say, "Are we doing something bad? It did not feel like that, and I want to do it again, but women loving each other seems to be wrong somehow."

Emily held her and said, "Some women have felt like this a long time back in history. People call them Sapphist after the ancient Greek poetess, Sappho, who apparently loved women. One does not hear much about them because they are very discreet, and a lot of people do not think women have any independent desire of their own. It is not illegal the way men who love men are, but it might be if we are open about it.

Let's just pretend to everyone else that we are simply very good friends and roommates."

"You seem to know a lot more about this than I do," said Hope. "You will have to teach me about it."

"I will," said Emily. "Not that I have had a lot of experience, but I have read some things since I discovered that I was a lot more attracted to girl than to boys. I am so lucky that I found you..."

*****

There were strict rules for female teachers: they were not allowed to marry as long as they held their job, they had to wear demure white blouses and dark-coloured skirts, they were not allowed to smoke or drink or behave in any unseemly way, neither in nor out of school. They could use bloomers for cycling to and from school but not in corridors or classrooms. First and foremost, they had to set a shining example for the girls they taught by being unfalteringly feminine and maternal in their behaviour.

Emily and Hope had made a solemn promise to the head mistress to abide by these rules. They would come to school every day from half past seven and stay till four o'clock or longer if they had more work to do. They would have regular visits by inspectors from the London County Council, who were in charge of education. The chief inspector was Mr C. W. Kimmins, and there was one woman who had been appointed to join the council, Ms Nettie Adler. She was the daughter of a chief rabbi and a member of the Liberal Party. Furthermore, she was aligned with the progressives in local politics. This Emily and Hope knew from the newspapers, and although they did not know her, they hoped that her presence might be a portent of better times for women's influence on politics.

They had been asked to teach various subjects in Forms One to Three for the first year. Their pupils would be eleven to thirteen- or fourteen-year-old girls, mostly from homes in the vicinity of the school. Hope and Emily were to come in on their first day of work to meet with the other teachers and discuss the curriculum for the school year of 1915-16.

In the morning, they had tea and toast in their tiny apartment, and they prepared a packed lunch to bring with them. They also brought pencils and pens, paper and just in case a box of chalk. They would be given the textbooks they were to use in the school, and they would also receive any further material they might have to use for teaching. They inspected each other's dress and agreed they both looked fine, and then they went to get their bicycles from the shed in the yard. Nothing could shake their proud feeling of absolute preparedness for the work ahead, and they were in high spirits as they rode their bicycles up Highbury Road and the hill to the school. They parked their bicycles and shed their bloomers before they went to the teachers' room on the ground floor. It was a large area with tables and chairs, and they were shown to the women's table where they sat down next to each other. When the schoolmistress came in, they stood up and said, "Good Morning, Miss Jacobs," in a chorus. Miss Jacobs asked them all to sit down, and after a short welcoming speech, she asked the headteacher of each form to introduce the following semester's curriculum. Hope would be teaching English, geography and history as her main subjects, while Emily would be teaching elementary math and science, natural history and English. They would also be expected to take care of their classes in cooking, sewing and physical exercise a few times a week. Besides, they would sometimes have to monitor the children's dinner breaks, where school dinners were served every day for the poorer students. They received the textbooks they were to use, and at four o'clock, they were permitted to leave and reminded to prepare the lessons for the following Monday.

On their way home, they shopped for a few essentials so that they could cook their dinner by themselves. Back in their apartment, Emily offered to cook, and Hope sat down to study her timetable and to prepare her first lessons. After supper, she washed the dishes, so Emily would have the opportunity to study for Monday's work. They agreed that they would spend their Sunday afternoon taking their bicycles to a nearby park to enjoy the fresh air. It was an unusually hot September day with not a cloud to mar the blue sky. They went to St James Park to have their picnic lunch, and after that they sat on the grass and talked.

"Let's go past Selfridges and have a look at the shop windows with all the beautiful things we cannot afford to buy. The weather is so splendid for bicycling," Hope suggested, and so they went to get their bicycles straight away

They cycled all the way to Oxford Street and to the department store that had opened six years ago. It had an impressive façade with every window beautifully decorated as appetisers to the store itself. The American, Mr Selfridge, who owned it had realised that shopping could be more than just buying the things one needed. It could be an adventure and a leisure time entertainment to walk around in the luxurious environment and just look at the merchandise without being harassed by sales people. Selfridges attracted many people with its ambience, its cultural and scientific exhibits and its whole atmosphere of welcoming everyone, especially women. It was closed on Sundays, so Emily and Hope strolled around and looked at the windows for almost half an hour.

After that they again got on their bicycles and rode home to prepare their work.

***

The next day, the school year started. The pupils all lined up in the schoolyard in their white pinafores, black velour hats, black stockings and lace-up boots. They carried a cloth bag with their school shoes for indoor use. The teachers went to get their classes and walk them in lines into the corridor outside the school room where they hung their bags, hats and blazers on a hook and changed from boots to indoor shoes.

Hope met her first form class and took them to their classroom where she was to teach them English for two periods. She had been given a list of names to check on attendance, and after writing her name on the blackboard, she spent the first hour making notes about every girl in her class, where they had gone to school before, how many brothers and sisters they had and what their fathers were doing for a living. She had 28 students present and two were missing, but she would check up on them in the break. Most of the girls had long hair worn in a single braid or hanging loosely down their backs. They were for the most part eleven years old, but a few were twelve.

All of the school rooms lay around a central hall which was used for assembly every morning at nine. Five minutes before the bell rang, Hope would tell the children to clear away their things and put them inside their desks before they went down the stairs for assembly. She reminded them that running on the stairs was not allowed. They should walk in a single file and keep to the left after herself, and they should remain quiet unless a teacher addressed them directly. After assembly, she wanted them to return directly to their classroom.

The classroom had large windows that looked out on the grounds around the school. Two girls would share a heavy oak school desk with a bench for sitting. The desktop could be lifted up, so that their things could be kept safely inside. The classroom walls were bare, except for a picture of King George V high up on one wall and a large blackboard at the front of the room.

At assembly, they would all sing a hymn, and the schoolmistress would read a piece from the Bible. Then she bid the new students in the first form welcome to the school and introduced the new teachers. Afterwards, the students would file back to their classes for fifty more minutes of teaching.

Hope had chosen to test their reading skills first. She had taken a set of readers, which she had brought to class before school began, and soon she had her notebook out to note down what she thought about each student's skill level. Most of the girls read very well, but she noted down a few who would need extra help in the future. Then the break came, and Hope went immediately to the head teacher and asked him if he had anything to tell her about the two girls who had been missing from her class. He did not know what had kept them away but advised her to make home visits and talk to their parents as soon as possible. He got the addresses from the school office and passed them to Hope, and she decided to go on Saturday if the girls had not turned up.

After the short break, she had to teach history and geography before the dinner break at twelve o'clock. She had decided to start with a lesson on British prehistory and then combine it with the teaching of England's geography. After each twenty minutes of teaching, she stopped to ask one or two students sum up what she had told them and to ask questions if they had any. They had lots of questions, and she answered them as well as she could.

When dinnertime came at twelve, the children who were entitled to free school dinners went to one part of the eating hall and sat down to eat. The rest of the girls brought out their lunches and sat in little groups eating and talking. Hope did not have supervision duties that day, so she sat in the staff room and lunched on the sandwiches she had brought, and Emily joined her a few minutes before the end of the break for a cup of tea.

"How was your day so far?" Hope asked.

"Fine, how was yours?" Emily said and then continued, "I taught English and introductory math and this afternoon, I have to teach a cooking class. I am afraid that I will make some terrible mistake, and the girls will catch me in it."

"You will not," said Hope, "I am sure of it. Tomorrow I shall switch classes with you for the afternoon and teach cooking to my class. And now I have to take them all out for an hour of physical exercise… It is all a little frightening in the beginning. By the way, did you have a full attendance today? Two of mine were missing."

"Mine were all there," Emily answered. "But we have to get back to our classes now. I will see you back here afterwards."

***

Hope went off to get her class ready for their hour of physical exercise. Since the weather was so fine and warm, she would take them out on the sports grounds and make them do some gymnastic exercises there. Soon she had them hopping and jumping and waving their arms in unison and then walk briskly around in a circle. After the physical exercise, she took them back to their classroom and got out some materials for sewing.

"How many of you have tried sewing before?" she asked. "Put up your right hand if you have."

About half of the girls had tried sewing before.

"The first thing you must all do is to sew a bag for your needlework. You will each have a piece of cotton cloth which you will use to make a bag."

She showed them how the piece of cloth was to be folded to make a bag. They each got a piece and were asked to stitch it together in the way she showed them on the blackboard and then show it to her. "When you get older, you may have a sewing machine, but for now, you have to learn the making of stitches that will hold really well when you do them properly."

A few girls had already finished their stitches when she stopped talking. While she waited for the rest of the girls to finish, she let those who had finished take out a book to read. She promised herself that she would bring some more books from the library to the class the following day.

Finally, all the girls had finished and shown her their work. Not everyone's bag was neatly square, but they would have to do. Then she showed them how to make double stitches along the loose stitches they had already made, and then how to pull out the loose stitches afterwards. Now they all had solid bags for their handiwork, so the next step was to provide all the bags with a cuff, through which they could pull a drawstring to close the bag. But that would have to wait for next week, so she dismissed the class. All the girls said in a chorus, "Goodbye, Miss Maundrell," and filed out of the room.

"See you all in the morning," Hope murmured in reply.

In the staff room, she waited for Emily while she began preparing for the next day's classes. Last Friday, she had received a schedule for the whole year, and she had noticed that apart from their summer holiday, they would have two days at midterm in October and a two-week break for Christmas. Apart from that, all of her days would be more or less like today. She liked the contact with the children and felt sure it would become something she loved doing, but today, she was really tired. When Emily turned up, she looked no less tired, and they decided to finish their work on tomorrow's lessons quickly and then go directly home to catch a nap before supper.

After a few weeks at school, they both got used to the work, and it no longer felt so exhausting every day. The two girls that had been missing from Hope's class on the first day had both turned up for school the next day. One had been too sick to attend, and the other had lost a baby brother the day before school started, so she had been asked by her mother to stay at home for the day. Both brought letters signed by their fathers explaining the situation.

***

Hope and Emily spent most of their summer holidays in London helping with the war effort. They did, however, spend the last week of their holiday in Calne, where Sarah and Eleanor thoroughly enjoyed hearing about their experiences at school. Hope and Emily were happy to speak about their girls, and Sarah and Eleanor would often laugh out loud when one of them vividly described the ups and downs in the lives of their students. Most of their girls were middle class and lived relatively comfortable lives. A few were brilliant and worked hard to improve themselves, while a few learned only the bare minimum to get through school until they could leave as soon as they were fourteen years old. The majority were in between, and time would show how much they could teach them in the three years they were under their care. Hope always tried to find something they were good at, so she could praise all of them at least once a week, but it was not always easy. She told her sisters about Millicent who had missed her first school day because her baby brother had died. She came from a big family and Hope had taken her aside one of the first days to comfort her after class. Millicent seemed to be one of the bright girls, and after that first time, she had come often to talk to Hope during breaks about how her family was doing and how she herself would never want to have babies. Hope understood very well how Millicent felt, and she always advised her to get as good an education as she possibly could, so that she would have other choices in life.

Emily told Eleanor and Sarah about the twin girls in her class, Annie and Lucy, who always tried to fool her by pretending that each were the other one. It took her several weeks to learn how to tell them apart. And then there was Brittany who excelled in math but had great difficulty in reading. She was a morose girl most of the time but showed signs of real intelligence when one talked to her. She had an excellent memory, and she really worked hard, but somehow, she had never really mastered the skill of spelling and reading. Emily wondered why and whether there might be a way for her to overcome her problem. She seemed to suffer from a kind of word blindness, but there was no explanation for the condition, nor any suggested cure except to work harder.

On their last Sunday of the vacation, Hope and Emily travelled back to London on the train. The school would start for them on Monday morning, but the children would not start until Wednesday. The extra days for the teachers would be for planning the details of the curriculum and the duty rosters of each teacher on Monday. On Tuesday, they would be planning the excursions to take place in the autumn, including a preliminary visit to the places chosen.

Wednesday morning, the children were back, noisy and boisterous after their vacation. It took some time to bring them back to order, but finally, they could lead them to their classrooms in a single file and start the morning.

Hope started by greeting them all. "Good morning, and welcome back from your holidays."

"Good morning, Miss Maundrell!" they yelled back in chorus.

Hope then took attendance, and luckily, everybody was present. "The rest of the time until Christmas," she began, "we shall move further ahead in all subjects, and from January we shall begin to repeat some of the learning from the spring in preparation for your exams in March. For now, you will all have to read a book and write a report to me on what the book was about, whether you liked it or not, and why. In history, we shall start to learn about the Viking Age and what it meant for Britain's culture and language. We shall draw pictures related to this topic, and we may visit a museum to see their collections from the Viking Age. Millicent, when was the Viking Age?"

Millicent was surprised to be the first one to be asked a question, but she quickly collected herself and answered: "I think it was from around eight hundred until the middle of the year one thousand."

"Excellent reply," said Holly. "It is usually counted from the attack on Lindisfarne in 793 until the Battle of Hastings in 1066. But more about that later.

"In sewing classes, you will learn how to knit and crotchet, but first, you shall learn to embroider your names onto a piece of cloth with cross-stitches. Put up your finger if you know how to do that already."

About a third of the girls raised their hands.

"You will have elementary math and science and natural history with Miss Emily Browne, and we shall both accompany you on excursions when our classes go together. That leaves only geography in which we shall learn about one of Great Britain's colonies, namely India. I have a brother in the Indian Navy. Do any of you have relatives who live there?"

Three of the girls raised their hands. One had an uncle working in a company in Calcutta, and the two others had an older brother serving in the British army. "Splendid," said Hope. "I am sure we shall have great fun on that topic. Now, until assembly, please take out your readers, and we will do a little reading. Nelly, will you begin, please."

The school days went on peacefully for the rest of the year and the beginning of 1916. In March, the examinations and evaluation started. Most of the girls did well in their exams, and in April, they all progressed to the second form.

Both Hope and Emily lost a few girls from their classes over the winter months. One girl died from diphtheria, and two simply disappeared. The school and the local education board contacted the parents and threatened to fine them, but to no avail. Four girls moved away from London with their parents and would hopefully continue their education in the towns they went to. Emily and Hope worried about each girl they lost but learned from talking to the other teachers that such losses were inevitable. They both got a new girl in their class and were busy helping them to fit in. Their lives consisted mainly of teaching and taking care of the girls under their supervision, giving useful advice on what to do in case of air raids and directing them to help where needed. In the evenings, they patrolled their assigned neighbourhoods, making sure that all windows were darkened and guiding people to safe places during air raids before they themselves sought shelter in an underground station or wherever they could find it.

**

They had spent Christmas of 1916 in Calne, and Sarah had told them the sad news of Hope's brother, Ernest, who had been murdered while he was Acting British Resident in Brunei. He had been trying to apprehend a Sikh sentry who had attacked a companion when he had been shot and killed. The murderer was caught and executed, but for Sarah and Eleanor, who remembered their little brother very well, it was very sad news. They had not heard from him for a number of years and were quite surprised that he had reached such a high rank in the years since they had last seen him. But most of all they found it difficult to accept that he was gone at such a relatively young age of only thirty-six and that now they would never see him again. Eleanor had a small stone put on her father's grave with Ernest's name on it, and they all went to the graveyard to pay their respects.

As 1917 rolled along, they were getting more and more emotionally exhausted by the war. In March, the Russian Tsar abdicated, and one month later, Lenin arrived in Russia to lead the Bolshevik Party. The revolution came in November, and the Russian war against Germany ended. The same year, the USA entered the war while President Wilson declared that it was 'the war to end all wars'. By the summer of 1918, ten thousand American soldiers arrived in France every day. In the meantime, the Germans had launched a spring offensive in the hope that they might end the war before too many Americans arrived. By using new tactics, they moved further into France and threatened to take Paris. Weak supply lines and lack of tanks and motorised artillery made the Germans unable to consolidate their positions, and in the end, the Allied offensive was able to stop them and force the Germans to retreat. In August, the Germans saw that they would lose and sought ways to negotiate a peace without losing everything. Peace offers were extended to Belgium and the Netherlands, but they were both rejected, and as rumours began to spread among the Germans that the war was lost, there were several incidents of mutiny.

In November, an agreement was reached. Germany would no longer be an empire and the Weimar republic was established. Armistices were signed by the Central Powers one after the other and finally with Germany on November 11. A ceasefire came into effect on 'the eleventh hour of the eleventh day of the eleventh month' until the peace treaty was signed at Versailles seven months later.

On the Wednesday when the armistice was declared, people over most of Europe were happy and relieved and many gathered in the streets to express their feelings and to sing and dance. Hope and Emily let their pupils out of class early and were caught up in the happy crowds.

They were both relieved that the war seemed to have ended but also appalled, and they grieved at the loss of lives and limbs it had caused to the young men of their generation and younger. Nine million young men had perished from the world and more than double that number suffered lasting damage from their wounds. Hope had had her thirtieth birthday during the war, and so had Emily a year before. The day after the armistice, they reflected on their lives that had been put on hold during the war. They both began to feel cheated of the best years of their life, and after a while, they slowly began to feel a need to make up for what they had missed. The taste for travelling and adventure that had only just been awakened during their trip to Cornwall almost five years ago came back to them. They wanted to see more of the world, and when Emily found out that her father, who had died recently, had actually left her a small sum of money, she had been surprised. She also felt grateful that her father had not let the cooling of their relationship influence his feeling of responsibility to provide for her future. Now they could afford another trip, maybe several in the future. But they agreed that they had better put the money in the bank for now and wait to travel until things had settled down.

Part Three
The Interwar Years I

During the war, Hope's and Emily's relationship had deepened. One evening after they had both been at a site, where a house had been bombed in the early evening, killing many of the residents, they had returned home in horror at some of the sights they had seen. That night they held each other close and provided much needed comfort after having helped carry bodies out of the ruined building. After a while, they kissed passionately, and Emily's hands began to roam over Hope's body and touch her everywhere. Soon Hope began to return Emily's caresses, and when Emily whispered that Hope should open her legs, she did so and let Emily's fingers go where they wanted. It felt wonderful and exciting, and Hope pressed herself against Emily's hand until she could bear the joy and excitement no more and let go of herself into the most exquisite feeling of abandon and pleasure she had ever felt.

After a while, Emily whispered, "I used to do that to myself when I was younger. Did you like it?"

Hope whispered a little hoarsely, "Very much. May I try to do it to you?"

Emily opened her legs and guided Hope's hand until it was in the right spot. "Rub me gently at first, and then increase the pressure when I am ready."

"How will I know when you are ready?"

"I will let you know."

Hope tried her best and only a few minutes went by before Emily whispered, "Now." Hope increased the strength of her rubbing and a few seconds later, she could feel Emily tensing up and finally sink back with a deep, contented sigh. After some minutes had passed in which they lay quietly next to each other, Hope sat up and looked at Emily. "I think I love you even more now. Will we ever do this for each other again?"

Emily also sat up and said, "Yes, of course we will, if both of us want to. I have loved you for a long time now, and to give that love a physical expression is something I have thought about before, but I did not want to offend you, so I held back. I am so happy that we both enjoyed it and can do it again." They kissed again and finally fell asleep.

***

Now that the war was over, it finally seemed that women would be allowed a greater part in society's affairs and that education would finally be more open to them. The first women had been allowed to study at university in 1878, and the first degrees had been awarded two years later. In 1883, the first woman to be awarded a doctorate in science had been the mathematician Sophie Bryant. In 1904, Millicent Mackenzie had become an assistant professor and later in 1910, she had been promoted to full professor of education, the first woman to hold a professorial title in a fully chartered university in Great Britain. Slowly and gradually, possibilities for women seemed to be opening up in a variety of fields, and after the war had ended, women over thirty had finally been allowed to vote in 1918.

However, during the last months of the war, people had gradually become aware of the reality of the pandemic of influenza that had only been a rumour during the war. It was called the Spanish Flu, since the Spanish newspapers had been the only ones able to report freely and without censorship on the progress of the disease. However, Spain was not the origin of the disease, and a definite origin was never found. It spread throughout the globe and killed maybe 50-100 million people. In England alone, 250,000 people died on top of those killed in the war.

Both Hope and Emily had gone through a bout of influenza in the spring of that year, but apart from a few days of muscle pain, fever and discomfort, it had been relatively easy to get through. But now it seemed to have returned in strength, and this time, it was deadlier, especially among young, otherwise healthy people. Those that had been hit by the first wave seemed to be immune to the second wave, so neither of the two women fell ill when their students began to show symptoms. Both lost girls from their classes, and even those who recovered had long absences from school. Some never returned, because their mothers needed them at home to help look after their younger siblings if their fathers were not able to work and make money after their war experiences. After the passing of the Fisher Act in 1918, it had become illegal to employ children under the age of twelve, but the unpaid housework and childcare carried out by girls had no restrictions until school attendance became compulsory in 1921. Still, it took years to be implemented all over Britain.

***

After the war, England was governed by the Liberal Party under Lloyd-George. A great many policies to benefit the poor were enacted in the first years after the war, such as the building of subsidised council houses, unemployment insurance and old age pensions. In 1919, a peace conference was held in Versailles, and the League of Nations was created with the purpose of never allowing a war like the one the world had just been through to happen again. So, the 1920s began on a hopeful note in Britain.

Unfortunately, America did not join the League of Nations because there was a majority in the US who preferred isolationism and feared that the US might end up in another war if the league tried to enforce all its rules.

The demobilisation after the war saw massive unemployment, and the national debt could not be repaid sufficiently from the war reparations. There were frequent labour strikes, and the question of Irish independence was still a cause of serious unrest. Women who had worked in men's jobs in the armour industries had only been paid half the usual wages that men earned, and now that the men were returning from the war, the women had to give up their jobs. Some happily returned to being mothers and wives, but for those who had lost their providers in the war, life became harder. The men, who had seen hell in the trenches and on the battlefields, were often profoundly affected and found it hard to find meaning in their lives. But slowly, most people became used to life in peacetime and things settled down. In 1921, unemployment rose to unprecedented highs, and poverty became widespread. The enfranchised part of the population had tripled when voting rights for all adult men and for women over thirty were introduced, and with this, the large gap between the upper class and the rest of the people gradually disappeared. Labour union membership grew, and the unions became stronger. In the elections in December 1918, both Hope and Emily proudly went to the polls and exercised their right.

They followed the newspapers avidly and went about their work as teachers. In 1919, the Sex Disqualification Act made it possible for female teachers to be married, although in practise it took longer before married women teachers were accepted in many places. Some sectors of factory work came to be considered women's work, but the work hours were long, and the pay was low. The unions were primarily for men, and although they saw equal pay as a goal, they did not really fight for it. The new school law of 1921 also had provisions for children with disabilities, for regular health checks and for aid to families who were especially poor. Things seemed for a while to be improving all over, and the post-war economy was recovering rapidly for those who were not laid off.

Hope and Emily had secure jobs as teachers, and in their free time, they went to lectures or concerts or spent time reading or talking together. Once they went to a lecture by the famous and controversial Marie Stopes, a paleo-botanist, who had turned into a crusader for birth control and eugenics. Hope admired her for her intellectual capacity and academic achievements, while Emily appreciated her mostly for her endeavours to liberate women from multiple childbirths and make their lives better. On their way walking home from the lecture, they discussed her views.

"What an impressive woman with all that dark hair piled on top of her head and those sad dark eyes," Hope remarked. "I heard she had a stillborn child recently."

"Yes," Emily replied, "it must have been very sad. But what did you think of her ideas?"

"She is definitely right about women's lives being ruined by too many childbirths," said Hope, thinking of her own mother's early death. "And she also has a point that it is detrimental to our country and our future if too many children grow up in poor and unfit families."

"I think so too," said Emily, "but don't you think that she was being too hard on the degenerative effects on the offspring? In my experience as a teacher, even very poor children can develop excellent minds if given a little help. And there are certainly many children of the rich who are much less gifted."

"That is true," said Hope. "I think the concerns she expressed about poor children being more stupid than better-off children are unfounded. I am much more concerned about the number of children being conceived and what that means for women's independence. Her ideas about birth control certainly deserve to be spread widely."

"That is true," said Emily, "and I am also concerned about whether our population could outgrow the available resources as Thomas Malthus predicted. Although it seems that the occasional wars have so far counteracted that tendency."

"Don't be so cynical," replied Hope. "I think that once the world has settled down after the Great War, we may have learned to avoid unwanted pregnancies as well as such meaningless bloodshed in the future!"

Emily stopped and grabbed both of Hope's arms as if to shake her. "I cannot help but think that your missionary childhood has been detrimental to your common sense. Why should things suddenly improve? It never has before in history."

But Hope glared back at her. "Come on now, aren't you the one who used to be the hopeful one? Can't you see that we must do our best to be optimistic, both for our own sakes and for the children we teach."

"Well," Emily said, "it is just that I hate to expect too much and then be disappointed. I want to be prepared that something may go wrong, so that it will not hit me so hard when it does. I like it much better to be pleasantly surprised when I am expecting the worst."

Hope looked at her thoughtfully for a moment. Then she said, "We are very different, but I suppose that is why we love each other. We complement each other and together we constitute a wholeness, don't you think?"

"I do," Emily agreed, "I think that without you my life would be a sad one. I love you more than I can express!"

**

A week later, they went for the first time to see one of the new American motion pictures that were becoming so popular in London. It was made by Charlie Chaplin and was called 'The Kid'. It began with a woman leaving a Charity Hospital with a new-born baby in her arms. She abandons him in a car seat with a note, but the car gets stolen. When the thieves discover the baby, they unload it near some trashcans, and Charlie, a tramp, finds him and brings him up. Together, they live as thieves and hustlers, while in the meantime, the mother has become a famous opera singer. She comes upon this little boy and, without knowing that he is her real son, starts helping him in various ways. The police want to take the boy away to an orphanage and Charlie protests but loses. He falls asleep and dreams of angels, and in the end, he is picked up by a car and taken to a house where he is happily united with his mother. Hope and Emily cried and laughed at this motion picture and became thoroughly enchanted with the story, Charlie Chaplin and the other actors. Afterwards, Hope remarked that even though none of the actors had said anything, she had felt completely taken in by the story and its characters. Emily agreed wholeheartedly, and they decided that this would not be the last time they went to see motion pictures. Charlie Chaplin, who had been born in England, was visiting London in September, and they both wanted to go and see him in person if they could get the time off from work. After work, they did go to the hotel where he was staying, but the crowds were enormous, so they gave up.

**

The year of 1921 ended with the signing of an Anglo-Irish Treaty which gave independence to the Irish republic except North Ireland which remained a part of Great Britain. The year had been turbulent and bloody with many incidents between the Irish and the British soldiers and police. During 1922, Britain gradually relinquished its power over The Republic of Ireland and left its military bases behind. Lloyd George had to withdraw as prime minister after his and Churchill's plans to fight a war against Turkey were defeated. He was followed by the conservative Bonar Law, who had to retire already the following year in May because of ill health.

Hope and Emily celebrated their classes' graduation in April and both celebrated their birthday in 1922, Hope her thirty-fifth and Emily her thirty-fourth. They began to make plans for their trip abroad. With their savings, they should be able to travel for a month in the summer, and they both wanted to visit Italy.

The time until the beginning of the summer holiday in July 1922 passed quickly, and the two women made a short visit to Calne to tell Sarah and Eleanor about their plans. Eleanor came to the station to pick them up with the horse and buggy the sisters had acquired just after the war. It hardly had room for three people, but they managed to fit themselves in. Hope was impressed.

"Now the two of you can get around in style," she said. "I wonder if we shall soon be picked up in an automobile when we come."

"Do not set your hopes too high little sister," said Eleanor. "None of us can drive an automobile, and I guess we would be too nervous to even try."

Sarah would be fifty-nine years old that year, but she was still very healthy. Eleanor was still only forty-five, and Hope knew that she would need only a small push to learn to how to drive an automobile, but she held off for now.

During supper, Hope and Emily laid out their preliminary plans for their trip. They would leave England on July 20 and go to Paris for their first brief stop before going on to Italy. In Italy, they planned to visit Venice, Rome and Naples. Sarah, who could still remember some of the places she had visited when travelling with their mother and father, told them what she remembered.

"I was born in Madagascar," she said, "but my earliest memories are of Creve Coeur in Mauritius. Warm and lovely place… that is all I remember. My brother Henry was born there, too. Then we went back to England for a while before we sailed for Japan. The time in Japan is what I recall most vividly. I was six or seven years old, I think. We lived in a very nice house in Nagasaki with a garden, and we had a Japanese maid who took care of us. Mrs Goodwin was also there almost every day. She was a great friend of our parents, and every time we had a new little brother or sister, she would stay at the house to help our mother cope. She also taught at the school nearby, and we all went there when we were children. There were other teachers, and mother also helped teach us about many different things."

Sarah stopped talking, lost in her memories of a happy childhood.

"We all grew up speaking both English and Japanese, and we had many friends from other countries as well," added Eleanor. "I forgot my Japanese after we moved to England and I started to go to school."

"Do you think you may ever go so far away as to Japan?" asked Sarah suddenly.

"Probably not," said Hope.

"I would certainly like to see China and Japan," said Emily. "Japan sounds like a lovely place, even though it must have changed a lot since you were there twenty-seven years ago."

"I am sure it has," Sarah commented. "After all, it has been through wars with both China and Russia, and it was on our side during the Great War. The Japanese are now members of the League of Nations, but their continued efforts to expand into China and Siberia may lead to conflicts."

Hope was surprised at how well Sarah seemed to be informed. She had not paid much attention to what the newspapers wrote about Asia, but apparently, Sarah had. She looked at Sarah with renewed respect.

"You have kept up your interest in Japan," she ventured. "I am surprised that you are so well informed."

"Well, I still read books and newspapers," said Sarah, slightly offended, "and when Henry visits now and then, we always discuss Japan and how things are there. He lends me books occasionally, and I read them. After all, we both lived there for a lot of years, even though Henry went off to school in Repton when he was around nine years old. I also occasionally hear from my old Japanese friends."

"How is Henry these days?" Hope asked.

Eleanor answered: "He is still a bachelor, and I doubt that will ever change. He is a grumpy school master, and I do not think he will ever stop trying to lecture us and everybody else about things. But he is an old dear when he comes to visit us in his shiny new automobile and takes us for drives around the countryside."

Hope thought about her uncle, Henry. She had not seen him for years. They were both teachers, but her brother was an old-fashioned grammar school master with a university degree, while she was a middle school teacher trained in a teacher's college. Maybe they did not have much in common after all. Still, she promised herself to write him a letter from Italy. She asked Sarah if she thought that might be a good idea, and Sarah confirmed that it would definitely please him.

Sarah kept up with all their brothers and sisters, and she told Hope that Arthur was still a career officer in the navy and away on a ship most of the time. Nevertheless, he had met an English girl in India in 1916 and had married her in Bengal. In 1921, Arthur and his wife had been on holiday in Jersey and also visited their cousin who worked as a cook in Gorey. Amy had been pregnant at the time and gone into labour six weeks early. Their baby boy was born prematurely and could not eat properly, and he only survived for a day and a half. He had been baptised Graham Barton, and they had buried him in Gorey. Sarah's eyes filled with tears as she told Hope about the agonised letter she had received from their brother, who was deeply worried about his wife's ability to recover after such heartbreak.

Bertha had married a cricketer and their brother William was also a cricketer of some fame, who had finally married after fathering two illegitimate children. Just before the war, his wife, Evelyn, had borne him a daughter whom they had named Diana. Sophia was married to an Irish clergyman and they did not have any children. How Sarah kept up with all of them, Hope did not know, but apparently, they all wrote Christmas letters every year, a custom Hope herself had almost abandoned. But she had no doubt that Sarah kept them all informed about each other as well as about how she herself was doing.

Trip to Europe with Emily in 1922

On July 21st, 1922, they got on the train to Calais and crossed the Channel to begin their holidays. From Calais to Paris, they again boarded a train, and the whole trip would take one day at the most. Already on the train ride through Belgium and Northern France they could glimpse the horrific damage done to this area where the trench war had played out. Although reconstruction had begun in many places, there were large areas where not a house or tree had been left standing, and even the soil had been upturned. Many unexploded grenades were still left in the ground, and some places had been declared 'red zones' in which nothing could grow for some time. This was where so many young men had been killed, and Hope and Emily felt compelled to pray silently for their souls, if for nothing else then at least to revere their brief existence and their suffering. In some places, there were ruins of houses blasted by artillery or burnt to the ground.

As they drew closer to Paris, they could see fields of wheat and grass with cows that seemed untouched. However, France seemed to be in a serious economic slump, even though they had been on the winning side of the war. The country seemed to recover very slowly under President Poincaré, but Germany was defaulting on their war reparations, and France herself had debts to pay after the war.

Europe was trying to get to terms with the many refugees from various places and suspicion of foreigners was still very high. Hope and Emily had acquired the passports with photographs that were now required to enter most countries. As British subjects, they had no problems when entering Belgium or France, and they were already getting used to the fact that one had to carry valid identity papers in order to cross borders, and they knew that these papers were the most valuable of the things they carried with them.

The French were determined to build up their country's defences, so that they would never be attacked by the Germans again. As part of this, they demanded high reparations from Germany to cover their war losses, but Germany had no way of paying what they demanded. The war had taken so many young men's lives that women had been obliged to step in and take many of the jobs that had traditionally been done by men. The self-confidence they had gained was impressive, and Hope and Emily found some optimism in that.

They had written to reserve a cheap hostel in the Quartier Latin, and to get there from the train station, they went by a bus and were let off in front of the road to their hotel. They rang the bell of the hostel, and the concierge let them in and took them to a small room with a double bed and a French balcony from where they could look down on the street.

"Breakfast is at eight o'clock, and curfew is at midnight," the concierge said, "and you cannot have any gentlemen visiting in your room. There is a room downstairs where breakfast is served and where visitors can be entertained in the afternoons."

"Oui, madame," the two women answered and smiled. Nothing was further from their minds than having male visitors. They unpacked their things and went out for an evening meal. Their hotel was near Boulevard de St Germain, and there were several restaurants to choose from. They picked one that looked relatively cheap and went inside to eat. The food was plain but absolutely delicious, and they drank a glass of red wine with it. This made them feel deliciously sinful, and they were in high spirits as they walked arm in arm back to the hostel. "I think I love Paris," said Hope. "Not that I would like to live here, but we could certainly go for holidays here again, don't you think?"

Emily laughed, "If you love Paris after one glass of wine, then let's have two of them tomorrow. But I agree with you. The food is good, and I think we will like the city when we see more of it tomorrow."

The next morning, they woke up early and went down for breakfast. There were several people there, and they shared their breakfast table with two young men who had travelled from Denmark and were going to Italy to study art. They introduced themselves as Olav and Peter, and they came from upper class families in Copenhagen. Their English was excellent, and they spoke French as well. Before they continued on to Italy, they wanted to see the art scene in Paris, and today they were going up to Montmartre, which was a thriving community of artists. Hope looked at Emily and then spoke.

"This is our first day in Paris, and we do not know our way about. Would you mind awfully to take us along? We will not bother you when we get there, if you will only take us there." Emily nodded, and Olav answered.

"We would like very much to have you accompany us up there, but you may have to make your own way back to the hotel tonight. Is that all right?" The girls nodded and did not ask what Olav and Peter had planned for the evening.

"Let's meet in front of the hotel in an hour," said Peter.

Hope and Emily went back to their room to get dressed for the trip. It was a warm day, so they settled for white summer dresses with broad belts and large decorated sunhats. They decided to wear sturdy walking shoes as they expected to walk a great deal.

From the hostel, the four of them walked together to the nearest metro station. They would be going to Anvers station and walk from there up the hill to Montmartre. On the way, they chatted about their lives. Hope and Emily told the young men that they were schoolteachers on their summer holiday, and Olav and Peter were still studying to become painters. They both said their parents wanted them to go into trade but that they had been given a year of freedom to travel and look around now that they had finished their university education. It would be their 'grand tour,' and they would be expected to settle down after they returned. Both Hope and Emily were a little envious of them, and Emily asked, "Do rich Danish girls also get to go on a year's trip around Europe paid for by their father's money?"

"Certainly not," Peter replied. "Not if they are nice girls. Why should they want to? They may go with their husbands once they are married, who knows."

"So, we are not nice girls?" asked Hope.

Peter blushed and said, "It is different for you two. You both do honest work and earn your own money. You certainly seem to me to be nice girls."

The train rolled into Anvers and they got off.

"Are you prepared to walk upward for a while?" asked Peter. "If not, we can find a carriage of some sort."

Both women declared that they wanted to walk, and they set off and were soon in the narrow streets climbing upwards towards the top of Montmartre. A variety of colourful shops and cafes appeared, and when they neared the top, a number of painters with their easels could be seen painting the streets and the buildings. At the top, the Basilica de Sacré Coeur, which had been finished in 1914 but only recently consecrated, lay as a beautiful and impressive landmark that could be seen from far away. The view from the top of the mount was breathtaking, and after looking a while, they walked to the Place du Tertre and found a small café that served lunch. Olav and Peter had a glass of wine but Hope and Emily asked for tea to drink. Over lunch, they talked about what they were seeing around them.

"What a lovely square this is," said Emily. "The artists must have a hard time making a living, but they make this place very colourful."

"Picturesque, I would say," Hope added and smiled. "I am glad we came here. Thank you for taking us, both of you."

They agreed to split up after lunch as the women had a long list of the places they wanted to see, and they had less time to spend in Paris than Olav and Peter. They said their goodbyes and began to walk down to the city below. They used the Eiffel Tower as a landmark and walked towards it down to the river Seine. On their way down, they passed the Moulin Rouge where Toulouse-Lautrec had painted the theatre's famous posters. They did not go all the way but stopped to see the Rodin Museum and the Church of Saint Sulpice on the way. Finally, they went into the Luxembourg Gardens to rest a while before they went back to their hotel.

***

The following morning had been set off for a visit to the Louvre where they bought picture postcards for their family and friends. The famous painting of the Mona Lisa had been stolen in 1911 and was lost for almost two years before it was returned. This had only added to the fame of Leonardo da Vinci's portrait of Lisa Gherardini, the wife of a Venetian silk merchant. As they looked at it, they tried to find out why this portrait in particular had become so famous. The slightly corpulent woman was standing, turned faintly to the right and with her hands clasped in front of her. On her face was a dignified half smile while her eyes looked somewhat sad. Her features were regular, framed by her loose dark hair which reached below her shoulders. In the background was a dreamy landscape, which conveyed depth to the picture.

Hope and Emily agreed that she was beautiful and mysterious before they went on to look at the rest of the art works.

There were so many other paintings and sculptures in the museum that they could not possibly see them all. They took a late lunch in a small café near Point Neuf and sat and enjoyed the sun for a while.

Later that afternoon, they stumbled over the bouquinistes, the booksellers along the quays of the Seine River. Their enthusiasm for browsing the many books and magazines on sale made them forget their tired legs, and although most of the literature was in French, the prices were not high, and they each chose several books to take back home. Hope bought poems by Baudelaire and Rimbaud and a few others, while Emily went more for novels.

***

After supper that evening, they planned the last day of their stay just strolling around the Latin Quarter. Here they came across a man and a woman, Henri and Claudette, who were working in a café. Henri was a painter and Claudette wrote poems, and they both worked in the restaurant business to survive. They told Emily and Hope about the Dada movement that had started in 1916 as a sort of protest against the meaninglessness of life. Its exponents were artists like the German Max Ernst, the Spanish Salvatore Dali and many others. They inspired surrealism and a variety of new art forms. Artists from all over Europe were becoming involved, and they were making contact across borders now that the war was over. Several of them had fought on opposite sides in the war, but this only united them in their feelings of absolute disgust for politics, and they refused to let anything stand above art and the enjoyment of life. Emily and Hope were very interested, so they stayed in the café for hours and bought several rounds of wine for all of them. Their long conversation with the couple and what they learned from them made them feel more hopeful for the future than they had done in a long time. On their way back to the hotel, they decided that they wanted to learn more about this new kind of art when they got a chance.

***

The next day, they were back at the station and found their train for Italy. They would go directly to Rome and Naples and then stop in Venice on their way back home. They got on the Simplon Orient Express, boarding a Wagon-Lit that would take them south through Lausanne and through the Simplon Tunnel to Milan and then to Rome. The train would be avoiding Germany, which the allies still did not trust completely. Their compartment converted into two beds at night and into a seating area by day, and it was quite comfortable. It was late afternoon when they left Paris, and after eating supper in the dining car, they sat reading in their compartment until the conductor came and converted the space to a sleeping car. When they went to bed, they were already in the south of France, and when they woke up the next morning, they had gone through the tunnel and were out of Switzerland and passing into Italy.

Hope and Emily had heard and read of the unrest in Italy and the new man who aspired to become the ruler, Benito Mussolini. The son of a blacksmith and later working as a stonemason himself, he had been a socialist from childhood, and when he moved to Switzerland to avoid military service, he also attended university courses in Lausanne. When he returned to Italy in 1904 during an amnesty for deserters, he served two years in the army. Then he became a schoolteacher for some years, edited a socialist magazine and became the secretary of the Socialist Party. He wrote extensively and became a leading figure among Italian socialists. Gradually, however, he became more and more critical of Marxism and egalitarianism, and when the war came, he was expelled from the socialist party for disagreeing with its anti-war stance. He then turned away from socialist ideas in favour of revolutionary nationalism in which national identity and loyalty had replaced class struggle. He formed the Fascist Party in 1914, and this new party often had violent encounters with both socialists and with the authorities. He was badly wounded in the war in 1917, and when he recovered, he became the editor-in-chief of his old newspaper *Il Popolo d'Italia.* He promoted the idea of fostering warriors who could lead the people in gaining 'vital space' for Italy to grow and prosper. That the neighbouring states might not like this was no problem for Mussolini, who believed that a small population of Italians would be much better than a large population of Slavs, who were inferior people in his eyes. The same was true for the black people of Africa. Mussolini wanted to promote lots of births in Italy in order for the nation to be numerically strong enough to conquer the lesser races in a larger territory, which could then be dominated by the superior Italians. He formed groups of armed former veterans, 'blackshirts', who were to keep order in the streets. The government was very shaky, and Emily and Hope could not help but be a little apprehensive about what they would find in Rome. *Would it be an unsafe place to be in?*

Hope and Emily arrived as planned in Rome at the Termini station and found a nice hotel nearby in the Esquiline, where the host spoke English. They asked him about the security situation, and he calmed them by saying that everything was very quiet just now, and that he would let them know if anything happened that could become dangerous.

"We would like to see the city, especially Saint Peter's Basilica and the Borgia Apartments, so may we book a room here," they asked, and they got a nice double room with a washstand in the corner. The hotel served dinner at 8 o'clock every evening, but the owner advised them to be back before darkness fell, because the city was unsafe for women, with frequent unrest and attacks.

***

The next morning, they had an Italian breakfast with strong coffee and rolls with jam. They would both have liked some strong tea, but they told each other encouragingly that they had not come abroad to live exactly like they did at home, and the coffee was actually quite delicious. Afterwards, the hotel manager told them how to find transportation for Saint Peter's Basilica in front of the station where they had arrived the previous day. They could take an electric tram, and they could buy their tickets on the tram. This sounded very easy and they soon found the right tram in front of the station. While they rode through the city, they looked for familiar landmarks.

"Rome was originally built on seven hills," began Emily, "and our hotel is actually on one of them, the Esquiline."

"I know," Emily replied, "but now that the city has grown so large, you would not notice that. I guess those hills were not all that tall to begin with. If you hadn't read the Baedeker, you wouldn't even be able to tell from just walking around, I suppose."

From the bus, they discovered the Pantheon and they also caught a glimpse of what they thought was the Trevi Fountain, and they decided to walk back that way to see more. But their first goal was the Basilica of Saint Peter and the Sistine Chapel, of which they had heard so much.

The bus stopped in front of St Peter's Square, and the conductor kindly showed them how to walk to the front of the church where they could buy tickets. On their way, they had not noticed any unrest, but they could see that many people still seemed poor and undernourished. Not that they themselves looked that well dressed or rich, because they

68

had deliberately not spent much on their clothing. They wanted to save as much as possible to make their money last as long as possible.

They walked across the large square and stopped for a moment by the fountain and the Egyptian Obelisk. It was said to be 4000 years old and had been brought to Italy by Caligula in 37 AD, and in 1585, Pope Sixtus decided to move it to Saint Peter's Square. It was one of several Egyptian obelisks in Rome, and it was unadorned. It was also said to have witnessed the crucifixion of the Apostle Peter in the year 64.

"Witnessed," Emily remarked drily, "where are its eyes?"

Hope and Emily walked up to the entrance of the church and passed the colourful Swiss Guards, who had been guarding the Pope since the fourteenth century. When they entered the church, they first of all noticed how enormous it was. It made the people standing near what was presumably the altar look very small!

"This must be the largest church I have ever seen," Emily whispered to Hope, who nodded and whispered back, "The largest in the world, I have been told."

The church had the shape of a cross, and where the two lines crossed, there was a fine dome erected on top. Along the aisles of the nave were numerous smaller chapels, each a piece of art in themselves. In the heart of the basilica were two staircases made from marble, which led to the lower chapel, built on the level of the old Constantine church on top of which the renaissance church had been constructed. St Peter's grave was supposed to lie underneath.

Hope and Emily wandered around the church and admired the marble and wooden interior as well as the numerous beautiful artefacts, which were all over the place. The gorgeousness of the surroundings was at the same time absolutely stunning and slightly nauseating in their opulence, although their beauty and perfection could not be denied. When they finally left the church, and stepped out on the piazza again, they were ravenous. They left the piazza to find a place to have lunch before they began to look for the Sistine Chapel.

Later, they entered the Borgia Apartments where the papal art collections were held. Walking through several rooms of lesser interest, they eventually reached the entrance to the Sistine Chapel, which was at the far end from the entrance. On their way, they passed other rooms that would have been interesting to take a look at, but they had to hurry in order to see what they had come for before closing time. After waiting a few minutes outside, they were able to enter the large rectangular room. It had a vaulted ceiling that they had to look at by tilting their necks backwards. There were arched windows down each side, but several of them had been blocked, so that they had to get their eyes used to the half-light of the chapel. But soon they could see the magnificent frescoes that covered the walls and ceiling. The ceiling was painted by Michelangelo between 1508 and 1512. The sidewalls were divided into three tiers of which the central one had two cycles of paintings, one describing the life of Moses and one describing the life of Jesus. They were painted in 1480 by four renaissance painters, Botticelli, Ghirlandaio, Roselli and Perugino, and their workshop apprentices.

Beneath these were hangings in silver and gold and above the two cycles of narrative frescoes was the upper tier with its gallery of Popes. Around the arched tops of the windows were lunettes containing the ancestors of Christ. These were painted by Michelangelo as parts of the ceiling. It was a beautiful room, but it was not until they finally bent their necks all the way backward and took in the ceiling that they realised its stunning magnificence. On the ceiling, Michelangelo had painted a series of pictures of God's creation of the world, his relationship with mankind and finally, man's fall from grace. One of the most famous frescoes by Michelangelo was God's creation of Adam. It showed God with a host of angels behind him stretching out his finger towards a naked man lying on a green hill. The man reached out and their fingers almost touched or maybe had just touched. The rest of the frescoes on the ceiling were also from the Genesis and showed the creation of the Earth, Noah's story and God driving Adam and Eve from the Garden of Eden after the snake had tempted Eve.

Hope and Emily were overwhelmed. Most of all they wanted to lie down on the floor and look at all the details of the pictures, but that was surely not allowed, so they just stood and looked up until their necks began to hurt. Hope's attention kept going back to the fresco of God and Adam and their outstretched hands. With such art, she supposed it was easier for Catholics to hold on to their belief in God, no matter how bad and cruel the world was.

She remembered the very strict and proper protestant churches in England. They had a few stained-glass windows with pictures, but they had no such unrestrained religious art like they had seen both in Saint Peter's Basilica and here. She was interrupted in her reverie by Emily, who complained that her neck was getting sore. She took Hope's arm and suggested that they go outside to the square to find a place to rest and perhaps have a cup of coffee. The museum would close soon, so Hope readily followed her.

"I am rather sated with religious art for today," Emily said.

"Yes, it is stunningly beautiful," Hope agreed, "but it is almost too much."

***

They then decided to explore something about pre-Christian Rome on the next day. "Let us go to the Colosseum tomorrow," Hope said. "I, too, have had enough for now of fine paintings depicting Christian motives. But I cannot help thinking of the immense riches that the Catholic Church have had at their disposal to do all this."

"So much money and talent spent on making people believe in God, instead of making them improve the world we are living in and making people's lives better," said Emily.

Hope shook her head sadly. "Not to mention the role played by religion in causing wars through the times." They sat in the hot July air and tried to cool themselves with the fans they had brought with them. While they waited for their coffee, they rubbed their sore necks.

"It is like there are two opposite sides to humanity, don't you think? There is a side devoted to beauty and reflection, and another devoted to destruction and the killing of each other because of religion or other delusions," Hope said with an involuntary shudder.

"Yes, I believe you are right," said Emily, "but I wonder if each human being may not contain both sides. Religion would explain that as the evil being the work of Satan, wouldn't they?"

"I guess so," said Hope, "but I do not believe it deep down. There must be some other explanation, I am sure. I just do not know what it is."

"Good and evil seem to be struggling," said Emily, "but maybe that is just the way we are seeing it. Maybe each of them simply exists to remind us that the other is there, too. Or maybe they are not really opposites like they seem to us..." she trailed off. They both sat silently for some time before they decided to head back to their hotel.

***

The next day, they set out to visit the Colosseum. They walked through Rome for most of an hour before they could see the ruins of the Colosseum, but it was an enjoyable walk through parts of the classical city. They passed the ruins of the ancient Forum where several archaeologist teams were working on excavation sites, and after a further walk, they reached the enormous walls of the Colosseum. The large amphitheatre had been built almost two thousand years ago and had been destroyed several times by fire or earthquakes. But it had also been rebuilt and restored so that now one could still see a part of the high outer wall. Inside, the floor was gone, but it was possible to use gangways to walk across the floor and see the lower parts and tunnels where wild animals and gladiators had been kept for the games. All around there had been seats for the audience with space for up to 50,000 spectators to sit. It was hard to imagine nowadays, but both women knew that these games had comprised fights to the death between gladiators and wild animals up until only a little over a millennium ago. Both criminals and the early Christians had been submitted to such cruel deaths in front of spectators who enjoyed the drama's mixture of fear and despair with its accompanying human pain, blood and gore. It was cooler in the shadows of the Colosseum's walls, and they shivered when they thought of what had been going on there in Roman times.

On their way back to the hotel, they witnessed a street fight between what looked like unemployed workers and the paramilitary forces called the blackshirts. It seemed to draw more people and get more and more violent, so Hope and Emily turned down a side street to get away from the disturbance and back to the safety of their hotel.

***

During their evening meal, they talked about their plans for the trip. "I want to go to Naples and see Mount Vesuvius and Pompeii as we have planned," Hope said, "and I would not mind leaving Rome tomorrow, actually. There may be a lot more things that we ought to see, but I really do not feel comfortable here. The atmosphere in this town feels very charged, like a volcano about to erupt."

Emily laughed. "So instead you want us to visit a real volcano that erupted only seventeen years ago and is still active?"

"I only want to see it from a distance, and I definitely want to see Pompeii, which was destroyed in the year 79 and then buried in ash and other debris for over a thousand years and forgotten until the 18th century. It is said that one can see how the people at that time were living just as they were suddenly killed by heat and ash. They left their houses in such a hurry that food was still left on their tables. Isn't that something we should see: the past kept as it was for all those years?"

Emily said, "Of course we should see it. It may be almost like travelling in time. I do think, though, that we should stay one more day to properly explore Rome. What do you say?"

"I think that will be fine," Emily said. "After all, we have both seen street violence before and survived, haven't we? But let us leave the day after tomorrow and hope that Naples is less tense."

On their last day in Rome, they had agreed to go to see the so-called Altar of the Fatherland near the Piazza Venezia, so they got on a tram towards the Capitoline Hill. The large structure had been built in 1885 in honour of King Victor Emmanuel II, who was called 'the Father of the Fatherland' because he unified Italy as one kingdom in 1861. It had been designed by Guiseppe Sacconi, and many Italian sculptors had contributed to it. There were stairways, columns, fountains, a sculpture of Victor Emmanuel on a horse and two statues of the Goddess Victoria in horse drawn carriages. The whole structure was 135 meters wide and 70 meters high. It was really more impressive than beautiful, but Emily and Hope had come specially to see one part of it, which had only the year before been designated as the grave of the unknown soldier.

The idea of commemorating all the unidentified soldiers who had died in wars grew especially strong in Britain and France after the Great War had ended in 1918. In Britain, a funeral had been held in Westminster Abbey on Armistice Day 1920, and in France, the Tomb of the Unknown Soldier was created under the Triumphal Arch, both with an eternal flame. The ide had caught on in other countries as well, and in 1921, USA, Portugal and Italy had also established such tombs. They would usually hold the unidentified remains of a soldier inside, found and chosen by the veterans of the war, but in Italy, the process had been slightly different. Eleven bodies of unidentified soldiers from different battlefields southeast of Rome had been dug up and taken to Aquileia's Cathedral in Northern Italy. One of those eleven bodies would then go on to be interred in the monument for Victor Emmanuel on the 4th of November 1921, the third anniversary of the Italian victory. In the cathedral where the bodies were gathered, the mother of a dead volunteer soldier from Trieste, Maria Bergamas, was asked to choose a body on the 28th of October. This was the first time a woman was allowed to play a key role in a national ceremony. The idea was to highlight the Christian idea of the *mater dolorosa,* the grieving mother, who like Jesus' mother had tragically and heroically lost her son.

Maria Bergamas then followed the body on its solemn journey by train to its final destination in Rome, where it arrived on November 1st after stopping 120 times in villages and cities for local communities who wished to pay homage to this symbol of all their lost young men. The ceremony gathered people from all walks of life to share their grief in unison despite the political rift that had gradually been created by Mussolini and his blackshirts.

After standing a short while in front of the Italian unknown soldier's grave, they walked away. Hope said: "If there is going to be equality between men and women, I guess women will be expected to serve as soldiers, too. Don't you?"

Emily's first reaction was to laugh, but when she realised that Hope was serious, she stopped laughing. "Getting the right to vote and play a role in decisions made on behalf of all the men, women and children is not much to ask for, is it. I have never thought of equality going much further than that. After all, men and women are basically different physically and mentally."

"I wonder," mused Hope. "We say that men are strong and women are weak, but we have both seen very physically strong women and also some men that were not very strong. Could that be more about what one is brought up to be? In farming, for instance, many girls become very strong because of the hard work they are expected to do."

"Yes," conceded Emily, "but women get pregnant and must care for the children. Men just do not have that instinct, nor the physical ability to care for babies."

"No," said Hope, "but women like you and I will probably never have babies, so why should our whole lives be determined by the fact that we are capable of conceiving them? More and more women are doing things that only men used to do, both intellectually and physically. There are women who fly airplanes, aren't there?"

This, Emily had to concede. They had both read stories about Baroness de Laroche in France and Bessica Raiche in America, who even built an airplane for herself.

They walked silently on through the Borgo area towards the Tiber River and over the first bridge to visit the small, boat-shaped Tiber Island. There was an old hospital and a church built on top of an ancient temple. They crossed the second bridge and entered the Travestere area where they found a small café and sat down for a rest. Emily picked up their conversation about men and women.

"I have been thinking about equality between men and women," began Emily, "but I cannot get beyond the biological differences. I do not think that men are better or worse than women at a lot of the things that men seem to have claimed for themselves in this world. Men have all the privileges but also the responsibility that goes with it. They are supposed to work to feed and protect their families, even if it means that they have to go to war and perhaps offer up their lives. Women have to protect their homes and their children as best they can in such situations. And to fill as many supportive roles as they can. Women, too, do go to war, you know. As nurses, drivers, couriers, and many other necessary services. Don't you think we have different roles to play?"

"That is definitely so now," Hope said, "but if women had more say in matters of state, they might influence decisions about whether there should be any war at all. It is certainly difficult to imagine a world in which men and women would be completely equal and could live in the way their abilities would take them, regardless of what they looked like between the legs when they were born. I do think it could be a better world, however."

"I wonder," said Emily, "but I do not think it will ever be a reality. I have read about matriarchal societies in the past, but never about societies where men and women had equal status and roles. It is interesting to imagine a world which is completely neutral as to whether a person is of one or the other in terms of sex."

They both fell silent again, thinking about what kind of society the future might bring.

After their coffee and cake, they felt rested and decided to take a look at the part of town they had ended up in after crossing the river. Trastevere was an ancient part of town with cobbled streets and many narrow alleys. It was a culturally diversified part of Rome, and Hope and Emily felt more comfortable there than they had done elsewhere in the city. There were no signs of the militant blackshirts, perhaps because resistance was strong and Trastevere was dominated more by a population of the socialist and communist working class. Emily and Hope could not read the Italian newspapers very well nor understand what people were saying to each other, so all they could do was attempt to gauge the undercurrents of political unrest.

When they finally found their way back to the hotel and told the manager that they would like to check out in the morning and go to Naples, he did not seem at all put out that they wanted to shorten their stay in Rome. On the contrary, he said that he thought that it was a good decision, given the political tensions in the city.

***

Naples is a paradise; everyone lives in a state of intoxicated self-forgetfulness, myself included. I seem to be a completely different person whom I hardly recognise. Yesterday I thought to myself: Either you were mad before, or you are mad now (Johann Wolfgang Goethe, 1787)

The next day, they took the train to Naples and found a place to stay before they walked around the city. They found a bus for Pompeii and bought tickets for the following morning.

Despite the proximity of Naples to such a large and destructive volcano, its inhabitants seemed carefree and happy. It was such a relaxing contrast to Rome with its tense atmosphere. It was not that its people were more prosperous, but they simply seemed more easy-going and cheerful.

The city had been founded by Greeks from Rhodes hundreds of years before Christ, and it had fought in alliance with Rome against Carthage. To Rome, it was a paragon of Hellenistic cities where they would visit and have summer villas. The Romans built aqueducts, public baths and temples, and several Roman emperors spent their holidays there from time to time. When the Western Roman Empire fell to the Ostrogoths, Naples, too, was subdued and became part of the Ostrogoth's territory until the Byzantine Empire seized control in 553. Over the next centuries, Naples was dominated by many different foreign powers until it finally gained its independence in the ninth century. However, by 1137, the Normans gained control of all the large city-states on the peninsula and Naples became a centre for art and education as well as for trade by sea. In spite of the many political upheavals and changes, Naples ended up being the second largest city in Europe in the seventeenth century, second only to Paris.

Italy did not begin to become a unified country until 1861. When Giuseppe Garibaldi managed to raise his 'Expedition of the Thousand' Italy eventually united as a kingdom. This led to an economic collapse for Naples and about four million people emigrated over the next decades until the Great War started in 1914, and Italy joined in 1915. Naples had by then become an impoverished and unhealthy city, plagued by many epidemics.

Hope and Emily arrived in the city with a clear expectation of entering a once great and powerful place now in a slump, and this expectation turned out to be mostly true, although improvements could be seen. One thing that surprised Hope and Emily was how important women had been in the political conflicts. During the war, women had taken over the jobs that had usually been considered men's work, but at the same time, they held protests to keep their men from being drafted to fight in the war. Some women had been in favour of the war, but the majority had chosen just to endure and try their best to keep their families fed. Those who had fought for the rights of women to vote were generally against the war. But towards the end of the war, the shortages became so dire that many women chose to take part in demonstrations against the lack of bread and the ever-rising costs of living. Some also took part in the many spontaneous strikes for better working conditions and for ending the war. The largest part of women's war participation was, however, charity. Women of all backgrounds had taken it upon themselves to help the families of the soldiers. Subsidies had been handed out, home visits organised and childcare provided. The women had kept soup kitchens open to provide hot meals, and many helped provide woollen vests and socks, underwear and heaters to warm up the soldiers' food rations.

Women were hired to work in clerical positions and even in the munitions industry, where they turned out to be able to work well enough to satisfy the industrialists. In the countryside, farmers' wives could earn extra money by sewing clothes for the soldiers, and artisans and small businesses were also continued by female family members of the drafted owners. The agricultural production was largely kept up by women, children and the elderly, and much transportation was kept going by women drivers. Female nurses were trained quickly, and some had even been sent to the front by the Red Cross.

Of course, there had been voices lamenting this 'distortion' of women's roles, but need had overridden the protestations, and after the war, it was clear that the mobilisation of women had been indispensable for winning the war. But what had come of it? Maybe it was too early to tell, but both Hope and Emily found it hard to see any progress for the Italian women now that the war had ended. Everybody seemed to be intent upon getting back to a normal family life and healing the wounds and scars from the war. Emily and Hope had observed this already in Rome, where they had soon grasped clearly how the war had changed Italy into a deeply divided country in need of a strong leader, capable of uniting people around a common goal. Whether Mussolini was such a man, they could not clearly divine. His followers had appeared to be very violent and intimidating, but who could tell whether that was just a phase that would pass.

Naples was poor and deeply Catholic and living in dangerous proximity to the large volcano, Vesuvius. The faith in the protection of the Neapolitan Patron Saint Januarius and the Virgin Mother was an important creed. The town's historic centre was very large and reflected the central role played by Naples all through history.

**

Having read that Naples was assumed to be the birthplace of the pizza, Hope and Emily set out to find a place where they could have pizza for lunch, and they soon found a small restaurant which specialised in pizza baking. There were several toppings to choose from, but they both settled for a pizza napoletana. They saw how other customers took slices and ate them by hand, so they did the same. It was a delicious and filling meal, and they had a single glass of wine with it and relaxed.

A man, who looked to be around thirty with slightly reddish hair and a moustache, came over to them and asked them in impeccable English if they were Americans, and happy to meet someone who could speak English, they told him that they were from London and were school teachers travelling in Europe. He introduced himself as Mr Anthony Jones from Southampton but added that he had gone to Italy in 1905 and met and since married his Italian girlfriend, so he was feeling more Italian than British. Living with his parents-in-law and helping them in their wine business, he had decided to stay when the war broke out. By being a British citizen, he had avoided the fighting and stayed with his family. His wife had borne him four children, but he had lost two of his three brothers-in-law to the war, so now he had to look after their wives and children, too. They had all looked forward to their business picking up after the war, and it was finally beginning to grow now. He also said that it had been a long time since he had seen any foreign travellers in Napoli and that he enjoyed speaking his mother tongue again. He asked what the war had been like in England, and Emily began to tell him about the many young British men killed in Flanders and France and about the bombings from the air in London, but Hope broke in.

"Let us not talk about the war anymore. Maybe we should try to look forward instead."

Anthony looked sad and said that he was not so sure that the future looked so bright either.

"All the resentments that came out of that war are not resolved. At least not in Italy, where there is a feeling of being cheated out of the things the country was promised in return for entering the war. The fascist nationalists are growing in power under Mussolini, and I am not sure that bodes well for Italy."

"But what do they want to achieve?" asked Hope.

"Well, you know that before the war Mussolini was a socialist and against the war, but he changed his viewpoint and began to support the war, because he thought that the war might bring back Italian greatness. He began to see himself as a revolutionary nationalist and to claim that nationalism was much more important than class struggle. He promotes the idea that Italy must get back the greatness of the Roman Empire all around the Mediterranean. Personally, I am worried that he may gain even more followers and utterly destroy this beautiful place." Anthony sighed and drank deeply from his wine glass.

Hope and Emily had listened intently while he spoke, and though they found it hard to believe that things were really that bad, they thanked him very gratefully for telling them of his worries and promised that they would follow carefully what happened. They gave him Sarah's address in Calne and told him to write them and they would reply. Before they took their leave, they asked him to give their greetings to his family and all the children in his household. In return, he asked them to come back to the restaurant on the day after tomorrow, so that he could take them for supper at his home.

***

The next day, Emily and Hope set out for Pompeii on the coach. In the autumn of the year 79 AD, Vesuvius had erupted violently and killed everyone in Pompeii and neighbouring villages and covered up the place with successive layers of many metres of ash. The event was documented by contemporary historians, but the site was abandoned and over the next centuries, even its name was forgotten. Only in 1599, parts of the walls were unearthed when the building of an underground canal was carried out, but they were covered up and forgotten again. In 1738, the city of Herculaneum was discovered when workmen were building a summer palace for the King of Naples, and ten years later, Pompeii was rediscovered during an excavation by a Spanish military engineer. In subsequent excavations, many intact buildings and wall paintings were revealed. Over the next hundred years, excavations continued and in 1863 when Fiorelli took charge of the work and realised that the hollows in the ground found here and there had been left by decomposing bodies, he devised the technique of injecting plaster into them in order to recreate the shapes of the people of Pompeii who had died in the disaster.

The newly discovered erotic frescoes on the walls presented a problem, as they were far too explicit and daring for the prudish time when they were discovered. Therefore, some of them were hidden away again or locked up. The artefacts discovered were moved to the Naples National Archaeological Museum where some of them were locked away in a so-called 'secret cabinet' which would only be open to men of a mature age and respected morals.

Hope and Emily walked to the site and found it to be much larger than they had expected. As they walked along the ancient paved streets, they tried to envisage how life could have been there before the eruption. They visited the House of Julia Felix, a large Roman villa, which had been converted into living quarters for several families after an earlier earthquake in 62 AD. In Julia's house, the walls had been decorated with paintings which depicted daily life in the Pompeian Forum. There were market stalls, people conversing, beggars and a scene from an open-air school. The city had been divided into rectangular blocks of buildings that contained shops, residences and inns. They saw the remains of the

79

House of Sallust with its atrium and water basin in the middle. They also saw the fantastic mosaics in the vestibule and other rooms of the so-called House of the Tragic Poet and the pictures of Greek myths in the atrium. That such beauty and so much hard work would have been destroyed in half a day by a force of nature... it was a distressing thought, and it left Hope slightly depressed. They walked around a few more houses and then sat down to eat the food they had brought and to talk about their experience.

"What an amazing mix of cultures," said Emily. "Besides the Greek and Roman remains, there was also a temple to the Egyptian Goddess, Isis."

"And it was all destroyed in less than a day," said Hope. "Isn't that the saddest thing?"

Emily did not answer right away. "Do you see only the sadness, Hope? Even before you see the beauty and the miracle of these lives being rediscovered after almost two thousand years? We all have to die some time, don't we? But we and our lives will not be forgotten. We become part of the pageant of human history—not a big part, but we are there. So were they! It does not matter if we are remembered as individuals, but we were here, Hope, we were here!"

Emily's words soothed Hope's momentary sadness. She turned to Emily and put her arms around her. "I adore you, Emily. You are my joy in life, and I do not know what I would do without you! You are right, I tend to see the sadness and melancholy in life, whereas you always see brightness and light. It was what made you so attractive to me when we first met, and it has never left you. I think that when the French use the expression joie de vivre, they must be thinking of someone like you!"

"You have it, too, Hope. You are also a joyful spirit. You just need to be reminded now and then, but it gives you a depth and thoughtfulness that I may sometimes lack."

They looked into each other's eyes for a long time and saw the love they shared for each other. Society might find such love unnatural and impossible but Hope and Emily had long ago decided that their true feelings for each other were right, no matter whether society accepted it or not. Actually, most of society had no idea what two women living together might be up to physically. Illegal sex was defined as penetration by the male penis of anything other than their adult, female wives or lovers. So, men could be punished for having intercourse with young children, animals or other men, and they often were. Women were not supposed to enjoy any kind of sexual intercourse, and if they could not find anybody who would marry them, they were pitied mainly for not being able to bear children of their own.

Even before the Great War, there had been more women in England than men, and the war cost a further 700,000 young men or more their lives. Their absence caused even more young women to be unable to find a husband or to remarry if they had lost their husbands to the war. The middle classes were worse hit than any other since more officers were killed than those of lower ranks. Emily and Hope knew from the beginning that as teachers they would not be able to keep their jobs if they decided to marry, so from the outset, they had not had any such hopes. Instead, they had sought love and tenderness in each other's company and with some experimenting, they had learned to satisfy each other's needs, both emotionally and physically. It was not something they spoke to others about, even though they felt that Sarah and Eleanor and perhaps others, too, might suspect as much, just as they themselves sometimes saw female friendships which they thought might be more intimate than just friendships.

They returned to Naples in the evening on the bus and decided to explore the city the next day.

***

They set out just after breakfast, determined to see as much as possible before they had to be at the restaurant at five o'clock to meet Anthony. They started at the main square of the city, The Piazza del Plebiscito, from where they could see the Royal Palace to one side and the Church of San Francesco di Paola on the other side. They were impressive buildings containing fine statues but Hope and Emily passed them by and went instead to see the Castel Nuovo. Built in the time of the first king of Naples, Charles I, in 1279, it was a powerful mediaeval castle with large round towers on all sides. The main gate had a triumphant arc in white marble, which was added in 1443 to celebrate King Alfonso V's arrival in Naples. Castel Nuovo was indeed an impressive landmark that seemed like a formidable deterrent to enemies.

They walked slowly back to Piazza del Plebiscito and on from there to a small square called Piazza dei Martiri. It had a tall monument in the middle for the virtue of martyrs, and around it in each of the corners were placed four lions. They had been placed there after the Italian reunification in the 1860s to each represent one of the failed rebellions against the Bourbons. They walked around the monument and looked for a place to sit down, but as they did not find any, they continued down towards the Villa Communale, the largest green area in the city. The park had been built by King Ferdinand in the 1780s on reclaimed land. Originally reserved for members of the royal family, it had become open to the public after the unification of Italy in 1869.

It was a large park along the coast, known for its aquarium and research station, which had been started by the Prussian zoologist, Felix Anton Dohrn. The public had been charged for entry from the beginning in order to help finance the research that was going on there, and Hope and Emily gladly paid their fee to get inside and look at the many wondrously varied creatures of the sea. In the park itself, there were a number of beautiful fountains to cool the air and to explore.

Eventually, the time came for them to go back to the hotel and change for dinner. At five o'clock they arrived at the restaurant as agreed, and Anthony was waiting for them there. He had an automobile with him and proudly showed it to them.

"I bought it together with my brother-in-law," he said. "We are both very interested in automobiles, and we take turns driving it. As you can see, it is only really meant for two persons to sit side by side, but I thought we could squeeze in the three of us if we tried to make ourselves as thin as possible. Have you ever been conveyed in such a contraption before?"

Since neither Emily nor Hope had ever been in a private car before, they shook their heads and gingerly let themselves be helped up into the seat. Anthony started the car and got in behind the wheel, and they started rolling down the street. After the first few minutes of nervousness, they started to enjoy the ride. Almost before they knew, they were at Anthony's home.

Anthony introduced them to his wife, Lisa, her parents, his two widowed sisters-in-law and the six children in the household aged from ten years old down to the baby Lisa was holding in her arms. Lisa smiled and said, "My youngest, Emilio. Born last year."

Lisa's English was charming but difficult to understand. Hope told Anthony to tell everybody that they were very sorry to intrude on his family without being able to speak their language. But nobody seemed to mind and soon they were all seated around a large dining table. Everybody fell silent as Lisa's father said grace, but as soon as he had finished and made the sign of the cross, everybody started speaking at once. Lisa served the children first, and they fell silent as they began to eat. Then she served her father and mother and the two guests, and then the rest of the adults. All got a heap of spaghetti on their plates with deliciously spicy tomato sauce. Fresh bread was also put on the table. Then several large pizzas were carried in with different toppings. They were cut into wedges so that one could try more than one kind. Lisa and her sisters-in-law were really good cooks, and Anthony said jokingly, "Now you can see and taste why I could never leave Italy!"

After supper, all the children were sent off to bed, and Anthony served them strong mocha coffee in tiny cups. Afterwards, he suggested that they walk back to their hotel with him and Lisa. Hope walked with Lisa behind Anthony and Emily, and Lisa asked her about her family. Hope tried to explain how she was the youngest of eleven children, and how her older sister had brought her up because her mother had died.

"You no mother?" Lisa exclaimed, and there were tears in her eyes as she grabbed Hope's arm. "Poor you!"

"My sister was like a mother to me," Hope explained, but she could see that Lisa was not convinced.

"I am a teacher now, like Emily," she said.

"But no husband," said Lisa, "and no children. You not lonely?"

Hope thought about how to answer. When you had to communicate with a very limited vocabulary, the conversation tended to become more direct and simpler than she felt comfortable with.

"In England, you cannot be married if you are a teacher, so I am not married. But I am not lonely. I live with my friend Emily who is also a teacher. We look after other people's children all day, so we never feel lonely."

"Oh," said Lisa. "I worked in factory in the war but hated it. Just wanted to go back to my children and Anthony and not feel so tired all the time."

Hope sighed. "I can understand that," she said, "and I hope that your children will soon be able to live in peaceful times."

"Oh yes, Signorina Hope, so do I!" Lisa smiled wistfully. "There your hotel." She pointed to the building on the other side of the street. Hope had not even noticed where they had gone, and now it was already time to say goodbye. She gave Lisa a quick hug and said that she would write them a letter. Anthony and Emily had come up to them, and both Emily and Hope thanked them for a wonderful evening and waved goodbye as Anthony and Lisa disappeared down the street hand in hand.

"What a lovely couple," said Emily as they got back to their room. "Anthony was telling me about how he loved living here, but he also told me about how frightened he had been during the 1906 eruption of Vesuvius. It had happened just after he had come out here and before he married Lisa, but he still remembered the sickening feeling of the earth under his feet moving and the rain of ash from the sky. Damages in Naples itself had been minor, and most of the people who had been killed or hurt had lived on the other side of the mountain."

"This happened just after he arrived here?" asked Hope. "Why didn't he move to a safer place?"

Emily laughed. "I don't know, maybe he had already seen Lisa."

"Yes, Lisa," said Hope. "I had quite a nice conversation with her about why we had not married and had not had children. Weren't we lonely? I told her that we could not marry and be sure to keep our jobs, but as friends, we were not lonely. She actually worked during the war, but she hated it and missed her children. I really liked her. She seemed so honest and direct, and even though some of that was because of her limited grasp of English, I felt that the greater part was simply openness and honest interest. I promised we would write letters to her and Anthony in the future."

"We certainly will," Emily said. "I will also want to know how Italy gets on from now on."

The next day was cool but sunny. It was a nice day for walking, so they simply meandered about the streets without any particular aim. The city had a certain dilapidated charm, and they could understand how it had attracted many foreigners before the war.

When they got home at lunchtime, a letter was waiting for them from Anthony who asked them if they wanted to come along with his family to visit the island of Ischia and the thermal baths the day after tomorrow, which was a Sunday. They went over to the address Anthony had written on the note and found Lisa to say that they would be delighted to come and asked what they should bring. Lisa told them to bring just bathing suits and towels, and they agreed to meet in the morning at the ferryboat in the harbour. Lisa sketched a map of how to get there from their hotel. She and Anthony would bring their three older children, Antonio, Maria and six-year-old Emma. The baby would stay at home with the other two children and their grandparents and aunts.

Lisa also told them in halting English that they should visit the Campi Flegrei to the west of the city. "Not beautiful place but grand to see the wildness of the living ground under the feet. In some places, *fumaroles*…I cannot remember the English word, but smoke coming out of the ground, and you can feel the power of God when you stand at the bottom of the Solfatara and smell the hellish smoke and see the mud boiling."

"I know," said Emily. "I have read about it. Solfatara is the crater of an old volcano, and I have heard that it is the sight of a lifetime."

"It sounds dangerous," said Hope, "but I guess we want to go there anyway to see what it is all about."

"I have also read that the ground rises up and down at times," said Emily. "Charles Darwin's good friend, the geologist Charles Lyell who wrote *Principles of Geology*, visited Campi Flegrei about one hundred years ago. We will certainly go there. Thank you, Lisa."

"We will see all of you on Sunday," said Hope. "We look forward to it."

***

The rest of the day they rambled around in Naples and soon found themselves close to the city's archaeological museum.

"We did want to see that, didn't we," said Hope. "It holds many things that were excavated from Pompeii and other things from Naples' past, too."

Emily agreed, and they went to buy tickets.

The museum had three floors, and they began looking around at the many glass cases filled with artefacts. It was all beautiful and interesting, but the way the exhibition was arranged made it hard to focus your attention on specific objects or find out what they had been used for and by whom. Instead, they focused on the sculptures and mosaics, but in the end, they tired of walking around. They found the door to the secret room with the pornographic material which had been removed from Pompeii, but it was locked, and only mature gentlemen were allowed in at specific times. Emily was annoyed. "Why are women not allowed to take a look? One would think it would be more harmful for men to look at people who are not dressed or who are indulging in erotic adventures. Men can do more harm if they are unduly excited, can't they?"

Hope hesitated to answer. Finally, she said, "I guess you are right in that, and their aggression is often directed against women, as we saw before the war during the women's demonstrations for the right to vote. But still, it is interesting why people of two thousand years ago had such a prurient interest in and apparent tolerance for carnal pleasures. I suppose that their pagan religion encouraged it…"

"That might be so," Emily replied, "and who says they were wrong, and we are right? We have been brought up in a culture steeped in Anglican Christianity, and we admire bodily innocence and purity. We find pleasure in abstinence and virtue, and even if we do not consider ourselves religious, we still cannot escape the conventions of the society we were brought up and live in."

"But," protested Hope, "what can we do about it? We are what we are because of how we grew up. We can change some of that, but if we tried to change all of it at once, where would that leave us? Small changes happen all the time and sometimes large ones. But every time changes happen too fast, they are accompanied by suffering and loss of

85

human lives. Think of the war that just ended, think of the revolution a few years ago in Russia…"

Emily bit her lower lip and looked thoughtful, "This is the same person who told me to envision a society where there was no difference between men and women? I can see what you mean, but still, I think that there are things we could fight to change or at least support the fight to change like we did with women's suffrage before the war and maybe still have to do when we get back."

Hope smiled. "We got rather far away from our starting point of this conversation, but I think we agree enough to go and find a café and get some refreshment, don't you?"

Emily did, and they wandered off. They soon found a café and had a small cup of strong coffee.

***

In the morning, they set out by bus to go see the Solfatara caldera and the Campi Flegrei. They got off at Pozzuoli and decided to walk along the Via Solfatara towards the Solfatara caldera. The whole area was volcanic with many craters, but Solfatara was the most accessible. The road was narrow with beautiful views of the Bay of Naples on their right along the way. They walked for a little more than an hour before they began to smell the sulphur of the caldera. It was a very unpleasant smell, but they kept on, and after a while, they did not feel the smell so badly. Soon they stood at the entrance to the caldera. It was huge, with nothing growing there, but apart from the grey stony ground, there were also some poisonous-looking yellow spots from where the odious smell and steam emanated. As they went down the low side of the caldera, the air became hotter, and occasionally, there was a small tremor under their feet which made them feel like small fragile bugs about to be thrown off a stone kicked by a huge boot. Lisa had been right. This was an awe-inspiring place, and it made both of them silent with a mixture of terror and fascination. Here and there they could see pools of boiling mud, and there was also a lake shrouded in vapour because the water in it was so hot. After walking around for about ten minutes, they had had enough of the foul smell and began to make their way out of the caldera and back on the road to Pozzuoli. As the smell grew fainter behind them, they found a place in the sun to sit down and have their lemonade.

"The smell of Hell certainly makes you thirsty, doesn't it," Emily remarked and laughed.

"Yes, it does," answered Hope, "and I am glad that we got to see it. But I am mostly relieved that we got away from there unscathed."

"We are not really away from it," remarked Emily. "This whole area lies in an old caldera, and it must be undermined by volcanic activity—all the way to and including the area of Vesuvius. I don't think I could live permanently in a place like this with the earth ready to blow up under me at any time. I know they say that it has been almost a thousand years since the last known eruption, and they call it dormant, but it seems to me that it is having an unrestful sleep from which it might wake up if you disturb it."

"Well, it probably will not," said Hope. "Let us go back to town and find a place to eat, and after that we can look around at some of the buildings and monuments that have been here for lots of years without being destroyed."

"I wonder what the Earth was like all those years ago before there were humans living here," Emily mused. "A young world that was still settling down…" she trailed off. "It might have looked a lot like the Solfatara crater, don't you think?"

Hope said that she was sure that as time passed, we would know more and more about all of the things that were still mysteries to us.

They were tired when they came back to Pozzuoli and found a nice little restaurant to sit down and rest. They ordered a pizza and a glass of wine each and finished with cups of coffee, and then they were ready to see the town. They first went to see the *Marcellum* food market where three tall columns stood. The century before, they had been thought to be part of a temple, but newer research had shown that they were instead part of an ancient market place. The three characteristic marble pillars had been on the frontispiece of Charles Lyell's book on geology in 1830. The reason they were so interesting was that they had stood intact for almost 2000 years, but even more that the pillars had small holes in them which indicated that molluscs had bored into them at some point, and since molluscs were sea creatures, the pillars must have been partly covered by the sea at some time. Either the sea level had risen and fallen, or the earth itself must have subsided at certain times below sea level. Many nineteenth century scientists had contributed to this discussion, even Johan Wolfgang Goethe, who published a journal article on the subject in 1823. Many thought that the theory of the land having subsided as much as three metres would have been impossible without the columns disintegrating. Lyell, however, in 1830 found other instances of subsiding or uplifting happening over long periods without the buildings being destroyed. Indeed, in 1538, a series of earthquakes had caused a similar upheaval with a new mountain resulting in this area, the 123-meter tall Monte Nuovo just west of the town.

Hope and Emily wandered past the pillars and could see for themselves the rings at different heights, made by molluscs. The site had been well excavated during the past two hundred years, but still there were a few people digging there, and for a moment, Hope and Emily stood and watched their work with interest. Then they left to find the Flavian Amphitheatre, which was said to be the third largest in Italy. It had been built during the reign of the Roman emperor Vespasian and finished by his son Titus in the first century AD. Titus' reign was short (AD 79-81) but it was marked by two major catastrophes of which the first had been the eruption of Mount Vesuvius in AD 79, and it was followed in AD 80 by the burning of Rome. Contrary to expectations, Titus had turned out to be a compassionate leader who in both cases operated with empathy and sought to relieve the plight of the victims. He was actually visiting Pompeii when the fire in Rome broke out and lasted for three days and nights. It was not of the proportions seen 25 years before under Nero, but it still destroyed large parts of Rome. Titus paid for the buildings destroyed in the fire, and he ordered the final construction of the Colosseum in Rome and the one hundred days of games and celebrations after it was finished. The amphitheatre in Pozzuoli was a construction much like the one they had seen in Rome, so Hope and Emily spent only a short time walking through the underground caves which were well preserved while the upper structure had suffered under various earthquakes.

On the bus back to Naples, they both napped a little. It had been an exhausting day, and they looked forward to going with Anthony and Lisa to the thermic baths the next day.

***

Hope woke up early and lay in her bed for half an hour before she got up. She was thinking about her sisters back in England, Sarah and Eleanor. She had begun a letter to them the evening before, and now she sat at the desk determined to finish it and tell them about all the things she and Emily had seen and experienced in Naples. While she was writing, Emily had woken up, too, so she quickly finished her letter. The two women kissed each other and went down for breakfast with the letter, which they asked the concierge to post. Then they set out for the harbour, following Lisa's hand drawn map. They easily found it and the ferry for Ischia, where Anthony and his children were waiting. Lisa was off to secure them good seats on the voyage, so Hope and Emily grabbed the hands of the girls, while Anthony took Antonio's hand. They boarded the ferry and began to look for Lisa and found each other almost immediately. Lisa had held four extra seats in the front of the ferry from where they had the very best view of where they were going. Antonio got his own seat while Maria sat on her mother's lap. Emma, to everybody's surprise, crawled onto Hope's lap and settled down. It was a sunny day, but as the ship began to move out in the Tyrrhenian Sea, the wind became rather chilly, so everybody got out scarves and light shawls to put on. Hope put her shawl around Emma's little body and held her tight. For a moment, she regretted never having a child of her own to snuggle up so closely to her with all the trust in the world. She looked at Emily next to her and then out to the sea and again to Emma now asleep in her lap. She lightly touched her lips to the child's head, before she looked out to the sea again. It was very calm and beautifully blue. The silence was only broken by the ship's motors and some quiet talking among the passengers.

After sailing along the coast for quite a while, they passed the small volcanic island of Procida on their right and began to look out for Ischia itself. Soon they could see it, and Emma woke up and wanted her mother. Emily and Hope stood up from their seat and moved to the rail to see better.

"You with Emma on your lap looked quite Madonna-like," said Emily.

"It felt like that in a way," replied Hope. "I have spent a lot of time with small children before I started my education as a teacher, you know, and children seem to feel safe with me."

"Haven't you ever wanted children of your own?" asked Emily.

"Have you?" Hope asked back.

"No," said Emily, "I like children, but I have never wanted any of my own. I do not want the biological messiness of conceiving them and bearing them, and the responsibility of bringing them up twenty-four hours a day frankly scares me."

"I never thought it was for me either," said Hope. "But only because I do not want to be tied to a man for the rest of my life. And you cannot really bring up a child on your own, I guess."

"We could adopt Emma and bring her up together," Emily said, and they both laughed at the idea.

"Why you laugh?" asked Lisa when they sat down again.

Emily said that they had just been laughing in sheer joy at the beauty of the scenery and the sea. They would not tell her that they had been talking about taking away one of her children…

***

The ferry laid to and they were let off on the waterfront. Antonio led the way to a spa that he and Lisa had visited before, the Casamicciola Terme in the hamlet of Bagni. It was a short walk from the harbour where they had arrived, so they set out walking. The old village of Bagni had been ruined by an earthquake in 1883, but the place had been rebuilt and now had several facilities for enjoying the hot springs and mud. They went to one of these places and had a brief lunch that Lisa had packed before they went in. Here they split up and Anthony and Antonio went to the men's section while Lisa took the girls to the women's section. She spoke briefly to the attendant before turning to Hope and Emily and asked them if they wanted the mud bath treatment. Both agreed and followed the attendant, while Lisa remained with the two little girls. "Meet you out here in an hour," she said and smiled encouragingly at them.

Hope and Emily were taken to a changing room where they took off all their clothes and wrapped themselves in the large sheets that were laid out for them. The attendants took them into the bathing room, where two large tubs of hot mud were waiting for them. A towel was wrapped tightly around their hair and then the attendants indicated that they should get into the tubs of mud. The attendants held up the sheets to protect their privacy until they had lowered themselves into the hot mud and were sitting comfortably with only their heads sticking out of the mud. It was unexpectedly pleasant once they had adapted to the heat, and soon, they were completely relaxed. They could not even muster the energy to talk to each other, so completely did they relax. After thirty minutes had passed, the attendants indicated that they should get up and they were placed on stools and rinsed off with lukewarm water and then led to a pool of hot mineral water. Here they soaked for about ten minutes before they were led back to the dressing room. When they came out, Lisa was waiting for them with Maria and Emma, and they all changed into their bathing suits and went to a sulphurous pool outside and got in. The feeling of sitting with their faces exposed to the outside air with the beautiful landscape all around them and their bodies floating in the hot water was like nothing Hope and Emily had ever tried before. Lisa and the girls' chattering in Italian ran together with the birdsong and the natural sound of the landscape, and while they held hands under the water, they felt a solemn, almost religious coming together of their spirits that was more joyful than words could express.

They had agreed to meet with Anthony and Antonio outside the spa around three o'clock, but when they finally got out of the water, got dressed and set their hair, they were almost a quarter of an hour late. They got two hansom cabs to take them down to the ferry, where they had time for some coffee for the adults and lemonade for the children before boarding the boat back to Naples. Lisa unpacked the last of her provisions for the children, and they all sat and talked about the day's experiences. Maria and Emma soon fell asleep while the others talked.

"Thank you for giving us this marvellous experience," said Hope to Anthony and Lisa. "I was actually a little nervous beforehand, but I cannot remember when I have ever before felt this wonderfully relaxed."

Anthony said, "Maybe you have come to understand some of the good sides of living in a volcanic area. There are compensations for the dangers that we live with."

"I wonder," said Emily. "Would it not be better to live in safe old England and just visit once in a while?"

Lisa interjected, "If volcano wake up, it no matter you be a visitor or one of those live here all the time. No way of knowing when it will happen."

"But it is not just the volcanoes," said Anthony. "The beauty of the bay, the food and not least the people also make it worth living here. I wouldn't exchange Lisa's cooking and our beautiful children for the dampness and blandness of English food. And I love the Italian language, even when it is used for loathsome political slogans."

"Hush," said Lisa. "Not talk politics such public place. Never know who listening."

They all fell silent at this until Lisa asked them about English schools. "We sometimes talk send Antonio to boarding school in England when he fourteen years. You think a good idea?"

"Does he want to go?" asked Hope.

"We have not asked him," Anthony told them. "But he will go if we tell him to."

"I have a brother who teaches at a boarding school in Repton," said Hope. "I can ask him, but I wonder if it will not be too hard for Antonio to live on his own in England."

"I do not know," said Anthony. "It may be even harder for him to live in Italy as a young man in the future. I want to make the best decision for him, but it is hard. I have begun to teach him English in the evenings just in case."

"Let us know if there is anything we can do," said Hope. "We shall be back in England after the summer, and we will do everything we can to help."

"Thank you," said Lisa. "Good to have friends in England, if we decide to send him."

Now Antonio had fallen asleep too, oblivious to the fact that he had been the topic of the conversation. They arrived in Naples and hugged each other goodbye, not knowing if they would ever meet again. On the next day, Hope and Emily had planned to start the last leg of their Italian visit to see the fabled city of Venice. They had about twelve days left before they had to start their journey back to England.

**

The train for Rome and Bologna miraculously left on time, and after settling in their seats, they waved goodbye to Naples, agreeing that so far it had been the most pleasant experience on their tour. Meeting Anthony and his family seemed a completely undeserved blessing and had given them a unique insight into how people in Italy lived their ordinary lives.

When they stopped in Rome after an hour and a half, the train paused for fifteen minutes before it slowly began to move towards Bologna, where they would have to change trains before they continued to Venice. They had thought about stopping in Bologna for a day or two, but when they heard that Mussolini had held a great fascist meeting for 50,000 people there on the 1st of June and declared that he would lead a full-scale revolt against the anti-fascist government, they had decided instead to get off in Florence and spend a little time there before getting back on the train to Bologna and then changing to the train for Venice.

After Rome, their train soon turned away from the coast and began to go inland towards Tuscany with its beautiful landscape. This land was originally inhabited by the Etruscans from whom the name derives, but around 100 AD, it came to be dominated by the Romans. In the fifth century, the Roman state collapsed, and like other parts of Italy, Tuscany came to be governed by a variety of different groups and families up through history. Its main cities, however, remained centres of art and civilisation, and Tuscany is considered the birthplace of the Renaissance. In 1861, Tuscany became part of the united Italy under King Victor Emmanuel II. For a brief period, Florence became its capital, until this role was taken by Rome in 1871. Through the city ran the broad river Arno, which could be prone to flooding now and then when the rains had been heavy.

They got off at the train station and found their lodgings in a new pension named Annalena in one of Florence's old buildings not too far from the Ponte Vecchio Bridge. The pension was on the third floor of an old building, and it was full of beautiful furniture and paintings. They were warmly received and accommodated in a room with a balcony from where they could see the Boboli gardens and the Pitti Palace. Emily and Hope had a cup of coffee in the lounge and went to see the art gallery in Palace Pitti. It was only three o'clock in the afternoon.

However, when they saw how large the palace was, they decided to postpone viewing the rooms that were open to the public until the next day, and in the meantime, they had a look at the garden. To their disappointment, the garden closed already at half past four, but they decided to come back and explore more of it after they had seen the palace the next day. Instead, they wandered down to Ponte Vecchio and found a bridge over the river with shops along its sides. This was the oldest bridge in Florence, and it seemed more like a shopping street, which simply extended over the river to the other side. The atmosphere was busy, and loud voices from sellers rang through the air. After they had reached the end of the bridge, they simply turned and walked back the same way that they had come.

***

After a good night's sleep and breakfast, they got ready to see the city. In the hotel lounge they met a British couple who introduced themselves as Mr and Mrs Harrison-Smythe, and when Hope and Emily had also introduced themselves and said that they were going to Palace Pitti, Mr Harrison-Smythe suggested that they all go together with him as their escort, and they gratefully accepted the company. The Harrison-Smythe's were from Brighton, and they had been to Italy many times before the war. Now that travel had become possible again, they had come back to visit friends in Rome, where they had lived a few years before the war began. Mr Harrison-Smythe was a man of independent means, and they were both writers and had no children. Mrs Harrison-Smythe also liked to draw, and they would be trying to write a new travel guide to Italy now that the war was over. Hope and Emily told them that they were both teachers, and that they had brought an old Baedeker.

"A new travel guide from after the war would really be useful," said Hope. "I must say that I applaud your efforts."

They arrived at the Pitti Palace, which had some years ago been donated to the city to be turned into a proper museum. It had originally been the town residence of Luca Pitti, a Florentine banker, but in 1549, the house had been bought by the famous and fabulously rich banking House of the Medici. It had then become the chief residence of the ruling families of the Grand Duchy of Tuscany. These families collected many pieces of great art, jewellery and other luxury possessions. When Napoleon entered Italy, he used the building as a power base, and it was later taken over by the appointed king of the united Italy. King Victor

Emmanuel III had donated the palace and its contents to the people in 1919, so that it would be a museum.

The work of turning the palace into a museum was still underway, and in the meantime, a number of galleries were open to ordinary people. When finished, it would probably become the largest museum in Florence.

They registered at the entrance and were allowed to see some of the renaissance paintings, which were hung in the downstairs galleries. The building itself was not beautiful to look at, but it was impressive by being so large and forbidding. It was built in the Roman style with large arched windows. Later additions were built in the same style. But as soon as they were inside, they could see that it would probably become a great museum once it was ready.

Inside the galleries were ceiling frescoes form the mid-1600s, paintings by Rubens, Botticelli, Titian, Raphael and many others. The Royal Apartments had decorations and furniture from the age of the Medici. A throne room designed for Victor Emanuele II had red brocade on the walls and some large Japanese and Chinese vases from the 17th and 18th century.

Hope loved the renaissance paintings of people. They were so lifelike, and their emotions were so obvious and shone so clearly through the paintings. They spoke to her heart much more than later art, and they had lots of time to look at each one, because Mr Harrison-Smythe took his time making notes about them. Emily was getting impatient and they were all getting hungry, so in the end they left for the gardens where they could sit and partake of their picnic lunches.

Behind the palace, the Boboli Gardens were laid out with a large amphitheatre, which was used for performances for the amusement of the Medici court. A large courtyard connected the palace and the garden.

They crossed the courtyard and climbed the stairs to the Boboli Gardens where they came to a fountain decorated with sculptures. From here they could see the amphitheatre, and they went and sat down there to eat their lunch. A short rest followed during which Mrs Harrison-Smythe napped, before they went further upwards towards Neptune's Fountain and the large statue by Giambologna named 'Abundance'. It was supposed to depict the first Victor Emanuel's wife. The slope behind the fountain led down to a pond, and everywhere there were sculptures among the trees. There were many places that seemed to invite one to sit down quietly to talk or to read a book, and Emily and Hope decided to do just that the next day. They found the grottos with sculptures and stalactites and after seeing those, they went towards the exit and left the garden. Their last view was of the fat, naked stone figure of a court dwarf astride a tortoise. Mr Harrison-Smythe told them that he was a real person called Nano Morgante, who had been at the Medici court in the 16th century. All the women found it distasteful and offensive and left as quickly as possible. But the image of the naked dwarf lingered in their minds.

***

They had dinner at the hotel with Mr and Mrs Harrison-Smythe and learned that they had both been in Scandinavia during the war. They could not go back to England because of the danger of sea-travel, so instead they had travelled around Denmark, Sweden and Norway, which had all declared neutrality during the Great War. They had tried to work on a travel guide to Scandinavia during those years, and when the war was over, they had submitted their manuscript with hand-drawn maps and sketches to a publisher. But they were doubtful as to whether it would ever be published. Now they had gone to Italy to see whether they could find inspiration for a new book. From Florence, they were going to explore the smaller villages of Tuscany before going further south.

Hope and Emily told them that they were only travelling in their holidays for the adventure and for improving their knowledge of the world, hopefully in ways that might benefit their future teaching. They would leave for Venice in a few days, but not until they had seen the famous Uffizi galleries and explored the city a little further. Mr and Mrs Harrison-Smythe had already been to the Uffizi galleries, so they would not be coming with them, but they might meet tomorrow night and say goodbye.

***

Emily and Hope got up early in the morning and after breakfast they walked around Florence until the gallery opened. Finally, they ended up outside the Uffizi Gallery on the other side of the river, Arno.

The Uffizi complex was built well over 350 years ago to house the offices of the Florentine magistrate. The inner courtyard was very long and narrow with a view of the river at the end. Many beautiful sculptures were standing in the nearby Piazza della Signoria and among the pillars of the Uffizi. From the beginning, the first floor had been intended for the display of the Medici's collection of art, but over the years, more and more sections of the palace were included in order to house all the art pieces that were collected. Both Leonardo da Vinci and Michelangelo were said to have stayed there to work and enjoy the beauty and recreation available. When the Medici dynasty lacked male heirs and declined, the collection remained and formed one of the first modern museums when it was opened to the public in 1765. Hope stood long in front of Botticelli's paintings of women, such as 'The Adoration of the Magi' and 'Birth of Venus'. She pointed them out to Emily for the beauty of the female figures, and Emily nodded thoughtfully.

"He painted women very beautifully, but I wonder about what kind of women he painted and whether he genuinely loved women. Or did he just paint a classical idea of pure women who had no resemblance whatsoever to the women of his day?"

Hope smiled at her and said that she did not know, but she preferred to appreciate the beauty of the pictures without thinking too much about the reality behind them. "Is that not what art is all about?" she asked. "To give us dreams and fantasies to carry around with us inside our hearts, so that we always know that the ugliness of reality can never get completely to the core of our humanity?" Emily put a hand on her arm and gave it a little squeeze.

"I am sure you are right," she answered, "but I can never see one without thinking of the other. Sometimes I wonder if it will ever be possible—or even desirable—to have only beauty and peace and get rid of all the ugly sides of human life."

Hope answered thoughtfully, "Maybe we need to have some of the ugly and evil in order to be able to appreciate the good and the beautiful... Christianity seems to say that if we die and go to heaven, there will be no more evil and ugliness. I cannot help thinking that heaven may be a rather boring place to spend eternity..."

Emily squeezed her hand and said, "Did we not agree to stay away from organised religion? I believe that we only have this life that we live now. Let us live it to the full!"

They both laughed and went on to see more of the exhibition. They stopped several times to admire paintings of naked women like Titian's 'Madonna of the Long Neck'. "It must have been because their motives were religious that they were allowed to paint so much nakedness," Hope said. "I am sure our old queen would not have liked it."

"I agree," Emily said, "but sometimes the fact that it was seen as art, made it more acceptable, don't you think?"

When they reached Rembrandt's 'Portrait of an Old Man in an Armchair', Hope said, "He looks a little bit like my father just before he died."

"Do you miss him?" asked Emily.

Hope thought for a while. "I miss having a father," she said, "but in truth, I do not remember him very well. Except that he was always very sad and serious."

They left the gallery in the afternoon and went for a late lunch in a restaurant on the square outside. After lunch, they took a walk in the Boboli Gardens. It was a hot day, but it was possible to catch a small cooling breeze here and there, and they soon found a small café where they could sit in the shade while they brought out their books and writing blocks. Hope wrote a letter to Sarah and Eleanor while Emily was reading Somerset Maugham's first book *Liza of Lambeth*. After an hour, they left the café and the Boboli Garden, this time looking more carefully at the naked dwarf and pitying him more than feeling offended.

***

In the end, they decided to stay one more day to take a day trip to Pisa to see the famous Leaning Tower, which had been built as a free-standing bell tower to the cathedral in the 12th century. It had begun to tilt already during its construction because the foundation was too soft on one side, and it had taken 200 years to finish it. The tower was almost fifty-six metres tall on the low side and more than a metre taller on the high side, which gave it a distinctive tilt of 5 degrees, which would slowly increase every year.

Arriving in Pisa, they soon found the cathedral complex at Piazza dei Miracoli and the four old religious sites of which the leaning tower was one. The others were the Cathedral, which was the oldest, followed by the Baptistery, a domed building almost as tall as the bell tower just west of the Dome. Then followed the leaning bell tower, and last the cemetery, Campo Santo, surrounded by a peaceful cloister. The buildings were used as a hospital.

Hope's and Emily's attention immediately went to the tower, which was leaning out from behind the cathedral. It was built in white marble with lots of pillars and arches around each of the eight floors, except the uppermost one, which contained the seven bells. Emily and Hope discussed whether they should climb the 296 steps to the top of the tower, but they agreed to see the other buildings first and then have lunch before they undertook the climbing.

They first entered the Cathedral, which was dedicated to the assumption of Virgin Mary. Its construction had begun in 1063 when the people of Pisa were engaged in travelling over most of the world. Inspiration to build the cathedral, as well as some of the construction materials, had been drawn from the foreign cultures they had

97

encountered. The cathedral soon got an Archbishop and was consecrated in 1118 by the Pope, Gelasius II.

It had a pretty and impressive interior with granite Corinthian columns along the nave and a large mosaic in the apse depicting Christ enthroned between Virgin Mary and Saint John. In the galleries behind the altar were twenty-seven paintings from the 16th and 17th century, depicting scenes from both the Old and the New Testament. Unfortunately, the church was also gradually tilting because of the soft underground on which it had been built.

From the Cathedral, they went to see the Baptistery, which was begun in 1153 but not finished until the 14th century. It was a very large building but comparatively austere in its interior. In the middle was a large baptismal font with a bronze statue of St John the Baptist in the middle.

The churchyard was located at the northern edge of the square and was said to contain some of the original earth of Golgotha, where Christ had been crucified. A century later, a cloister had been built around it, and the cemetery had been completed in 1464. The outer wall contained forty-three blind arches and two elaborate doorways, while the inner wall had round arches. It used to contain many Roman sculptures and sarcophagi, of which some were still left there. The walls were covered in frescoes depicting scenes from the Old Testament and the Genesis. The most famous fresco was called 'The Triumph of Death', painted by Buonamico Buffalmaco about ten years before the Black Death hit in 1348. It became famous as a 'painted sermon' and later inspired other artists. Emily seemed especially drawn to the gruesome man-eating monster from hell with its many eyes.

There was also a hospital and other buildings in the square, but Hope was hungry, and Emily also wanted to sit down, so they found a suitable café and ordered spaghetti and coffee.

When they had rested and eaten, they went back to the leaning bell tower to ascend the stairs. They counted the steps as they walked, but soon got each other confused about the exact numbers and gave up. The stairs were worn and somewhat slippery, and even inside the thick walls with few external visual clues, you felt a slight vertigo from the uneven steps of the inclining tower. They came out where the bells were hanging and caught their breath for a moment before they looked at the bells. There were seven in all, tuned to a musical scale, and they all had different designations. They climbed the last few steps before they finally came outside and stood in the open area that went all around the tower. The iron parapet was not very high, but the view, especially towards the cathedral, was splendid. They walked around the cupula and

Hope asked Emily if she could recall what Galileo Galilei had used the tower for. "I believe he threw down two spheres, one large and heavy and another one much smaller to prove that they would reach the ground simultaneously, regardless of their weight."

"Oh, right," said Hope, "and he proved Aristotle wrong."

They had come to the stairs again and began the descent. It was easier than it had been coming up, and soon, they were on *terra firma* again. They blinked a little when they re-emerged into the bright sunlight, and they walked once more around the base of the odd tower to experience the dizziness it produced.

"I wonder if it will just lean more and more and then finally fall down," Hope said.

Emily shook her head. "I do not know. I hope they will find a way to save it. And if not, I hope it will not hurt anyone." After coming back to Florence, they packed their trunks and laid out their travelling clothes before they went to dinner. Tomorrow they would go to Venice.

***

In mid-afternoon, they arrived in Venice and crossed the long bridge into the city itself, which had been built on 117 islands and was riddled with canals and bridges. Before the war, many British writers, poets and artists had lived there and enjoyed the decadence and free lifestyle among the rich architectural wonders of the past. During the war, Venice had been a large naval base, and the city had been full of sailors and soldiers. The great basilica of St Marco's had been surrounded by sandbags for protection, and lots of great works of art had been removed to safer places. There had been some bombing by Austrian planes in 1915 with the railroad bridge as the main target, and a bomb had hit the Carmelite Church of Scalzi by mistake and destroyed it.

Hope and Emily found a *vaporetti* to take them close to their hotel, the *Internazionale* in Calle Larga. It was situated in a fifteenth century palazzo, and it was run by a Jewish-Hungarian immigrant, Signora Zoe Lustig and her Italian husband, Ugo Serandrei. Emily and Hope were warmly welcomed by Signora Lustig and shown to their room overlooking the street below. It was a small guesthouse with only twelve rooms, and the temporary stop that the war had caused to tourism still made it relatively easy to find rooms.

Hope and Emily immediately loved the room with its fine old furniture and the quiet surroundings. The only sound they could hear was of people walking and talking in the streets and the occasional singing of the gondoliers when they passed nearby. They went to bed early and enjoyed the clean sheets and the exhilaration of knowing that they would wake up to a probably sunny day and be completely free to make their own plans for the day and for the several days to come until they would have to start their journey home.

Breakfast was brought to them in bed. They each got a tray brought in with legs under it to keep it steady. On the tray was coffee with milk, rolls, butter and some jam. When they had finished, they took turns going to the bathroom to freshen up before they got dressed to go out. During the war, women's dresses and skirts had gotten shorter and simpler, and Hope and Emily had been among the first to shorten all their dresses to mid-calf and make new and looser outfits for themselves that felt much more comfortable for cycling and for work. For going around Venice, they chose dark skirts and white blouses on top, and they wore their comfortable shoes for walking. Before they had left England, they had both had had their hair cut in a short bob style, Emily's hair was brown and smooth while Hope's hair was unrulier and tended towards a natural curl. They usually wore a straw hat with a simple ribbon to protect them from the strong sun.

They went outside and into the streets and just took a walk around the neighbourhood to acquaint themselves with the layout of the nearby streets and bridges. They carried a street map with them so as not to get lost. They walked slowly through the streets and crossed a bridge, and soon they found themselves on St Mark's Square and decided to have a look inside the Basilica.

It had been opened to the public after the war, and they were offered a guided tour by an Italian gentleman who spoke English. He took them inside, and they were immediately overwhelmed by the glow of the golden mosaics and the enormous amount of marble used to build the edifice. Many of the treasures were spoils of earlier wars from especially Constantinople but also from other places. The beauty and grandeur were almost too much to take in. The gentleman explained that he was a professor of Byzantine art from the university but that he tried to take the few tourists in Venice around the church to earn a little extra money for his family. Emily offered him a small amount, since they had to save on money themselves, and he graciously accepted to give them one hour of his expertise. He told them his name was Moretti, so they respectfully addressed him as Professor Moretti.

He told them about the history of the church, which had originally been the private chapel of the Doge but had been open to ordinary people for a long time now. It was said to house the earthly remains of St Mark, one of the four evangelists. The bones had been smuggled out of Alexandria by Venetian merchants in the year 848 and brought to Venice.

Then the Doge built a whole new church for his tomb. At that time, the possession of such a valuable relic had helped make the city rich. Trade had flourished and with it also cultural exchange. St Mark's symbol was a winged lion armed with a sword, and this became the city's emblem.

Inside, the church felt huge. It consisted of five enormous domes supported by five arches, and the light glittered all over the mosaics. The professor explained that this effect had been created by placing the small squares of the mosaics in different directions, so that they would better catch the light from all angles.

The mosaics represented the gospels, the professor said, but it was hard for Hope and Emily to find any recognisable stories in them until Professor Moretti pointed out what they should look for.

The church was full of treasures. There were pieces made from gold and silver, rare glassware and other precious materials. Many of them came from Venetian raids on the Holy Land, when they took part in the fourth crusade in the twelfth century. Under the high altar were the remains of St Mark and once they went behind the High Altar, they could see the Golden Pala. It was made from pieces of enamel stuck onto a golden leaf and littered with precious stones. It had taken centuries to finish in all its glory, and Hope thought it was more precious and grander than actually pretty. She was getting a little dizzy from all the riches that surrounded them and was happy when they finally went outside.

The famous four horses from the Holy Land that used to ornament the façade of the church had been removed to Rome for safekeeping during the war, but now they were back in all their beauty and splendour. The façade had so many lovely details to look at, that they decided to stay in the square for a cup of tea or coffee and just enjoy the view. They asked Professor Moretti if he would join them, but he begged off and went to see if he could find more tourists to show around.

"How sad," said Emily, "a great professor and teacher reduced to playing tourist guide to earn pocket money enough to survive..."

Hope nodded and said, "I hope the country will quickly regain its footing now and be able to recover enough that Professor Moretti can concentrate on his work as a teacher and scholar. He seemed such a nice man."

"The slow recovery after the war seems to be one of the things which enables us to travel so cheaply, don't you think?" said Emily.

"I don't really know," said Hope. "People at home are also suffering in the aftermath of the war. London was heavily hit, too, and many lost their lives or their health in the war. And now the unemployment has risen so fast. It leaves a lot of people dissatisfied all over Europe, and I wonder if it really has been the war to end all wars, as they said it would be."

"Now we are getting morose, aren't we?" said Emily and attempted to change the subject. "That splendid church ought to cheer us up. Think of all the effort and craftsmanship that has gone into building it and all the treasures they have managed to collect there. Not that one was cheered by all that cruelty and greed that has gone before it... Now, let's go and see more of Venice before we become all gloomy. Let's go to the Rialto Bridge."

They finished their tea and biscuits at the Café Florian and found the price to be almost double what they would have paid anywhere else, but at least they had now visited the oldest and perhaps one of the most famous cafés in Europe.

Hope carried their Baedeker guidebook which was published long before the war but still very useful. Using its street map, they soon found the Rialto Bridge over the Grand Canal. It was an A-shaped bridge built to make room for ships to pass underneath, and the whole bridge was covered with a roof and walls, with just a few places from where one could see the broad canal. On both sides of the bridge were small shops selling food and other things such as antiques and Italian souvenirs. Hope and Emily wandered up the stairs on the bridge and looked at the wares on sale—a market on a bridge, what an extraordinary thing. They bought some fruit to bring back to their room, and then they crossed back over the bridge and returned to their hotel for supper.

Over the next five days, they crisscrossed Venice and saw both The Palace of the Doges, which they explored with the help of their Baedeker. The book went through the art works in great detail and both girls enjoyed the gorgeous paintings on the walls and the ceilings, which were painted by famous painters of the renaissance, such as for instance Tintoretto. After seeing the Scala dei Censori, they went along a narrow passageway to the Bridge of Sighs which connected the palace to the prison. Down a stairway were the dungeons where torture and executions took place. Back on the Bridge of Sighs, Hope read from the Baedeker that the bridge had 'probably never been crossed by any prisoner whose name is worth remembering or whose fate deserves our sympathy'.

"I wonder if that is so," said Emily. "There must have been some who were innocent of the crimes they were accused of."

"Yes," Hope added, "or maybe their so-called crimes would not have been considered punishable by death today."

Both women felt a shiver and were glad when they were outside in the warm sunshine again.

Another day they went to visit the Museo de Correr, which was also near the Palace of the Doges. It had started as a private collection by Teodoro Correr about the history of Venice. He had bequeathed it with his palace by the Grand Canal to the city of Venice after his death. His collections included both works of art, documents and individual objects which reflected the history of Venice. He had also donated funds to make the collection open to the public, and this had happened in 1836. The contents of the collection were then catalogued and organised, so it could be used by scholars, and the best pieces were exhibited to the public. The collection grew larger as other families donated to it, and it was moved to Fondaco dei Turchi, the old Ottoman-Turkish Ghetto, which had been restored in the 1860s.

The exhibitions presented items to describe Venetian life and the culture of Venice in its heyday before it was conquered by Napoleon. Besides the many paintings and sculptures, there were fine manuscripts, maps, woodcuts, topographical and navigational instruments, armour, weapons, and a large collection of coins. Emily became bored before Hope and suggested that they should go and have some Italian coffee soon. They had both gotten used to drinking the strong coffee served in Italy. They actually liked it and found it a superior stimulant to tea. Hope agreed that they needed something to refresh themselves, so they left the rather dusty museum and went into one of the side streets to find a café.

"Let us take the boat to Murano tomorrow to see the glass production," Emily suggested.

"Maybe we can also visit Burano. It is famous for its lace I have heard," said Hope. "Let us see if we can visit both tomorrow."

They got up early the next morning to catch a vaporetti to Murano. Sailing in the lagoon was pure pleasure as the water was calm and the sun was warm. They reached Murano in slightly under one hour and found a charming little island. Glass workers and shops selling the famous Murano glass chandeliers and other glass objects in various colours were everywhere. Glass had begun to be made in Venice long ago, but in 1291, all the glass manufacturers were removed to the island of Murano, because they presented a constant fire risk in the city. For hundreds of years, the Venetians had held a monopoly on the making of fine glass, but some of the artisans travelled to other places in Europe and brought the secrets with them. By the end of the 16th century it was a secret no longer, and many other places in Europe began to be able to make both optically clear glass and metal-coated mirrors.

Hope wanted to buy two fine glasses inlaid with gold and have them sent to Sarah and Eleanor, but Emily persuaded her not to. They were too fragile to be sent all the way to England, and they had to be careful with their money. Hope finally acquiesced and they both agreed that they would buy small presents that were easy to transport. Instead, they would try to make some drawings, and Emily sketched the two glasses in her sketchbook while Hope decided to try to use her watercolours to reproduce the delicate colours later. Finally, they bought two decorated glass beads and took one each as a sign of their firm friendship and love for each other. They would each have it put on a chain when they were back in the city.

At noon, they had lunch next to the vaporetti stop and were ready to get on the boat to the smaller island of Burano. They would only have an hour or two there if they wanted to get back to the city that evening, so after they had arrived, they walked around to look at the lace shops and at the ladies who sat out in the sun working on the incredibly intricate patterns. It was said that the first lace was a gift of foam from a mermaid to a fisherman, who took it home and dressed his bride in it. It was so beautiful that soon all the women in the island were trying to reproduce it, and that is how the island's reputation came about. Many laces were created by several women working together, each doing the parts that she did best.

Hope and Emily stared longingly at the incredibly intricate works, and in the end, they each bought a small lace-trimmed handkerchief in spite of all their firm intentions not to buy anything. But they wanted something to remember this little island by, and a lace handkerchief was always a part of a lady's wardrobe anyway, wasn't it? Not that they ever saw themselves as ladies, but they were both able to act the role from looking at the many ladies they had gotten to know through the suffragette movement.

Back in Venice that evening, they agreed to spend their last day in Venice walking through the streets and across the bridges, and they would each find a nice chain for their glass pearls.

Back in England

The journey home was long and uneventful, and they arrived back in London on August the fifteenth. School would start on Monday, September the fourth, but they were expected to start a week earlier to prepare. That left them a few days to get settled back into their apartment and a weekend to visit Sarah and Eleanor in Calne. When they arrived in Calne, they were met at the station by Eleanor and her buggy. They embraced warmly, and Eleanor commented on how sun-tanned they had both become.

"You do not get a skin-color like that in England," Eleanor commented. "I must say you both look very healthy!"

"It will soon fade," said Hope, "but how are you two doing?"

"Oh, we are both in excellent health," said Eleanor. "We live quietly from day to day and are happy as long as nothing terrible happens. The war was bad and the Spanish flu also, but since then we have had a stable life with our friends and our work. We are really not very adventurous, either of us, you know."

Hope could not help but feel that their lives were rather dull compared to her own, but she did not say anything. She was happy to have this stable point in her life. In a way, it gave her freedom, because she knew that her sisters would always be there for her and always love her, no matter what.

Emily asked if they had kept the newspapers from the time they had been away.

"Of course," answered Eleanor. "We kept them for you. Nothing much has happened in England over the summer, but you may have a look for yourselves."

Sarah was waiting for them at home with tea and scones, eager to hear about their adventures. "We got your last letter from Florence, thank you so much," she said to Hope. "You write so vividly that we could almost feel as if we were there ourselves!"

"Did you write about Pisa?" asked Emily.

"Yes," Hope replied, "I sent it the morning we left for Venice."

When they sat down for their afternoon tea, Hope told them about what they had seen in Venice, and Emily supplemented here and there with her own observations. They brought out the lace handkerchiefs they had bought in Burano and gave them to Sarah and Eleanor, who were impressed with the fine handicraft, which was more ethereal than any lacework they had ever experienced before.

Finally, Sarah asked about Italy and what the political atmosphere had felt like. Emily shook her head sadly and said, "It was ugly, especially in Rome. Like a volcano about to explode."

"Yes," Hope added. "I would call it menacing with all those blackshirts watching everybody. Thankfully, we only got a good look at them in Rome, where we saw a street fight going on."

"We have seen some reporting in the newspapers," said Eleanor. "I wonder if Mr Mussolini will not grab power one of these days."

"I am sure he will," said Emily.

Hope told her sisters about their promise to help the friends they had made in Naples, Anthony and Lisa Jones, when the time came for their oldest son, Antonio, to get his education. "Could we speak to Henry about getting the boy accepted at Repton in a few years, if Lisa and Anthony decide that he should get his education in England?"

"I have already mentioned it to Henry after I got your letter from Florence," Sarah said. "And he is willing to do what he can, since the boy is a British citizen. Let us return to the subject when the time is closer."

After tea, they went for a walk around Calne and visited the family grave in the churchyard. Sarah and Eleanor had had a stone made in honour of their mother's memory, even though she already had a gravestone in Nagasaki. They had also had a small stone put down for their sister, Edith, who had died in New Zealand last year. It was placed next to the one for Ernest. Sarah visited the grave once a week, sometimes with Eleanor, and they kept it very nice and tidy.

Part Four
The Interwar Years II

Back to Work

On Sunday afternoon, Hope and Emily returned to London and began to get ready to start work. The school year began, and both Hope and Emily were happy to be back as they rode their bicycles to school in the mornings. They felt well prepared for the new school year and looked forward to meet the new girls whom they had just gotten to know back in April and would be teaching for the next three years.

Since the Education Acts of 1918 and 1921, it had been prohibited to let children under fourteen be employed, and all children between the age of five and fourteen had to attend school. For the teachers in the lower secondary schools, this meant a slightly more stable school day with all the children present most of the time. All schools had to have medical inspections at regular intervals, and a school nurse had been employed. Besides, the League of Nations had agreed on an International Labour Act on the work of children and women, adapted in 1919, and this had further reinforced the prohibition against children, women and young people's working in dangerous occupations and at night. In 1920, a Consultative Committee on Education had been established by the government with William Henry Hadow as its chairman. Hadow's committee was working on the question of whether the curriculum for boys and girls ought to be as similar as it was now or whether there should be more differentiation. It concluded that since girls had household duties besides their schoolwork and because they had a weaker constitution, they must not be overburdened by homework and too heavy a curriculum. Instead, they should learn domestic skills and hygiene. Hadow also put great weight on both girls and boys learning aesthetic pursuits such as music. His and his committees' recommendations had a large influence on the way schools in England developed in both structure and content, but many of the new ideas took a long time to be implemented because of economic restraints. Hope and Emily followed Hadow's work with interest. They were both anxious about what it might mean for their future work. Their salaries had not been raised as much as they had hoped for after the Fisher Act had been passed in 1918. In the years after the war, many female colleagues had been fired when the men returned from the battlefield.

Hope and Emily had left the National Union of Teachers in 1920 in order to join the National Union of Women Teachers, which pursued a more feminist and international agenda, and which was much more approachable and friendlier than the NUT. Here they made new friends who were much more sympathetic to their views, not only on education, but on matters of inequality between men and women as well. Women's salaries were only eighty percent of that of men for the same work, which, it was said, was justified by the men's role of providing for their families. This and the marriage bar, which meant that women who got married could be dismissed, the lack of a salary scale for women who were promoted—all of that had become issues to fight for. Women over thirty had finally been included in the franchise during the war and had been voting for the first time in 1918 when David Lloyd George had been re-elected for the Liberal Party. In 1922, the next election was to be held in November, and Hope and Emily intended to vote once again for the liberals.

On the first day in school, all their students wore prim blue pinafores with short-sleeved blouses underneath. The blue pinafores were shorter now, and pretty with the white socks and black shoes. The sun was shining warmly on the first day, and everybody seemed happy and very lively. The girls were happy to see their friends again after the long holiday and were chattering away.

Emily and Hope came out in the school yard and got their girls to separate into those for Emily's class and those for Hope's. It took a few minutes to get the girls lined up in a neat line, and then they led their classes to the homeroom. They each had thirty-five girls in their class.

Hope began her day by wishing everyone welcome back from their summer holidays. All her girls were present as she began her talk, "I hope you have all had a good time during your vacation and are ready for some hard studying this autumn. I would like you all to spend the first class writing me a short essay on how you have spent your break from school, so if you would please get out your pencils, I will distribute a piece of paper to each of you. This year we shall spend more time on writing, spelling and composition, and you will each have one hour to finish your work. But first, let us look at how to compose an essay. I briefly talked about composition before our break, but does anyone remember what I said about composition?"

A few hands went up, and Hope picked Ann to reply.

"An essay must have a beginning, a middle and an end."

"That is right," Hope said, "but remember that it must also have a title. This time, I have given you a title, 'My Summer Vacation,' but if you can think of a better one that fits your essay, you are welcome to use that instead, as long as your essay is about your recent summer vacation. Anyone, how would you start such an essay?"

A few other girls held their hands up. Hope picked Moira, and Moira said, "Miss Maundrell, you told us that we should always define when and where we are writing about, so I would start by defining the time and the place."

"Excellent, Moira," Hope said, "and the third thing to remember is that your essay should also stick to the topic all the way through. And it should end with a few sentences to sum up what the whole essay has been about."

She finished handing them each a piece of paper and reminding them not to talk while writing. "When you have finished, please come up and leave your sheet on my desk and remember to write your name on top. You may begin now."

All the girls began to write. Some wrote freely while others wrote slowly and laboriously. A few were not writing at all, so she went to each of them and encouraged them to get started. Their individual essays should give her a good idea about what she needed to teach and who might need more help than others with learning to write and spell correctly.

When the class was over, she collected the essays and took all her girls out in the schoolyard to get some fresh air. Her next lesson would be reading. In the afternoon, they would do history and later geography. She was going through the same curriculum that she had taught with her previous two classes but using the experience she had gained to alter her teaching somewhat according to what she had learned along the way about what caught the student's interest and enthusiasm. This year, she had discussed with Emily how they could add something about the recent war and present-day politics and maybe get their students started to follow the news with more understanding. It was ambitious for eleven and twelve-year-old girls, but they were determined to try.

When Hope got home in the evening, she had brought all the essays her students had written with her to correct them. She showed some of them to Emily who wanted to try something similar with her class. Today, she had taught reading and elementary math and science, but the next day, they would switch classes for the last part of the day with Emily teaching math and science to her class and Hope taking Emily's class in history and geography. Twice a week they would do that, so that the students would benefit from what they both did best. This was an experiment which the school had agreed to try out when they had suggested it.

While Hope was reading through the essays, she wrote down her impressions and concrete suggestions in her notebook. Here, Hope had all the names with some space after each, which she planned to fill in with whatever key words about each girl that might give her an idea of what they would need from her. She began with Elly Abner, who had written a very short essay on how she had spent all summer in London helping her mother look after her younger siblings and doing various work around the house. This was characteristic of most answers, but a few had spent some of the vacation with relatives in the country and playing with their cousins and bathing in the sea. A few of the essays were so poorly written that Hope made notes to herself about giving them some remedial help with English. A few were exceptionally well written with almost no spelling mistakes and a vivid vocabulary. Hope could not help wishing that all her students were of the latter kind, but soon, she determined that wishful thinking would not do anyone any good. She would do her job of teaching to make all the girls at least better than when they started in her class.

Next week, the school would assign positions for selected girls as head girl, deputy head girl, various class and other prefects etc. Both Hope and Emily had to find a few girls who might have the potential for such roles. The head girl would always be chosen from the upper forms, but the next day, both she and Emily would talk to some of the most promising girls and look for the potential leadership qualities, which might make for a fine deputy head girl among those in the lower grade. Besides being excellent students, girls chosen for such positions had to have enough charisma to make the other students look up to her and follow her directions when needed. When correcting the essays, Hope had already made notes of some of the possibilities, and all the other teachers would have been doing the same. Later in the week, they would discuss their results and by Friday, they would all have a list of names for the pupils to choose from.

***

In December, the Irish Free State was established as a British dominion, and the three years of the Irish independence war ended. However, six provinces opted out of the new state and chose to remain a part of Great Britain, while members of the Irish Republican Army refused to swear allegiance to the British monarch. Peace was not yet in the cards.

1922 also saw the establishment of the British Broadcasting Company, and Emily rigged a small crystal radio, called a 'cat's whiskers,' so they could hear some of the broadcasts at home. Thus, they managed to hear in January of 1923 the first broadcast from the outside when the National Opera Company performed Mozart's 'The Magic Flute' from Covent Garden. Although the sound quality was not very good, it felt like pure magic to Hope and Emily that they now had a contraption in their home that made it possible to actually hear sound transmitted through the air to their house. "Emily, you are just so clever," exclaimed Hope when the transmission was over. They had not dared to invite any guests to listen as Emily was still unsure whether her apparatus would work properly.

***

On the first of September 1923, just before noon, a horrific earthquake struck Eastern Japan and destroyed most of Tokyo and Yokohama and the surrounding areas. Because of the timing, many households were in the process of cooking meals over open fires, and this greatly added to the disaster. Huge fires arose and killed more people than the initial earthquake. In the aftermath, many people believed rumours that the Koreans in Japan had taken advantage of the chaos and sought to enrich themselves by robbing abandoned property and even poisoning the wells. Vigilante groups would kill a great number of Koreans before the police could restore some semblance of order.

It took over a week before people in Europe could gain a full picture of what had happened, and when Hope and Emily visited Sarah and Eleanor in their autumn break, they met Henry who had also come for a visit. Sarah was still upset about the terrible earthquake in which she seemed to have lost at least one old friend who had moved to Yokohama. She had written to the people she had kept in contact with over the years to find out how they were doing. Sarah's school friend, O-Haru, who had been her own age and a close friend, had perished in the fires with the rest of her family, and Sarah grieved over losing her in such a horrible way. To Henry and Eleanor, it was not a personal loss, but in the evening, they all spoke about their happy childhood in Japan. Hope and Eleanor had only vague memories of life in Japan, but they could see how deeply it touched Sarah and Henry. Emily tried to understand how and why such a distant catastrophe could affect the four siblings, and she felt their emotions keenly and listened patiently to their memories. They had all experienced minor earthquakes when they were children in Japan, and Hope and Emily thought back to their visit to the Campi Flegrei north of Naples and shuddered at the thought of the immense forces locked in the volcanic parts of the earth.

Sarah and Henry were old enough to remember the eruption at Krakatau in 1883 and its aftermath of widespread dust and lowering of temperatures over most of the world. Their parents and teachers had spoken about it, but only Sarah had felt some of its effects. Henry had been in school in England and only remembered the grown-ups talking about the extraordinary red sunsets that summer.

The epicentre of the earthquake in Japan had been under the sea in Sagami Bay, so it had not had any effect on the atmosphere, but the ground had shaken violently and created ten-metre-high tsunamis as well as landslides in many places. The death toll was thought to be more than one hundred thousand people. When Sarah ended the evening by suggesting that they all prayed in silence for a moment, nobody disagreed.

***

The early 1920s were a relatively prosperous period for those who were in employment, but as unemployment rose, more and more families found it difficult to manage. The wartime had made some people very rich, but the great majority had to struggle to make both ends meet. Among the young rich, who had been too young to fight in the war, a new culture emerged. These 'bright young things' listened to jazz music, went dancing and cut the length of their hair as well as their dresses. The young men drove automobiles, and in many upper and middle-class homes, electric light, telephones and radios became installed. However, workers and their families still lived in poverty, and when a worker lost his job, his family often had to go hungry. This led to political unrest and the rise of radical political movements. Hunger marches became more common, and when England returned to the gold standard in 1925, the situation worsened. Salaries were lowered as exports suffered, and gradually, things got more difficult as the decade approached its end.

Hope and Emily followed the political situation as closely as they could from the newspapers, but their daily routine did not change much as they taught their classes and occasionally tried out various new ideas in their teaching. In 1923, as their students graduated from their lower secondary education, they were happy to see a larger percentage than usual elect to continue their education in the upper secondary school.

A general election had taken place on September 6th, 1923, and the Conservative Party under Mr Bonar Law had formed a new government.

At the end of that year on New Year's Eve at 12 o'clock, the bells of Big Ben were transmitted on the radio for the first time. Emily and Hope had gone to a celebration with friends from the National Union of Women Teachers and had a great time. 1924 looked to become a fine year and they were both full of optimism as they started teaching their classes after Christmas.

Antonio

They regularly heard from Anthony and Lisa in Naples. The elections in 1924 had brought Benito Mussolini a landslide victory, but soon, he was in trouble over the disappearance and eventual murder of Giacomo Mateotti, a socialist who had spoken up about Mussolini's violent tactics to win the election. People in Italy and over most of Europe were convinced that Mussolini had ordered the murder, and his influence waned for a while. But in January 1925, he took responsibility for the fact that the murder had been committed by overenthusiastic fascists, and after that, he began to create the totalitarian dictatorship of Italy. Hope and Emily felt the anxiety behind Anthony's cautious comments on politics, and with Henry's help, they began to prepare for Antonio's schooling in England as they had promised. After a great deal of talking and pulling strings, he finally got accepted in April 1926 when he was 14 years old. When he arrived with Anthony in England, Henry went with Emily and Hope to welcome them.

Hope and Emily had moved to a new and larger apartment by then. It was also in Islington, but it had three rooms and a larger kitchen with room for a small dining table. But best of all, it had an indoor toilet. When Antonio was not at school, he could stay with them in a room of his own. On the day of Antonio's arrival, they had gone to the station. Antonio travelled with his father, and Hope and Emily immediately recognised Anthony and the tall boy at his side had to be Antonio. He had grown a lot since they had last seen him, and he was almost a young man now and rather handsome. Anthony greeted them with hugs and brought lots of greetings from Lisa and the rest of the family. He and Antonio would stay in London for a few days before travelling to Repton to get Anthony installed in the hoarding school. They went to Hope and Emily's apartment for a cup of tea and to see what would become Antonio's room in London on holidays. He seemed to like it but was also somewhat overwhelmed that it would be all his to stay in alone.

After tea and biscuits, they left the flat and went to the hotel where Anthony would be staying with his son before they went to Repton, Anthony wanted to show Antonio the king's palace and the government buildings on the next day, and in the evening, they wanted to take Emily and Hope out for dinner to thank them for their assistance in the matter of Antonio's schooling. The day after that they would get on the train for Repton, where Henry would pick them up at the station.

Antonio had not been saying much, but what he had said had been in impeccable English, so Hope was reassured that he would be fine as far as language was concerned. She thought that he was probably just shy and overwhelmed by leaving Naples and his large family behind to live in a completely foreign place, and she made an effort to make him feel as comfortable as possible. When he had called her 'Miss Maundrell' a couple of times, she asked him to look upon her and Emily as aunts and call them Aunt Hope and Aunt Emily respectively. During their supper, which they took at the hotel where Antonio and his father were staying, they agreed that Antonio would come to London in his first summer holiday from school and spend some time in Calne.

When Hope and Emily left for the evening, they both fell strangely disappointed. They had both looked forward to having Antonio around, but their experience had only been with girls, and they felt awkward around this young man, whom they hardly knew and who was so shy and formal.

"Well, said Hope, "we shall only have to see him during holidays, and maybe it will become easier with time, but I do wonder what we have let ourselves into."

Emily nodded and said, "I do not think he will be any trouble, but I do hope that he will become easier to talk to when he is by himself. But let us face it, we have absolutely no experience with boys of his age, and I am sure that it will take a while for him to get used to us, as well. He is probably feeling at least as awkward as we are."

"I am sure he is," Emily replied, "and we should never forget that things can be very hard for him, too. He will miss his mother and his family, and he will have a lot to get used to."

***

Anthony had just returned to Italy when the news reached England that an attempt had been made on Mussolini's life. On the seventh of April 1926 in Rome, a middle-aged Irish woman named Violet Albina Gibson had gotten up close to him and shot directly at his face twice, but Mussolini had escaped with a bloody nose because he had leaned back to acknowledge the crowds waiting for him, just as the shot rang out. Violet was a religiously and mentally confused woman with an obsession with martyrdom, but she came from a noble Irish family and the whole affair was quietly resolved by declaring her a mental case and returning her to England, where she would pass the rest of her life in an asylum. Mussolini seemed to have reacted very calmly to the whole affair, being mostly offended that an old ugly repulsive woman had nearly taken his life.

***

Back at work, Hope and Emily soon got too busy to think much about Antonio. They both had a class of new girls to deal with and a lot of administration on top of it this year. With their seniority in the school, they had been given more responsibilities and that meant more work as well. Nevertheless, they faithfully kept up a correspondence with Antonio every week and told him about their lives, so he wouldn't feel too alone in England.

On May 1st, the coalminers went on strike and were subsequently locked out because of a conflict over planned reductions in their wages. Two days later, they were joined by many others in a general strike, which meant that printers, dockworkers, ironworkers, transport workers, and steelworkers all joined the strike. Since there were no newspapers, the BBC began to broadcast news five times a day, and the government declared martial law. The general strike ended after nine days, but the coalminers continued for some months until they had to give up, and martial law was not rescinded until December.

During the summer, Antonio came up to London to spend a few days with Hope and Emily. Henry had accompanied him as far as London because he was planning to spend some time in the British Library, so Hope and Emily picked up Antonio at the station and took him home with them for supper. They were planning to take him along to Calne to visit Sarah and Eleanor in a few days, but first, they were going to show him a few things in London. Over supper, they asked Antonio about his new school. At first, he answered hesitantly, but when Hope asked him how often he heard from his family, he brightened somewhat and told them that he thought he was one of the boys in school who received the most letters. "I get a letter from my parents every week and one from you Aunt Hope and Aunt Emily. And sometimes, my mother sends me letters or drawings from my little sisters and brothers. Some of my old friends write, too. I write them back in Italian, so I will not forget my first language. None of the boys in school speak Italian, and I do not think anyone in Repton does either…"

"Excellent," said Emily. "It will be very useful when you grow up that you are fluent in both English and Italian."

"Aren't you learning French and Latin, also?" asked Hope.

"Yes," answered Antonio, "I like Latin very much and I think I am doing well. But French is very hard, and my teacher is not very patient. He says that my pronunciation is 'atrocious'—I did not know that word, so one of the other boys explained that it meant terrible."

Both Hope and Emily laughed and said they would practice pronunciation with him during the holiday.

"How do you like the other subjects?" asked Hope.

"I like most of them," said Antonio, "but some of the teachers are rather boring, so it is hard to be attentive all the time. But I try hard."

"How are you getting along with the other boys?" asked Hope. "Have you made any friends yet?"

"Most of those in my class are very nice," said Antonio. "It was hard to talk to them the first couple of weeks, because I was very uncertain about how to get along with English boys, and I think they were also feeling that I was a stranger. But after a while, I got a few friends, and now it is easier. I am not the only foreigner in the school, after all. There are three from overseas colonies, two from Africa and one from Palestine, I think. They are not in my class, though."

When they had finished their meal, Emily asked what Antonio would like to see in London for the next two days before they went to Calne.

Antonio hesitated. "Can we see a movie?" he asked. "I have never seen one."

"Certainly!" Emily exclaimed. "Let us all go and see Charlie Chaplin in 'The Gold Rush' tomorrow afternoon."

Hope agreed. "If you have never seen a movie, Charlie Chaplin has to be the best way to get started. Let's buy tickets tomorrow morning and then watch the matinee showing. Is there anything else you would like to see?"

"If possible, I would like to go and see one of the big department stores like Harrods or Selfridges—not to buy anything, but just to see them. Will that be possible?"

"Yes, of course," said Hope. "Let's go to Harrods in the morning, then we can have lunch and go to the cinema afterwards. Those are very easy wishes. Then maybe we can do something more serious the day after tomorrow, e.g. British Museum."

They made sure that Antonio was comfortable in his room and that he had something to read before they said good night. "Good night, Aunt Hope and Aunt Emily," Antonio said and closed his door. Emily and Hope looked at each other when they were back in the living room.

"He is a very nice and polite boy," said Hope. "Do you not think that we will get along fine over the next years?"

"Yes," said Emily, "but it must be very hard for him to be in England all alone. I hope we can compensate a little for the absence of his family."

"This is the way thousands of British boys and girls have grown up for generations," Hope said, "most of them from a much younger age, and if their parents were overseas, they would not see them for several years. They seem to have survived very well."

"I know," said Emily, "but I cannot help wondering whether it is a good custom for young boys or girls to grow up without their mother close by. It may make them stronger in some ways, but wouldn't it damage them in other ways that we do not know about? Your mother went to boarding school and hated it, didn't she?"

"I never knew my mother, so I do not really know. But Sarah has told me that she had a very rough time there and that she was actually expelled. But she agreed to let my brothers go from the age of nine, and eventually, three of my sisters went, too. But none of them went to the Missionary Children's School where she herself had been sent. And when Eleanor and I became old enough to go to boarding school, we could not afford it."

"Anyway," said Emily, "I went to a boarding school for girls when I was twelve years old, and I guess I was fine, but I remember feeling very lonely in the beginning. Let us do our best for Antonio—at least he is much older than English children are when they are first sent away."

***

The next morning after breakfast they took a bus to Harrods at Knightsbridge. Antonio was overwhelmed by the size of the department store and the variety of goods for sale. When they got to the Egyptian escalator, he looked around at the magnificent décor for a long time and finally said, "I will take my mum here one day!"

Hope hugged him and said, "Yes, that would be a great idea. I am sure she would love it!"

They walked around the store and looked at all the things on offer for almost an hour. They finished by visiting the food court where Hope and Emily bought them a few things for lunch, which they took into Hyde Park, where they found a bench to sit on while they partook of the delicious food. After walking around in Hyde Park for a while, they got on the tube to Leicester Squarer and went to the cinema. Emily bought their tickets and they found their seats.

The film opened with long rows of gold prospectors on their way to Klondyke and passing over the icy Chilkoot Pass. Soon, a lonely prospector appeared in overlarge shoes and with the characteristic walking style of Charlie Chaplin. As he passed dangerous cliffs, a large black bear appears and follows him, but no harm comes to our hero. We see another prospector, Big Jim, finding a large lump of gold and rejoicing in his good fortune. Later, a storm comes on and we see a small cabin with a big man inside, looking at a poster showing that he is a wanted man. He hears someone and goes outside the cabin to see who it is, and in the meantime, Charlie Chaplin enters and starts looking for something to eat. The big man comes back and angrily tries to throw him back out in the storm.

In the meantime, Big Jim's tent has blown away with Jim hanging onto it for dear life. The storm blows him right in through the open door, but he comes back and rescues our little hero from the criminal. Stuck in the raging storm for days, the three men grow more and more hungry and finally decide to draw cards to decide who has to go outside to find food. The criminal leaves and Charlie and Big Jim are alone in the cabin. Thanksgiving comes around, and Charlie is cooking one of his boots in a pan of melted snow to feed them. They share the boot and eat it slowly and laboriously.

This scene made Antonio laugh out loud, and he was absolutely riveted by the film for the rest of the time it played. Hope and Emily had never heard him laugh so much since they had met him in Italy four years ago. After they got outside, Antonio was still chuckling as they talked about the movie and recalled several scenes over and over again.

After dinner, Anthony thanked them for a wonderful day, and Hope and Emily finally felt as if they had been able to break through the boy's reserve, and they all felt comfortable around each other. The next day, they had planned to go to the British Museum and afterwards to go look around the bookstores in the neighbourhood. Antonio was greatly impressed with the museum and seemed especially interested in the collection of Egyptian mummies and the other Egyptian artefacts. Hope told him as much about Egyptian culture and history as she could remember, and they went to look at the so-called Rosetta Stone from 197 BC, a decree from Ptolemy V who ruled from 204 BC to 181 BC. It was a black irregular fragment of a stele with incomplete inscriptions in three languages. When it had been found in Rashid in Greece, the part of it that was in Greek had been relatively easy to read, while the side in Egyptian hieroglyphs was unintelligible. The third side was written in Demotic, another Egyptian language. The stone was black with the writing in white, about one metre high. Over the years, scholars had painstakingly used the Greek text to reproduce the two other inscriptions and understand them as well as guess at the missing parts. Antonio was fascinated by the detective-like character of this work and by the Egyptian hieroglyphs, and later, when they went to the book stores, he used his pocket money to buy a couple of books on Egyptian history to take back to school after the holidays.

When they got back home in the afternoon, they began to pack to go to Calne the next day. They would stay in Calne for a couple of weeks with Anthony until he had to go back to Repton. Henry would come and stay for a few days and then accompany Antonio back to school.

Sarah and Eleanor welcomed them warmly at Calne station, and Sarah immediately put her arms around the boy in a gesture of unconditional love. The boy seemed to enjoy her affection and hugged her right back. Maybe Sarah understood better that the boy needed physical attention after leaving his home and family, Hope thought. Eleanor followed suit and hugged the boy, and they all walked from the station to the house. Hope and Emily got their usual room in Hope's old bedroom. Antonio was put in the room that Sarah and Eleanor had used to rent out to Mary. Since Mary had moved back to Guernsey, Sarah and Eleanor had decided to convert her room into an extra room for sewing. However, in anticipation of Antonio's visit, they had put in a bed for Antonio to sleep in.

The long summer days were spent in walks over the hills and into the wood or on trips to visit nearby farms. Antonio learned how to help around the house and to shop for them all. Sarah cooked delicious English dinners and even tried a few Italian recipes to please Antonio. In the evenings, they read books and talked about Italy and England, their families and other things. Antonio was remarkably intelligent and well spoken for his age, and one could easily hear that he was used to talk about a lot of topics with his parents.

On the last day before Hope and Emily had to return to school, Henry arrived in his automobile to take Antonio back to Repton with him. His presence rather ruined the easy and relaxed mood that Antonio had grown used to while staying with the four women. Everyone became more formal and subdued, except for Sarah, who stayed her usual self and even joked a little bit about Henry's stiffness and insistence on being very formal and teacher-like when Antonio was around. On the spur of the moment, Hope decided to go with Henry and Antonio to Repton and visit the school. Only Sarah had ever seen the school where Henry worked and lived, and Hope wanted to see Antonio there, too. Emily would return alone to London and wait for Hope there.

The next day on the trip to Repton in Henry's car, Antonio wore his school uniform and looked very handsome. They started early and planned to stop for gasoline and lunch in Stratford-upon-Avon, so that

Antonio could see William Shakespeare's famous birthplace. It took them about three hours to reach Stratford with a few breaks on the way. Hope and Antonio sat next to each other in the back seat of the car and talked about Shakespeare, while Henry occasionally interrupted with a few words. When they reached the town, and found a place to park the car, they went on foot to see the sorry remains of the Shakespeare Memorial Theatre, which had burned down in March and was now a ruin. With the help of volunteers, it had been possible to save many of the precious documents and portraits kept in the theatre's museum, but the fire had spread to surrounding buildings and caused great devastation. The wind changed in time to save the library and art gallery, so those were fortunately still standing.

After viewing the site, they went for lunch at a nearby inn, where Henry told them of a visit he had paid a couple of years ago to the memorial theatre to see a performance of 'King Lear'. Hope had read the piece, but Antonio asked eagerly what it was about. In school, he had learned about Shakespeare, and he had read both 'Macbeth' and 'Othello' in edited versions. Henry briefly recounted the story. "You see, Antonio, the old King Lear wants to divide his kingdom among his three daughters. But first, he puts them through a test in which he asks them how much they love him. The two youngest flatter him, but the oldest, Cordelia, refuses to put her love into words, which cannot describe how much she loves her father. This infuriates Lear, so he deprives her of her inheritance. The French king then offers to marry Cordelia, even though she has no inherited land. In time, Lear is betrayed and undermined by his two younger daughters, and he flees their house to wander around the heath with two loyal companions, his fool and a loyal nobleman named Kent. Here he meets another nobleman fleeing from family trouble, namely the young Gloucester. Gloucester's father wants to help King Lear but is caught and blinded by Lear's daughters. Meanwhile, Cordelia has turned up in Dover with a French army to help her father. In the end, everybody kills each other in various ways, and when they are all dead, England ends up in the hands of the elderly Kent, the husband of one of the younger daughters and the legitimate son of Gloucester."

Antonio did not look like he really understood the intricacies of the play's plot, but he nodded and decided to read it for himself later. After lunch, they walked through the streets of Stratford until they came to Shakespeare's birthplace in Henley Street. The old yellow timber-framed house had been bought by a charitable foundation and restored in the 19th century, and behind it was a lovely and tranquil garden.

Hope was very glad to have seen the birthplace of one of her favourite writers, and Antonio seemed to enjoy it, too. But Henry was eager to get to Repton, and soon, they were on their way again. Passing through Birmingham, they reached the school in Repton in time for afternoon tea. The school consisted of a collection of yellow-brownish brick buildings in a small park with an impressing stone arch entrance. Henry took them both first to see the school's chapel and then to tea in his rooms before he walked Hope to the station. She had given Antonio a hug and said goodbye with as much warmth as she could, but Antonio had already retracted into his schoolboy persona and seemed embarrassed to be hugged.

* * *

On the train back to London, Hope was glad that she had spent her day off with Henry and Antonio, but she had not liked the school much. It was the first time she had been to a boys' boarding school, and it somehow did not feel very welcoming to women. This was the kind of place where England's future leaders grew into adulthood, and it seemed so detached from real life, full of fixed rules and traditions, which had very little to do with the outside world. When she thought of her older brother who had spent almost all his life in such surroundings, she could not really feel the person behind what he had become. She thought of Sarah, only one year older, who had played with him when he was a little boy, and she could not imagine the kind of boy he had been. She wondered again about the boarding schools that England was so proud of. Were they really the best places for young boys to get their education?

* * *

When the October break came around in 1926, Antonio had been invited to stay at a school friend's house near Birmingham, so he had written to say that he would like to go there and not come to London until Christmas. Henry had vouched for the friend's family, so Hope and Emily gave their permission.

That year, the famous mystery writer, Agatha Christie, suddenly disappeared from her home in Surrey without a trace. Emily was sure that she must have been abducted and murdered by one of her fans, but Hope was not convinced, and indeed, nothing pointed in that direction. On the third of December, she had kissed her seven-year-old daughter goodnight, then gotten into her car and never come back. One of the greatest manhunts seen at the time, involving one thousand police men, hounds and even airplanes was set in motion, but to no avail. Two other famous mystery writers, Arthur Conan Doyle and Dorothy Sayers, were consulted in the case. Speculation was rife, and the press was filled with interesting theories as to what might have happened. By the second week of her disappearance, the news had spread around the world and even appeared on the front page of the *New York Times*. At one point, her abandoned car was found. It had apparently suffered a minor crash, but Agatha Christie was nowhere near it. Finally, after eleven days, she was found in a spa hotel in Harrogate, living under an assumed name, namely that of her philandering husband's mistress. Emily and Hope had to accept the story that was put out, namely that Archie Christie had asked her for a divorce, and this had brought on a kind of fugue state or amnesia caused by depression and perhaps trauma. When her husband came to take her home, she claimed to have no memory of what had happened... They could not help speculating about what had really caused this desperate attempt to get away from her life.

A few days before Christmas, Hope and Emily went to pick up Antonio from the station and brought him back to their apartment. His autumn visit to a friend's house had been a success, and he had experienced British upper-class life with some amusement. He told Hope and Emily about Peter, his friend, and Peter's parents who had sold their stately home in the countryside and now lived in a large house in Birmingham. Both Peter's father and his mother had gone into business when they had moved from the estate, and they were doing reasonably well financially, but they had a great deal of trouble abandoning some of their aristocratic habits, which they could no longer afford. Peter could not really remember much about their life before the war, but he had heard from his mother about the huge staff they used to have and how they never used to do anything for themselves. Now they were making do with a cook and a maid, and both of Peter's older sisters were working in offices. Peter's mother was an interior decorator, and his father had started a farm machine factory. They were all expected to be there in the evenings, dressed for dinner, which the maid would serve. Hope and Emily had not known much about the aristocracy before the war except what they had read in books, so they enjoyed Antonio's description. He had really been very observant, and he had a talent for noticing the amusing nuances of manner and describing them to Emily and Hope.

After spending a few days in London, they would go to Calne to spend Christmas Eve and then return to London to spend the rest of the holidays with Hope and Emily's friends. They were going to take turns going out with Antonio so that they would have every second day to work on preparations for the end of the school year in March. On the first day, Hope would take Anthony to visit the Victoria and Albert Museum in Cromwell Road in South Kensington. It had started out as an exhibition of contemporary design and architecture promoted by Prince Albert, but from 1899, it had been renamed the Victoria and Albert Museum and greatly expanded. As they walked around the galleries of beautiful textiles, sculptures, wallpaper and furniture, Antonio's interest was clearly flagging, so Hope cut their visit short and took him across the road to visit the natural history section of the British Museum. This, too, was an imposing building, and in the central hall they found 'Dippy', the enormous, 32-metre long replica of the skeleton of a diplodocus found in Wyoming in the USA. Dippy had been a gift from the Scottish-American industrialist Andrew Carnegie who had paid 2000 pounds for the casting of the skeleton, which proved to be a great attraction in London. Antonio was fascinated, too.

"Is it real?" he asked. "And how old is it?"

Hope read from the sign: "It may be over 154 million years old, and it says that it is the longest of the so-called dinosaurs. This is a cast of the original bones, which were found as petrified fossils during the construction of a railroad in Wyoming. Sorry, but that is all I know."

"But, Aunt Hope, the Earth did not even exist that long ago! God created the earth and all its living creatures less than ten thousand years ago—I do not remember the exact number of years, but it was not millions!"

Of course, Hope thought to herself, he has had a conservative religious upbringing and probably never heard of Darwin or Wallace. *Should I tell him more about it?* She decided to discuss it with Emily first, so for now she just replied, "Well, maybe God created the fossils, too, just to give us something to wonder about." Antonio looked at her doubtfully, but Hope had already moved on to some of the other exhibits in the side galleries.

The visit to the natural museum was fascinating, with its mixture of familiar life forms, some quite unfamiliar. Especially the galleries of fishes, reptiles and amphibians had many strange looking creatures to look at. They walked around for a while until Antonio was beginning to look tired, and Emily suggested that they leave and go home. On the way home, they would shop for supper at the market, and Antonio helped Hope find some spices that could make the food a little more like Italian food. They also bought some tinned tomato soup, some baked beans, cauliflower and bread. Finally, they bought a cake for dessert. When they came home, Emily had tea waiting for them, and Antonio told her about 'Dippy' and how big it had been.

"Aunt Hope told me that it was 154 million years old, but how can that be true when the world is much, much younger?"

Emily looked at Hope inquiringly. Hope felt like a mother who has finally decided to tell her child that Father Christmas and the tooth fairy were stuff made up to make the world of children seem more magical than it really was.

"You see, Antonio," she began. "Religion may not know everything there is to know about the world. People have always been curious and wanting to know more about their surroundings. You know that there are people in the world who do not believe in our version of God, and some of them endeavour to find truth and proof to explain what they discover. That is what we call science."

"I know that," said Antonio with a smidgen of contempt in his voice. "Are you telling me that science has proven that God does not exist?"

"No, no, not at all," Emily and Hope protested. "We just think that science has made some discoveries that the Bible could not have quite foreseen, and we must take that into account when we describe the world. This does not mean that God does not exist, only that the Bible may not consist of facts only. For instance, science has shown that the earth is probably vastly older than we used to think and that it was inhabited by animals that then became extinct for one reason or another. There was a scientist in Scotland, Charles Darwin—we saw a statue of him in the hall of the Natural Museum. He published a book called *The Origin of the Species* in 1859. It presents a theory of evolution, which we think is very compelling in its analysis of how life evolves. You should read it when you feel ready and make up your own mind."

Antonio looked doubtful. "I have heard of Darwin, of course, and his theories may certainly have some truth to them, but they do not mean that God was not the original creator of the world, do they? I was just surprised when I heard the age of Dippy, because I had not known that the earth was millions of years old."

"I am sorry," said Hope. "I thought for a moment that your church rejected all modern science, but obviously, I was wrong. Emily and I were both brought up in the Anglican faith and know very little of the Catholic Church. It seems we were rather prejudiced, and I apologise."

"That is all right," said Antonio. "Frankly, I am rather bored by religion and would like to know more about science and find out as much as possible about how the world works and why. Please do not worry about my religious views. You cannot offend me by telling me things that I do not already know. I think I am old enough to handle it." He smiled.

Edith started laughing, and soon, Hope and Antonio joined in. For the first time, they felt a sense of complicity and relaxation. Hope realised that she and Emily did not have to take on the heavy responsibility of parenting for Antonio but could look upon him as a younger brother. He was already basically settled in life by the careful and loving upbringing he had received from Anthony and Lisa, and he did not need extra parents. Instead, they could behave like older sisters to Antonio and simply share whatever they wished with him and help him explore the world.

***

They arrived in Calne the day before Christmas. It was a very cold winter, and it kept snowing. Luckily, Sarah had stocked up on food, because as the snow blizzard became worse, it became impossible to go out. For several days, they were stranded inside with only the radio to tell them what was going on in the outside world. As soon as the roads were passable after a day of thaw, they said goodbye to Sarah and Eleanor and set off for London. They put Antonio on the train to Repton where his school would have someone pick him up at the train station. There was still a lot of snow everywhere, and some days, traffic would come to a standstill. Towards the end of January, another blizzard hit, and the river Thames could no longer be contained in its basin. Many underground stations were flooded, and river water came into Westminster Hall as well as the House of Commons. A number of people drowned or died in other ways directly connected to the weather that winter.

***

When they had been to Europe in 1922, Hope and Emily had become acquainted with avant-garde movements in art and literature. They had tried to follow the developments of Cubism, Futurism, Dadaism and Surrealism, but it was as if almost everything avant-garde was happening on the mainland with very few repercussions in England. After the war, many European artists had moved to New York and some American artists got involved, but in the 1920s, after the prohibition laws had been enacted in the USA, they all seemed to have congregated in Europe and especially in Paris. The avant-garde movements impacted not only paintings and literature but also music, theatre and performances. Many new magazines came into being for shorter or longer periods. While Hope and Emily had been in Italy, they had looked for evidence of such movements, but had been unable to find any. The word surrealism was coined by Guillaume Apollinaire in 1917, and the movement grew in Paris in the 1920s. The surrealists wanted to show the world in surprising forms to challenge the normal perceptions of reality and to shock the bourgeoisie. They did not always agree among themselves and several different manifestos were published. The one published by Andre Breton in 1924 had so far seemed to be the most widely accepted. It proclaimed automatic writing and drawing as well as dreams as ways to explore and reveal a deeper reality.

Hope and Emily sought out lectures about the subject, but they were few and far between in London. The library, which they frequented, had very little on the subject, even in French. In England, the disillusion and lack of meaning in the world, which inspired European artists both before and especially after the Great War, did not really resonate. Instead, the Design and Industries Association, inspired by the older Arts and Crafts movement, the Parisian Art Deco and the modern German Bauhaus, had taken the lead by, among other things, decorating the London Underground with colourful and modernist posters. Frank Pick and others sought reconciliation between art and corporate business interests and maintained that beauty lay in anything that was 'fit for purpose'. Frank Pick was the joint assistant manager of the Underground Electric Railways Company in London from 1921 and a founding member of the Design and Industries Association, and he once compared the underground transportation system to a mediaeval cathedral where art could be made and enjoyed by thousands of people every day. He brought order to the tumble of posters that had hitherto filled the walls of stations by introducing standard sizes and positioning. He teamed up with architects in designing new stations both inside and outside, so that over time the London Underground took on a characteristic look inspired by Art Deco in which beauty and purpose could combine to please the daily users. He streamlined the lettering and design of station names and invented the red circle behind the sign to make it stand out.

Hope and Emily liked the new pleasing design, but they were still looking for more bold and experimental art that could comment on life in a less commercial and practical manner. They found some in literature such as the poems and writings of T. S. Elliot, James Joyce, Ezra Pound etc. Many of these writers were originally Americans who had settled in Europe and stayed there, and their international outlook and bold writings were attractive to Hope and Emily. In the years from 1927, they had begun to save up for a visit to Paris again, but they had decided to postpone such a trip until after Antonio had graduated. Maybe they would go in the summer of 1930.

In May 1928, the Representation of the People Act passed the Parliament, and the age for women to vote was lowered from thirty to twenty-one and finally gave women equal suffrage with men. This was greeted with pleasure by Hope and Emily, although they would have liked to have seen it happen much earlier. This added five million more women to the electorate and actually saw women voters becoming the majority with 52.7 % of the electorate in the 1929 general election.

1928 had also been the year in which the first novel about lesbianism was published in England. The author was Radclyffe Hall, and the book bore the title *The Well of Loneliness*. Radclyffe Hall had been baptised Marguerite, and from an early age, she had fallen in love with women. She termed herself a 'congenital invert,' a term taken from the physicist Havelock Ellis, who studied human sexuality and wrote extensively about it. In *The Well of Loneliness,* she did not write explicitly about sex, but she wanted to take up the subject of homosexuality in order to change people's perceptions. However, a campaign led by the editor of *The Sunday Express*, James Douglass, under the title 'A Book That Should be Suppressed', turned public opinion against her. The book went to court accused of 'obscenity' and promotion of unnatural relationships between women, and all copies were ordered destroyed. But the publicity generated by the trial only made the book more well known. Hope and Emily both read it and approved of the publisher and the writer's bravery, but they did not like to see themselves as 'congenitally inverted'. Their way of life seemed more like a rational choice and a private matter, so they could not help feeling some regret at the ensuing scrutiny of women who lived together. They had always been meticulous about never showing any public displays of affection, never speaking in public about their feelings for each other but always maintaining that their living together was just based on friendship and practical considerations. They knew of the American term, 'Boston marriage,' which was used for an arrangement where two women who were economically independent of men co-habited simply by preference and without any romantic intentions, and they hoped that this was the impression they were giving to co-workers, friends and acquaintances. They had not needed to worry, since most people saw them simply as two spinsters who had set up house together for lack of better choices, women who had not been able to find a husband because of the war and the profession they had chosen.

***

The 1920s were an age of optimism, and new consumer goods made life easier and more fun. The pre-war optimism was slowly returning after the devastating war experience, and where some sought comfort in various interpretations of communism, others chose to despise the increasing 'Americanism' with its attending admiration of technology, commercialism and cheap conveyor belt entertainment. Everything seemed to have sped up from communication to transportation. Fascism was gaining ground and promoted mass movements of nationalism, racism and the belief in a strong leader rather than in democracy. Through violence, fear, propaganda and use of the new mass media, such as movies and radio, they turned many people away from the democratic political culture. Sir Oswald Mosley had become a member of Parliament after the war, first for the conservative party, but later, he crossed the floor and eventually became a member of the Independent Labour Party. He was a brilliant speaker and was re-elected in 1926. But only a few years later, the post-war optimism cracked as more and more people lost their conviction that the Great War had been the war to end all wars.

On September the 20th, 1929, the London Stock Market crashed after the arrest of the top British investor Clarence Hathy and his cronies. This sets events in motion that culminated in the Wall Street crash where stock prices hit rock bottom on Black Tuesday, October 29th of the same year. It was followed by The Great Depression that lasted for 12 years. Unemployment rose sharply in most manufacturing sectors, and world trade diminished by half. In heavy industries, the output fell by a third, and in 1932, the country had 3.5 million unemployed workers. Raising taxes and cutting public spending helped only a little and caused great dissatisfaction in many people. London and the nearby counties suffered less than other areas, because growth in electrification and mass production of electric goods, such as cookers, washing machines and radios, was doing very well. Also, the motor industry grew rapidly in towns like Birmingham, Coventry and Oxford. The number of motor vehicles on the roads doubled in the 1920s, and agriculture also flourished. But regions that had depended on mining and heavy industries suffered greatly. In some towns in the northeast, unemployment rose to 70%. Unemployed workers marched to London to present their case to the government but to little avail. Like in the hunger marches of the early 1920s, groups who had been laid off because their employer had gone out of business initiated such marches and elicited some sympathy but very little concrete action.

In Italy, a general election in the spring of 1929 had made Mussolini the de facto dictator of Italy. Letters from Anthony and Lisa began to sound worried about what Antonio should do after school. He would be graduating the following year, and while he was missed enormously by his family, concerns for his future made especially his father wonder whether coming back was really the best thing for his son. In the end, Antonio became the one to decide.

"I am going home next year," he declared. "I want to be with my family again and help them through whatever will happen in the future. Italy is my home, and as much as I like and admire Britain, I love my family more."

Thus, it was decided, and on March 31st, 1930, Antonio left by ship and train for Italy. He was now a young man, fully capable of making up his own mind as well as travelling alone to Italy. Hope and Emily were sad to see him go, because they had really grown fond of him over the past four years. They were also a little worried about how he would find Italy after his years in England, but they comforted themselves by thinking about how happy his family would be to have him back among them. In September, he would enter the University of Naples to study, and they were sure he would excel.

After Antonio had left, Hope and Emily immediately started to plan their summer vacation in Paris. During the 1920s, Paris had become a gathering place for people of many different nationalities, who wanted to live cheaply and try new things. Many wanted to be writers, painters, musicians, singers, dancers, or entertainers of one kind or another, and a number of them got started on the road to fame and glory. By 1930, *les années folles*, the crazy years, were gradually grinding to a halt as the depression began to hit France as well, so Hope and Emily would be just in time to experience its last glory that summer. 1930 was to become the last year for rich American tourists to enjoy the favourable exchange rate and spend freely on fashion and alcohol in France. The poorer artists began to move out, too, when the depression hit Paris in 1931.

Trip to Paris

Hope and Emily would go by train to Dover and get the ferry to Calais and then take the French train from Calais to Paris. It would take them almost a day to get there, and they had decided to find a hotel on the Left Bank of the Seine, near the Luxembourg Garden and the famous cafés, where the artists and writers were known to gather. On their way into the city, they noticed that the Eiffel Tower had become an enormous advert of light bulbs for the Citroen Motor Company and agreed that they found it vulgar and ugly. They had picked Hotel de Saint André des Arts in the street by the same name, very near the Luxembourg Gardens.

It was a small and old hotel with five floors, stonewalls and exposed wooden beams, which Hope found very charming, and it was cheap enough that they could stay for the three weeks they had planned. When they had checked in and placed their luggage in their room, they went for a short walk around Montparnasse. They soon found their way down to the river Seine and walked along it until they turned left and eventually reached Boulevard Saint-Germain from where they could go to the famous Café de Flore and have a glass of wine before they went home to bed. They sat for a while and watched people go by, until Emily said, "This is the life, dear. Here we are again in Paris! Let's toast to that."

They both raised their wine glasses and smiled. The world was full of problems, but here they sat in Paris with all of three weeks in front of them and could feel for a while as if nothing else could possibly matter. They continued to watch people and occasionally remarked on what they saw. They noticed a few well-dressed women in long flowing summer dresses and pretty bell-shaped hats, but this was not a district where fashion dominated the view.

The next morning, they set out for the famous bookstore and lending library called 'Shakespeare and Company' in Rue de l'Odéon. It had been set up by a woman, the American Sylvia Beach, with some help from the more experienced French bookseller Adrienne Monnier, who owned the bookstore across from it. Shakespeare and Company attracted especially expatriates in Paris who would come to buy or borrow, not only books that had been banned in their home countries, such as James Joyce's *Ulysses*, and D.H. Lawrence's *Lady Chatterley's lover*, but also other newer literary works. Emily was determined to buy some of the books that one could not buy in England and smuggle them back. Hope held back a little and suggested that they borrow them and read them first and only bought a few that they really liked.

When they entered the bookstore, they were greeted by a slender woman with short, dark and unruly hair, who welcomed them and introduced herself as Sylvia. She was about their age, and she had been sitting by a table in the store. Behind her, the wall was full of framed photos and a few ageing posters, but the rest of the store had books on every wall. The place was well lighted from the windows, and comfortable reading chairs were placed here and there so that the room looked more like a living room than a store. They immediately liked it very much, and when Sylvia came over to greet them, they told her their names and that they had come from London yesterday to visit Paris for three weeks and learn more about what was happening in literature and the arts. She invited them to look around and explained that while the books in the front were for sale, she also ran a lending library for those who could not afford to buy all the books they wanted to read. For a monthly fee, you could become a subscriber. Then she asked if they could read French, and when they replied affirmatively, she pointed across the street to another bookstore. "My best friend, Adrienne, runs that book store, called *La Maison des Amis des Livres*. It is also both a library and a bookstore, and you should take a look there as well. Please ask me anything if you think I might be of help."

Hope and Emily explored the bookcases for a while. They found a copy of *Ulysses* published by Shakespeare and Company and they decided to buy it despite its bulk—it was 730 pages long. They knew that Sylvia had spent a lot of time and almost all her money to get the book published, and that Joyce had later sold the rights to Random House for a great deal of money. However, he had shared none of this profit with Sylvia as far as they knew.

They asked Sylvia if she could recommend any new women writers to read.

"Certainly," she said. "Do you prefer poetry or prose?"

"Both," said Emily.

"Gertrude Stein, whom you probably know, wrote this one in 1914," Sylvia took a book from a shelf entitled *Tender Buttons. Objects. Food. Rooms*.

"Yes, I have heard of her," said Emily, "but I have not read this one. It looks very interesting."

Sylvia also showed them Djuna Barnes' *Ladies Almanack* and told them a little about her. "She and many other women like myself have moved to Paris after the Great War, partly because of the freedom we experience as expatriates, partly because it is possible to live on very little money. Gertrude Stein and Alice Toklas have lived here for many years even before the war and they host literary salons with lots of food, both for the body and for the soul. Others like Nathalie Clifford Barney and her painter friend Romaine Brooks do the same, especially for women poets. Some gather here at my bookstore for the readings we arrange to hear what others are working on. French writers come, too, to be inspired by the expatriates' discussion and vice versa. For the past ten years, we have been a kind of community where everybody can feel at home and find some help when they need it."

"That sounds wonderful," said Emily.

"It has been," said Sylvia, "but in the past year, more and more of the regulars have gone, and I am not sure that the good times will last."

"Is it because of the economic crash in America?" asked Hope.

"I guess that is part of it, though France is still managing to stay out of the economic crisis. But I am afraid that it will hit us very soon. Another reason is that many people fear that the unresolved conflicts from the Great War may lead to new wars in Europe."

"Blimey!" said Hope uncharacteristically. "Do you really think so?" She looked horrified. "But what about the League of Nations? What about the Kellogg-Briand Pact that was signed here in Paris less than two years ago? It made war illegal, didn't it?"

"Some of my American friends do not think it will help. As for the League of Nations, they point to the fact that America never joined and that several countries are threatening to leave the league if their demands are not met," Sylvia replied. "The Kellogg-Briand Pact is seen as a purely idealistic attempt to pretend that the world is better than it is. I don't know." Then she changed the subject.

"How would you like to look at some of the magazines that regularly report on everything cultural that is happening in Paris?" she asked. "Do you know Janet Flanner, who writes for *The New Yorker*? Her 'Letters from Paris' might be just the kind of information you are looking for. I have a few of the latest issues, and I also have several copies of *Transitions*, which is published by Eugene Jolas and his wife, Maria. Why don't you both sit down, and I will make you a cup of tea while you browse them."

"That is very kind of you," Hope said, and Emily chimed in, thanking her. They sat down at the table in the back and began to read. Hope held up a 1927 issue of *The New Yorker* and said, "Here is an article about the dancer Isadora Duncan who died so tragically a few years ago. Miss Flanner writes really marvellously well, and I feel that we have missed something by not following the developments in dancing and ballet. I wish we had seen her perform." Emily nodded.

"I am reading Flanner's article from last year about Edith Wharton, who lives south of Paris and still writes books. Do you remember when we both read *The Age of Innocence*? Such a lovely and insightful novel. Miss Flanner has written a portrait of her, which I find rather unkind. She calls her 'cold'…"

"Does she now?" Hope said, "Maybe she knows better, being a fellow expatriate American. I just thought the cool way in which she wrote reflected her upper-class background and the time she wrote about."

Sylvia now brought them each a nice cup of hot tea and sat down with them.

"The book store is not busy at this time of the day, so I thought that I might sit down and talk to you for a few minutes. We have a reading planned on Friday, which you might want to come and hear. You will be most welcome. We do not have so many activities in the hot summer months, but some people are dropping by, and we are planning to have a poetry reading. We will have to see who will be available, but I am sure Janet will be there, and perhaps an American named Henry Miller…"

"We would love to come," said Emily. "Thank you for inviting us. Should we bring anything?"

"Some wine and cheese would be nice, but you do not have to. Anyway, what do you do besides reading when you are in England?"

"We are both teachers at a high school for girls," said Hope. "Our students are from twelve to sixteen years old, and we want to teach them in a way that makes them think and act like independent beings."

Emily added, "We have been together ever since we graduated from teachers' college, and in our twenties, we were supporters of the suffragette movement, so education for girls is something we feel very strongly about. We want our girls to know about strong women who they can emulate." Sylvia nodded her approval.

Hope continued, "In England, it can be still be difficult for most women to be accepted in many fields, but there are hopeful signs. We hope to get inspired by the international environment here in Paris, so we can better open up our students to the world, both geographically and spiritually."

"That is very admirable," said Sylvia. "Countries that want to censor great authors like James Joyce and D. H. Lawrence need strong people to stand up for the freedom of their people to judge for themselves what they wish to read. You should not think, however, that the French in general are more tolerant than other people—they are not. They just tend to leave artists and foreigners alone as long as they do not bother anyone else."

**

It was around noon when they left Sylvia's bookstore with the books they had bought. The day had grown hot, and after buying some bread and cheese for lunch, they decided to spend the afternoon in the Luxembourg Garden. Sylvia had told them about 'La Ruche' in Passage Danzig, where artists lived cheaply. It was a three-storied octagonal building, shaped somewhat like a beehive, and it had originally been used for one of the pavilions during the 1900 World Exposition. Afterwards, it had been bought by Alfred Bourget and rebuilt on his land to make studios for artists. Although the building was behind heavy iron gates and one could not go inside without an invitation, they had decided to go the next day just to see it from the outside.

In the Jardin du Luxembourg they found a place to sit and eat, and they began to read the books they had bought. Emily embarked on *Ulysses* straight away, while Hope debated for a while whether to read Gertrude Stein or Djuna Barnes, but eventually settled for Barnes' *Ladies' Almanack*. It had the extremely long subtitle: 'showing their Signs and their Tides; their Moons and their Changes; the Seasons as it is with them; their Eclipses and Equinoxes; as well as a full Record of diurnal and nocturnal Distempers, written & illustrated by a lady of fashion'. Besides, it had illustrations done by Djuna Barnes herself. In sharp and witty terms, it described a circle of women friends around 'Dame Evangeline Musset,' who Sylvia had told them apparently was drawing on the real person of Natalie Barney and the women who frequented her salons. Hope did not know any of the women and found the novel a bit perplexing. She looked at Emily, who seemed engrossed in *Ulysses*.

"I am going to stretch my legs and have a look around," Hope said. "I will leave my things with you, if you don't mind."

"That's fine," said Emily. "I will stay here."

Hope got up and looked around. The garden and the palace had been created in the 17th century; it modelled the Pitti Palace in Florence, and it was laid out in a geometrical way with straight and diagonal paths, square lawns and an octagonal fountain in the middle. It did not look as if one could get easily lost, so Hope set out in the direction of the fountain. In its basin, children were sailing model boats while their mothers or nannies sat in chairs and watched them. Along the centre were a number of statues of women, and Hope soon figured out that they were former queens of France. There were many other sculptures here and there in the garden. But more interesting than the sculptures were the living people who were out to enjoy the sunshine and who were walking or sitting here and there. An elderly lady was feeding the birds, and Hope imagined that she could tell native Parisians from the tourists by their clothes and behaviour; the Parisians were less loud and more elegantly dressed, she thought. After a while, she went back to Emily and suggested that they find a café and have a cup of coffee. Emily immediately agreed, and when she had gotten up and packed their books, she began to tell Hope about what she had been reading.

"It is quite interesting and sometimes funny," she said. "I think I am going to like it. The dialogue is rather straightforward so far, but in between, there are various casual references to classical Greek literature, that are not always clear. So, I would say that I have a demanding read in front of me… Will it be OK if I keep the book a while before handing it over to you?"

"Certainly," said Hope, "especially if we can take turns reading it aloud to one another now and then. I started on Djuna Barnes' book, and I think it would be even more fun to read if one knew the real people she writes about. But even as it is, it is quite interesting."

They had reached the Boulevard St Germain and went into the Café de Flore, where they sat down outside and ordered two coffees. At the next table sat a strikingly beautiful, dark-haired young woman engrossed in reading a book. She seemed very intense, and they watched her a little while.

"I wonder what she is reading," said Hope. "She looks like a student or a young teacher."

Another young woman came into the café and sat down at the same table. "Comment ça va, Simone," she exclaimed after she had lit a cigarette. "Have you heard from Jean-Paul recently?"

Hope turned her head when the two women began to talk animatedly. But it wasn't polite to listen to other people's conversation, so instead she turned her attention to Emily and asked her what she would like to do next.

"Why don't we have a late supper and then go to hear some jazz music? Let's go to Montmartre and see if we can find 'Chez Bricktop'."

They had talked about this amazing person called 'Bricktop' before they came to Paris. Her name was actually Ada Smith, but because of her mixed parentage as the daughter of an Irish woman and a Black American man, she had strikingly red hair, which had earned her the nickname. She had started performing in vaudevilles at an early age, and she gained recognition from people like Cole Porter. In 1924, she had moved to Paris where Cole Porter hired her to teach his houseguests new dances, such as the Charleston, and soon, she ran two clubs, where she brought in performers and sometimes performed herself. In 1929, she had started her own nightclub in Rue Pigalle called 'Chez Bricktop,' and she was known as the queen of café culture as well as for smoking cigars. Many famous people frequented her clubs, and she had Duke Ellington, Mabel Mercer and Josephine Baker among her protégées.

Hope immediately agreed, so they went back to their hotel to nap for a few hours. Then they left their books behind and changed their clothes into something more suitable if the night should turn out to be chilly. They would find a place to eat in Rue Pigalle and then go to 'Chez Bricktop' afterwards. They got on the metro at Odeon and arrived in Pigalle about 40 minutes later. They found a place to eat and sat down with a glass of wine to wait for the food. They knew that they should not arrive too early since the action would not really begin before ten o'clock, so they lingered over their food and talked. At ten, they got out and went along Rue Pigalle until they found the grand entrance to 'Chez Bricktop' in number 66. They saw that the half-black English singer, Mabel Mercer was featured and looked forward to hearing her sing, but most of all they looked forward to seeing the formidable 'Bricktop' woman. They were seated at a table to one side, but the place was not so big that they could not see the stage, and besides, the central tables were already filling up. They ordered some wine and sat sipping it and waited for the performances to begin. They noticed that the audience consisted of white people who looked wealthy, but also of some that looked more casual. There were a number of black people in the audience, too. To Hope and Emily, they were a rare sight, but everyone seemed very comfortable in each other's company, and after a while, they stopped noticing. A slightly plump and very charming woman wearing a feather boa slung around her neck came out and mounted the stage to welcome her guests—this was Bricktop herself. The audience applauded, and then 'Bricktop' began by singing 'Embraceable You' by Gershwin. Hope and Emily had never heard anything like it, but they loved it right away. 'Bricktop' then introduced the people in the orchestra and the next singer, Mabel Mercer. As soon as 'Bricktop' had stepped down from the stage, she lit a cigar and to Emily and Hope's surprise, seemed to enjoy it. Mabel Mercer then came on stage and sang several songs, which they did not recognise, but she sang so distinctly that they could make out almost every word. When she stopped for a break, the orchestra played on, but people began to talk. Emily said to Hope, "I think I could fall in love with this music. It has such deep feelings, and when the orchestra plays, you almost cannot sit still."

"Quite so," said Hope. "Let's look for similar places back in London when we go back. And why don't we buy a few sheets of scores and try to play them ourselves on our piano in school." They stayed in the nightclub for a few hours and enjoyed the mood and the atmosphere before they found a taxicab to take them back to their hotel.

"What a night," said Hope, "this is far beyond my usual bedtime…

"We could probably get used to it," said Emily and yawned, "if we did not have our work to get up to every morning."

"Maybe so," said Hope. "I do not think that I would be comfortable living that way. It is fine to do now and then, but I do not think I am cut out to be a creature of the night."

Emily was already half asleep, and Hope added, "I do not think you are either…"

The next morning, they slept late and missed breakfast. It was a beautiful day like the day before, and they decided to go and see where so many of the artists lived in La Ruche. Behind the gates, they could make out the overgrown garden and the upper floors of what seemed to be quite a beautiful, but dilapidated building. Nearby was a market, where fish and meat were sold, and the smells drifted over the area. It was early afternoon and rather quiet except for the sounds coming from the market. They left and walked along the narrow streets to the Paris Catacombs, which was also on their list of things to see. It took them almost an hour to get there, but they were in no hurry. They had both brought their jackets because they knew it would be colder at a depth of twenty metres underground.

From the mid-1700s, the stone mines that provided the so-called Lutetian limestone and plaster of Paris had been used to build the city. In time, these early tunnels had been forgotten and buildings and roads established on top of them. A few began to collapse in the 18th century, not least the large collapse in St Germain de Près in 1774, and when about a hundred feet of street collapsed, the shoring up and consolidation of the large network of underground tunnels was begun, and an inspector of safety was appointed. This led to the inspection and filling in of the old tunnels, and small parts of them were turned into ossuaries to relieve the overflowing and increasingly unsanitary cemeteries in the city. The cemeteries in the city were gradually emptied of bodies, which were moved to shafts in the tunnels. They were opened to the public in 1874 after some of the bones had been arranged in pleasing and artful ways.

It was these ossuaries that Hope and Emily wanted to see. They could not tell why, but somehow, they both found it fascinating that they existed. At the entrance, they waited a short while until a few more people had assembled, and then the guide signalled that the tour would start.

First, they went down a long staircase and then straight through a stonewalled tunnel for a long way until they reached the first ossuary. It had an engraved message in French over the main entrance, 'Stop! This is the Empire of Death,' and the guide told them that there were skeletons of around six million dead people in there.

It was cool underground, and the theme of the caves did not help the chill. Row after row of wall panels and whole rooms constructed from skulls and other bones, set in patterns. Here and there, heavy pillars stood to reinforce the low-ceilinged stone roof. Most of the people in the group stopped talking after they had entered and fell silent as they saw the bones. Some stood still and read the inscriptions, which in some cases indicated from which cemetery the bones had come, and pondered over them, while others walked by, lost in thoughts. Everybody seemed to take only shallow breaths as if to take a deep one might be to breathe in death. Finally, after what seemed forever, they were able to climb the stairs to the outside again. They walked through a few streets before they found a nice-looking café and sat down and ordered two glasses of white wine.

"Now, what did we do that for?" said Hope who had turned quite pale. "It made me feel quite queasy to look at and to think about all those dead people who were once alive."

"Sometimes we must do things that are hard," replied Emily, "I believe that one of those things is to realise how we will all end up one day. Not necessarily on display in an ossuary, but just as dead. It depressed me, too, and I must admit that I have no real appetite for food now. Let's have one more glass of wine."

Hope agreed, and the waiter brought then an extra glass of wine and asked them if they would order their lunch. Hope asked for soup and bread for both of them and said to Emily, "We must eat a little bit, too, or we shall get drunk."

While the soup and bread were served, Emily continued their conversation.

"Since we are both agnostics, we do not expect to continue life after death, do we? We do not even want there to be an afterlife, am I right?"

Hope nodded, "That is not why it was so difficult to see the ossuaries. I think it was more the thought of the people who had worked to arrange the bones so carefully. What was going through their minds? What did they think? Did they think of the bones as simply material for decorations or a practical way of storing them, or did they think that they were honouring them by making a monument of their bones?"

"It was probably a bit of both," said Emily. "It seems to have been a custom in many cultures to let the body decompose and then dig up the skeleton to place it somewhere else—in a vaulted charnel house near the churches."

"Let us eat our soup and change the subject," said Hope. "Let us just walk through the city until we find a nice park…"

"Or we could try to find the grand mosque," suggested Emily. "It will be on our way back."

"Fine," said Hope. "Let us eat and get out of here."

They set out along the Rue St Jacques, turned right and walked along Rue de Monges and soon found the entrance on a corner. The mosque had been built in 1926 as a sign of gratitude to the Algerians who had fought for France in the Great War. It had a tall minaret in the back, and they found themselves in a tranquil garden where they could sit down by a small round metal table and order tea and biscuits. There were a few other customers, but the general impression was so quiet that they all seemed to speak in hushed tones. The mosque itself was a beautiful place decorated with tiles and colourful geometric patterns, especially around the windows and doorways. The mosaics were only decorative; there were no representations of human beings. Hope wondered why and asked Emily if she knew, but Emily shook her head.

"I do not know, but I have read somewhere that there is a prohibition against making images of persons. I do not know if that is true or why. Maybe the culture just became fascinated with geometry and patterns and developed their aesthetics in that direction."

Hope looked at her and said, "Maybe they never thought that stories should or could be told in pictures. I do not suppose a lot of people were able to read, so stories would have to be told and retold, and people would have to form whatever images they could in their minds…"

They left the café and went to look inside the mosque. Here they saw the various halls from the stone-tiled corridor running around the edge. There was a large empty room with a variety of carpets laid out to cover the floor and another one with intricately patterned floor tiles with a fountain-like structure in the middle. It did not look like any churches they had ever seen, but it felt like a holy place in which they did not belong, so they hurried out into the garden again. They sat down and had some more tea and pieces of strange sweet candy. It felt somehow as if in the middle of Paris, they had stepped out of Europe and into a world they did not know at all. "You were born in Japan," said Emily. "That must have been a very different world, too. Not like this one but in a completely different way?"

Hope tried to think back to her early years, but no matter how much she tried, she did not detect any memories whatsoever that she could fix to Japan. In the end, she shook her head and said, "I really do not remember anything about it. I was only six years old when we left, and I remember my father and Sarah and our house, but nothing I can identify as Japanese. We should ask Sarah when we get back home."

They left the mosque and bought some bread and ham to have supper in their room. They also bought a bottle of cheap *vin ordinaire* to drink with it. As they sat down to enjoy their improvised supper, they began to feel very tired and they went to bed as soon as they had cleared up the remains of their meal.

***

The next morning, they felt rested and ready for new adventures. It was their fourth day in Paris. Over breakfast, they talked over their plans for the day.

"Yesterday was an unusual day," said Emily. "Artists, bones and Muslims… Let's do something more traditional today."

Hope suggested that they should go and see the Panthéon, and Emily readily agreed. They had seen it from a distance as it lay on top of a hill, and they knew that it was a former church which had been turned into a mausoleum for distinguished Frenchmen. Inside, it held the famous pendulum, hung there by the scientist, Léon Foucault in 1851, to demonstrate the Earth's rotation. It was only a short walk from their hotel to its impressive neoclassical façade, where they entered. Light came through the windows of the dome, and they could see the beautiful frescoes which decorated the ceilings. It had not escaped their attention that the whole thing was built in honour of the 'grand hommes,' the great men of the fatherland, and they wondered whether any women had ever been interred there. They found only one, namely the wife of the great and famous chemist, Marcellin Berthelot, who had apparently died just before him since they were both interred in 1907.

"Who were they?" Hope asked Emily, who had done all the science subjects when they were students.

"I do not know about his wife, but he was a chemist who worked with thermochemistry and proved that inorganic substances could be synthesised into organic material if manipulated correctly. He also did work on explosives, I think."

"I wonder whether any women may ever end up here on their own merits," Hope mused.

"I wonder, too," said Emily. "There are a number of women scientists in the world, also in France, who would deserve to be honoured for their achievements. For instance, Marie Curie, who has already won the Nobel Price twice for her research. And many others… but I guess it will be many more years before such women will be recognised on a par with men."

They went up from the crypt and went to the middle of the building where Foucault's pendulum was suspended from the central dome, 67 metres above. It was a 28-kilo bob made of lead coated with brass, and it swung lazily over a centre platform with measures around it and tiles in the shape of Greek Meander Keys. They looked at it for a while. Hope could not quite see how this proved the Earth's rotation, and she did not ask Emily for fear that the explanation would be too complicated for her to grasp. She simply accepted that it was so and let herself be mesmerised by the slow swinging back and forth of the pendulum.

Once they were outside again, they drifted down Rue St Jacques to the entrance to the Sorbonne University, where they stood in the square in front of the famous place of learning. The main building itself was domed and had columns at the entrance. The University had over 11,000 students in various buildings spread around the Quartier Latin and more and more were women and foreigners. In 1925, the *Cité International Universitaire de Paris* had been built in a park in the 14th arrondissement in order to provide housing and meeting places for the students and visiting professors. In the square in front of the main building of the university there was a nice fountain. They did not feel comfortable entering any of the buildings, and they might not be allowed if they tried, so instead they sat down at a small café and took turns naming some of the many illustrious alumni that had walked here through the ages: Erasmus of Rotterdam, Honoré de Balzac, John Calvin, Voltaire, Victor Hugo, Francis Xavier and many more. Their list was awfully short of women until they thought of Marie Curie who had taken over her husband's professorship after he died tragically, but they could not think of any more women. The Sorbonne had accepted women students in 1880, but maybe it had not occurred to them that women might be able to teach, too...

"I wonder how many intelligent and gifted women the world may have missed by keeping them in kitchens and nurseries and telling them that was all they were good for?" asked Hope.

Emily thought about it.

"Many, I am sure," she said, "but wouldn't you agree that men and women were born different and have different roles to play as well as different aspirations in life?"

"Perhaps," Hope replied, "but we do not know, do we, until we try to do everything differently. I do not think that men in general are born more intelligent than women in general, do you?"

Emily laughed. "I do not know," she said. "Sometimes you ask the oddest questions."

Hope smiled and said, "I know, but I cannot help thinking about such things, and you are the only one I can ask about them without people thinking that I am dumb or crazy."

"You are neither dumb nor crazy," protested Emily, "and you know that. You just tend to question everything under the sky, whereas I prefer to think of things that can actually be answered. You are much more philosophical than I am, that's why."

Hope looked at her with affection and said, "You are the anchor of my ship. I could not do a thing without you!"

***

They left the Quartier Latin and walked to the metro station near Notre Dame. They had decided to go to the Chateau de Versailles to see the museum of French history. The trip by metro would take about one hour, but they longed to get out of the city and to see the famous rooms and garden, which were said to be exquisitely gorgeous. In the 1620s, the Boulogne forest had become a favourite hunting ground of Louis the Thirteenth. He had built a humble hunting lodge in 1623 so that he could spend the nights there. A few years later, he built a larger place which became the beginning of the palace.

His son, Louis the Fourteenth, saw greater possibilities and began the building of the larger palace that would become one of the grandest palaces in Europe. He held fantastic parties and ceremonies there, and by the end of the 17th century, it had become very famous. His own son, Louis the Fifteenth, however, was not so fond of the grandeur and size of the rooms, so he let the place be neglected the first few years and never enjoyed living there permanently. When he died in 1774, his son, Louis the Sixteenth took over and married the notorious Marie-Antoinette. They lived at Versailles until they were forced to flee in October 1789, when the revolution broke out. Louis was executed in January 1793, and his queen, who symbolised the arrogant luxury of the court, was executed in October the same year. When Napoléon Bonaparte came to power in 1799, he did not want to take over Versailles as his residence, and it was decided to make it into a museum. It had been the place chosen for the signing of the peace treaty that ended the Great War, and it was still famed for its gorgeous interior decorations and its collections of art. Besides its formal garden, symmetrically laid out in front of the palace, it also housed a large park around a central canal. The symmetry was a perfect example of how nature could be tamed and controlled with a lot of work and money, but somehow, neither Hope nor Emily found it beautiful. The interior was something else. They could not possibly see all of it in what was left of the afternoon, but they very much wanted to see the Hall of Mirrors where the Treaty of Versailles had been signed. They also saw the War Room and the Peace Room, which were smaller but no less gorgeous, decorated with gold and marble with paintings in the vaulted ceilings and crystal chandeliers. They marvelled at the luxury, but Hope couldn't help herself when she whispered to Emily, "No wonder that it all ended in a revolution! It is perhaps more of a wonder that it has not happened in many other places…"

"Remember Russia," Emily whispered back, and it was certainly true. The Russian Revolution never seemed to end, and under Stalin, there had been continued purges of people suspected of being counterrevolutionaries, who were either executed or sent to Siberian work camps.

They walked through the seven rooms which were called 'The King's apartments' and had been used for official occasions. Besides, there were also private apartments of the king and queen, but they were not open to the public except on guided tours. Like the rest of the palace, the official rooms of the king were beautifully decorated in luxurious materials and colours. This time, however, they were less easy to impress.

"In a way, it is nice that we can now see how royalty and rich people used to live," said Emily, "but it is also painful to see this and think of how many people could have been fed and educated if the money had been spent differently."

Hope hesitated. "Of course, you are right," she said, "but maybe there would not have been so much beauty created by artists and builders. And don't you think that it also drove progress and creativity?"

Emily shook her head. "No, I don't actually. I think progress and creativity is driven by the human intellect much more than by the consumption of the rich and privileged. We might have less gorgeous art, but we would have progressed more if so many people had not been hungry and downtrodden all their life."

"You sound like a communist," teased Hope.

"People who think that there should be more justice in the world are hardly communists," Emily said. "They just think that a fairer distribution would help us all avoid war and violence."

"Sorry," said Hope, "I did not mean to offend you. I agree with you fully. It was just your use of a word like downtrodden that made me think of communist rhetoric. I wonder why we humans cannot live in a more just and equitable society?"

"I wonder, too. I really do. Do you think it has anything to do with the seven deadly sins in the Catholic Church like greed and pride, for instance? I guess they are a rather clever collection of concepts that are despicable and evil. However, I cannot see any way to improve the world without making matters worse. We can all try to make ourselves better people in whatever ways we can, but we cannot really change the whole world, can we?"

Hope said, "What if women were the ones in power instead of men? Mothers? They would never agree to a war if it might get their sons and husbands killed, I suppose. They are in general much more compassionate and perhaps better at discussing things rationally."

"We do not know that," Emily protested. "If women had all the power, there is no guarantee that they would do better than men—we have never seen any evidence that they would. We shall have to see how they do, now that at least they have a small voice in politics."

"Too small," sighed Emily, "much too small…"

***

The next few days passed leisurely for Hope and Emily. They went for walks and read and talked. They visited Sylvia's bookshop again and learned that the planned reading would be by Paul Valéry, who would read of some of his new poems. They had heard of Valéry but had never read anything by him, and he had not been translated into English, but their French should probably be good enough to appreciate his reading, they thought. To prepare themselves, they went across the street to see Adrienne Monnier's shop and find something by him in French. Adrienne received them warmly and invited them to look around. She was dressed in a long, heavy velvet skirt with a silk blouse and a dark tightfitting waistcoat. Her straight fair hair was combed back, but her eyes were friendly and lively. They spoke French together, and on Adrienne's advice, they ended up buying *La Jeune Parque*. She explained that the *Parque* was the youngest of the three goddesses of fate in Roman mythology, and this was supposed to be her soliloquy spoken in hexameters on a beach just before dawn. The poem spoke about her uncertainty about whether she should remain an immortal without human feelings or whether she should choose the pain and pleasure of a human life. That sounded very interesting to Hope and Emily, and soon, they were really looking forward to the reading on Friday in Sylvie's bookshop.

Friday came, and they went to Shakespeare and Company around seven o'clock in the evening. They had bought two bottles of wine and some bread and cheese, which they put on the table. Several people had already arrived and were sitting or standing around in the bookstore reading or talking. It sounded like most of them were French, and they recognised Miss Monnier talking to Sylvia. There were also a few others that looked familiar but none that they recognised. Sylvia came over and introduced Janet Flanner, and she pointed out André Gide and his friend, the poet and translator, Valery Larbaud. Then she left them with Miss Flanner and they spoke briefly about movies. But soon Paul Valéry stood up and everybody applauded. He had become a member of the prestigious *Académie Française* in 1925 and was now very much in demand to write essays and give lectures all over Europe. He began by reading some extracts from his work in progress, *Variété*, and after that, he read a number of poems. His voice was sonorous and melodious, with a certain emphasis on the rhymes that made it quite hypnotising to listen to, even when you did not understand every single word. Hope and Emily felt very privileged to be there among all these interesting people, and they felt a certain longing to live like them, here in a foreign city full of people from all over the world. When Valéry finished reading, everyone applauded and after Sylvia had thanked him, she pointed towards the table. This seemed to have been the signal that many were waiting for, and they threw themselves upon the free food and wine on the table. The less hungry stood around and chatted with each other, wineglass in hand.

A young man came over to them and introduced himself as Valentin and asked them in French whether they spoke Esperanto. Esperanto was an artificial language invented and developed by L. L. Zamenhof in the 1880s, and it was intended to make international communication easy and unambiguous. It had won widespread recognition and been suggested as a common language for the League of Nations after the Great War, but France had voted against the proposal. The first world congress for Esperanto had been held in France in 1905. Hope and Emily had noted all this with sympathy, but they had not done anything to become active or to learn the language, so they had to disappoint the young man, and he turned elsewhere. Another man came over and introduced himself as a newly arrived American writer, Henry Miller, and they asked him if he had had anything published yet. "I have written three novels, do you see, but I haven't found anyone who wanted to publish them. So, I have come to Paris, to be free of American puritanism and small-mindedness, don't you know, and to try to write a new and much better novel, you see. Tonight, I have come for the free food and drink, don't you know. My French is not yet good enough to understand Paul Valéry, unfortunately."

He was refreshingly honest, and his American drawl and his deep voice was quite attractive. "Are you writers, too?" he asked.

"Heavens no," said Emily, and Hope added, "We are readers and schoolteachers from England on holiday. The owner of the bookshop, Miss Sylvia Beach, invited us." Miller looked around for Sylvia and said, "I have to speak with her, you know. Pleasure meeting you ladies, though," and then he went over to greet Sylvia and Adrienne.

Hope and Emily spoke again to Janet Flanner who asked them if they had ever been to see the Louxor Palace du Cinema in Barbès. When they shook their heads, she offered to take them along the next day as she was planning to go and see a surrealist movie with her friend, Solita Solano. They thanked her, and she said she would come to pick them up at their hotel at two o'clock in the afternoon. People were beginning to leave, and Hope and Emily left, too, and went back to their hotel.

The next day, Janet and her American friend with the exotic name picked them up and took them on the metro, and half an hour later, they were in Montmartre. First, they went to a small art house where they could have a quick lunch before seeing Luis Buñuel and Salvador Dali's short surrealist movie, 'Un Chien Andalou,' which had come out the year before. It lasted less than 20 minutes, and it was difficult to make much sense of, but they recognised its surrealist intention and the attempt to shock and challenge bourgeois conceptions of the medium. They just had time for a cup of coffee before Janet and Solita took them over to the Louxor to show them its Egyptian façade with colourful mosaics of flowers and animals. One of the first talkies from 1929, an American movie called 'Dynamite' by Cecil B. DeMille was featured as the five o'clock show, and they bought tickets and went inside. Solita had to be somewhere else, so she left while the other three went in. It was a very large and luxurious theatre with plush seating for about a thousand people. Hope and Emily settled down with Janet, and the film started.

The story was about a socialite who needed to marry before the age of twenty-three if she wanted to inherit her grandfather's millions, and she ends up paying a mineworker who is convicted and about to be executed to marry her. At the last minute, the conviction is overturned, and he is released. After many troubles and terrible entanglements, the two fall in love with each other and settle down. Hope and Emily enjoyed the drama intensely as it was playing out on the screen, and when they went out for dinner afterwards with Janet, the three of them had a discussion about the role of film. They had all liked *The Andalusian Dog*, but when it came to the American 'motion picture' as Janet called it, opinions were more divided. Janet said that one was easily taken in by the sight and sound, and that the dramas they portrayed were too far – too removed from reality to mean anything that was worth spending time and money on. "But it was fun," protested Emily, "and very entertaining."

"I can see," Hope said, "how films like that portray a fantasy world full of fantasy people and invented problems that have very little to do with the real world, but as entertainment, it is very efficient, isn't it? And I do not see why the medium should not be used to convey more real and serious dilemmas that would make the audience think."

"Have you any idea of the amount of money it takes to make a feature movie?" Janet asked them. "It is not something poor artists can afford. The people who can afford to pay for the production of a movie with colours and sound want to make sure that their investment will pay off in ticket sales. They go for safe things like cheap thrills and improbable events, not for experiments and quality."

"I had not thought of it that way," said Emily. "And films are so seductive that they can be used to make many people believe they are real…"

"Exactly," said Janet. "Imagine someone using movies to convince people that an enemy is so evil that you simply have to go to war to get rid of him. A movie could also be used to present a false reality in such a convincing way that it would make people act differently."

"But books and newspapers—and speeches—can do that, too," said Emily. "Isn't that what propaganda is all about?"

"Yes," said Janet wearily. "I just worry that modern moving pictures with sound and colour could become an even more effective tool for propaganda and in a more indirect way, too, by making people think that they are just being entertained and not influenced to see the world in a certain way."

"True enough," said Hope. "But I also think that movies may expand our horizons and teach us about peoples and places where we can't easily go."

They continued talking for a while and drank some more wine. When they were going back on the metro train, Hope and Emily thanked Janet for taking them along and said they hoped to see her in London if she ever came that way.

Just before they went to bed, Hope said to Emily, "Don't you think we have a wonderful and stimulating life? We meet such interesting people and learn new things all the time."

Emily agreed with a smile. "Yes, and we have each other to share with and to cherish." She fell asleep with Hope in her arms, feeling happy and contented.

***

Over the next few days, they greedily drank in as much of Paris as they could manage. The car company Citroen, which advertised so prominently on the Eiffel Tower, had become very successful after the Great War. In order to create more work for demobilised soldiers after the war, France had shortened the work hours, but the labour unions were not satisfied, and strikes happened intermittently.

Like London, Paris had its great department stores, which employed thousands of women. They had grown and extended their selection of goods, and Hope and Emily visited *Au Bon Marché* and *Printemps* and enjoyed the beautiful décor as well as looking over the many beautiful things for sale. Paris fashion and perfumes had become well known all over the world, and the department stores had many rich foreign customers.

The cafés near St Germain du Près became their favourite watering holes, and they particularly liked the literary and artistic ambience of *Les Deux Magots* and *Café de Flore*. Both of these were on street corners and made for entertaining people-watching as well. Occasionally, they walked through the Luxembourg Park and visited *La Closerie de Lilas* on Boulevard de Montparnasse, which was more peaceful and withdrawn behind its many tall plants, so it was wonderful for both reading and letter writing. It was said that Russian revolutionary Lenin had visited there while he was living in Paris from 1908 to 1912.

Hope and Emily walked all over central Paris and got to know their way around rather well. When the time for their return drew near, they went to Sylvia's bookshop to say goodbye and to wish her luck in the future. They asked her to give their greetings to Janet Flanner and everyone else they had gotten to know, and they bought a few of her magazines to read on the train back.

Back in England

When they had returned to London, they went to visit Sarah and Eleanor in Calne. Sarah walked more heavily now that she was sixty-one years old, and Eleanor, who was forty-seven, did more of the physical work now. However, both were healthy, and their quiet life was all they seemed to want. They both went to church every Sunday and helped out with the poor and sick in the parish when needed. They lovingly welcomed Hope and Emily and wanted to hear everything about their visit to Paris. They did not share the younger women's enthusiasm for everything new in art, music and literature, but they liked to hear about it and derive a vicarious experience. Neither Sarah nor Eleanor ever blamed them for their unconventional thinking and their opinions, not even when they spoke about religion. Sarah was incredibly tolerant, and Eleanor always followed her older sister's manners and behaviour. Although both Hope and Emily liked to debate, they never tried to argue with Sarah, nor she with them, so a visit to Calne was always a relaxing and reassuring experience.

Back in London, they started work again at the school. The depression was heavy in the early 1930's and the number of unemployed rose. In Germany, the National Socialist Party was on the rise, and when Adolf Hitler became the Chancellor of Germany in January 1933, Hope and Emily thought back to what Sylvia had said in 'Shakespeare and Company' three years ago, namely that some of her friends were thinking that a new war in Europe would come sooner or later. They knew that many in Germany had felt very angry and unhappy about the war reparations demanded of them, but although developments in Germany were reasons for disquiet, they also admired the efforts made there to bring order and stability to the country.

The Nazi Party, as they were now calling themselves, was extremely anti-communist, and when the Reichstag burned down in February 1933 shortly before an election, a communist was arrested as the arsonist, and Hitler blamed all communists for plotting against the government and began to persecute them openly. At the election on March the fifth, the Nazi Party won over 40% of the votes. Although Hitler had not been able to win the two-third majority necessary to gain dictatorial powers, he succeeded in getting an Enabling Act passed a few weeks later that made it possible for him to take absolute power in the country and pass laws without the consent of the Parliament. Now he could begin his terror regime against all those he thought were against him. He began with a national boycott of all Jewish shops, orchestrated by Joseph Goebbels, the Minister for Propaganda.

Emily's Illness

However, something happened which completely shook Germany out of the minds of Emily and Hope. An evening in the late spring of 1933, Hope detected a small lump in Emily's breast that she had not felt before.

"What is that?" she asked, alarmed. Emily could not feel it at first, but when she let Hope guide her fingers, she felt it as well. "That's funny. It does not hurt at all, I do not know what it is… do you think I should go to the doctor?" asked Emily with rising concern in her voice.

"You must," said Hope. "We need to know what it is."

Emily promised to go as soon as she could get an appointment, and Hope offered to come with her, but Emily said, "We can hardly be away from school on an ordinary day, both of us. I will go alone, and then you can come with me later if he thinks it is serious."

Emily went to see the doctor, and he felt the lump carefully. Afterwards, he said, "I do not think it is anything serious, but to be sure I want you to go to St Bartholomew's Hospital and see Dr Keynes. He will decide whether to do anything further. I will write you a letter, which you must take to the hospital to get an appointment. But as I said, I am pretty sure that you have nothing to worry about." Emily thanked him and waited outside until the nurse brought her the letter, which she would take with her to the hospital. "You should go there today and give them the letter, and you will get an appointment in a few days."

When Hope returned from school, Emily was waiting for her with a meal she had prepared. "What did the doctor say?" she asked as soon as she was inside the door.

Emily gave her a hug and said: "He said that he was almost sure it was nothing serious and that it would probably disappear by itself. But he wanted me to go to Bart's to see another doctor, just to be sure, he said. I went there already and gave them the letter, and they promised to write me in a day or two with an appointment. Let's not worry, the doctor sounded very sure that it was nothing to worry about."

Hope could not stop worrying all the same, and she could feel that Emily was not quite as calm either as she pretended. But they had to wait to hear from the hospital, so worrying would not do any good anyway. Hope suggested that they should go for a walk after supper. It was a lovely spring evening, and she would bring Emily up to date on what was happening at in the school.

As they walked, the looming fear of the disease they both feared to name walked with them. But Hope managed to keep their conversation light by telling Emily about what was happening at school. "You know there are some of the girls in your class and mine who are also girl guides in their free time. They have asked the school whether they can have an afternoon where they invite all the pupils in the school and their families to a gathering at the school to fund their activities and recruit more members. They will do all the preparations and cleaning up afterwards if the school will just let them borrow the premises. We will discuss it when we meet on Friday. What do you think?"

Emily thought it sounded like a great idea. "I think that the girl guides learn a lot of useful things, they are physically fit, they learn how to live outdoors, cooking and sleeping in tents and how to get along with each other by being kind and practicing good deeds. I think I would have liked it very much when I was a young girl. I vote for giving them permission."

"I do, too," said Hope. "I think it is very nice that girls nowadays believe in themselves and their skills. Let's hope that our school will back them in this. Perhaps we can offer to be supervisors?"

Emily hesitated a moment before she replied, but then she said, "Yes, let us do that."

Any plans for the future had become rather difficult to talk about, Emily realised. It all depended on whether her lump was benign or not. Hope put her arm under hers, immediately understanding why Emily had hesitated before her reply.

"It will be fine," she said as reassuringly as she could. "You will be fine!"

The letter from the hospital came, and Emily's appointment was late the following day, so they agreed to go to the hospital together after school. Bart's was in Smithfield, so they went on bicycle and entered the gate.

Dr Keynes was a good-looking middle-aged man with sharp features and dark hair combed away from his forehead. When they finally got in to see him, he palpitated the lump carefully. He asked Emily about her age and when she had first menstruated, whether she had children, whether she was working and at what, and many more questions. Finally, he said, "Miss Browne, I recommend that we remove the lump once and for all, and then I will take a look at it in the microscope."

"Will I lose my breast?" Emily asked with trepidation. What she was really afraid of but did not dare to put in words was whether she would lose her life. Hope, who was sitting on a chair behind Emily, put out a hand to her shoulder and squeezed it to comfort her as well as herself.

Dr Keynes said, "If I find anything untoward in the microscope, I would maybe like to remove more of the breast tissue and put some small tubes of radium inside your breast to make sure that nothing will remain to bother you later. You will not feel it in there, and the radium will dissipate in a few days. I know that many surgeons recommend a more radical approach, but I think that limited surgery combined with radiation is safer and less painful for the woman. But this is, of course, only if I find anything suspicious in the tissue that I remove. If not, I just leave you with a slightly smaller breast and peace of mind..."

He waited for Emily to give her consent, and she looked over her shoulder to see Hope's reaction. She had tears in her eyes as she looked at Hope, so Hope, who was not less scared than Emily, had to suppress her own feelings and look optimistically at Emily as she said, "I will be with you all the way, no matter what happens."

Emily turned back to Dr Keynes and said, "When can you do the operation?"

"We should not hesitate," he said and brought in the nurse and asked her, "When is the next opening in my schedule for a breast operation? What about Monday morning?"

"Yes, sir," the nurse said, "there are no other operations scheduled for Monday morning."

To Emily, she said, "Please come with me now, Miss Browne, and I will give you an appointment to come in on Sunday evening and tell you how to prepare."

They said goodbye to Dr Keynes, who said, "I will see you on Monday, and your friend can come in later in the day when you wake up from the anaesthesia."

This was Thursday, so they would have to wait three days.

"What should we tell the school?" asked Hope. "You may have to take at least one or two weeks to recover, won't you?"

"I do not want them to know anything about it," said Emily. "We shall have to come up with some other explanation for my absence…"

They spent all evening trying to come up with a scenario they could convincingly tell at school. Finally, they decided that Emily should tell the headmistress about her problem and ask for her cooperation in keeping it a secret from the rest of the school. They would tell anyone else that Emily just had a persistent cough and she would have to go away for a thorough examination of her lungs.

The next few days felt like the longest days in their life. On Friday, Emily had seen the headmistress, who had actually been very reassuring and told her that she had a friend who had now lived twenty years after a similar problem was discovered, and she was still very well. Saturday and Sunday they spent mostly at home until it was time for Emily to go to the hospital. They were received by a nurse who found a bed for Emily in a large ward, and the time had come for them to say goodbye. They hugged outside the ward for a long time before Emily pushed Hope away and said, "I will see you tomorrow afternoon after school."

"I love you," Hope answered and left with a heavy heart.

When she came home, she went to bed, but it was difficult to sleep. It had been a long time since she had slept alone, and although she finally fell asleep, she woke up several times during the night, and each time, her concern for Emily would make her cry. She even tried praying to her father's God, but all her attempts at prayer ended in anger towards this God, who could not or would not help her or Emily. She envied the sincere believers who were able to put their faith into an all-powerful supernatural being who cared about them. Not that they ever got what they prayed for, but then at least they could say there had to be a deeper, unfathomable meaning to that which befell them. And then accept it meekly as, "God's ways are inscrutable." That was not for her, she knew.

Somehow, she got through the next day at school and rushed out and home as soon as she could. Visiting hours were from seven to eight, and she wanted to be there as soon as they would let her in. At five minutes to seven, she parked her bicycle outside the hospital, and precisely at seven, she arrived at Emily's ward. Emily was asleep, so she sat down and gently reached for her hand. This woke up Emily who smiled at her and said, "Sweet Hope, I am all right! The doctor removed the lump, and a little while ago he came to tell me that he had found nothing suspicious, and that I would be able to go home as soon as my wound was sufficiently healed in five to six days."

Hope broke down in relieved tears. "Oh, Emily, I was so worried for you! I hardly slept at all last night. Are you in pain now?"

"Only a little sore," said Emily. "They gave me something for the pain a little while ago, so I feel very relaxed. Just a little tired."

For the next hour, they held hands, Hope sitting on the edge of the bed, and Emily lying down under her covers, dozing off from time to time. When the nurse came to tell them that visiting hour was over, Hope bent down to kiss Emily on the cheek, careful not to touch the bandaged breast as she did so.

"Do you want me to bring you anything tomorrow?" Hope asked before she left.

"A newspaper," said Emily. "I hope I will be more awake tomorrow."

***

A week later, Hope went to pick up Emily from the hospital. She paid the bill and they got a cab back to their apartment, where Hope helped Emily up the stairs.

"Really," said Emily, "I had no idea that one could get so weak from being in hospital six days! I shall have to regain my strength over the next week by walking and cycling a lot."

"Take it easy," said Hope. "You have to get completely well before we expect you back at school. Your temporary replacement is managing well, so you do not have to worry."

"Hope," Emily said when they were back in their apartment, "I have not looked at the wound yet. I turned away whenever they changed the dressings. But I think Dr Keynes removed the whole breast. Will you help me change the dressing tomorrow and look at it?"

"Of course, I will," Hope answered. "Remember, I worked in a hospital for almost three years before I decided to become a teacher. Not that I did much apart from scrubbing floors and comforting some of the children, but at least I am not totally unprepared."

In the night, they slept side by side. Emily lay on her good side and held Hope's hand until they fell asleep.

After breakfast the next morning, they decided that the time had come for them to face their new reality. Hope unwound the bandage which covered Emily's left breast and shoulder. Under the bandage, the wound was covered with a thick gauze pack fastened to the skin with strips of sticking plaster. Emily had been right; the doctor had removed the whole breast.

"I think we had better let this gauze alone until you go back on Friday to have the stitches removed," said Hope. Emily stared mutely at the flat pad of gauze where her left breast had been. Finally, she said, "Can you love a one-breasted woman?"

Hope stared at her. "Do you really think my love for you would be any less strong because of that! I would love you in any shape or form, even leg-less and arm-less! Oh, Emily!"

She hugged her gently to avoid putting pressure on the wound. "Don't you remember the Greek Amazons who cut off one breast to be better warriors? You are my Amazon, a strong and brave fighting woman."

A tear or two rolled from Emily's eyes, and she wiped them away saying, "Oh, Hope, you are so precious to me. I don't know how I could think that you would stop loving me. I am sorry, but all this has been a bit unnerving, and I am not my usual self."

For every day that went by, Emily became a bit stronger, and on the following Friday when they went to see Dr Keynes, he seemed very satisfied with Emily's progress. He removed the stitches and the drain and asked his nurse to place a lighter bandage on the wound. Emily was told to wear the bandage until she was felt sure that there was no more discharge from the wound. When Emily had dressed, Hope was allowed into the room again. They were told that from now on Emily should just see her regular physicist if there were any problems with the healing of the wound. The lump had contained some suspicious cells, but Dr Keynes felt completely sure that he had been able to remove all of them and that Emily would be fine from now on.

Emily asked when she could resume her work as a school teacher, and Dr Keynes said that she should do so when the wound had healed or earlier if she felt strong enough.

The sun was shining brightly when they again stood outside the hospital. They were both feeling happy and relieved to have put this nightmare behind them. When they came home, Hope pulled out a package and gave it to Emily. She opened it and found a number of thick pads each in small cloth pouches. When she looked inquiringly at Hope, her best friend said with a smile, "I asked around and found out that one can buy brassieres for women who want to look more buxomly than nature made them. They are rather expensive, so I simply stole the idea from them and decided that we could try to make pouches for your camisoles, so that nobody will notice that you only have one breast. Do you like it?"

Emily was in tears again. "You did that for me? Oh, thank you so much! I had already been thinking that I might have to change my dresses so as to disguise what had happened, but this is a much better solution. Let's get to work!" It took them only a few hours to put pouches in all of Emily's camisoles and to try them out with various dresses. In some cases, they had to reduce the stuffing in some of the pouches and add to it in others, but in the end, they were satisfied with their work. The stuffing was made from buckwheat hulls and kapok, but Hope suggested that they could try other fillings until Emily decided what she liked best.

In the end, Emily decided to go back to school after the summer holidays were over, but she visited her class one of the last days before the summer to introduce herself to the pupils who had started in April but whom she had hardly gotten to know before she had to go into the hospital. She also said hello to her old colleagues and reassured them that she was quite recovered and would be back after the holidays. She spoke with her temporary replacement and got a report on her pupils and what they had studied in her absence.

***

Hope and Emily decided to go to Calne to spend a week with Eleanor and Sarah. They spoke about the recent appearance of the Loch Ness monster on the second of May, but they also discussed the situation in Europe after the signing of the Four-Power Pact in July. None of them felt reassured after Germany, France, England and Italy had all signed it, because it seemed to be such an empty gesture with everything else that was going on. They recalled the news of the burning of all books with 'un-German ideas' that had happened in Berlin in May.

"And they say it was students who initiated it," Hope said. "Students! They are the very people that we all need to be open to new ideas of all kinds."

Emily shook her head. "They must have been drunk and egged on by the brown-shirted Stormtroopers. But I agree with you. If students begin to burn books in the street, it will end badly…"

"I read that they have fired all teachers who are of Jewish origin," said Eleanor. "They are blaming all the things that they do not like on the Jewish people, including their losing the war. Many of their most clever scientists, who are Jews, are getting out of Germany and moving to America."

"There are small groups who openly resist and want Hitler to restore personal freedom," said Emily, "but they get thrown in prison."

"Or sent off to a re-education camp, I have heard," said Hope.

They did not tell Sarah or Eleanor about Emily's surgery, and they hardly ever mentioned it among themselves. When the holidays were over, they both returned to their work and their usual lives. The work kept them busy, and when they were not preparing for their classes, they read books, listened to the radio and knitted or made small repairs to their clothes. Once a week, they splurged on cinema tickets. Before the film began, there was usually a news reel or two produced by Pathé News, which put pictures to some of the news they had heard on their radio.

They received letters every three months or so from Italy, where Antonio worked as a bureaucrat in the local government of Naples. His letters were full of humour that somehow told them more about the situation in Mussolini's Italy than straight facts might have done. In return, they told him family news and news of England's struggle to recover after the great depression. In his last letter, he had told them that he was getting married in a few months to a beautiful and sweet girl from Naples called Martina. He included a photograph of her and invited them to the wedding, but they had to thank him and congratulate him while at the same time telling him that they could not afford to travel at this time. They did not tell him that the main reason was that Emily's surgery had cost them most of their savings and, to be honest, most of their zest for adventure, too.

Emily still went to Bart's to see Dr Keynes every six months, but so far, the wound had healed nicely, and there were no signs of a recurrence. After three visits, he had told her that she should come back in a year if there was no change, and he considered her cured.

***

Hope and Emily followed the news intently and still remembered how Sylvia had shocked them in Paris by saying that some of her friends were convinced that a new European war would be coming. In 1934, Hitler had become the 'Führer,' and clips from the Nuremburg Rally had been shown in the newsreels. It was a weeklong rally with hundreds of thousand people in attendance, and it had been filmed by Leni Riefenstahl, who was a gifted film director and producer. These small insights into how Germany was changing worried the two women. They often discussed whether Adolf Hitler was a brilliant speaker and ruthless dictator or whether he was truly a crazy, mad person. The fact that so many Germans followed him enthusiastically and that the European leaders seemed to take him seriously meant that it was difficult to just consider him mentally ill. But on the other hand, as staid, middle-aged British teachers, they could not quite fathom the hysteria that accompanied his every appearance in public. Most of what he talked about, as far as they could follow the German words, was glory and honour when it was not hateful rants against his opponents and those who were not pure-blooded Germans. Especially Jews were a frequent topic of his rants.

"I wonder why the Jews always become the target for hate?" said Emily.

"Haven't they always been, somehow? Maybe because the Bible says that they killed Jesus," Hope replied, "but I do not know whether that is quite true. The Romans who were in charge of the land, must have had something to do with it, too, but nobody hates the Italians, at least not for that reason."

"Xenophobia has always been a cause of hatred," Emily said, "but Jews have been living in many countries for too long to be considered as 'foreign,' so it must be the fact that they have a different religion, although it is a very peaceful religion with no imperial ambitions."

"Yes, well, that is true. Christianity is much more expansionist, actually. But that does not explain why Hitler has decided to focus his hatred on the Jews. I do not think that religion has much to do with it."

"He blames Germany's defeat in the last war on what he calls 'the Jewish conspiracy to take over the world'. He thinks that wealthy Jews are trying to take over the banks and the newspapers, and they think of themselves a people especially chosen by God," Emily said.

Hope protested. "But most Jews are dirt poor farmers or workers. Some have gotten an education, so that they can get well-paid jobs as teachers or physicians, and some have worked hard and gone into business on the same terms as everybody else, and they may have become rich. Just like a lot of non-Jews. I just do not understand why Hitler hates them so much…"

"They are simply a convenient scapegoat, I think," Emily said. "If one wants to really get people together, hate is a great unifier."

Hope nodded. "That must be it. My heart weeps for the people he has targeted. With these new Nuremburg laws defining full-blooded Jews as well as one, two, and three-quarter Jews on the basis of their parentage, and allowing only Germans without any trace of Jewish blood to de defined as real Germans, he is really going too far."

They were having this conversation over supper one evening in late October 1935. Hope had bought some pies and bread, and Emily had brought home a bottle of white wine because it was Saturday. Later that evening, they would go to the cinema to watch the new mystery film by Alfred Hitchcock, *The 39 Steps*.

***

Germany, however, was not the only place to be upset about. The League of Nations was unable or unwilling to force their members to abide by the rules, for instance as they had been when Japan took over Manchuria in 1931. The Japanese delegation had subsequently walked out when they were criticised and afterwards just left the league. Neither were they were able to intervene when Germany had broken the Versailles Treaty and openly announced that the country would introduce military conscription and rearm in the spring of 1935.

In 1936, a civil war broke out in Spain, and the League of Nations could only look on as nationalist frenzy took over the world. Mussolini had gone to war in Ethiopia and forced its emperor, Haile Selassie, into exile in the same year.

King George V had died in January 1936, and the Prince of Wales took over as King Edward VIII. He was in the midst of notorious love affair with an American woman called Wallis Simpson, who had been divorced once and was in the middle of her second divorce, because the new king wanted to marry her. This caused a constitutional crisis in England, and in the end, King Edward abdicated in December 1936, and his brother, Albert, had to take over as George VI.

In the spring of 1936, Hitler again broke the Versailles Treaty and entered the demilitarised zone west of the rive Rhine river with 30,000 soldiers. Such a move was expected to provoke the French and the British into some kind of retaliation, but again, they did not act. They chose to believe Hitler when he declared that he was committed to peace and would make no further demands in Europe.

Hope and Emily were actually relieved to see that Britain and France did nothing. They did not believe Hitler's promises and reassurances, but at least there was no war in Europe this time. It had been decided before Hitler came to power that Berlin should host the Olympic Games that year, after they had been cancelled in 1918 during the Great War. When Germany tried to exclude all non-Aryan Germans from participating in the games, many countries protested that it was against the Olympic spirit to exclude athletes because of race or nationality. There were proposals to move the games to another country or to boycott them altogether. But in the end, the Nazis agreed to compromise a little by letting a few German half-Jews participate and by promising that all athletes from abroad would be equally welcomed and treated with the utmost hospitality. In the end, 5,000 athletes from fifty-one countries participated, and most of them as well as the foreign visitors were impressed by the excellent facilities and a Berlin that had been cleaned of any signs of anti-Jewish propaganda as well as the presence of any undesirable people. They had unceremoniously been moved to a camp well outside of town.

Hope and Emily were not all that interested in sports, but this event had many political implications, which were interesting. The games were obviously used as propaganda for the new Germany and the superiority of what was called 'the Aryan race'. The theory of an original Indo-European or Indo-Iranian race, who called themselves *Arya*, had come from linguistic evidence of a common Indo-European language, which could be reconstructed internally as a kind of Proto-Indo-European. When anthropologists adopted the concept in their studies of races, some had concluded that this language must have been spoken by a superior race, which had ended up dominating Europe. The characteristics of this Aryan race became idealised as tall, blonde Nordic types that, if kept pure, would end up dominating the world because of their inbred superiority. To Hope, with her missionary background, this was pure hogwash. She was convinced that all humans were basically created the same and that any differences were only individual and cultural. To Emily, whose background was science, it did not appear to be other than pseudo-science made up for purely egotistical reasons. Mainly, they both felt that human beings had more in common than what might separate them, and they deplored Hitler's definition of some people as *Herrenvolk* and others as *Untermenschen*, with terrible consequences for the people of Germany. There were even some British people, such as Oswald Mosley and his British Union of Fascists who had swallowed such theories and were trying to emulate the German Nazis. But Hitler was aware of the worries his rhetoric caused in Europe, so while planning a war in secret, he spoke often of Germany's peaceful intentions and of the meaningless killings that the Great War had brought with it. He convinced many that he was only making reasonable demands and would stop in time for peace to prevail.

The enormous Hindenburg Airship, which had carried out its maiden flight in March 1936, flew passengers between Europe and the United States. However, only a year later, it burst into flames when trying to moor at the Lakehurst Naval station in New Jersey. Its balloon was filled with highly inflammable hydrogen and when it exploded, everything, including the small passenger cabin with thirty-six people aboard, caught fire, and many were killed. With this, the confidence in the future of the big airships completely disappeared.

In 1936, when civil war in Spain had broken out, Francisco Franco became the leader and generalissimo of Spain in September. He started a ruthless dictatorship and persecuted communists, atheists and other opponents.

Back in England, the impressively large Crystal Palace, which had originally been built from glass and iron in Hyde Park for the Great Exhibition in 1851, caught fire and burned down. After the exhibition, it had been moved to Sydenham Hill in South London and rebuilt, and there it was used for exhibitions, concerts and events. In November 1936, a fire was discovered, and the fire alarm sounded, but in spite of all efforts, the fire only grew and could be seen from far away. When it was over, the former pomp and glory of the magnificent Victorian building was gone forever. Shortly after, when the king abdicated and married Wallis Simpson, many saw it as having been a harbinger of bad times to come.

***

In 1937, Emily felt a small lump near what was left of her breast. At first, she thought it might just be a benign cyst, but she went to Bart's after all and asked her doctor just to be sure. Dr Keynes did not appear perturbed, but he talked her into having it removed just in case. So, in March 19 37, Emily went into the hospital again. This time the surgery took even longer, as Dr Keynes removed any remaining tissue he could find as well as a number of lymph nodes.

"Was it cancer?" Hope asked him bluntly when she saw him after the surgery. Dr Keynes looked at her and hesitated. His hesitation gave her the answer, but he asked her to follow him into his office and offered her a cup of sweet tea.

Then he said, "You are her friend, and she has no husband or other relatives?"

Hope told him that she and Emily had lived together for more than 25 years and considered each other their closest relative. He seemed to understand, and after collecting his thoughts, he said, "Do you really want to know the unvarnished truth, although you must keep it a secret from the patient as long as possible? She must stay strong and hopeful at all costs, you know."

Hope felt her heart sink all the way down to her stomach, and she had to fight to not start screaming in despair. "I want to know," she whispered.

Dr Keynes then explained that Emily had cancer and that even though this time he had put some radium tubes in her chest to kill off any stray cancer cells, he felt that it might already have spread through her lymph nodes to other organs in her body. She might still recover well from this surgery and live on for a year or more, but the cancer would reappear eventually, and there was nothing he could do about it. "But," he added, "if you love her and wish to keep her for as long as possible, you must not tell her. She needs to keep up the conviction that she will get better. It is very important that she does not give up. Can you do that, even if it means that you must lie to her?"

Hope could not stop her tears now, and Dr Keynes handed her a handkerchief. "She will not wake up for some hours at least, so why don't you go for a walk outside to get some fresh air and get a hold on yourself before you go and see her?"

Hope did as he said and found herself in the street in front of the hospital. She crossed the road and entered Postman's Park where she sat down almost automatically on the closest bench and wept with sorrow and despair. After a long time, she got up and began looking at the memorial tablets on the walls under the half-roof. Postman's Park had originally been three smaller graveyards, which had been turned into a public park, when inner city graves were moved outside the city for health reasons. The park had been opened in the early years of the century as a memorial for heroic self-sacrifice, and over the years, various tablets had been put there with inscriptions. Hope idly read some of them. Some were very old, while others were more recent. 'Sarah Fields, a pantomime artiste, Prince's Theatre, died of terrible injuries received when attempting in her inflammable dress to extinguish the flames which had enveloped her companion, January 24, 1863.' There were mostly men but also quite a few women were memorialised on the plaques. Hope read about Alice Ayres, daughter of a bricklayer's labourer, who in 1885 by intrepid conduct had saved three children from a fire in a house in Union Street but perished herself and about Mary Rogers, a stewardess on the railway steamer 'Bella' which had gone to ground and sunk in March 1899. Mary had voluntarily given up her life belt for a passenger and gone down with the ship.

Hope drew in a deep breath. Now that she knew about Emily's prognosis, she almost wished that she did not. There was nothing heroic about dying from cancer, but perhaps she could be heroic in her own way by keeping Emily hopeful and happy as long as she could. She had to be brave and optimistic for Emily's sake, and she was going to start now! She returned to the hospital and washed her face with cold water from the bathroom tap, and then she waited by Emily's bed until she began to wake up from the anaesthesia.

Emily was groggy and nauseous for the first few hours, and eventually, Hope just assured her that all was well, the surgery had been successful, and she would be back in the morning.

When she got home, she wrote a long letter to Sarah in which she told her the truth. Hope needed someone to confide in, and the only person she could think of was her older sister who had been like a mother to her, and whom she trusted more than anyone to support her all the way. A few days later, she got Sarah's reply. As she had hoped, Sarah supported her and promised to help in whichever way she could and to never betray her confidence. She would come up to London and stay in their spare room where Antonio had stayed as soon as Emily returned from the hospital, and she would help them keep house while Emily recuperated.

As promised, Sarah was there when Emily was allowed to leave the hospital, and she soon got better with all the attention she got. Sarah was an excellent cook and managed to cheer them both up. Hope kept up her work, and Emily was soon ready to start again when April came around. Sarah had to go back to Calne after a week, and Hope felt strong enough to be alone with Emily without breaking down and blurting out her worry for the future. Dr Keynes had given Emily the perception that she was now cured, and soon, they returned to their daily life and old routines as best they could. Emily kept her fears to herself, and Hope did her best not to show hers. Never before had they had secrets from each other, but Hope firmly believed that Emily's life depended on her ability to keep her own sadness and hopelessness to herself. Emily, on the other hand, felt that Hope should not suffer under her own fears, and the result was that they avoided the topic.

The summer passed, and Emily remained well. Hope even began to believe that the doctor had been mistaken and that Emily might stay well.

On top of their own misfortunes and worries, it seemed that the world in general was crumbling, too. 1937 saw war break out between China and Japan when Japanese troops invaded Shanghai. The persecution of Jews in Germany got worse, but Emily's health remained the same although she occasionally complained of back aches and pain in her ribs Dr Keynes prescribed pain medication but did not suggest any other treatment at this time. He asked Emily about fatigue, and she admitted to feeling more tired than usual. So, he prescribed plenty of rest and less hard work. At the end of the year, she had a long talk with the headmistress, and it was agreed that for the next four months she could work shorter hours, and then they would have to review the arrangement in April when the next school year began.

They spent Christmas in Calne, and in the days after Christmas, Hope and Emily sat in the house alone one day, when Emily suddenly said, "I am never going to be well, am I?"

Hope was startled, and she began to say, "Of course you are, sweetheart, you just have to be…"

Emily interrupted her and said exasperatedly, "Stop lying to me, Hope. I cannot bear it!"

Hope began to cry, and Emily said, "I know you too well. Since I left the hospital this spring, I have felt your sadness, Hope. I am sure the doctor must have told you something that he would not tell me. You must tell me, because I cannot bear for there to be anything unsaid between us." Now there were tears in Emily's eyes, too.

Hope put her arms around her, and for a while, they cried in each other's arms.

Finally, Emily said, "Now tell me," so Hope told her through tears.

"Dr Keynes said that the disease was spreading, and he could not do anything about it. But I should not tell you, because you would live longer if you did not give up." Now she was sobbing, "Emily, you cannot die. I wouldn't know how to live on without you!"

They held each other, and after a while, Emily said, "Thank you for being open with me! I have known for quite some time now, and it has been horrible not to be able to talk about it to anyone."

"Sarah knows," said Hope. "I had to have someone to confide in when I had been told that I could not talk about it to you."

"And Eleanor?" asked Emily.

"I do not think Sarah has told her," Hope said. "She would not do that."

"Maybe we should talk to them both tonight," Emily said. "I probably cannot return to work in April, and you will need some support when that happens."

"Not financially," said Hope. "We can manage on my salary and our savings."

"I was thinking of emotional support," said Emily, and Hope started crying again.

After supper, they told Eleanor, and they all held hands while Sarah read from the Bible the age-old words of comfort from David's psalm: "The Lord is my shepherd; I shall not want. He maketh me lie down in green pastures: he leadeth me in the paths of righteousness for his name's sake. Yea, though I walk through the valley of the shadow of death, I will fear no evil for thou art with me…"

Although Hope and Emily no longer believed in any religion, the well-known words in Sarah's clear voice brought them both comfort and regret for their loss of faith.

Later after they were back in London, Emily said to Hope, "I do not want to be buried from a church and lie in a grave for you to visit. I want to be cremated, and I want you to try not to mourn me. Please Hope, live a good life for many years for both of us."

"I cannot promise you not to mourn! I cannot bear to think of you leaving me…"

Hope broke into fresh tears, and Emily let her cry for a while. Then she said, "Hope! Please stop crying and listen to me. I have made my own peace with what is going to happen, so please do not make our last time together full of tears. You have to remain strong for me and let me go, when the time comes."

Emily sounded very calm and determined, and although Hope felt overwhelmed by grief, she pulled herself together and looked Emily in the eyes and said in a small voice, "I promise!"

In March of 1938, Emily stopped working as a teacher. She was now in so much pain that she could no longer manage bicycling back and forth, and some mornings, she had to be helped out of bed and into her dress by Hope. After a couple of weeks, she simply stayed in bed, and she became short of breath just by going to the toilet. On the days when she worked, Hope had a neighbour's wife look in on Emily every hour to see if she needed help. And every evening, Hope helped her eat a little, and then she read the day's newspaper to her.

***

In March, Germany had engineered an annexation of Austria, which they euphemistically called the Anschluss, and Czechoslovakia was worried about its own fate. There was no doubt that Hitler wanted to take part of Czechoslovakia, too. Apparently, his generals worried that German military strength was not sufficiently strong yet. Besides, Chamberlain wanted to preserve peace at almost any costs. So, he asked Hitler for a meeting to find a peaceful solution. Chamberlain flew to Germany in September 1938. He agreed to let Hitler take Sudetenland, and later, France agreed, too. The British and French ambassadors made Czechoslovakia give up the areas along the Germen border, but when Hitler insisted that he wanted more, Europe was on the brink of war. In the end, a summit meeting in Munich was agreed on with Hitler, Mussolini, Chamberlain and Daladier, the French prime minister. Czech participants were there but had to wait outside the door. The four leaders signed an agreement that allowed Hitler to take the Sudetenland from October 1st, and the Czechs were told so. Hitler had achieved his desired 'Lebensraum' without firing a shot.

November 9, 1938, a terrible thing happened which became known as the Kristallnacht or 'the night of broken glass'. A young Jew in Paris had murdered an official in the German Embassy the day before, and as a revenge, the SA and members of the Hitler Youth all over Germany broke the windows of Jewish shops, desecrated synagogues, broke into Jewish homes and beat up the owners and killed almost one hundred Jews.

There was international outrage over this terror perpetrated by the Nazis, and American and European sympathisers in many cases changed their views. Jews in Germany who were claiming insurance were asked to pay for the damages themselves with the government confiscating their insurance money, and they now had to transfer their property to non-Jews.

***

For Hope, the night of November 9 was less violent, but it was the night she lost Emily. Eleanor had come up to London for two weeks to help Hope with practical things and to sit with Emily when Hope worked. When she had to leave, Sarah had come to take over. Dr Keynes had offered Hope a bed in the hospital, but neither Hope, nor Emily had wanted to be apart any more than necessary in whatever time Emily had left. Instead, he prescribed tincture of opium for her pain in gradually increasing dosages, which kept her asleep much of the time. Hope kept on working as a teacher, and her colleagues supported her and helped out whenever they could. Their friends and neighbours brought food and other small gifts to ease their burden. Since May, they had had a telephone installed, so that Emily could call for help if she needed it.

On the seventh of November, Hope had asked the headmistress for leave from the school to be with Emily. The headmistress showed great compassion and generously granted her a week without pay and even said that she might ask for more if she needed it. The next two days, Hope and Sarah took turns sitting by Emily's bed, and in the evening, she finally drew her last breath; Hope was sitting there listening to her. Emily's breathing had become very slow, almost as if she had to remind herself to breathe every time she had paused. When she stopped breathing altogether, Hope called out to Sarah in a panic. Sarah came immediately and put her ear to Emily's chest. Then she shook her head and closed Emily's eyes for the last time. After opening the window in the room, she took Hope in her arms and said, "It is over, dear Hope."

Now that it had finally happened, Hope felt only emptiness inside. Sarah made her call Dr Keynes, who came in the early morning and wrote a death certificate. Hope also contacted the funeral director and arranged for the cremation to take place. The next day, she informed the school, and Sarah helped her write the death notice for the newspaper. On the day of the funeral, Sarah, Hope and Eleanor went to the chapel of the crematorium and held a small ceremony to celebrate Emily's life, and to their surprise, most of their colleagues and Emily's class as well as older girls who had once been taught by Emily were all there and filled the little chapel to capacity. Quite a number of their friends had turned up, too, and even Hope's brother, Henry had come. They all stood in silence as Emily's coffin was carried from the chapel to the crematorium. When the doors were shut, Hope thanked them all for being there to say their last goodbye to her friend. "We shall never forget you, Emily!" she finished. She had managed to get through the whole thing without any tears, even when Henry drove her home with Sarah and Eleanor. Hope had no more tears to cry, and she felt empty and hollow inside. Sarah served them all tea and cake in Hope's apartment, and Henry offered to drop off Eleanor and Sarah off by the station when he left. Sarah decided to stay another night before she took the train back the next morning, and Henry and Eleanor took off.

"I think I know how you feel," said Sarah. "When our mother died, I felt the same loss of meaning and bewilderment about the future..."

"I loved her," said Hope simply. "I do not feel anything right now except emptiness."

"It will take a while," said Sarah. "But promise me that you will get busy from tomorrow. While you keep busy and do what you have to do every day, it will gradually recede, and you may even have days, where you can forget about it and be happy again."

Hope looked at her sister for a long time. "You had me and the other children to take care of. I have nobody!"

"Nonsense," said Sarah. "You have a lot of young children in your class who need you, and if that is not enough for you, the world is full of people who need help. Get busy, and get on with your life!"

Hope was taken aback by her sharp tone. Had she been too busy pitying herself? Death was commonplace, especially in times like these. Who was she to feel that her personal tragedy was the end of the world?

"Sarah," she finally said, "I love you, and I promise to do my best to live a useful life from now on."

They embraced and sat a little while listening to the news on the radio before they went to bed.

Part Five
The War

Hitler had promised at the meeting in Munich that the Sudetenland would be his last territorial claim, but nevertheless, he aimed at grabbing all of Czechoslovakia because of its strategic advantages. He terrorised the Czech government, and he bullied the old and sick president of Czechoslovakia into signing a document surrendering his whole country to Germany. But this would be the last territory Germany could conquer by terror alone. France and England, who thought that Poland would be next, let it be known that if the Germans tried to invade any more territories, there would be war.

Alliances were formed on both sides in preparation, France, England and Poland against Germany and Austria. The only unknown factor was Stalin's Russia who had not yet chosen sides. Both England and Germany wanted to sign an alliance with Stalin, but the British did not really trust Stalin and therefore delayed approaching him. Hitler did not like the Bolsheviks either, but he realised that he could not afford a war on both the eastern front against Russia and on the western front against England and France, so he planned to take care of the western front first and save Russia for later. In August, he succeeded in signing a non-aggression pact with Russia, which made war inevitable.

In the months after Kristallnacht, people from the World Jewish Relief and other organisations got together and attempted to save as many Jewish children as possible from Nazi Germany, Austria and Czechoslovakia. They succeeded in getting the English Parliament to give temporary visas to an unspecified number of refugee children under the age of 17 and transport them to England on the so-called 'Kindertransport' program. They would require private citizens in England to sponsor the children and guarantee that they would be taken care of and not be a burden on the British society.

Hope wanted to help these poor children, but she also wondered whether she could be of any help to a traumatised child after her own loss. She talked to her friends and colleagues and the headmistress, and in the end, she went to Calne and talked to Sarah and Eleanor about taking in a child. Everyone she spoke to seemed to think it would be a good idea for Hope to take on this responsibility and offered their help in any way they could. By early March, she was convinced and offered up herself as a sponsor of a child. As she had almost no experience with infants, she wanted a somewhat older child, and she asked the headmistress if she could accept an extra girl child, who could fit into one of the school classes, so that she could take the girl with her to school every day. She promised to teach the child English as quickly as possible and help her with her school work while she was there, which would probably be for six months or so until it became possible to return to Germany or until her parents managed to get out and go somewhere else, where they could have their child back with them. The headmistress agreed but asked that Hope take the girl into her own class and carry the full responsibility for her behaviour. In the middle of March, she went with Sarah to Dovercourt Bay, where the children who had no sponsor were placed in a summer camp until foster families were found for them. As new groups of children were arriving every week, any sponsor was encouraged to take one or more children with them without much checking of whether they were fit to bring up children. They asked Hope about whether she was an orthodox Jew, to which she had to answer no, but when the camp authorities heard that she was a teacher living alone in a rather large apartment in London and that she had permission from her school to take the child with her to work every day for the duration, they readily accepted her as a sponsor. She was allowed to walk around at teatime to look at the girls of the appropriate age and to choose one. Both Hope and Sarah felt uncomfortable about this situation and finally asked the camp supervisor to point out a girl, aged about thirteen or fourteen, who would like to go to school in London and to live with a teacher. The camp supervisor said something in German to the girls, and three put up their hands. She pointed to one of them, and a tall girl with long black braids came over and introduced herself in heavily accented English by saying, "I am Anna Meisler."

Hope pointed to herself and said, "I am Hope Maundrell, and this is my sister Sarah." She pointed to Sarah. "Where are you from, Anna?"

Anna, who had learned a little English from her mother answered, "From Wien," and the camp supervisor quickly added, "She means Vienna." Hope knew that, but she did not say anything.

Then they followed the camp supervisor into the office, where they were told that Anna was thirteen years old, born in Vienna on January 14th, 1926. Her father, a high school teacher and political activist, had been imprisoned in 1938, and Anna and her mother did not know where he was or if he was still alive. Her mother had decided to put her on a Kindertransport after that. They got a sheet of paper with Anna's parents' names, her mother's address in Vienna and information about schooling and whatever else they had been able to learn about her past.

Her mother had been a kindergarten teacher until she had been fired because of her Jewish heritage. They had then lived with an uncle where Anna's mother had helped with housekeeping.

When all the papers had been signed by Hope, and Anna had packed her few belongings, they went back to London on the train. Sarah stayed for the evening but went back to Calne on the train Sunday morning.

When they got back from the station, Hope sat down with Anna and tried to converse with her in English. Anna seemed quick to pick up new words, and Hope wrote them down for her and made her read them out. After an hour and a half, Anna looked tired, so Hope took her for a walk. Anna was curious, and Hope pointed out various shops and said their name in English, which Anna then repeated. When they came to the pedestrian crossing, they held back while a double-decker bus passed them, and Anna stepped back a couple of steps and turned her back while covering her head with both arms. Hope immediately realised that the girl had never seen one before and might have taken fright, so she stepped back, too. "Bus," she said to Anna, and Anna repeated, "Bus," and added, "Bi-i-ig bus!"

Emily smiled and said, "Yes, a very big bus. We call it a double decker. I will write it down for you when we get home."

On Monday, she took Anna with her to school to introduce her to the headmistress and to make the necessary arrangements. Since Anna was thirteen years old, she was a bit too young to follow Hope's third year class, but they agreed that until she learned English, she could spend the days there anyway. She could listen and read on her own under Hope's supervision. The headmistress could speak a little German and explained to Anna that a new school year was about to start, and as soon as she was able to speak English, she would move to a class with the girls of her own age, but until then, she could stay in Hope's class.

Anna was happy to be going to school soon, and she was committed to learning English as fast as possible. When they got home, Hope gave her pencils and a pen, and on the way home, they had bought stationery, so Anna could write her mother and let her know where and how she was.

Hope kept up her efforts to teach Anna English, and by June, she was already speaking and understanding very well. Her mother wrote her letters regularly, but there was still no news of her father's fate. When the summer holidays began, Hope took Anna with her to Calne to meet her sisters. Sarah, she had seen before but had no clear memory of, and Eleanor, she met for the first time. She was warmly welcomed and hugged, and she was given Emily's old bed to sleep in. Hope had felt a pang of longing when she had shown Anna where to sleep, and she almost let her tears flow. But then she thought of how much Emily would have liked for this poor young Jewish girl to take over her bed when she herself no longer had any use for it.

In the evening after Anna had gone to bed, Sarah said to Hope, "I know that you are not very religious yourself, but should you not think of the girl and her Jewish faith?"

Hope thought for a while, and then she said, "I had not thought much about it. I have been so busy teaching her English, and I guess I did not think that I had much responsibility for her spiritual well-being. She still has her mother, and hopefully also her father in Austria."

Eleanor added, "Things in Germany and its occupied territories do not seem to get better for the Jews. It may very well lead to war in the near future, and then I guess she will not be sent home any time soon. Don't you think that you should find a rabbi in London and ask his advice?"

"I guess her parents would like me to do that," Hope said hesitantly. "I will think about it when we get back to London and see what the possibilities are."

This was something she had not given much thought, but Sarah and Eleanor were right. Anna was not her child, and maybe she had a duty to keep up Anna's connection to her Jewish heritage. Especially if her stay was to be prolonged…

Hope and Anna stayed for three weeks in Calne. They returned to London in the middle of August 1939. After they got back to London, she tried to find out what Anna herself thought about the subject.

"Anna, listen," she began, "you have told me that in Vienna you went to a Jewish school."

"Yes, we were not allowed in German schools, but even if we had been, my parents would probably have wanted me to go to the Jewish school."

"I guess you learned about Jewish holidays and Jewish culture, didn't you?"

"Oh yes, we had to observe all the Jewish customs and learn why they were important. But I learned lots of other things, too."

"I am sure you did," said Hope. "But here in England, I have sent you to an ordinary school, and since I myself am not Jewish myself, I do not know much about Jewish customs, and I cannot help you observe them in your daily life. Would you have preferred to be placed with a Jewish family?"

"No, Aunty Hope," Anna said. "I am a Jew like my parents and my family has always been, and I will remain one in my heart. But under the present conditions, I am very lucky to have been taken in by you, and if possible at all, I would like to stay until I can go back to my parents when things return to normal and Herr Hitler allows it. I promise I will be good!"

"Oh, my dear Anna, I am certainly not trying to get rid of you. You are the sweetest girl and very bright! I am just worried about whether I am doing too little for your spiritual life…"

"Spiritual? What does that mean?" asked Anna.

"Oh," said Hope, "it means everything about what you believe in and so on. Your religious life. I cannot give you a Jewish lifestyle, and I cannot give you an alternative, since I am not religious myself. I want you to grow up and choose for yourself what you will believe in and how you will live."

"As long as I can live safely with you while Vienna is such a dangerous place for Jewish children and Jews in general, I will be fine," said Anna. "I wish my mother and my father were here too, though. But I am sure Hashem will forgive those of us who have come here and been unable to keep all the rules, as long as we stay true in our hearts."

Hope spontaneously gave her a quick hug and said, "Anna, you seem to have thought of this a great deal, and you seem much older than your years. I hope that you will be reunited with your parents soon, but I am going to miss you when you leave."

***

Things were not going well, however. On Friday, the first of September, Germany invaded Poland, and on the third, England and then France declared war on Germany. For almost a year, the government had worked on a plan to evacuate children and to some extent their mothers from the large cities, which they assumed would receive heavy German bombardment. On Thursday, Hope and Anna had been sent home from school to prepare for evacuation of the whole school the following day. They were to bring a suitcase with clothes plus a gas mask, and all children got a piece of cardboard to attach to their clothes bearing their name, the name of their school and the name of the station from which they would be leaving the next day.

Hope tried to comfort Anna, who did not want to go. "I shall be going with you, because all the teachers are being evacuated, too. We are going to the countryside, so try to think of it as a nice and fun trip away from school." But Anna was inconsolable and felt that she was getting even further away from her mother and her home. Also, she was worried about what would happen to her parents now that there would be a war. Hope was very worried, too, but she tried to conceal her feelings. After all, Anna would be just one of the many children that she would have to look after in Huntingdon, which was their destination, so she had to be cheerful and positive.

When they arrived at the school the next morning, all the children lined up to walk to the King's Cross station from where they would be leaving. The teachers walked along with them to keep them in order. They lined up on the platform ready to board the train that would take them to Cambridgeshire, where the school had managed to make arrangements with the Huntingdon Grammar School. This school had just completed a new school building and they had agreed to lend it to the Highbury Hill High School for the duration. The pupils and teachers were billeted among families in the area and in summer camps until families could be found for all.

***

Hitler had invaded Poland as expected, and England would stand firmly with Poland, so German bombings of British cities could start any moment.

For most of the children, this was an enjoyable trip, and they passed the time on the trip singing songs. Even Anna cheered up for a while and tried to learn the English songs. The grown-ups joined in and tried to suppress their weariness at the depressing thought that Britain would have to fight another war against Germany, which they had thought that they had thoroughly defeated only twenty-two years earlier.

When they arrived in Huntingdon, Hope and Anna and one more schoolgirl, Lily, from Hope's class found themselves billeted with a farmer's family close to the school. Anna and Lily went with Mr and Mrs Mason to their new home, while Hope had to stay with the children until they were all safely accommodated. There were not places enough for everybody, so cots were set up in the school's gymnasium for the rest of the children. Three younger colleagues were chosen to stay with them for the time being, while Hope was allowed to go to Anna and Lily for the night.

On Sunday morning, they were all to assemble in the school yard to receive instructions and to practice how to wear their gasmasks and where to find shelter in the case of an air raid.

Sunday afternoon, Mr Mason showed them around on the farm, and Mrs Mason showed them the kitchen and got them all engaged in preparations for tea. After tea, Hope and the girls went for a walk around the area.

Huntingdon was originally a market town on the northern bank of the river Great Ouse. The farm was very close to the Portholme Meadow and the weather was warm and sunny, so they had a very nice walk and returned to the farm feeling refreshed and more carefree than they had felt for days.

On Monday, they went to the new school where they started the day by practicing how to get their gasmasks on in a hurry and how to get to the nearest bomb shelter quickly and in good order. When the exercise was over, they began their normal classes, and after a bit of chaos, everyone settled down to what would soon become their daily routine.

For a while, it seemed that nothing much was happening; the expected bomb raids did not appear, and people began to speak of the 'phony war'. Some children wanted to go back to London, but the Highbury Hill High School discouraged this. Anna had not heard from her mother since the outbreak of the war, and she did not know whether the letters she wrote herself ever reached Vienna.

France, which shared a border with Germany, had started to build a wall of fortification towards the German border in 1929 to make sure that the Germans could never attack France across the border again. The last few years, before the war broke out, they had also increased defence fortifications to the north in case the neutral Belgium should be overrun by a German army trying to invade France that way. The Maginot Line had been expensive to build, but at least it would defend France against something like the last war's trench warfare. French soldiers stood by the Maginot Line where they were joined by a contingent of British soldiers, and on the other side stood the German army, waiting for the signal to attack. This stand-off continued through the winter and into the spring of 1940, but a British naval blockade in the meantime threatened Germany's provisions of iron ore, coal and other things transported by sea. When Russia attacked Finland, and the French and British allies joined in to protect the Finns, Hitler became worried that the allies would cut off the flow of iron ore from Norway to Germany. So, in order to prevent that from happening, he simply invaded Denmark and Norway who were not really prepared to defend themselves. Denmark soon surrendered, while Norway held out for over a month, but eventually, Hitler overcame the resistance and secured Norway as well. With supplies guaranteed, he could now turn his full attention to France.

On the tenth of May, Germany bombed Rotterdam and attacked Holland, Belgium and Luxembourg. France and England rushed to stand against the Germans to the north, but German troops cheated them by attacking instead through the Ardennes forest, which had been thought too hard to penetrate and, therefore, was only lightly defended, The

Germans then moved quickly north-west towards the Channel to attack the Allied forces. The British, French and Belgian soldiers retreated to Dunkirk where they seemed trapped between the German army and the sea, doomed to perish. However, while the Germans debated whether to let their air force finish them off or let the army go after them, an amazing evacuation was carried out by a flotilla of different British ships from destroyers to fisher boats. They managed to rescue almost all the British and 60,000 French and Belgian soldiers, while British planes helped by attacking the Germans from the air.

After that, the German army turned south and took Paris, and on the 17th of June, the French gave up and surrendered to Hitler. Now only Britain was left to fight the Germans. In May, Winston Churchill had replaced Neville Chamberlain as prime minister and his rousing speeches became a great morale booster for both the British forces and civilians.

Anna was withdrawn and dispirited, and Hope and Lily both did their best to cheer her up, but to no avail. She cried herself to sleep every night for several months. They went to school as usual, but their free time was reduced as they helped out on the farm, grew vegetables, mended clothes and tried to think of ways to stretch supplies as more and more goods were rationed. The news from the war was not good. The Battle of Britain had begun in August after Churchill had flatly refused to negotiate with Hitler, and London came under bombardment, as did many other big cities in England. The Germans flew almost daily, and where their bombs dropped, houses were destroyed, and people were killed. The Royal Air Force shot down many German planes, but they also suffered great losses themselves. In desperation, the British conducted a small but successful air raid on Berlin, which made Hitler retaliate by bombing London continuously in terror raids for fifty-seven days in a row, starting on the seventh of September. In retaliation, the British bombed both Berlin and other large German cities, and the Germans rained bombs on cities such as Birmingham, Manchester, Liverpool and Coventry.

In Huntingdon, they could occasionally see and hear the planes flying over them, and they spent several nights shivering in the bomb shelter built by the school. Their thoughts and hopes went out to the brave men in the Royal Air Force who risked their lives to defend their fellow citizens. Anna often cried, and Hope knew there was no way to comfort her except to hold her and talk to her.

One night, Anna asked her, "Do some people in England also hate Jews?"

"Why do you ask that?" Hope said. "Of course they don't." Then, Anna told her that several times she had noticed children in the school whispering about her, and once she had met some village children who had said to her that she was 'a dirty Jew'. Hope was aware, of course, that there were British citizens who had admired fascist thinking and even formed a British Union of fascists under Oswald Mosley. But after Winston Churchill had become prime minister, Mosley and his agitators had been interned and their party forbidden. She told Anna about that and added against her better knowledge that England was now solidly against Hitler and his ideas of racial superiority. "There are always some nitwits who will say dumb things because they do not know better. Please, pay them no attention!"

By Christmas, Germany had realised that they could not bomb the British into submission, and the nightly raids came to an end. Instead, Hitler decided to turn his attention to the East and wage war on Russia, as had been his plan all the time. The 'Lebensraum' he sought for Germany really lay to the east, and he had only fought France and England in order not to have to fight on two fronts at the same time. He hated the Slavs and thought them an inferior race, which he would have to annihilate to reach his goal of a world dominated by the pure Germanic race. His plans for attacking Russia had to be delayed for a few weeks because of Mussolini's attack on Greece. When Britain reacted by going into Greece, Hitler had to intervene on Mussolini's side and to bring the Balkans under control first, but in June, he began his surprise attack against an unsuspecting Russia. It was a three-pronged attack targeting the three cities of Leningrad, Moscow and Kiev, and at first, it was very successful. But the sheer vastness of the country and the fact that Russia could mobilise twice as many men to fight as Hitler had expected soon created problems for the German supply lines as well as for the stamina of their foot soldiers. Germany had counted on a summer war, and when winter set in and Stalin mobilised Siberian troops who were used to operate in freezing temperatures, the Germans were forced to retreat from Moscow in December 1941.

On the heels of the German army had followed SS units who dealt with the many Jews in Russia. Many were killed by firing squads, men, women and children, but this took time and cost precious ammunition, so more efficient ways of killing large number of people were eagerly sought after. Various ways of using gas were tried, and by the end of 1941, the gas called Zyklon B was settled upon. Jews would be put on trains and transported to camps in Poland to be exterminated like vermin. News of this got out in 1941 or 1942, but the allies' leaders were unable to do anything about it, and some of them probably thought that it was hyperbole and propaganda. Not until Germany fell in 1944-45 did knowledge of the full extent of the horrors become widely known to the public.

***

Hope and Anna, as well as the other girls and teachers of the school, eventually settled down as much as they could in the cramped conditions and with the food and clothes that were always in short supply. They grew vegetables and bred chickens, cleaned and mended, and Hope made sure that their studies were not neglected either. Anna had found a good friend and companion in Lily, and the two of them were often engaged in secret pursuits and whispered conversations that Hope knew nothing about. She was not worried, however. She was actually glad to see that Anna, in some respects, remained the teenager she should normally be.

Once a week, she demanded that Lily write a letter to her parents in London, and since Anna had no one to write to and already kept up a diary, she usually took her for a long walk to give her a chance to unburden herself of whatever worries she might have.

Oh, how Hope wished she still had Emily by her side to discuss all that happened. The longing felt like a permanent pain in her chest that she could ignore for long stretches of time, but then suddenly, it would return with a vengeance that almost took her breath away. She felt that the war had closed over England like a suffocating bell jar, which might explode if she gave in to her anger and frustration.

***

On Sunday the seventh of September in 1941, in the morning, Japanese airplanes had unexpectedly attacked the US marine and airfields in Pearl Harbour, Hawaii, thereby drawing America into the war. The war on China had been going on since 1937, and in 1940, Japan had entered a tripartite pact with Germany and Italy in which they promised each other mutual support in case any of them were attacked. Japan had not informed Italy and Germany about their plans ahead of time, so it came as a surprise. However, Japan had attacked in this case, so the mutual support clause did not apply, but Hitler chose to grab the chance to use his U-boats in the Atlantic and cut off supplies to Britain. On the ninth of December, Germany, too, declared war on the United States. Contrary to what Hitler had imagined, the American President

Roosevelt decided not to use the greater part of his forces to fight Japan in the Pacific but instead put them to help the British in Europe.

One day in the spring of 1942, Hope took both Anna and Lily with her on a brief visit to Calne to see her two sisters. All three of them were happy to get away from Huntingdon for a couple of days and see something else. Sarah was in good health in spite of her seventy-three years, but Eleanor looked tired and seemed to be in pain. She cheered up when Hope and the two young girls arrived. They sat down for dinner and talked about the two years that had gone by since they had last seen each other, and Lily told them about her background and her life in London, where her father was employed by the government and her mother was a nurse. She had two, much older siblings, a brother and a sister, who were both working for the government. Sarah told them that they had recently had a visit from Hope's brother, Arthur and his wife Amy. They had been evacuated from Jersey and now lived in Bath, and Arthur had returned to work for the Royal Navy.

Eleanor and the two young girls went to bed early while Sarah and Hope talked on for a while.

"How are you really, my sweet Hope?" Sarah enquired.

"I am too busy to think about how I am most of the time, and I suppose that is a good thing. After Anna came, we had only a few months before we were evacuated, and I haven't had much time to reflect on anything other than work since. But how are you, Sarah? You were always telling such nice stories about your youth in Japan and your Japanese friends?"

Sarah thought for a while. "Do you know, I have always been able to talk to Henry about Japan, but now he will not hear or talk about it anymore. What happened to that place? The things we heard from China in the past years have been frightful, and then their pact with the devils, Hitler and Mussolini… And on top of that they have attacked America… I cannot reconcile the Japan I knew with what has happened there since. They seem to have been contaminated with all the worst sides of European history. It is like a new disease, and they have absolutely no resistance against its virulence. I can hardly bear to think about it." Sarah had tears in her eyes, but she went on. "Hope, I cannot explain it, but I know it is going to end very, very badly for the Japanese, and the Japan that I grew up in is gone forever."

Hope put her arms around Sarah and said nothing. *What could she say?* Her childhood memories of Japan were long gone, and she saw only the monstrosity of what the country had become. She hoped the war would end badly for Japan, as she did for Germany. She tried not to think of Italy and Antonio, who were also on the enemy side of the war, and she had not heard from the family in Naples since the war broke out.

Sarah was getting old and frail, she could feel as she held her. She was now seventy-three years old, and she would not be here forever. She kissed Sarah on the cheek and said, "My dear Sarah, I love you so much. You are the best mother and sister anyone could have had, and I am grateful for the way you brought me up and supported me in everything. Let us retire to bed now and get some sleep."

"Yes," said Sara, "let's do that."

After staying a couple of days in Calne, Hope had to go back to Huntingdon with the two girls.

***

During that same spring in 1942, Hitler decided to leave the siege of Moscow as it was, and instead march towards Stalingrad and the rich Russian oilfields in Caucasus. In the beginning, the German army progressed speedily and overstretched their supply lines. When the battle of Stalingrad delayed the Germans and winter set in again, the German field commander wanted to surrender but was ordered to stay and fight on to the last man. Meanwhile, the dead from the battles and those who had frozen to death piled up and were covered with snow, and in February of 1943, the battle was over. Germany had lost in its attempt to conquer the Soviets, and the Allied forces began to believe that they might win the war.

In 1943, the Highbury Hill High School for Girls moved back to London. Hope and Anna returned to find that their apartment still stood, with only a little damage from the bombs, although many houses in the area had been turned into rubble. Anna, who had finished her schooling that year, decided to join in the war effort and got a job in a munitions factory while Hope started a new class of thirteen-year olds and signed up for the Women's Voluntary Services after school. London was by no means safe from bombs yet, so often the sirens signalling an air raid would force them into air raid shelters in the middle of whatever they were doing to spend long hours awaiting the all clear signal. Everybody was sleep-deprived and bone-tired, but the spectre of a victorious Hitler was even worse, so people plugged on.

In the Atlantic Ocean, the German submarines had been a terrible force and had sunk many British ships, but England and the United States made several leaps in technological progress, such as long-range radar and breaking the German cipher code, which had so far been thought to be unbreakable. Gradually, the tide turned, and the Allied forces began winning the naval battles. When the British decided to share the information they got from breaking the German code with the Russians, the Russians were able to prepare well for Hitler's plans to finally crush them in a large tank battle at Kursk, and the Germans got crushed instead.

That same summer of 1943, the Allied forces had managed to land in Sicily and were now fighting their way towards the north of Italy. Winston Churchill and Franklin D. Roosevelt had met in Casablanca and decided to forge ahead in Italy and attack Germany from the south. Roosevelt went along with this plan but wanted to keep the main part of his forces ready to attack Germany from England.

Mussolini's forces soon caved under the attack from the south, and Mussolini himself came under attack from his own king who had now decided that he had better shift to the Allied side. He eventually jailed Mussolini and disbanded his Fascist Party. When Italy surrendered in September 1943, Hitler was enraged and invaded northern Italy all the way down to and including Rome. The Allied advance was stopped for months in Anzio until reinforcement was finally sent in and Rome was captured. But the Germans dug in and managed to hold the Gothic line north of Rome until the end of the war.

In November of 1943, Sarah telephoned to tell Hope that Eleanor had caught pneumonia and was not expected to live. Hope immediately arranged to go to Calne on a Friday afternoon to help Sarah look after Eleanor and keep vigil at her bedside. Sarah was looking old and worn out when she opened the door, and Hope immediately took her into her arms and held her for a long time without words. In the early spring, their brother Henry had been killed when a German stray bomber had hit his school. The loss of their brother had been a great sorrow to them all, but especially to Sarah and Eleanor who had known him the best. Hope, who had been in the midst of moving back to London with Anna and the school, had not been able to go to his funeral at the time, so this was her first visit back home since she had been there with Anna and Lily.

When she saw Eleanor, Hope knew immediately that she was at the end of her life. Eleanor lay in her bed, completely emaciated and hardly conscious, and when Hope grabbed her hand and squeezed it gently, Eleanor only moaned and did not seem to recognise her. Her breathing was laboured and unsteady, and the doctor who had been in earlier and would come again in the evening tonight had told Sarah that there was nothing more he could do for Eleanor except pray for a miracle.

Hope persuaded Sarah to go and lie down to rest a bit while Hope took over. She sat by Eleanor for an hour, and there was no change in her condition. A neighbour had arrived with some food for them, and the parson's wife also came by to see if she could help. In the evening, the doctor came back and looked at Eleanor. He had her turn on her side with Hope's help and listened to her lungs, and then he shook his head. By then, Sarah had come back slightly rested from her nap, and they both sat with Eleanor the next few hours until she suddenly stopped breathing for several minutes. They waited, but Eleanor never breathed again. Hope went to call the doctor who would come the next morning to write the death certificate, and then she called the funeral home and the vicar to arrange the funeral for Sunday afternoon.

Hope and Sarah washed Eleanor lovingly and made up her bed as best they could with clean sheets. Then they dressed Eleanor in her favourite dress, combed her hair and laid her out under a sheet with a Bible under her folded hands. Sarah prayed with tears in her eyes for the sister she had lived with most of her life. Hope felt very sad, too, but mostly worried about what would happen to Sarah now that she was all alone in Calne. *Should she offer to take her back to London with her? But London was still very unsafe while the bombings were going on, and would Sarah even feel comfortable in the city after living almost all her adult life in a small village like Calne?*

The next morning, she broached the subject to Sarah, but as it turned out, she need not have worried. Before Christmas, Sara had already arranged to move into the nursing home in Calne run by the church. She thanked Hope for inviting her, but she wanted to stay in Calne, where she knew everybody and felt safe.

After Eleanor's funeral was over, Hope stayed an extra day to help Sarah pack her things and arrange for some of her furniture to be moved to the nursing home. When she had to leave on Monday evening, she kissed Sarah and promised to be back over Christmas.

***

Finally, it seemed that the war was turning. Plans had been worked out in great secret for 'Operation Overlord' in which the Allied forces would cross the Channel and invade Europe. The question of when and where still had to be decided, but finally, the invasion was settled for the fourth of June across the Channel to the beaches of Normandy. German forces had gathered near Calais, where the Channel was relatively narrow and where they expected the British forces to come across from Kent. On the British side, an elaborate plan of camouflage and deception was set in motion to make the Germans believe that such would indeed be the case. The ruse had worked, but the fourth of June dawned with exceptionally bad weather, and in the end, the invasion had to be postponed to the sixth of June. By the evening on that day, the Allies were successful in establishing their first bridgeheads on the Normandy coast. The Germans resisted and moving forward was a slow and painful operation. Over the rest of that year, the Allies met with many setbacks but still gradually made more progress, towards the Rhine River. From the other side of Germany, the Russians were progressing through Poland and towards the Oder and Neisse rivers. When they reached Maidanek, they found the first concentration camp, which was a shock to see. Even though the Allied powers had known about Hitler's maltreatment of the Jews and had heard stories about the brutality against them, the reality of whole camps built for the express purpose of exterminating them with such ruthless efficiency was worse than they had been able to imagine.

Word of the unspeakable horrors of the German concentration camps was becoming public knowledge, and Anna was becoming more and more depressed. Now that they were back in London, she had finally reconnected with her Jewish faith, and it seemed to help her to meet other Jews and to talk with them. Hope could only try to empathise, but she was as horrified as Anna over the stories in the newspapers.

As both the Russians, the Americans and the British closed in on Germany and many of the German generals realised that the war could not be won, a coup against the Hitler and the Nazis was planned by a group of conspirators led by Colonel Claus von Stauffenberg, who was Chief of Staff and Commander of the Home Army. On the twentieth of July in 1944, Stauffenberg carried a briefcase with a bomb into the meeting room and placed it next to Hitler. Stauffenberg then left the room, and the bomb went off as planned. Unfortunately, another officer had moved the briefcase, and when the bomb went off, Hitler was shielded by a massive oak table and seemingly only slightly hurt. After that, Hitler instituted a purge of the army and many were hanged or shot.

Hope had been back to Calne to visit Sarah during Christmas, but it had been a rather depressing trip. Sarah had seemed content enough staying in the nursing home, but she was losing her memory and her hearing. Hope had stayed with her and taken her out for small, slow walks in the vicinity, but she could feel Sarah's lack of zest for living now that Eleanor was no longer there. She was, therefore, not surprised when she received a phone call in early February 1944 that Sarah had passed away peacefully. Anna went with her to the funeral and comforted her but Hope just felt empty and too emotionally exhausted to really react much. The war had brought so many losses by now that she felt that she had cried all her tears and did not really care anymore whether she lived or died.

Towards the end of the war, Hitler had begun using newly invented flying bombs to hit Britain and carrying enormous loads of explosives they were devastating when they hit. The V1s and the V2s only stopped coming when Hitler's troops had been forced so far back into Germany that the range of these bombs could no longer reach England. Meanwhile, the Allied forces continued into Belgium and Holland, and on the twenty-fifth of August, Paris was formally liberated by Free French troops under General Charles de Gaulle.

When winter fell, and the roads became muddy, the Allied forces needed new supplies and halted their progress. Hitler saw an opportunity to make a last-ditch surprise attack sheltered by a thick fog, and his forces succeeded in creating a bulge in the Allied front line. The ensuing 'Battle of the Bulge' was initially a German success, but it could not be sustained for long, and in December, the Allied forces were moving in on Germany proper, crossing the Rhine in early March 1945.

In the east, Russian troops were venting years of accumulated anger on the German civilians, and in the ensuing panic, many tried to escape by going west to meet the Americans. Others chose to commit suicide rather than submitting to the Russians troops.

In Berlin, Hitler was hiding with his closest allies in a bunker under the German Reichstag in Berlin. On the thirtieth of April, he shot himself and his mistress Eva Braun after making Admiral Karl Dönitz president of the Reich. A few weeks later, it was all over. Germany surrendered unconditionally, and Europe was free.

People all over Europe were almost ecstatic in May of 1945. Finally, the threat of sudden death from the skies was gone, the dark curtains could be removed from the windows, and one no longer had to spend nights in air-raid shelters or an Underground station. The hated gas masks could be put away, and the work of reconstruction could begin. Not to mention that spring was well under way, and in London, the parks filled up with green leaves and pretty flowers. The daffodils had been the harbingers of change, and even Hope cheered up slightly at the sight.

The Jews of the Kindertransports and others who had become displaced in the war could now with the help of the Red Cross begin to find out what had happened to their family members. Anna lost her job in the factory and instead began to help out at the Association for Jewish Refugees and to learn Hebrew in the evenings. Although she and Hope saw rather little of one another, they remained close and loving. It had been a long time since Hope had gone with Sarah to pick up the confused and forlorn thirteen-year-old, and now she was almost eighteen and had grown into a beautiful young woman.

Part Six
The Post-War Years

By the end of the nineteenth century, some Zionists had begun to move into Palestine to settle in what they considered the original Jewish homeland and to revive the Hebrew language. The dream of returning to Jerusalem had been a part of Jewish ritual prayers and tradition for centuries, but in the nineteenth century, it crystallised into an organised Zionist movement, which worked to create the beginnings of Israel. The British government supported the idea and in the mid-nineteenth century, it was openly discussed to make a Jewish homeland in Palestine under British protection. The Austro-Hungarian journalist, Theodor Herzl, wrote a book in German in 1896 called *The Jewish State*, and he was convinced that the only way to get rid of anti-Semitism would be to create such a state. For this purpose, he created the World Zionist Organisation together with Nathan Birnbaum, and they held their first congress in Basel in 1897.

During the next decades, widespread pogroms against Jews in Russia created waves of emigration to Palestine. The new immigrants founded the city of Tel Aviv, where Hebrew was used as the language in some schools and in the university. The Jews also bought land and farmed it, and the first kibbutz was formed in 1909. In November 1917, the Balfour Declaration had been adopted after a great deal of discussion about its wording. It declared that Britain favoured Palestine as 'a national home for the Jewish people,' and that this must not 'prejudice the civil and religious rights of existing non-Jewish communities in Palestine or the rights and political status enjoyed by Jews in any other country'.

In 1918, the League of Nations had endorsed the declaration, but over the years and during the Second World War, enmity between the Jews and the Arabs had grown more and more bitter, and eventually, a civil war broke out.

The Zionists, who had waited years for England to fulfil its promise of creating a Jewish homeland, became impatient and started terrorist attacks on the British in Palestine, but England was concerned about protecting the Anglo-Arab relationship and the whole of the British Empire, which contained many Muslims. So, even after the war, when the German atrocities against the Jews became clear, England continued the 1939 restrictions on the annual number of legal Jewish immigrants to Palestine. When a ship full of Jewish refugees illegally tried to go to Palestine in 1947, the British refused to let them land. In the end, the ship was sent to Hamburg from where it had come, and the Jews were violently forced to disembark. The situation was getting untenable, and when England had to give up its mandate in Palestine, the United Nations chose a two-state solution and partitioned Palestine into two sections, an Arab one and a Jewish one. The Jews declared the independence of the state of Israel on the fourteenth of May 1948.

In the meantime, back in England, British fascism had resurfaced immediately after the war, but this time, Jewish organisations fought back, and in 1946, 'The 43 Group' was formed. They turned out to be very successful in fighting fascist demonstrations and infiltrating the fascist organisations. Hope was worried about Anna's future and wanted her to go to university, but Anna clearly had other ideas. She had long anticipated that her parents had not survived the war, and in 1946, she was finally able to have her worst fears confirmed. Her mother was registered as one of those who had perished in a German concentration camp in Poland. She never found out what had happened to her father, but she accepted that he must have died, too. On the day that she had found her mother's name in the records, she sat down with Hope in the evening for a long talk. They had just learned about the bombing of the King David Hotel in Jerusalem, targeting the central offices of British mandatory authorities and the headquarter of the British armed forces. The bombing was carried out by the Irgun as a response to recent British raids on Jewish agencies, and it resulted in great destruction, ninety casualties and forty-six injured.

Both Hope and Anna had been horrified by the attack on the hotel, but their reactions were very different. Where Hope saw it as yet another tragic outcome of the war, Anna saw it as an unfortunate result of Britain's failure to live up to the promise of letting the Jews have a homeland in Palestine. Hope realised that Anna's new work with the Association for Jewish Refugees and the people she had met through that work had caused a change in her. She was increasingly committed to the Zionist cause and tried to explain to Hope that she could not just stay in Britain and get a university education while her people were fighting for their future fate. Hope could well understand that the Jews needed their own country, but somehow, she had thought that Anna had become like a daughter to her and would stay in England now that she had no more attachments to Vienna. But Anna continued, "I have met a young man, David, and I would like to bring him here to meet you soon. He, too, is Jewish but he was brought up in the Jewish faith here in

England, in Birmingham, and I met him in Hebrew class. He has been helping me with my language studies."

"Of course," Hope said, "by all means, bring him here. I will try to make kosher food for him with your help. How serious are you about him?"

Anna blushed a little before she answered. "Pretty serious, I guess. We have been talking about emigrating to Palestine together and helping to build up the new Jewish state."

Hope was stunned and blamed herself for not talking more to Anna in recent months, so she would have been able to see this coming. She had been aware that Anna was studying Hebrew and spending a lot of time with her Zionist friends, and she had been delighted at Anna's deep interest in her heritage, but somehow, she had never thought of Anna moving far away from her as a possible consequence of this. She had seen Anna's interests more as a natural reaction to what had happened to her and her family, and as a search for answers to why it had happened. *Had she been naïve?*

"You look very surprised, Aunty Hope," said Anna, using her more childish name for Hope for the first time since they had been evacuated in 1939. They had agreed then that Anna should stop calling her 'Aunty' so that the other children should not feel that Hope was more to Anna than to any of the other school girls who were away from their families during the evacuation years.

Anna continued. "I do not want to live away from you, but I have realised that I will never be English. I will always be a Jew, and that has more meaning for me and my life than anything else. After all that has happened, my duty is clear, and I must join my people in their homeland to help make it a reality as best I can."

"But it is so dangerous," said Hope weakly, seeing at the same time in a flash that in Anna's eyes all of her life had been 'dangerous' in a way that Hope would perhaps never understand. She continued immediately and said, "I will miss you so very much."

"I will miss you, too," replied Anna. They embraced, and Hope wiped a tear from her eye. Just then, life seemed to be all about losing the people she loved.

When Sunday came around, Anna brought David to meet Hope. He was a handsome young man, perhaps four or five years older than Anna and a few inches taller. He had been in the RAF as a flight mechanic during the war, and after the war, he had decided, like Anna, that he needed to know more about his Jewish background. His parents had been very liberal Jews before the war, and though they had kept the sabbath and arranged for his bar mitzvah when he became that age, he had gone to an English school and lived a rather secular life up until the war ended. When the news about the concentration camps had become common knowledge in 1944, he had been shocked and sad but also angry and determined that he had to do something. When he had met Anna earlier that year, they had very soon found each other to be kindred spirits and fallen in love.

David was very polite, but Hope encouraged him to call her Hope instead of Miss Maundrell, and soon, they spoke quite unforced about the war and some of the problems which had come up with the mass-demobilisation of the army. Hope could not help liking this young man, and while they were setting the table for dinner, she said so to Anna, and they both smiled. They sat down at the table and ate the fish and vegetables, which Anna had bought from a kosher shop, and enjoyed their meal. When Hope asked them whether they wanted tea or coffee after dinner, they both asked for coffee, and Anna offered to make it.

As soon as Anna had left for the kitchen, David bent forward and said, "Would you mind if Anna and I got married next year? We both want to."

Hope laughed a little. "You do not have to ask me, but of course I will not mind. You are both splendid young people, and I hope you will be very happy together. But do you really intend to emigrate to Palestine? How do your parents react to that?"

David said that he and Anna were quite determined to emigrate, either within the British quota if that was possible or illegally if they had to. "My parents do not know yet, and I do not think that they will approve. But I am a grown man now, so I do not need the approval of my parents, so I have decided to tell them nothing about it before we actually have a date for when we can leave."

"Have they met Anna?" Hope asked.

"I am taking her to Birmingham to meet them as soon as we have a couple of days off. They know that I have met her and love her, so they cannot wait to meet her."

At that moment, Anna came back from the kitchen carrying a tray of tea for Hope and coffee for her and David.

"What are you talking about?" she asked.

"David just told me that you both wanted to get married, and I congratulated him on his excellent choice," said Hope and got up to hug Anna.

The rest of the evening, they discussed plans for the wedding, and Hope asked many questions about Jewish weddings and about Birmingham, where their wedding would take place. Anna had only been at one wedding in her life when she was a child in Vienna, but

David said that he was sure that his parents would want a rabbi's blessing.

"If we end up with a Jewish wedding," Anna asked, "will you take part in my mother's place, Hope?"

"If you tell me exactly what to do and when, I will do my best," promised Hope with some trepidation.

***

In the general election in the last year of the war, the Labour Party had surprisingly won, and Clement Atlee had replaced Winston Churchill as Prime Minister. It was the first Labour government ever in Britain, and they soon set about creating social reforms and a welfare state while gradually dismantling the British Empire.

In May 1947, Hope went by train to Birmingham to attend Anna's wedding to David. She stayed in a hotel but spent most of her time before the wedding with Anna and David and his mother. They would hold the wedding in David's parents' garden, where David had his father to help him raise the canopy *(chuppah)* under which he and Anna would be married. They talked to the rabbi who would officiate at the ceremony, and they laboured over their marriage vows *(ketubah)*, which they would both sign on the day of the wedding together with two official witnesses. They would also exchange rings, and Hope went with them to find two suitable rings, which she had decided should be her gift to the couple.

On the wedding day, the weather was perfect. David's parents accompanied David to the chuppah, and afterwards, Hope walked with Anna along the garden path to join them. Nobody was able to see that Anna had been weeping in Hope's arms only minutes before when she had been overcome with sadness for her own parents' demise. Now she looked radiant in a simple knee-length dress with long sleeves and a veil that covered her long black hair. David was wearing a dark suit and a blue kippah on the top of his head. The rabbi said some prayers in Hebrew and then blessed a cup of wine, which bride and groom both drank from. He then handed David a piece of white cloth and David wrapped the glass in it before he put it on the ground and broke it with his foot. Hope had been told that this very old custom was to remind the couple that life contained broken things, too. She liked that thought, and she was prepared when all the guests got up and shouted 'mazel tov' in congratulation.

The young couple would be leaving England in the next few days, but apart from a promise of help from a Jewish resistance group, they still did not know exactly how they would reach their goal. Hope feared for their fate on the journey and in the war-torn country they would arrive in, if their emigration was successful. She kissed them both goodbye when she left and made them promise to write her as soon as they could. Then she left with a heavy heart, not sure whether she would ever see them again. The next morning, she got on a train back to London.

***

In 1947, the winter months of February and March had been exceptionally cold all over Europe and in England, and an unprecedented snowfall prevented the transport of coal. A shortage in energy supply followed and forced many businesses to close for the duration. Cattle were known to have frozen to death in the fields, vegetables also froze in the ground, and a food shortage became imminent. On the tenth of March, however, milder weather began, and a thaw set in. The large amount of thawing snow could not be absorbed in the frozen ground, and massive floods overran large parts of the Thames Valley. When a winter gale came a week later and brought lots of snow and rain, flooding became even worse in the towns and properties around the rivers. Dykes broke down in several places and water flooded over fields and houses. The flood lasted nearly a week, but even when it was over, the consequences in terms of lower production output and losses of farmland and produce still plagued the country. It would take a long time to repair the damage, and the Labour government was blamed for its poor management of the crisis and almost lost the following election in 1950.

Hope was nearing her retirement age. She had had her sixtieth birthday in 1947, but she was still in good health, so she decided that although she might have to stop working at Highbury, she would continue teaching as long as she was able to in some shape or form.

In 1947 in April, she retired from the school with some regret but also happiness in her newfound freedom. *What would she use it for?* She decided she would start looking for those of her siblings who might still be alive after the war. She read the letters she had inherited from Sarah's estate, and thus she learned that William had emigrated to the US in 1932, and the newest letter Sarah had kept from him was from 1934, when he had decided to move from New York to the west coast. That was thirteen years ago, and she wondered if he was still alive and if so, how he was living. She also found a letter from Arthur, who had been only three years older than her. She had a vague memory of him from before he went away to school. He had written to Sarah just before the war broke out, and he had to leave Jersey, and Sarah had told her that he had been in Bath during the war. *Was he back in Jersey now? The old letter had stamps from Jersey Island, and there was an address in St Helier written in the upper left corner of the envelope.* She decided to write him and his wife to see if they still lived there. She composed a letter and sent it to the address on the envelope, and several weeks went by. Then, one day, she received a letter from an address in St Helier, the largest town on Jersey. It was written by Amy, Arthur's wife.

April 11, 1947
My dear sister-in-law, Hope,

Arthur and I are both very well and happy that our island is free again. When the horrible Germans left, we got our house back in St Helier and plan to enjoy our old age in peace here. Arthur is not a very good letter writer, so he asked me to pen this reply to you. We would very much like to see you and share this beautiful island with you. Can you come down in the summer? We run a small guest house with five rooms, which we rent to tourists in the summer months, but if you come, we can save one for you at no cost. We look forward to making you comfortable and showing you around. Do you have a telephone? If you do, we can make further arrangements, but if you do not have one, we shall send you the information in a letter about how to come here. We shall meet you at the harbour, so please come.

Yours faithfully
Amy and Arthur

Hope looked at the telephone and contemplated calling them immediately, but she stopped herself. *It might be awkward after all those years.* Instead, she wrote them a letter back and thanked them for the invitation. She would go in August if that would suit them and spend a week there. She would have to go by train to Poole and then get on a ferry to take her first to Guernsey and then on to Jersey. She really looked forward to meeting her long-lost brother and his wife and also to visiting the island, which lay so much closer to France than to England. The bailiwicks of Jersey, Guernsey and the Isle of Man all had the status of being Crown Dependencies, so its residents were British citizens, but during the war, they had been ruled by German occupying forces from June 1940 to May 1945. The British had decided not to fight for the Channel Islands after France had fallen to the Germans, and the people of Jersey had helped evacuate troops from of Saint Malo on the coast of Brittany. Even the French General Charles de Gaulle had been evacuated from Southern France via Jersey to England. A few days later, the Germans arrived in the islands to occupy this tiny part of the United Kingdom, and before that some of the inhabitants had chosen to evacuate their children and, in some cases, themselves as well to England. Arthur and Amy had been among those who left, not because they had any children, but because Arthur had been recalled to help during the war.

***

In August, just before Hope left for Jersey, she received another letter, this time with Italian stamps. It was from Antonio who had survived the war as had most of his siblings but not his father, who had died from a lung disease already in the first year of the war. His mother, Lisa, was still alive and in reasonably good health, and he asked Hope if she would come to Naples and visit them. She promised herself that she would write him a long letter from Jersey and tell him about all that had happened in the years that had gone by. She thought that she might take him up on his invitation the following year if she could afford the trip.

***

When the ferry neared the harbour in Jersey after a mostly pleasant trip, Hope immediately spotted an elderly gentleman and his wife on the pier. The man looked very much like the photograph she had kept of her father, and both he and his wife had the right age for him to be her brother. She got off the boat and went directly towards them and said tentatively, "Arthur?"

They both turned to look at her and said, "Eva Hope?"

"Yes, I am Hope. Amy and Arthur, so very pleased to meet you."

Amy stepped forward and gave Hope a hug, and Arthur put forward both of his hand and took hers.

"My baby sister," he said, "it has been such a long time…"

"Let us go home and have some tea," Amy suggested, and Arthur took Hope's trunk and started walking.

"We live just up the street," said Amy and Arthur, and Hope began to follow. Amy had plainly been beautiful as a young woman, but now she looked a bit gaunt and had several deep furrows in her face. Arthur had a long beard and a ruddy face, and he, too, was rather thin. Nevertheless, they both looked very healthy.

They came to a large house with a garden in front, all very nicely kept. "This is our house," said Amy. "And as I wrote to you, we run a guest house, so there are some people staying here, a family with their son and two elderly gentlemen. You will meet them for the evening meal but let us take you to your room first. They went through the garden gate and up to the entrance in front. They entered a large hall and took the stairs to the upper floor, where Hope got the front room overlooking the garden and beyond it, the sea. The room had a large bed, two armchairs with a table between them next to the window and a large armoire and some bookshelves. It also had a small writing desk with a chair pushed under it. *It is perfect*, thought Hope. Amy showed her the bathroom and the toilet in the corridor and left Hope to get ready before she came downstairs.

Downstairs, Amy and Arthur had two rooms to themselves. In one of them, the table was set for tea, and Amy had baked scones and served them with jam and clotted cream.

"We follow the French custom and serve a hot evening meal for guests at seven o'clock, and if they want an English tea, they usually take it in one of the many cafes in town. They can have it here, too, of course, but they must say so in the morning before they go out, and most guests do not want to make up their minds so early," Amy explained.

Arthur broke in and asked Hope about what she knew of their siblings' fate during the war.

"I am sorry to say that I have not been able to find out much," said Hope. "Most of what I know is what Sarah told me before she passed away. There are not many of us left alive anymore. As you know, Ernest and Edith are gone. Sophia also died before the war. Bertha married an Irishman, but we have not heard from her since. During the last war, we lost Sarah and Henry and Eleanor. Eleanor and Henry died in 1943, and Sarah lived a year longer. As you know, Sarah was like a mother to me, and losing her in one of the darkest years of the war was very sad. I tried to find William, but he has emigrated to America, and as I understand from the last letter he sent to Sarah, he moved out west even before the war started. Have you heard anything from him, Arthur?"

"Last I heard was before the war began, I think it was in 1937. He was in California growing raisins, he said. He probably still is, don't you think? The war was not fought inside America, after all."

"I can try to write to him if you still have the address," Hope said, and Arthur went to a cupboard and took out a box of old letters and began to look through its contents.

"I think it was in the other box," he finally said. "The one we lost during the war. But what about you, Hope? What has life been like for you?"

Hope told them the basic facts of her life—that she had been a teacher, that she had never married but had lived with a dear friend, Emily, who was also a teacher. Unfortunately, Emily had died of cancer just before the war. She, herself, was now retired, but she thought she might want to go on teaching in some capacity or other. But what about them?

Amy said, "We met back in India where I was living with my father after my mother had died. We fell in love and were married in 1916. Then we decided to move back home after the First World War, and we settled in a small cottage in Bath while Arthur joined the Royal Navy there. Those first many years we only saw each other when Arthur was not away on active duty, but we went on holidays together every year. In 1921, we visited Jersey for the second time, and that was when we lost our baby boy. After that, the doctor told me I could not get pregnant again."

"Oh, Amy," said Hope. "Sarah told me that, and I felt so sorry for you."

Arthur took over. "In 1938, I retired, and we decided to settle in Jersey and live the rest of our days near the ocean. We bought this house and started a small guest house. But then the war broke out and I was recalled, and the following year, Amy managed to get away from Jersey before the Germans invaded. We went back to Bath and lived there until the war was over, and then we came back here. The house had been taken over by some German officers for the duration of the occupation, and it took quite some work to restore it when we moved back."

Hope looked at Arthur and asked if they had visited Calne while they were in Bath.

"Only once," said Arthur. "It was hard to travel, and we had very little money. We went to Calne when Sarah wrote us about Henry's death and Eleanor's illness in 1943. We spent an afternoon with Sarah before we had to go back. It was such a sad occasion. But she told us about you and how you were doing, and if you had not written to us, we would definitely have contacted you."

Amy added, "We were lucky to get away from here during the war. I have since heard from our friends who had stayed that they had a very difficult time."

"In 1940, the Germans bombed St Helier," Arthur said. "We were shocked when we heard, since we knew that the island had already been completely demilitarised. But nobody had told the Germans, apparently. When they finally came, they took over completely, requisitioned whatever they needed, vehicles, buildings, furniture and other things. They changed Jersey's time zone from GMT to the European time zone, forced the people to drive on the right side of the road and changed the money to occupation money called *scrip*. They took people's radios, too, so that nobody could listen to news from England. The people who hid their radios would try to keep the rest informed, but if they were discovered, they were sent to jail and, in some cases, deported to Germany. Not all of them came back."

Arthur continued, "You will also see along our coasts how they built a lot of fortifications and dug tunnels to defend the island against attack. They imported foreign workers to do it and treated them very badly. And all for nothing... the islands were never attacked."

"And people nearly starved in the last year," Amy said. "Fewer and fewer ships came, and my friends were running out of all the supplies they usually imported from England or France. Tea, soap, salt etc. Food was so scarce, but in December of '44 just after Christmas, when they all thought they might starve to death, the Germans finally allowed monthly Red Cross packages to come in by ship, thank God!"

"It must have been terrible for the people here," said Hope, "but as you know, England was quite bad, too. At least the Channel Islands were not bombed, except for that first time. I was evacuated with my whole school to Cambridgeshire from the day the war broke out and until 1943, when we returned to London. While we were in the countryside, life was mostly peaceful, but after we returned to London, the bombs kept falling on all the large cities. Especially the new rockets, V1 and V2 were frightful. We had hoped that The Great War in 1914 would be the war to end all wars. How naïve we were!"

"But," said Arthur, "those infernal bombs the Americans dropped on Japan... maybe that will be able to keep the peace."

"They dropped the second bomb on Nagasaki where we lived as children," Hope said. "Apparently, it destroyed everything and killed many thousands of people. It makes me sick to my stomach to think of it. I am only glad that Sarah did not live to experience that. She lived there for so many years and had some friends she was still in occasional contact with through letters. Sarah would have been devastated, I imagine."

"I am sure you are right," said Arthur.

Amy got up. "I have to supervise the preparation of our evening meal," she said. Hope offered to help, but Amy said that she should go and unpack and make herself comfortable before dinner. If she felt like it, they could take a walk after dinner and have a look at the town.

Before the war, Jersey had been a popular vacation place for tourists from England. It had sandy beaches, lots of sunshine and prices were cheaper than in England. After the war, the tourist business had picked up again, and when Amy and Hope went for their walk in the early evening, the promenade along the coast was quite lively. It was low tide, so they had a view over the lowlands with sand intermixed with small pools of water.

"Here you can see the sea bottom," said Amy, "and when the tide comes in, all this will be under water all the way up to this promenade. If one gets caught unawares down there when the tide rushes in, it can be quite problematic, so you must check the schedule of the tides before you go down there." Hope said that she would certainly do that. Beyond the promenade, they could faintly see the outline of the coast with quiet coves and rather dramatic cliffs in between. As they walked, Hope commented on the beauty and asked Amy what their daily life was like. Amy hesitated a little before she answered, but then she said, "I have been thinking of our future for a while. Right now, Arthur's pension and the guest house are making us enough money to live on, but some things are getting harder as we grow older. And we have no children to take over from us, so I guess that in a few years, we shall have to sell and move into something smaller. We are thinking of Gorey where our son is buried. It probably has the best view of the sea in Jersey, which means a lot to your brother. It would be the perfect place for us to grow old. I don't think the captain could live away from his ocean, and I am beginning to feel the same way."

"You call Arthur 'the captain'?" asked Hope.

"Well, not to his face," Amy replied. "But everybody has called him 'captain' for so long now, and I have gotten so used to it, that I sometimes use it myself… Sorry, but he seems to like it, so…"

"OK," said Hope, "maybe I will, too, in that case."

"What will you do with yourself, now that you have retired?" asked Amy.

"Next spring, I will go to Naples in Italy," said Hope. "When Emily and I were traveling before the war, we met an Englishman who lived in Naples with his Italian family. They became our friends, and when they wanted to send their oldest boy, Antonio, to school in England, we helped them arrange it, and Antonio stayed with us in London for all his holidays. He went to the school where my older brother, Henry, taught, and he also met Sarah and Eleanor. After he went back to Italy, we kept in contact for as long as we could, but when the war broke out, correspondence with Italy became impossible. But then, just before I came down here, I received a letter from Antonio inviting me for a visit. His mother Lisa is still alive, and I would love to see her and Antonio one more time."

"That sounds wonderful," said Amy. "Did you and Emily travel a lot?"

"Not really as much as we would have liked to," said Hope. "We had so many dreams but not a lot of money. We were able to travel a couple of times to Europe before Emily passed away. But then the war came, and Jersey is the furthest I have travelled since 1930… seventeen years ago, it must now be now."

Hope looked so sad that Amy put her arm around her shoulder and gave it a tiny squeeze.

"You and Emily must have been like sisters, Hope. I can understand how much you miss her."

Sisters, thought Hope… But she decided not to tell Amy how close they had really been. She would never understand. Instead, she answered, "Yes, she was my best friend ever," and let the topic rest there.

***

Over the next week, Hope explored first St Helier and then more of the island. She borrowed Amy's bicycle and went to St Aubin, St Mary and even as far as the 13 kilometres to Piémont on the northwest coast one day. She came to love the beautiful vistas of the coast and the remains of old castles. She also saw the German-built fortifications, but now they were empty and could not spoil her tranquillity and enjoyment of the place. First, she cycled along the bay towards the east and paused in the old fishing village, St Aubin, from where she could see St Aubin's Fort across the water. It was accessible by foot at low tide, but nothing about it looked inviting. She sat down in the shadow of a café and brought out the sandwiches that Amy had pressed on her. After eating and drinking a cup of tea, she walked a little along the old railway track before she decided to return to Arthur's and Amy's place. Tomorrow, she would go in the other direction towards the east. The island was no larger than she felt sure that she could go anywhere by bicycle and return the same day.

When she returned in the afternoon, she helped Amy with getting supper ready at seven o'clock, and then she sat down and ate with Arthur and the guests. She had met the Middleton family with their seven-year-old son over the meal yesterday and found them very agreeable. The two elderly gentlemen whom Amy had mentioned the day before had both been out, but today, they were both there. Amy introduced Hope by saying, "Mr Davis and Professor Young, this is my sister-in-law, Miss Hope Maundrell, who is here to spend the week with us." Both men got up and bowed to Hope, before they shook hands while introducing themselves. Mr Davis was a retired tradesman from Birmingham and a widower, while Mr Young had been a university professor of history at Oxford. He had never married. After his retirement, he was working on a book about the German occupation of Jersey.

After dinner, Hope helped Amy clear the table and the woman, Lis, who Amy had employed to help, finished washing the dishes and cleaning the kitchen, while Amy and Hope made the dining room ready for breakfast.

The next morning after breakfast, Hope set out again on her bicycle. She could feel a bit of soreness in her leg muscles after yesterday, but it soon disappeared as she cycled along the road towards St Martin and the eastern coast. She would go directly to Gorey and see the famous mediaeval castle of Mont Orgueil and the ancient dolmen at Faldouet. And then she would take the longer road along the coast on her way back home to St Helier.

As she passed by Gorey, she could already see the castle down by the coast and the sea beyond it. *No wonder Arthur and Amy want to live their final days here,* she thought. It was really beautiful. The castle was built in the years from 1204 to defend against Norman attackers from the coast, and when it could no longer do so, it was used as a prison until the end of the seventeenth century. The Germans used it during the war, but it was in such a generally dilapidated state that people could not go there, so Hope had to enjoy the view from the beach. She could not help wondering why this small beautiful island bore so many marks of war and had been defended so heavily throughout the centuries. Then she realised that, of course, their geographical position between France and England must have made them strategically important in all the wars that had been fought since the 13th century. The islands were like immovable ships in a heavily trafficked lane, destined for countless collisions over the years.

*** *

Hope got on her bicycle again to find La Pouquelaye de Faldouet dolmen, and with some help from the locals, she found it in twenty minutes. It was a stone-age collection of large stones, probably as old as 6000 years or more from when Jersey was still connected to the European continent by a land bridge. Nobody knew who had built them. The large stones had been placed to form an entrance to a chamber, covered with a very large and heavy stone, supported by smaller stones. They could be found in various places in Jersey, and although it must have taken a lot of heavy work to build them, their purpose was still unclear. Most people thought that they had been used to bury people in.

Hope sat down on a smaller stone and took out her drinking bottle. She had some water and began to feel hungry in spite of the heavy breakfast Amy had served in the morning. She looked at her new wristwatch, which she had received as a parting gift from her colleagues on her last day at Highbury Hill. It was already near one o'clock, and she decided to return to Gorey and get something to eat before she started back to St Helier.

On the ride along the coast, she passed the Royal Bay of Grouville and saw the sandy beach below. A few people were sitting and watching while their children played at the water's edge. When the road was about to round the headland at the southeastern tip of Jersey, she reached La Rocque. Before turning into St Clément bay, she saw a square whitish defence tower built a couple of hundred years ago on a tidal island. A little further along the bay there was another tower, this one round with a part of the upper tower painted in white. She guessed it had to have been built in the 1780s. This part of the coast had been heavily eaten into over the centuries when it had become flooded at high tide, but now it was more solidly defended from such ravages of nature. Various rocks of different sizes stuck up from the beach and the water, and Hope enjoyed the wildness of the coast as it varied between sand and cliffs. Soon she was back in St Helier, where she quickly washed herself and slipped into a clean blouse before going downstairs to find Amy already busy in the kitchen.

"Where did you go today?" asked Amy, and Hope told her about Gorey and its old castle and about the dolmen she had visited.

"It is hard to understand that humans lived here more than 6000 years ago," said Hope. "I wonder who they were. I have read that Jersey had a land bridge to the continent at that time, so I guess they wandered here from Europe…"

"Maybe they found themselves cut off from the continent when the sea level rose," Amy said.

"I guess so," said Hope, "or maybe they just liked it here so much that they did not want to leave."

"Could you cut the cucumber in slices?" said Amy, and soon, they were both busy in the kitchen.

***

That evening as they were sitting in the drawing room, Arthur asked Hope how she liked it here in the island. "I love the landscape, the sea, and most of all the peace and quiet. I do not miss the big city at all," Hope said.

"How about coming back next summer?" asked Arthur. "And every summer for that matter. It has cheered Amy and me up tremendously to have you here, and if you would like to do that, I would start building a small extension towards the back so that you would have more room to live in and more privacy."

"Yes, wouldn't that be a great idea," Amy chimed in. "So much cheaper and healthier than London, I am sure."

Hope was startled by this suggestion. "Thank you, Arthur and Amy," she said. "Can you give me some time to think about it, please. It would be a tremendous change, so I must get used to the idea. But I would certainly like to come next summer, if I may."

"Of course, dear, please come! But remember that we are not getting any younger, any of us," Arthur added. "I would like to get to know my little sister better before I leave this world."

Arthur had a gruff way of speaking, and he rarely betrayed any emotion. Hope could not help thinking why he had not made any effort to contact her before the war. But then she thought of Sarah, who had stayed in contact with all her siblings throughout her life and been content to take on the role as the central point for all of them and keep them all informed about each other as long as she could. The eleven children that her father and mother had brought into the world in Madagascar, Mauritius and then Japan had been sent to school in England from a young age, except for Sarah who had stayed in Japan with her parents until her mother died and her father retired from the mission. She had been like a mother to Eleanor, Hope and Arthur in Japan, and after Arthur had also gone away to school and her father had died, there had been only her and Sarah and Eleanor left in Calne. She remembered having met all her their siblings when her father had been alive and for his funeral, but after that, the family had been scattered to the four winds, and although Eleanor had eventually chosen to stay in Calne with Sarah and herself, and they had seen Henry regularly, the rest of the siblings had simply grown apart. *Now most of them were dead or had disappeared forever. Maybe Arthur was getting sentimental in his old age, but then maybe she was, too.... Here they were, two surviving children of Eliza and Herbert, with no children of their own. Why should they not get to know each other in the last years of their lives?*

Hope had no reservations about Amy. She had liked her at once, and she knew they would get on well with each other. *What did she have to tie her to London, now that she no longer had her work? Her familiarity with the city? Yes, the city had many attractions but maybe not so many now that she was getting older.* She would have to think hard about this before she came back next summer.

She stayed in St Helier for the next two days and helped Amy and Arthur around the guest house. The young woman, Lis Miller, came in the mornings to clean the guest rooms, while Amy cleared the breakfast things away and set the table for supper. Arthur kept the accounts, worked in the garden and made repairs around the house. The guests were out most of the day.

Professor Young told them over supper that day that he wanted to go and visit the former German Hohlgangsanlage 8 in the St Lawrence Parish, which had been opened to the public last year.

"What is it?" asked Mrs Middleton.

Professor Young told them that it was a tunnel system built by the Germans as part of the so-called Atlantic Wall during the war. Jersey had several such tunnels and they were all supposed to be part of a much larger net of tunnels and fortifications on the islands. Since the Channel Islands were the first British territory to come under Germany, it had been especially important to Hitler that they should be heavily protected. The Germans had used the tunnels to store weapons and food and other things. Professor Young had been there last year when they were opened to the public, and this time, he wanted to see if there was any possibility of turning one of the tunnels into a monument or a museum for the many slave labourers who had suffered and perished there. He would be going across the island by bicycle, and Hope asked if she could come with him. At first, he seemed hesitant to agree, but after Hope told him that she had already been cycling around the island for two days and that she had taught history in school, he softened a bit and said that she could come if she promised to be quiet and not talk too much. Hope was slightly offended by his male arrogance, but she did want to see this German 'hohl-something,' whatever that meant, and she would like to go with someone who knew what he was talking about.

***

Actually, as they rode their bicycles towards Lawrence parish, Professor Young turned out to be a great deal more loquacious than he had seemed at the guest house. He told her that 'Hohlgangsanlage' was German for an 'installation of hollow passages,' and the Germans had constructed many such long tunnels in Jersey for storage. Some of them even had rails, so that things could be transported back and forth by train wagons. It was believed that they had planned to create twenty-five such structures in all, using forced labour from their occupied areas. They had also employed local people, but they were treated better than the foreigners and were paid salaries. Eventually, the war had ended, and the great tunnel system had never been finished. Some of the tunnels had been taken over by the British military and used for storage, but most were abandoned and looted for scrap metal. The one they were going to see today was tunnel number eight, and the Germans had given it the designation, Ho8. This one had been converted into an emergency hospital after the Germans began to fear an Allied invasion in 1943. The construction had been undertaken by, among others, the organisation 'Todt', the German construction and engineering conglomerate, named after their leader, Fritz Todt, who died in a plane crash in 1942. The Todt Organisation was continued under the architect, Albert Speer, who became minister for armaments and war production. As the war progressed, more and more forced workers came to the island to work on the tunnels in twelve-hour shifts and with very little food, and many starved.

Hope could hear that he had enjoyed teaching, and she asked what she hoped were sufficiently intelligent questions along the way. As they neared St Lawrence parish, she asked Professor Young about his earlier research and why he had become interested in the tunnels.

"I have always been interested in the Channel Islands and their history. My mother was born here, so I came often as a child. When I went to university, I studied the history of Normandy and the wars between France and England in the middle ages. I studied the old fortresses and who had possessed them etc. But when the war ended, and I retired, I decided to rekindle my interest in Jersey and look at what had happened here during the war. Last year, I went to see the German Underground Hospital when it first opened and after talking to one of the people who looked after it and seeing the great interest people were showing, we got to talking about turning it into a more lasting memorial to the people who had worked and died here. One of the problems with establishing a monument here is that according to old Jersey law, the landowner, who owns the land above the tunnel, actually owns the underground as well, all the way to the centre of the Earth. The British Army who liberated Jersey gave permission for this tunnel to be opened to the public and made a gift of it to the Jersey people, but it was not theirs to give, so the owner is probably going to sue for his right of possession, and we are sort of waiting to see how things develop."

"You keep saying we," said Hope. "Who else is involved?"

"We are a small group of army historians and interested citizens of Jersey, and we hope we can get the landowner to join us, too."

When they reached the cave entrance, they rested their bicycles against a tree.

There were already a number of people there waiting in a line for the guide who would take them in. Professor Young and Hope joined the line and awaited their turn. When they reached the front of the queue, an elderly gentleman with a large moustache and a fresh flower in his buttonhole greeted them from his chair. "Hello, Professor Young, nice to see you again."

"Hello, Jim. May I introduce you to my companion, Miss Maundrell, this is Jim Sutherland, who guards this entrance."

They greeted each other, and Professor Young took out his wallet to pay the entrance fee of sixpence per person. They entered the tunnel with a group of people, led by Mr Sutherland, who explained what the various rooms had been used for. They saw the hospital beds, the operating theatre, and various rooms that had been used as offices, the telephone exchange etc. As they walked in a line behind Mr Sutherland, it was eerie to listen to their voices echoing in the tunnels.

Mr Sutherland told them that the tunnels had been dug by drilling and blasting, mostly avoiding the hard granite and instead following the loose shale rock to save time. This had meant that they had to be shored up with concrete to avoid rock falls, and in fact, there had been relatively few accidents during construction. Malnutrition and starvation had cost more workers their lives than accidents.

"Amazing," said Hope when they were outside again. "So much work done, and it was never really used."

Professor Young said goodbye to Jim Sutherland, who was getting ready to take the next group through, and then he turned to Hope and said, "The Germans built at least twenty-five of these, or rather, they planned to, but only tunnel one was completed before the war was over. The rest were only partly finished or remained at the planning stage. This one, number eight, was close to completion, and in 1943, it was decided to turn it into an underground hospital to treat the soldiers who might get wounded in the final attack on England."

Hope shuddered, "Fortunately, that never happened."

Professor Young went on. "You saw how many people lined up to see this. They have been coming every day since the tunnels were opened. Don't you see what it might do, if it was turned into a proper museum, both to commemorate those who lost their lives in this small corner of the world, and to tell future generations what the war was like for the people of Jersey who lived through it? We must have museums and memorials everywhere that show war, not as a glorious fight between heroes and villains, but as it really was. Death, dirt, hunger, fear and suffering…"

"I certainly agree," replied Hope. "In part, we want to forget the horrors and do our best to move forward with our lives, but you are right. If we allow ourselves to forget, it may all happen all over again. But I suppose that even if we do our best to remember and make succeeding generations remember, it may be part of human nature to react to what is perceived as unjust by striking back, don't you think so?"

Professor Young was quiet for a while as they sat on the grass and shared tea from the thermos flask that Hope had brought with her.

"I guess so," he finally said. "But we must keep trying. Try, try and try again, as they say, there really is no alternative."

"I like the idea of a museum," said Hope. "Let me know if there is anything I can do to help."

The professor thought a little while.

"Do you mean that?"

"Certainly."

"Well," Professor Young said, "you used to be a teacher, so administrative work would not be completely outside of your experience, would it?"

"I can keep order in documents, write letters and reports and so on, if that is what you mean."

"I certainly need that," said Professor Young. "Let me think about it for a while. Give me your London address, and I will write you later. You might indeed be of some help."

Hope wondered what she had gotten herself into, but since she had nothing better to do and this was an exciting project, she decided to just wait and see, and let the chips fall where they may.

***

On the way back to St Helier, they talked only occasionally. They felt tired and decided to make a stop in Millbrook to have tea before they started on the rest of the way home. Millbrook village had grown up around the station on the now defunct Jersey railway between St Helier and St Aubin. It had a church, St Matthew's, which Hope had heard about and wanted to see, and Professor Young fortunately agreed to go with her after tea. St Matthew's Church was nothing special on the outside, but it was also known as 'the glass church'. This was because of its interior, which had been done by the French glass sculptor, Rene Jules Lalique. Lalique had been a neighbour and friend of Florence Boot in the South of France, and Florence Boot was the widow of the fabulously rich entrepreneur who had started Boots, the chain store pharmaceutical outlets. When she had offered to pay for the interior decorations to be made by her friend, the parish had gratefully accepted the gift in memory of her late husband.

The front door to the church had two frosted glass angels, and when they went inside, they could see the full splendour of Lalique's art-nouveau decorations: the cross over the altar adorned with motifs of the Jersey lily, the glass angels, the opalescent panels and the unique glass font… It was a very special place of shifting light that signalled a purity, which might seem almost cold. Hope shivered a little inside the church, and the professor noticed at once and asked her if she was a true believer, too. Hope shrugged and replied: "I am the daughter of a missionary, but I guess I am a lost sheep. I do not seem to believe in anything supernatural at all."

"I see," said the professor and stayed silent for a while. Then he said, "We ought to be getting on home or we will be late for supper."

"Of course," said Hope, and they went to get their bicycles. On the way back to Helier, she thought about whether the professor might have been offended at her answer, but she really did not care.

I am too old to worry about what people think, she mused. *I wouldn't mind working with him on the Jersey Tunnels project, but if my lack of belief offends him, I probably would not like to work with him anyway. I will find other things to do.*

They made it back half an hour before dinner, and Hope thanked the professor for an interesting and enjoyable day.

"It was indeed very agreeable," he said.

Then they went to their rooms to get ready for dinner.

***

On Sunday, Hope got on the ferry and returned to London after saying fond goodbyes to Amy and Arthur and after promising to come back the next summer. She had written to Antonio while she was in Jersey, but she would wait to post the letter until she was back in London. She had written that she would visit them in the spring of 1948, if they could have her in late April or early May.

Back in London, she began to look for a temporary job where she could make a little extra money for her trip, and since she had remained a member of the National Teachers' Union, it was not difficult to get a part time job as a special teacher. She applied for several part-time jobs and found one where she would be teaching extra English to immigrant children from Eastern Europe whose parents had come over as part of the scheme for European Volunteer Workers. She was to teach two afternoons a week until April 1948, and the salary was not much, but at least it could be saved up for her trip to Italy.

***

The year before, the crown princess had become secretly engaged to a navy lieutenant named Phillip Mountbatten, whom she had met when she was only a teenager. The engagement became public in July 1947 after the princess had celebrated her twenty-first birthday in April. Her parents had initially been hesitant to agree to her marriage to this man who had no fortune but was a prince of Greece and Denmark, with rather too strong familial relations to Germany. He had changed his last name into his mother's maiden name and converted to the Anglican Church when he had become a British citizen, and he had renounced all his titles except his military rank in the British navy. The day before the wedding, he had been granted the title, Duke of Edinburgh, but there were still many who did not approve of the wedding because of the recent war. But Princess Elizabeth stood firm, and the wedding was planned for the twentieth of November 1947.

Since King Edward VIII had endangered the monarchy by choosing to abdicate in 1936 in order to marry a twice-divorced American woman, his younger brother, Bertie, had reluctantly succeeded him to the throne. The royal family had been shaken to its foundations, and the new king had been very unhappy to become the king. He chose to adopt the name, King George VI, and with the help of his wife and the mother of the two beautiful young princesses, Elizabeth and Margaret, he actually did very well and became an extremely popular king.

In 1936, Hope and Emily had followed the story of Edward and Wallis with fascination, but after Emily had become ill and died, Hope had not taken much of an interest in royal matters. Then the war had come, and like most other British people, she had looked up to the king and the prime minister and supported them with all her heart. Nevertheless, she had voted for Clement Atlee in 1945 because she believed that Britain needed a labour prime minister to lead the country in peacetime. And she felt that she had been right in her choice. Atlee's politics had led to more welfare and peace in Great Britain. The Empire, however, had begun to crumble. The Balfour declaration in 1926 had defined the dominions as 'autonomous communities within the British Empire,' and in 1931, their full legislative independence was confirmed in the Statute of Westminster. After that, these states became referred to as the British Commonwealth, which shared a monarch, but nothing else. As more and more former dominions became independent republics, some joined the commonwealth, but many, like India, which gained independence in 1947, did not.

When the big royal wedding was held in Westminster Abbey, there was still rationing in England, and the queen was said to have saved up her rationing coupons to pay for her splendid wedding gown. Even Hope felt some excitement about this marriage of the crown princess and had spoken to Amy about it on the phone. She had even invited Arthur and Amy to come and stay with her in London for the big event. In the end, only Amy came, as Arthur did not quite feel up to a London visit.

On the day of the wedding, the two women got up very early in the freezing weather, dressed warmly and went to find a place outside Westminster Abbey from where they might see the carriage processions of first the queen and Princess Margaret, followed later by the king's mother, the Queen Mary, and other special guests. Finally, King George VI and his daughter, the crown princess arrived in the gorgeous Irish State Coach, which had very recently been restored after a fire. The wedding ceremony was transmitted worldwide on BBC radio, and afterwards, when Hope and Amy hurried to a tearoom to get warm after standing for hours in the street, the radio was on so that they could hear much of it.

The bride had eight bridesmaids, one of whom was her sister, Margaret. There were also two small pageboys. The guests were families, nobles, and royalty from foreign countries, all dressed to the nines. The groom's three German sisters were not invited and neither was the bride's uncle, the Duke of Windsor and former king who had abdicated in 1936.

Hope and Amy thought the bridegroom a dashing young man with his fine military bearing, and they also found the glimpse they had gotten of Princess Elisabeth's wedding dress a divine sight.

Amy was staying in London the whole week in London with Hope, and the two women had gotten closer, so Hope became more and more sure that moving to Jersey would be the best thing for her to do. She liked the thought of growing old near the sea and in a small and quiet community, and she would not mind making herself useful by helping Amy and Arthur with their guesthouse every summer. In the winters, when there were not many tourists, she could read books and do some knitting or sewing or go for long walks. The only things she might miss in London were the easy availability of the variety of book stores and cinemas and the feeling of somehow being where things happened.

However, London was also dirty and unhealthy with its frequent heavy fogs and the smoke coming out of factory chimneys all year round. Every winter, it got worse when ordinary people also began to heat their houses with coal. Compared to the fresh sea air, which was so plentiful on Jersey, it was really no contest.

Hope would, however, take one last trip abroad and visit her old friends in Naples first. She had written to Antonio that she would come for a week in May 1948 if they could receive her then. She was a bit apprehensive about travelling alone the long way by train alone, but she was still very healthy, and she looked forward to revisiting Europe where she and Emily had had such a happy time. When Antonio wrote back and said that he would come to Rome and meet her in his car, she began to get her passport in order and ordered train tickets for Rome.

***

An evening in December, her phone rang. It was Professor Young from Cambridge who asked if she could meet him when he came up to London after Christmas for some meetings.

"Certainly," Hope said, and they agreed to meet for lunch in the restaurant at his hotel on Russell Square. She wondered what he wanted to see her about. She had almost forgotten about him in the months that had passed since they had met in Jersey.

In January on the day they had agreed on, she went to Hotel Russell and into the restaurant. Professor Young was already sitting there, nursing a cup of coffee. He got up and pulled out a chair for her, and she thanked him and sat down.

It was a gorgeous dining room, designed by the same architect who had also designed the first-class restaurant on the ill-fated ship, the Titanic. Hope looked in awe at the luxurious decorations, and Professor Young said, "I always stay here when I come up to London. It is so conveniently located near the British Museum, the best book stores and the London University buildings. I have taken the liberty of ordering us a light lunch, if that is all right with you?"

"That is fine," Hope said, "and thank you again for letting me join you on your trip to the Jersey War Tunnels."

"Not at all," said Professor Young. "It was a pleasure."

Lunch was served, and while they partook of the meal, they discussed the upcoming Olympic Games, last year's royal wedding, the fact that Cambridge had decided to allow female students as full members from this year and, unavoidably, the weather.

Finally, when they had coffee afterwards, Hope asked how the project on creating a memorial to the people who worked on the Jersey War Tunnels was coming along.

"Well," said Professor Young, "that was actually why I asked you to meet me here. Do you remember that I spoke to you about the need for help in keeping a check on the correspondence and records? I am trying to find out who the owner is but so far, without much luck. Nobody is living at the property now, so it is difficult. Eventually, if it all progresses well, we may need an attorney to draw up the papers, but until then, our group agreed that I could ask you if you would be in charge of our archives and correspondence."

Hope took her time before she answered.

"Well, I might be free to do so from June this year. But I am actually planning to move permanently to St Helier from this summer to live with my brother and sister-in-law and help them with the running of their guest house, you know."

"But that would be perfect," exclaimed Professor Young. "We have been talking about the benefits of having our archive in Jersey rather than in Cambridge where it is now. It would be so much more convenient to have it close to the Jersey authorities while the legal issues are being cleared up. Eventually, it will be housed at the museum, I suppose, but until then, St Helier would be the best place."

"How large is the archive?" asked Hope.

"At present, I have everything in a few boxes that can easily be moved to a location in Jersey. But it is bound to grow larger with time, so we shall have to rent some office space in St Helier for you to work in. And there is the matter of paying you for your work. For the present, you may need only a few hours per week, and we shall apply for some funding, but right now we are prepared to pay the rent and furniture and an honorarium of five pounds a month. It is not much, I know, but we will also pay for stationery and stamps and other supplies you may need."

Hope had never thought she would hear from him again, but apparently, he had been busy in the meantime, working out precise plans and getting the group's consent for the details. So, he had been sincere in Jersey when he had dangled the prospect of work in front of her. She would love to take on a small office in St Helier and do this kind of work. And they would even pay her. She almost accepted without hesitation, but she stopped herself and asked if she might think about it for a few weeks and get back to him, and he accepted that. They parted amiably outside the hotel with the professor heading off to the antique book stores and Hope heading for home.

Hope sat in her London apartment and thought about her life. *When Emily had died in 1938, the apartment had lost all of the lustre it had had when they were living there together. When Anna had moved in the following year, she had done her best to make it into a nice and cosy place for the girl to feel safe and comfortable in. Then the war came, and they had been evacuated to the countryside for almost three years. Hope had made sure that they stayed together, and when they finally returned to Hope's apartment, the property had still been standing, and they had continued to live there. There had been the bombs and shortages to worry about, but they had managed somehow. By the time the war had finally ended, Anna had grown into a young woman, only to learn that the war had made her an orphan. She had grieved and sought comfort among other Jewish survivors, and in the end, she had married and moved to Israel with her husband. Hope had not heard from her since she had left with David almost two years ago, and she had no idea where they lived or whether they even were alive.*

The apartment held many happy memories but also many sad ones. In the end, it was not difficult to leave it behind and start a new life in Jersey, so she wrote first to Arthur and Amy that she would move down there by the middle of June. Then she wrote Professor Young and told him that she would be happy to work on the Jersey Underground Hospital project from August. She went through her things to see what she wanted to take to Jersey and what to get rid of before moving. She would send ahead all her books and photo albums, and a few other keepsakes, and when she got back from Naples, she would pack a trunk of her clothes and have them sent as well. Over the spring, she got ready to leave her old life and start a new one in Jersey

Italy

In April, Italy had held a general election and the Christian Democracy had been victorious. Their leader, Alcide de Gasperi, had continued as the president, and the government formed in 1948 managed to keep all communist and socialist parties out of the coalition. After the war, the USA had been eager to form an alliance with Italy, so that it might not become part of the Soviet bloc, and massive aid had been given to the Christian Democracy. Hope had followed this in the British newspapers, and she felt reassured that it would be safe to go to Italy now.

When the time came to leave for Naples on May sixteenth, she boarded the train to the ferry and then again, the train on the other side. The last time she had passed this way had been in 1930, and Emily had been with her. As she sat there, looking out of the window, she thought of the warm companionship they had enjoyed but forced herself to not get lost in the past, but instead, focus on the here and now. She took out the two books she had brought for the trip and tried to decide which one to start with, *The Diary of a Young Girl* by Anne Frank or *Doctor Faustus* by Thomas Mann, just translated into English. She chose the diary of Anne Frank and was soon caught up in the near-namesake of her own Anna and her life in hiding from the Nazis in Holland. She knew from what she had read about the book that Anne Frank would not survive the war, but still, as she read, she found herself hoping for a miracle that would make the book end differently and reveal that Anne was still alive and maybe living in Israel like her own Anna... bruised by all the sadness she had experienced but still alive and helping to build a new life for Jews in the new state of Israel which had just been proclaimed by David Ben-Gurion two days ago.

***

The train passed through Europe as Hope slept, and when she woke up the next morning and had her breakfast, they had already reached the outskirts of Rome. Antonio was waiting for her on the platform, and luckily, he was able to recognise Hope, for the young man she had sent back to Italy in 1930 looked nothing like the grown man who waited for her on the platform. He seemed larger and much more muscular than she remembered him, and his elegant dress showed that he was doing well. He embraced her, and as soon as he said, "Welcome, Aunt Hope," she recognised his voice and his smile.

"Antonio, is that really you!" she exclaimed. "I hardly recognised you. I am so glad to see you again, alive and well!"

"Me too," Antonio smiled. Then he took her trunk in one hand and put the other under her arm, and together they walked to his car, which was parked in front of the station. It was a red Fiat Topolino station wagon with a rear body made with a wooden frame and wooden panels—a so-called 'woodie', Antonio told her. He helped her into the front passenger seat, and they rode south out of Rome and after a while, they found themselves on the road along the sea.

"It is a long drive through the region of Lazio to Campania and Naples," said Antonio, "but there are very beautiful views of the Tyrrhenian Sea. And we can stop wherever you want when you need to stretch your legs. We will stop for lunch in two or three hours, and I have brought something to drink for us as we drive."

As they drove, Hope had time to look at Antonio in profile. He looked a lot like his father, but his dark hair and brown eyes were from his mother's side of the family.

"How is your mother these days?" Hope asked.

"Mama is very well, actually. She enjoys being the old matriarch of the family, and she welcomes every new grandchild with delight. My two aunts both died, so mama is the family's only representative of the older generation, except for my uncle and aunt who live in a separate house. Mama and Martina get along very well, and together with my younger brother they run the wine business successfully."

"And you?" asked Hope. "Aren't you involved in the business?"

Antonio shook his head. "Only marginally. My education brought me a fine job in the Campania local administration of import and export, so I am a bureaucrat now. It is a good and secure job, but I am thinking of running for a post in government in a year or two... who knows. I would really like to work on the development of Naples and the province of Latina now that the war is over."

Hope was surprised. "You want to be a politician?" she said.

"Yes," Antonio answered, "I wish to play my part in making Italy a better and more prosperous country. If I am successful in local politics, who knows where that could lead... I am a Christian Democrat, and I joined the party in 1944. I did not want to see Italy run by communists or socialists with strong ties to the Soviet, so I felt I had a part to play in avoiding that."

"So, you favour the American connections," Hope asked.

"Actually, not really," said Antonio. "We may be very dependent on the United States for now, and that is to our advantage, but in the long run, I hope we can work for a strong and commercially united Europe. I think it will be the only way to avoid future European wars."

"That sounds excellent," said Hope. She was feeling quite proud of this young man, who she had briefly helped raise.

They rode a while in silence. Then Hope said, "Tell me about your family and everybody living with you."

Antonio began: "There is my mother whom you have met. She is now seventy. Then there is my wife, Martina, and our little boy, Alessandro, who will be two tomorrow. On our boat trip, you met two of my sisters, Maria and Emma, do you remember?"

Hope remembered them, not least Emma and the way the little girl had snug up to her after falling asleep on the boat...

"I remember them very well," she said. "Are they still living at home?"

"Maria is married to a pianist and lives in Rome. They have no children. Emma is still living at home; she got married very young, and her husband was killed in the war shortly after. She has been helping out with the business and the children. She also draws and paints, and sometimes her drawings are bought by magazines as illustrations, but now I think she may have met someone… how do you say…for keeps— although she is being very secretive about it."

Hope laughed. "Yes, you may say 'for keeps'; I understand what you mean."

Antonio continued. "My three younger brothers all live with us or nearby, but only Emilio works in the business. Arturo is not married, and he works as a teacher, and Gabriel will move out soon, because he and his wife will move to Sorrento and open a new wine shop.

"My cousins, who were living in our house with their mothers when you were here last, have all emigrated to America before the war started. We have recently had a letter from the oldest, and they appear to be doing fine now that the war is over. The boys served in the American army and have now been demobilised and begun their educations on the GI bill…"

Anthony had stopped talking when they entered Gaeta, and now he parked near a restaurant and declared that he was starved. Hope was actually quite hungry, too, and she needed to go to the loo, so she readily got out of the car and followed Antonio to the entrance.

They had a leisurely lunch, and Antonio told her about the city of Gaeta.

"Here we are a little more than half way to Naples. Gaeta suffered a great deal after 1943 when the Italian government surrendered to the Allies. The Germans were afraid that the Allies would land there, so they decided to move all the town's inhabitants out of the town and place them in camps. The Germans wanted to be ready to defend the harbour at all costs. The people were allowed back to rebuild after the Allies had occupied Rome, but it was hard to get back to its former prosperousness and importance. It is, however, still a popular holiday spot and it is famous for its tasty olives."

"They really are very good," Hope confirmed while putting another one in her mouth.

"I am sorry, but we have to drive on right away, as I promised Mama that I would have you back in time for our evening meal. We can always drive back some other day if you want to see more of the town. I have a holiday this week, so I am free to take you sightseeing," said Antonio.

"You do not have to take me sightseeing," answered Hope. "I would like to get to know your family and to meet Lisa again, more than anything else."

"Maybe I can take you and Mama and Martina on short trips from Naples to Sorrento and maybe even to Amalfi… you have not been there before, have you?"

"No, and I also thought I might revisit Pompeii. Can we do that one day?"

"Yes, easily," said Antonio, "and we can even include a visit to Resina or Herculaneum, as I think you say in English. It is smaller than Pompeii, but in some ways even better preserved."

"That sounds wonderful," said Hope.

***

They drove into Naples and arrived at Antonio's home around six o'clock. Lisa stood in the doorway to receive them, and Hope recognised her immediately, even though her black hair had turned white and her face was wrinkled like her own. The two women embraced, too overcome by all the time that had passed and all the sadness that lay between them in the twenty-five years that had passed since then. Here they were, two survivors of so many losses and hardships and the bond they had created so many years ago still intact. They both had tears in their eyes when they let each other go, and Lisa immediately took Hope's arm and led her into the house with Antonio following them. Hope was offered a chair by a young woman carrying a child on her arm, and Antonio introduced his wife and son.

"I have heard so much about you from Antonio," Martina said. "I am very happy to meet you." Hope could see that she was even more beautiful than the picture Antonia had sent her, and the baby looked happy and well fed.

A woman around thirty entered and said, "I am Emma, and Mama says we have met before, but I guess I was too young to really remember."

Hope stared at the young woman standing in front of her and tried to reconcile the image with the sweet little girl who had slept so trustingly in her lap on the boat trip all those years ago.

"Emma, Emma…" she said and stood up to embrace her. "I certainly remember you as an absolutely adorable little girl. What a beautiful woman you have turned into!"

Only Emilio was at home as both his brothers were away on business, and now he approached Hope and said hello. "My English not good. Benvenuto!"

"Hello, Emilio," said Hope. "You were just a baby when I last met you, and here you are a strapping young man. It is amazing…"

Emilio did not understand all she said, but Antonio translated, and everybody laughed.

Hope was shown to a small room on the second floor by Lisa. "It is only a small room, but I hope you will be comfortable. The bathroom is next door on your left, and my bedroom is the second door on the left. If you need anything, just ask. We eat at seven, so please come down when you are ready."

"Lisa, your English has improved so much! How did that happen?"

"When Antonio left for England, I begged Anthony to teach me more, and he did. We spoke English together in the evenings for at least one hour every day until he died…"

"I am so sorry that he is not among us anymore," said Hope. "He must have died a few years after Emily. Both you and I had to get through the war without our beloved one…"

"Oh," said Lisa. "You and Emily were…" She paused and then continued, "It must have been terrible for you to lose her. How did she die?"

"Breast cancer," said Hope. "Yes, it was terribly sad, and I still miss her."

Lisa looked a little uncomfortable, so Hope quickly said, "I will get ready for dinner and come down at seven."

Lisa gave her a quick hug and said, "Yes, I will go and help Martina get everything ready," and then she left and closed the door.

***

Hope washed her face and hands and quickly changed into a fresh blouse while she was contemplating what she had said to Lisa. *Maybe she had revealed too much by comparing her love for Emily to Lisa's for Anthony. On the other hand, she did not want Emily to be remembered as 'just a friend'; they had been lovers, and they would have been a married couple if the law and the church had permitted it. Sarah and probably Eleanor had known and accepted it even though they had never spoken openly about it… Well, that was the way things were, and probably always would be, but it was not fair!*

When Hope came down for dinner, she was seated between Lisa and Anthony. The Italian food was just as delicious as she remembered it, but she was tired after the long journey and could not eat very much. Lisa seemed to understand and said, "You must be quite tired, so please feel free to retire whenever you want. We will understand…"

"Actually," said Hope, "I am ready to fall asleep in my spaghetti, so if you will excuse me, I would like to just say good night for now and go to bed."

Lisa announced to the table in Italian that their guest was very tired and wanted to be excused, and then she went with Hope upstairs to make sure that everything was as it should be before she said good night and left.

Hope lay awake for a while in the unfamiliar bed until sleep finally overtook her.

***

When Hope woke up the next morning, the house was quiet. She went to the bathroom and washed herself all over, before she went back to her room and quietly got dressed. She was feeling well rested when she went down the stairs and met Martina, who had started to prepare breakfast in the kitchen. She smiled and said, "Good morning. Did you sleep well?"

"Yes, Martina, thank you. I slept like a baby," said Hope. "Can I make myself some coffee, please?"

"I have already made coffee," Martina said. "Please sit down at the table and let me bring you a cup. Would you like some bread and jam, too?"

"Oh, yes, thank you," said Hope, suddenly feeling ravenous. She sat down at the table and enjoyed the morning stillness, while Martina prepared a few slices of bread and jam and brought the whole thing on a tray for her. Martina went back to the kitchen to prepare breakfast for the rest of the family. Gradually, the house woke up. First to join her was Lisa and soon after, Emilio and Gabriel. They both greeted her warmly in Italian and had a quick breakfast before they left for the wine company next door. Arturo also came down and greeted Hope warmly before he left for the school where he taught. Lisa told Hope that he was an English and French teacher at a high school in town and Hope looked forward to talk to him about teaching later. Soon after, Emma came down carrying little Alessandro in her arms and sat down to feed him the porridge his mother had prepared. Finally, around nine o'clock, Antonio appeared and sat down. He looked at Hope, "I do not usually sleep this late, but since this week is my holiday, I felt like indulging myself a little."

"Of course," replied Hope. "I hope you had a good rest."

Lisa had gone to the kitchen to help clear the breakfast things away, and Martina had come in to take Alessandro from Emma to play with him. Emma had gone to the kitchen to help her mother.

"So, what should we do today?" said Antonio. "Should I take you and Mama for a trip to Pompeii and Herculaneum?"

"If Lisa wants to go, I would be delighted to go there, but let us ask her first."

Just then, Lisa came in from the kitchen, and Antonio asked her if she would like to come along with them to see the two old ruined cities. Lisa turned to Hope and said, "If that is where you would like to go, I will come with you. I went to Pompeii once with Anthony, but that was a long time ago, so I would not mind going again, and I have never seen what they have dug up at Resina, so yes, let us go there."

An hour later, they were ready to depart. Lisa and Hope sat in the back seat while Antonio drove. This time, they rode in another Fiat with seats in the back. The front seat was taken up by a picnic basket with drinks and food for the trip, which Lisa had prepared.

They had decided to start at Resina's Herculaneum, which was the smaller of the two sites and the one located furthest to the south. After a little less than an hour's drive, they reached the town of Resina, where they parked the car. Then they walked downhill on the main street towards the archaeological site. A little over ten minutes later, they reached a ramp leading down to the paved roads of the part of the city that had been laid bare. The view over the site from the ramp gave an impression of how deeply the houses and streets had been buried under rock and ash.

When they had bought their tickets and a map, they entered the site. They decided to go first to see the male and female baths, which were next to each other. Lisa explained that they had both drawn water from a deep well and that the water had been heated by a large furnace. The hot water had been carried around the baths in lead pipes and had worked as a kind of heating system for the complex. They admired the floor mosaics and what was left of the walls, and then they went into some of the other buildings that were open. Some of the walls still had fragments of well-preserved frescoes and fine mosaics, but most had been removed and brought to the archaeological museum in Naples or to other museums around the world.

They noted the mosaic of Hercules and Amphitrite, which they found when they entered what seemed to be a wine-shop at the front with amphorae still in place on its shelves. Behind the wine-shop, they stumbled on what seemed to be a place for dining, with couches along the walls and a serving table in the middle. On one wall was the beautiful mosaic, almost untouched, depicting Neptune and his wife, Amphitrite, in light blue robes that left them semi-naked. They stood next to each other on a yellow background and with various border decorations. In the same house, parts of the originally wooden second-floor were left, carbonised by the heat of the pyroclastic flows, which had followed the eruption.

***

The tragedy, which had hit Herculaneum, Pompeii and other villages in the area so many years ago had been buried underground by the emissions from the volcano and almost forgotten. Pompeii had been buried under four meters of ash, while Herculaneum had lain forty meters below the surface of today. Therefore, it had been much more difficult to excavate and much of it was still underground with present-day buildings and people living more or less on top of it. Thanks to the violent eruption of Mt Vesuvius in 79 AD the earth was very fertile and attractive to later farmers. The first archaeological endeavours in the eighteenth and nineteenth century in both Herculaneum and Pompeii had been treasure hunts for beautiful statues and artefacts to take away to private collections in Europe. Only in the beginning of the twentieth century, when the excavated sites were beginning to decay from exposure to the elements and from the endless curiosity of visitors, had there been attempts to gain some control and protection of the sites.

After leaving Herculaneum, they agreed that they would find a place in the shade to sit down and enjoy their lunch before moving on to Pompeii further south. When they came to Pompeii, Hope could not help thinking of her visit there with Emily twenty-five years ago. They had still been in their thirties, and Hope remembered the conversation they had had about the past. She had pointed out the tragedy of what had happened that day in AD 79, when people's lives had been snuffed out in a few hours, and Emily had reminded her of the joy of being able to see how they had lived so many years ago and how they were all part of a wonderful pageant of history moving along. She felt somewhat ambivalent about Emily's words now. It seemed to her that history was mainly a succession of tragedies broken by moments of oblivious happiness followed by more tragedies. She took Lisa's arm and tried to tell her about her conversation with Emily that long time ago. Lisa nodded as she listened, and then she said, "We should not try to understand such things, I think. I have learned to put my trust in God no matter what happens. Life has to be a mixture of happiness and tragedy, because how would we understand one without the other. This is the way God has arranged it, I think, and His ways are beyond our understanding."

Hope gave up trying to explain and thought how neat it must be to have an unshakable faith in submission to a god who directed the world in a meaningful way beyond human understanding. *What was wrong with herself that she was unable to believe like that? Was she too self-centred?* She thought again of Emily, who had not believed in a god either. What was the expression she had used then about her? Oh yes, *joie de vivre*—joy of being alive.... *Was that all? Should she stop measuring everything by what had gone before and instead live in the here and now?* She would have to think about that some more, but for now, she would at least try to practise it.

***

Lisa had noticed her thoughtfulness, and now she asked if Hope was tired. "A little," answered Hope, "these cobblestones are hard on your feet, aren't they?"

Lisa smiled and said, "Yes, they are not for old ladies, are they? When I was here with Anthony, we were still very young, and I did not even think about it. We were so much in love that I probably felt as if we were hovering over the ground." They both laughed and trotted on. In the interior courtyards, green grass and a few bushes were growing. They lent some comfort to the desolate ruins of the unroofed buildings. There were more visitors than Hope had seen the last time, but there were also some places that had been hit by Allied bombs during the war, and in 1944, a large earthquake had contributed to the destruction. Many ruins were being removed and used for the construction of Italy's new roads. If Italy wanted to preserve these ruins for the future, something had to be done soon. She said so, but Antonio explained that despite the enthusiasm and the hard work of the present Superintendent of Antiquities, Professor Amedeo Maiuri, it was hard to get sufficient funding, and the excavations were not an immediate priority for the Italian government.

***

When they had returned to Naples, Hope said that she wanted to revisit the Archaeological Museum the next day to see the various treasures that had been added over the last twenty-five years. Antonio went with her and on the way there, he asked her whether she wanted to see the secret room?

"Has it been opened up for everybody?" she asked surprised.

"No," said Antonio, "but I managed to get special permission to take you there, if you want to take a look. I remembered you and Aunt Emily telling me how angry you felt the last time you were here, that only men of a certain status could get permission to access it. That is still the case, but I have a friend in the Antiquities Office. He got permission for you and me."

Hope chuckled at how priggish the Italians still were about their own ancient culture. *Had not Adam and Eve walked naked in the Garden of Eden?* She had no special inclination to look at pornography, but her curiosity made it impossible for her to refuse this invitation. At the same time, she was a little embarrassed to accept it, so she made Antonio promise not to tell the rest of the family about it.

"Do not worry," said Antonio. "I will not tell anybody, and besides, Mama would get very angry with me if she knew about it."

At first glance, the museum had not changed much in the way exhibitions were arranged. There was still a model of the city of Pompeii, which gave good impression of its size and extent, and it was thought to have had around twenty thousand inhabitants at the time of the eruption. The heavy ash and stones from the sky had made the roofs cave in, so only parts of the walls remained. Herculaneum, on the other hand, had filled up from the bottom with lava and clay, so that one could see multi-storeyed buildings, in which wood had been carbonised from the heat.

When they got to the mezzanine and the first floor, Hope could see that items had been added here and there which she did not remember seeing on their first visit, but the overall impression remained the same, beautiful sculptures arranged according to their material, frescoes and mosaics on the walls and glass cabinets full of smaller things like vases, utensils, drinking cups, etc. When they came to the Secret Cabinet, a guard unlocked the door and stepped aside so that she could enter.

"I have seen it before," said Antonio, "so I will let you look alone. I will be just out here waiting for you."

"Thank you," said Hope and entered, feeling a little bashful but glad to be allowed to look around on her own, so as soon as she was alone, she decided to take a good look and be guided by her curiosity rather than her prejudices. She already knew that the ancient Romans had not had any shyness about showing the naked body; rather they had thought it beautiful enough to decorate their houses and public places with. But this room was not a display of nudity alone. She first looked at a male figure, probably a god, having sexual intercourse with a goat lying on its back. An impossible sight, and she almost laughed out loud as she understood that it was an example of humour rather than of obscenity. She looked at the various statues of the god Priapus with his enormous erect member. She knew that it was meant as a symbol of fertility, but still, it seemed grotesque and more laughable that titillating. There were also frescoes of men with young boys and men with women engaged in sexual encounters, and she looked for scenes with women engaged with women, but as far as she could see, there were none in the collection. After less than ten minutes, she knocked on the door and was let out.

"So, what did you think?" asked Antonio.

"It was very interesting," answered Hope noncommittally. "Thank you for providing this opportunity for me."

Antonio looked at her and asked if she had thought it embarrassing. Hope said that she had found some of the sculptures rather amusing and that she had felt intrigued by the idea of a society that had not seemed at all embarrassed by such displays in the public space. She wondered whether it was Christianity that had caused the change…

"Well," said Antonio, "I see the introduction of Christianity as an opening of peoples' eyes to right and wrong, and that might well include modesty as opposed to lack of shame—an awareness of how to behave in a civilised society…"

Hope did not agree with him. She saw nothing more civilised in the present-day society than in what she knew of ancient Rome. Actually, she felt that the sexual mores of the Pompeiians had been a great deal more civilised than, for instance, the shameful acts of war the world had been engaged in recently. But she did not say so. Instead, she thought about Emily and how much more fun it would have been to have experienced this and discussed it with Emily. Indeed, she almost regretted having agreed to accept the permission on her own. *Was there anyone she could ever discuss it with? Or could she find some books about the ancient Romans and their thought about nudity and carnal relations? Probably there might be some, if not in English, then perhaps in French?*

She changed the subject and suggested that in the afternoon they might take Alessandro and Lisa to the park, Villa Communale, where she had been with Emily. Maybe Martina would come, too?

After lunch, they waited for Alessandro to finish his nap before they set out again. Instead of Martina, Emma came with them, taking turns with Antonio, carrying Alessandro, when his little legs could not keep up.

The park was close to the sea, so it was nice and cool. The trees, pavilions and statues provided some shade, and they found a nice place

227

to sit down where Alessandro could run around freely. Hope thought he was such a happy child, the absolute centre of the family. Antonio told her that Martina was expecting her second child around Christmas but that she had not told anyone yet. She would wait until it began to show.

Emma said that she wanted to show Hope around a little, so Hope got up and took her arm to walk with her. When they were away from the rest of the family, Emma said that she only wanted to get Hope to herself, so that she could ask her some questions.

"As you know," Emma began, "I was married very briefly, and my husband died in the war."

"Yes, I am very sorry, Antonio told me about it. It must have been very hard for you."

"Yes and no. It was not a very happy marriage. But did Antonio also tell you that I am seeing someone special?" asked Emma.

"Yes."

Emma paused briefly, and then she said, "You were never married, were you?"

"No."

"But you lived with a woman friend?

"Yes, her name was Emily."

Hope was beginning to get an idea about where the conversation was going.

"Did you love her?"

"Yes, I loved her dearly, but why are you asking, Emma?"

"My whole family thinks I have a new boyfriend, and I don't know how to tell them that she is a girl. I have met a wonderful woman, and I want to share my life with her, but I do not know how."

Emma had tears in her eyes.

"Oh, poor Emma! I really do not know what to say, but I can see that it must be very difficult. Emily and I were very discrete. We were both teachers from a time when teachers were not supposed to marry and have families, and at the time, I do not think many people thought it strange that two spinsters lived together. And even if they did, it was not something that people would mention in polite society. I think my sisters knew and accepted our love for each other, but it was never something we talked about."

"I can't tell my family," said Emma. "I cannot imagine the pain it would cause them. It would be a terrible scandal that they would never live down. And the reaction from our priest is unbearable to think about. Don't you have any advice?"

"I do not know the Italian society and culture well enough to give you any useful advice, I think. Could you move away from Naples to a larger city for work or study and to live more anonymously? I think there are artist's communities in most large towns who have more diverse and tolerant life styles, where the two of you would be accepted. In Paris in the 1920s and early 1930s, there was such a community of women, who were quite open about living together in couples. Emily and I spent a summer there in 1930—but I guess the war put an end to it or suppressed it completely…"

Emma pulled herself together and said, "Thank you, Aunt Hope. I am glad you let me talk to you and took me seriously. I know you cannot solve my problems, but I was not wrong in thinking that I might talk to you about them. It gets so lonely at times…"

Hope squeezed Emma's arm. "Yes, it does indeed. I hope your friend gives you the comfort you need, and you have my very best wishes for a happy future."

They walked back to the rest of the family, and Emma immediately went to play with Alessandro. Hope sat down next to Lisa, while Antonio began to clear away the remains of their afternoon meal. "What did you and Emma talk about?" asked Lisa.

"This and that, nothing special," said Hope. "You know I have always had a special fondness for Emma, since when she was a little girl. It was really marvellous for me to see that she has grown into such an accomplished woman, you know. It gives me hope that the world is moving on and renewing itself, even if some of us are growing worn and decrepit."

"Decrepit," said Lisa. "I don't think of you or me as decrepit. I think we have been blessed with a good and strong health, which will last us a while yet."

"You are right," said Hope. "I am so happy that I got to meet your beautiful family once more in my life. I wish Emily and Anthony could have been here with us, but that was not to be, so we must honour them by our own joy, Lisa, don't you think?"

"I certainly do," said Lisa and got up together with Hope when the rest of the family was ready to leave.

***

Hope's last few days in Italy were spent with Antonio taking her and Lisa on an overnight trip to the Sorrentino peninsula. They would stay overnight in Sorrento, and the next day they would drive along the beautiful, old road along the coast to Amalfi. This would all be new to Hope, because she and Emily had not gone further south than Pompeii. They would go all the way to Salerno and then turn back to Naples.

They got up early in the morning and packed overnight bags before they had a quick breakfast. By seven o'clock, they were ready to say goodbye to those family members who were awake, and then they set off towards Sorrento. The first half of the journey was familiar from their trip to Herculaneum and Pompeii, and after they had passed Pompeii, they came to the small town, Castellammare di Stabia, which had grown up on top of the old town of Stabiae. It, too, had been buried by the debris from the AD 79 eruption of Vesuvius. It had been a much smaller port than Pompeii, but it had been known for its luxurious villas along the headland overlooking the sea. They had been described by Pliny the Elder and had actually been discovered in the 18th century, but the excavations had been buried again, and nobody knew exactly where. They made a short stop to stretch their legs at a place with a panoramic view of the Naples Bay, where they could see Mount Vesuvius across the water, looking almost as if it had two peaks, one a little larger than the other. It looked so peaceful, but they all knew that the tranquillity of the view was deceptive, and that one day, the beautiful and brooding mountain might again rain destruction over the communities along the bay.

Back in the car, they continued until they reached Sorrento and their hotel Tramontano. It was an old, palatial hotel, which had had many famous guests staying, such as Goethe, Byron, Shelley, and Keats. The Norwegian dramatist, Henrik Ibsen, was said to have finished his play, 'Ghosts', there.

Hope could not help wondering how Antonio could afford such a stay. He probably had 'connections,' thought Hope and decided to just enjoy it. They checked in and agreed to meet in half an hour for lunch.

Sorrento was an ancient city, favoured by Romans for its fertile land and pleasant climate. Not much had been preserved from that time, except the Greek Gate, which had stood steady and heavily since around 400 BC. Other ruins of the old city wall had been recently discovered but were not open to the public. Wars had plagued the area over the years until it became part of the State of Italy in the 1860s, and it had drawn tourists ever since.

They found a restaurant on Piazza Tasso and had a delicious meal. Antonio said that this area was also famous for its limoncello liqueur, and they should try that tonight before going to bed. It was strong, but great for helping one's digestion. They decided to stroll through the narrow streets and alleys next to the piazza and look at the many different shops. Hope wanted to find some presents for Arthur and Amy, and she ended up buying a fine music box made of wood and decorated with a pretty inlaid design of roses.

Finally, they walked towards the beach, but did not take the steps all the way down. Lisa and Hope were feeling a bit tired, so they opted for coffee and rest in a small café, before they turned back to the hotel. It was a lovely warm afternoon without being too hot, so they sat in the sun outside and felt very relaxed and lazy.

Hope began to tell them about her plans to leave London and move south to the island of Jersey, where her brother and sister-in-law lived. She had to explain where Jersey was, and Antonio explained it to Lisa in Italian.

"Oh," she said, "I did not even know that there were islands in the Channel. What will you do there?"

Hope explained that Arthur and Amy ran a very nice guest house in St Helier, and she would help to keep it going for a few years until they could all retire. "It is such a quiet and beautiful place compared to London, and Arthur and Amy are my only surviving family as far as I know. They have no children, and neither do I, so maybe we need each other now."

Antonio remembered how close Hope had been to Eleanor and Sarah and how their brother, Henry, had been a fixture in their lives. As a young schoolboy in England, he had experienced both the exhilaration of being free of the ties of family and the desperate loneliness of that freedom. Hope and Emily had been a wonderful support to him, as had his teacher, Henry. He also remembered the warmth he had met when they visited Calne. He could certainly understand how Hope would prefer to spend the later years of her life with whatever remained of her family, rather than living by herself in London. Lisa, who had spent her whole life at the centre of a large family, found it hard to even imagine the kind of family that had been Hope's, but she felt intensely sorry for her and spontaneously reached for her hand under the table.

"I hope you will be very happy with your brother and his wife," she said and squeezed Hope's hand before she let it go.

Hope smiled at her and said, "I am sure I will."

***

The next morning, they got back into the car and set out along the Amalfi coast to Salerno, from where they would return to Naples. After leaving the bay of Naples and crossing the peninsula, they were in the bay of Salerno. They reached the fishing village of Positano, with its houses clinging precariously to the mountainside, which descended steeply to the sea. Antonio took them along the beautiful coastal road to Amalfi, which had been cut into the cliff side in the nineteenth century to connect the many small villages, which had so far been accessible by boats only.

They drove slowly and carefully along the narrow and constantly winding road with steep cliffs rising on the left and stunning views of the blue sea far below on the right side. Here and there, bright colourful villages clung to the cliff sides, and there were also places along the side of the road to stop and pause by the most breath-taking views. Thus, it went on for about fifty kilometres before they reached Vietri sul Mare, where they had decided to have lunch. They parked the car and found a nice little place where they could rest and have something to eat.

From Vietri sul Mare, they took the road going north towards Pompeii and from there, on to Naples. They arrived home just before Martina and Emma were ready to serve the evening meal, and they were all rather tired after the long drive. Hope still had one day in Naples before she had to catch the train back to England. She chose to spend it quietly with the family to fasten all the impressions firmly in her mind, knowing that this might well be the last time she ever spent with them. From now on, they would communicate by letters only.

In the evening, however, she took a long walk with Emma to stretch her legs before going to bed. Emma told her about Felicia, the woman she had fallen in love with. Hope recognised her need to talk openly to someone about her secret, and she listened patiently. Felicia was a painter but supported herself by working in her brother's pizzeria a few hours every day. They had met each other sketching in the city park the previous last summer. When they had struck up a conversation, they had immediately felt a mutual sympathy, and over the next few weeks, they had grown closer. Their physical relationship had developed slowly until one evening when they had been alone in Felicia's room and they had kissed passionately, and one thing had led to another. That evening, Emma had gotten back very late, and to fend off the family's questions about where she had been, she had told them that she might have found a 'special friend'. They had all assumed she was talking about a man and asked a lot of questions, but she had refused to say anything more until she was more certain. That was about two months ago, and the pressure for more information was getting unbearable.

Hope sympathised and encouraged her, but she felt keenly that she could not advise her in any practical way. Finally, she said, "If at all possible, both of you will always be welcome to visit Jersey for a holiday. And please write me and tell me how everything is going for you."

Emma promised to write to her, and Hope asked her if she could read books in English. Emma confirmed that she had already read several

English novels, prompted by her father and brother, so Hope promised to send her a book about love between women.

***

The next day, she said her goodbyes to everyone in the family and hugged Lisa and thanked her profusely for taking such good care of her. Then she got into the red Fiat with Antonio, who would drive her to Rome Termini, where she would start her long journey back to London. Antonio carried her luggage on to the train and made sure she was comfortable before he kissed her cheeks three times and wished her a pleasant journey home. As the train left the station, Hope took a deep breath and leaned back in her seat. *What a wonderful time this had been!* She was glad that she had decided to go do one final trip, in spite of her age, before she settled down for good in Jersey. She was still healthy, and although she tired more easily than before, she saw no reason to stop living before she absolutely had to.

***

Hope spent the first weeks of June making the last preparations for moving to Jersey. She had already completed all the necessary registrations, so now she said goodbye to her friends and former colleagues and sent off the clothes for summer and winter she would need. The last week in London she moved into a cheap hotel and felt almost like a tourist in her own city.

First, she obtained a pirated copy of Radcliffe Hall's book, *The Well of Loneliness*, and packed it inconspicuously among a few magazines and other books. She sent it to Emma, just as she had promised, and hoped that it would not be stopped in customs. Then she bought a number of books for herself, including a large German-English dictionary, which she thought she might need for her work, and had them shipped to Jersey. The rest of the time she spent somewhat sentimentally visiting her favourite museums and galleries in London, and the last night, she went to the cinema to see the recent movie, 'Anna Karenina', with Vivien Leigh in the title role.

Jersey

The next morning, she went by train to Portsmouth and boarded the ferry. The weather was a bit rainy, but nothing else signalled that the trip might be anything other than pleasant, and indeed, as the ferry left the

English coast, the sun came out. She hoped this might be indicative of the whole venture—leaving the rainy British shores for a life in sunny Jersey.

At the ferry station, Amy and Arthur were waiting for her just like the summer before, and this time, there was no hesitation before they warmly embraced each other.

"We are so glad that you decided to come down here," said Arthur. Amy seconded that, and they walked back to the guest house together. Hope was glad to be back, but as they walked, she could not help wondering whether she would ever come to think of this delightful place as her home. *Well, she had made up her mind, and there was no going back, was there?*

Over tea, she made it clear that although she would help out with the guesthouse, she would not be staying with them forever. She would have to find herself a place nearby to live and to work. She had already told them of Professor Young's offer of paying the rent and a small honorarium if she would start up the archive and take care of the correspondence for the tunnel project, so she would be looking for a small apartment with both an office and living quarters.

"You can stay here as long as you wish," Amy assured her. "It should not be too hard to find what you want, and we will help you. But for now, take some time to settle down. Professor Young has booked his usual room for August, and you can help each other set up his archive. For now, I should get the evening meal ready, so please excuse me for now."

"I can help you," volunteered Hope, but Amy told her to go and unpack and get ready for supper. Arthur set about checking the tables in the dining room. There were seven guests apart from themselves, so he made sure that there were plates, glasses, napkins and cutlery for ten people. He also set out the small trays with salt and pepper and various condiments. Hope went to her room and changed into a clean dress and an apron before she went down to help.

After breakfast the following day, she started looking through the local newspaper, *Evening Post*, to see if there were any offices or shops for rent within her price range. She did not see any, so she decided to seek the help of a real estate agent.

Amy came and asked Hope if she wanted to come shopping with her, and Hope immediately said yes. Amy was a well-known person around the shops, and she introduced Hope as her sister-in-law, who had just moved to St Helier and was looking for a small apartment with an extra room for an archive. They also called in on an estate agent and asked him whether he knew of any suitable place. Amy assured Hope that this would bring results soon, and she was right. A few days later, the estate agent called that he had found two places for rent which might suit her, and if she would care to see them, he would call on her in his car and take her along to both of them this afternoon.

The first place was on the outskirts of the town near a forest. It was a small, self-contained cottage with a little garden in front, and it looked very nice. The price, however, was more than Hope wanted to pay, and the house was too remote to be practical for going to the guest house on a daily basis. It was not really what she had envisaged for her purposes.

The second place was quite different and lay on a busy street in town. It was an apartment that had originally been inhabited by the owner of the drapery shop on the ground floor. When he had died, his son had taken over the business but had not wanted the apartment, since he had bought a house with a garden a little outside St Helier. The apartment had thus been put up for rent. It was within easy walking distance of Arthur's and Amy's guesthouse, and the price was very reasonable. There were three rooms, a small one and two slightly larger ones with an entrance from the front staircase. The back stairs led down to the shop and the courtyard, but the door to the shop would be kept locked except for emergencies. There was a reasonably sized kitchen and a toilet inside the apartment, and Hope decided that it would fit her purpose very well, so she agreed with the agent that she would take it over from the first of August. Until then, she would have free access to do the necessary repairs and redecorations, as she wanted.

In the evening, she took Arthur and Amy to see it, and Arthur immediately offered to put up new wallpaper in return for Hope doing some of his chores at the guest house.

The next six weeks they spent their time divided between the guest house and the apartment. Arthur took down all the old wallpaper and put up new and cheery patterns. They laid rugs on the floor, and Amy sewed new curtains. Arthur put up bookshelves and cupboards in the room intended to hold the archive. Hope found a used desk to work by, and the people she bought it from gave her a chair to use with it. She had sent her bed and her favourite chair from London, and when they arrived and she put them in, the apartment began to look liveable. By August 1st, she was ready to move in, and she was looking forward to show Professor Young what she had accomplished. They had been corresponding regularly in the meantime, and the professor had sent her money to pay for the rent and renovations.

They met that evening over dinner, and Hope promised to pick him up from the guest house and take him to the new office the next day. As they walked through the streets of St Helier, Professor Young told her that he had found out that the land above the tunnel was owned by a company based in England, but so far, he had not been able to find our further details.

The professor was pleased by her office arrangements, and they went through her filing system and her book-keeping, which was still only in the beginning phase.

"I am very pleased to have secured so capable a person to run this side of things," he said. "I will be spending this summer talking to some of the people who worked there while the tunnels were being built to get their testimonies about how things were, and I may ask you to type my notes and file them, too."

"I can do some interviews for you, too," offered Hope.

"Maybe I will ask you to do that," Professor Young replied, "but first, we have to find some people who will talk to us. Some people feel that working for the Germans, while the rest of England was putting their lives on the line to resist, is something shameful that should be forgotten as quickly as possible."

Hope had not really thought about that aspect of the whole sorry sad thing.

"But Britain abandoned them, didn't they?"

"Yes, but there are some who think they might have resisted more than they did. I, personally, do not think they had much choice in the situation, but it may be a somewhat touchy topic for some. So, we have to be diplomatic and careful when talking about it."

***

The war had been a dreary time for the people left in Jersey, shifting between anxiety, real fear and boredom. Just getting through every day, trying to make do with what was available without thinking too much about what was not, had been a challenge. All were waiting and hoping that things would not end too badly, that there would come a time when it was all over, and life would return to some kind of normality that would not be too unbearable… Some people would help the Germans by pointing out the transgressions of others, and some young girls were later denounced for fraternising with the enemy. A few cooperated directly with German officers to bring goods illegally to the island and sell them on the black market. The anger and suspicions provoked by such behaviour still drew long shadows and made healing difficult. Hope realised that, for the time being, she had better leave the interviewing to Professor Young. More time would have to pass before the war years might become a part of daily conversation. The relief and happiness they had all felt when the Germans surrendered and left, and they could start to rebuild and recover, lasted for a while. But after that first euphoria passed, many of them had losses to assimilate: the loss of family members and friends, the loss of property ruined by the occupying forces, the humiliations and horrors they had suffered, the loss of their pre-war innocence and the gradually growing knowledge of the atrocities committed everywhere and especially on the Jewish population. One simply had to focus on the future while managing the here and now as best one could.

After the war, working people in England were encouraged to take summer vacations once a year in order to relax, so that they could return rested and full of energy to work afterwards. New tax regulations had made it attractive to marry before April 6, because a couple could then file a joint return for the preceding year and save a sum of money in taxes. A lot of young people had postponed their wedding till after the war, and by using this tax advantage, they could afford a honeymoon. Soon, Jersey had a booming business catering to honeymooners, with large hotels and bus tours and special entertainment for the young couples. Small guest houses were rarely used by honeymooners, but still, Arthur and Amy also gained from the influx of tourists to the island. Many of the people who had spent their honeymoon in Jersey would come back year after year to enjoy the beaches and the many beautiful places.

Hope took Professor Young back to the guest house for their evening meal, and over the next two weeks, they met frequently to discuss the archive and the new material the professor brought back from his interviews. Hope typed all of them and filed them with any additional information that was provided.

***

Life continued quietly as she helped Arthur and Amy run the guest house in the summer months and worked on the archive during the winters. She kept informed about what happened in the larger world through the radio and by reading the newspapers available on her almost daily visits to the Public Library. There were war tribunals going on in Nuremburg and Tokyo, and some of the worst criminals, who had been apprehended, were executed or got long prison sentences.

She read about the US offer to make money available to Europe to rebuild their countries and their economies after the war through the Marshall Plan. In 1947, the Soviet Union and the Eastern European buffer zone of countries they had gained after the war refused the

American offer of economic aid, because they saw it as an investment in setting up an anti-communist bloc among the European countries. When the negotiations ended, a clear division of Europe into east and west had been established, the east dominated by the Soviets and the west by the Americans. When the communists were victorious in China, too, the Americans began to feel seriously threatened. And when the three western sections of Berlin joined together and began to use the new West German Reich mark as their currency, the Soviets responded by cutting off all access to the beleaguered city. The three air corridors, agreed upon with the USSR earlier, became the only route into the Allied sectors of Berlin, and through them, the air lift of food and other necessities was established. The combined strength of the Allied powers managed to get a steady stream of aircrafts flying to Berlin and back from bases in West Germany. They brought many tons of food, coal and other necessities into West Berlin for over a year until the blockade was formally ended in 1949.

Like a shadow over all post-war negotiations hung the poisoned cloud of the existence of nuclear weapons. At first, the Americans held the monopoly on how to make them, but when Truman finally told Stalin that they had this devastating bomb, Stalin did not seem surprised. It turned out that he knew all about the Manhattan project and the details of how to make a bomb from his spies. He had already started his own project, which was delayed only by the scarcity of uranium.

In January 1946, the newly formed United Nations had met in London and discussed the future of nuclear weapons. A commission was formed for nuclear energy, and proposals were heard for eliminating all use of nuclear weapons, but they were all rejected because of mutual distrust. Soon after, the United States began testing different kinds of plutonium bombs in the Marshall Islands at the Bikini Atoll after moving the residents away from the area. At the same time, the Soviets were working feverishly to complete their own nuclear weapon, and in 1949, they successfully managed to test their first plutonium bomb. A few years later, both sides had enough nuclear weapons to be able to completely destroy each other, and a new concept entered the world, 'mutually assured destruction' or in short, MAD. The purpose was to deter the enemy from making the first strike.

**

In Jersey, Hope followed the news on the BBC and from the newspapers and sometimes discussed them with Arthur and Amy. Arthur took what he called the realistic stance, namely that once something new was invented, it would be impossible to un-invent it, so the only solution to the existence of nuclear weapons on two sides of a conflict was to keep the terror balance going. Amy and Hope did not agree with him and felt sorry for the children who had to grow up with the threat of sudden annihilation.

But most of the time, the three of them were concerned about how to make the guest house friendly and welcoming with healthy and hearty meals while rationing was still in force for many goods. Gradually, through the 1950s, people became more prosperous, and there were plenty of summer guests. In the winter of 1952, Professor Young suddenly caught pneumonia and passed away, and without his strong support, the project could not continue, so Hope had to give up the archive work. She made an agreement with the public library to turn the archive over to their collection for safekeeping. After that, she gave up her flat and moved in with Arthur and Amy again, but they were already planning to sell their house and business in the spring of the following year and fulfil their dream of moving to Gorey. They had found their dream house with a view of the sea and bought it. They wanted Hope to come with them, but Hope had already made up her mind not to intrude on Arthur and Amy and their life as old-age pensioners. The years in Jersey had been wonderful and she loved both Arthur and Amy, but frankly, she missed England a bit, and now that she had no more work to do, Jersey felt too remote and quiet for her. The thought of living there alone and on her own if Arthur and Amy should die before her was unbearable. She had decided to move back to England again and resume contact with her old friends. After almost five years in Jersey, she felt healthy and full of energy, and she began to look for a position back in England. She hoped she could find temporary work in a private school somewhere and do some teaching again.

***

In February 1952, the king had died from a lung disease to the great sorrow of the country. His eldest daughter, Elizabeth, and her husband returned from a trip to Africa to take over the throne. By then, Winston Churchill had become Prime Minister again, despite being in his late seventies. Hope wrote letters to friends from her old school and looked for temporary positions in the vicinity of London.

The following winter, on the night between January 31st and February 1st, a violent storm combined with a spring tide had caused great floods along the coasts of the North Sea, and especially the Netherlands had been hard hit. Almost two thousand people lost their lives, and so did even more farm animals. Many neighbouring countries sent aid and the Red Cross collected money to help the survivors. The Dutch government began the Delta Works and built a whole series of dike rings to prevent similar disasters in the future. England's east coast was also hit hard by the flood in many places, and although the death toll was not as high as in Holland, many places were devastated, and 30,000 people had to be evacuated from their homes.

Part Seven
Recovery

Life in Caversham

After some time, Hope found that the private Queen Anne's School in Caversham needed an extra school librarian, who could also teach English and history from time to time as a replacement teacher, when other teachers were absent. Hope applied for the position and got it from April 1953. It was a contract position, so she would have to have her contract renewed annually, but that suited her very well, since she had no plans to work beyond the age of seventy.

When the time came to say goodbye to Arthur and Amy, it was more difficult than she had anticipated. There were tears in both her and Amy's eyes when they hugged, and in spite of Hope's promises to visit them, they all realised that they could not be sure that they would ever see each other again, Amy and Arthur were both 68 years old, and Hope was 65.

The year before, Hope had at long last received a letter from Anna and David in Israel. They were living on a kibbutz in northern Israel and had two children, a boy named Akiva who was three years old and a baby girl of two months, named Esther. They were healthy and happy, both had had military training and were working and living on the kibbutz. They invited Hope to come and visit them for a while and take part in life in the kibbutz. Hope had written a letter back to say that she would look into the possibilities but that she might have become too old to undertake such a journey.

In Caversham, the school had helped her find one of the new prefabricated council row houses that had been built after the war. It had two rooms, a bathroom and a kitchen, a small garden in front and a yard in the back. The bathroom had hot running water and a flushing toilet, and the kitchen had a refrigerator, a water heater and a built-in oven. To Hope, having all these conveniences to herself seemed like an unprecedented luxury. She bought a bicycle and a new radio and various things for her kitchen and began to look forward to her new life.

She went to the school several times to meet the librarian and learn how it was organised, and she met some of the teachers of the 11-13-year-old pupils she might have to teach. Her first teaching duties would be to take over for a teacher of English, Mrs Hall, who was pregnant with her first child. Mrs Hall had an insurance, which granted her thirteen weeks of maternity leave, and she fully intended to come back to her job when the thirteen weeks had passed. Most women would quit their job when they got pregnant to be full-time housewives, but when Hope met the twenty-five-year old Mrs Hall, she saw how the times were changing.

They met in the teachers' room one of the last days of March, and Hope, who had herself become rather grey and wrinkled, saw a young, radiant blond woman come over and introduce herself as Mrs Hall.

"Miss Maundrell?" she said, and when Hope got up from her chair and stretched out her hand, Mrs Hall said, "Please call me Wendy," she said. "I feel so much more comfortable being called by my first name by people who are older than me."

Hope liked her attitude and said, "Well, in that case, you can call me Hope. How do you do, Wendy?"

Wendy was wearing a wide jacket over her skirt and looked quite pregnant. She indicated her protruding belly and said, "As you can see, I shall be having a baby in about six weeks, and I feel rather heavy, but apart from that, I am fine. How are you? I hear that you have recently moved here to Caversham. How do you like it?"

"It is very nice," said Hope. "The school helped me find a nice little prefab to live in, and I have just about settled down. But tell me about your classes and what you want me to teach them while you are away."

Wendy talked, and Hope took notes for the next hour or so. Then she looked up and asked Wendy what her students were like.

"Since this is a boarding school, and a rather expensive one, my students are generally well-mannered and quite motivated for study. They have varying abilities, of course, but you had better make your own assessment of that. I will leave you the lists of their names and their latest grades on my shelf." She indicated a wall with a number of pigeonholes, each with the name of a teacher on them. "I am planning to stop working on the first of May, so we will have plenty of time to talk before then. You shall be working in the library as well, I understand?"

"Yes, I shall be the assistant to the school librarian, Mrs Lily Jones."

"Good luck," said Wendy. "I hear she can be a bit of a dragon at times, and the girls in school fear her... By the way, won't you come over for supper on Sunday and meet my husband, Gordon? He is also a teacher, and we actually live in a prefab, too, not very far from you, I guess, so you can probably walk there in less than five minutes."

"I would be delighted," Hope said. "But are you sure you can manage at this time?" She looked at Wendy's belly.

"Being pregnant is not a disease," said Wendy. "Of course, I can manage, and Gordon will help me. Have you no children?"

"No," said Hope, "when I first became a teacher, we were not supposed to get married. Actually, one might have gotten fired just for marrying, let alone having children. Besides, I never wanted marriage anyway."

"You will have to tell us more about how things were then when you come over for dinner, won't you."

"You want my life story," smiled Hope. "I warn you, it is a long tale."

Wendy gave her the address and drew a small map for Hope, and then they said goodbye.

***

The following Sunday, Hope wore her best dress, a blue shirtdress with a pattern of small white flowers, and over it, she wore a light brown cotton coat and a hat that matched her dress. She was still slender and felt that she looked quite nice in her new black shoes with their low heels and her black handbag. When she rang the doorbell, Wendy came to open the door.

"Welcome to our humble abode," she said. "Please, come into the parlour and meet my husband." Hope entered and took off her coat, and then she followed Wendy into the living room. Gordon was sitting in a chair and immediately got up to greet their guest.

"Gordon Hall," he said. "I am pleased to meet you, Miss Maundrell."

"Pleased to meet you, too," said Hope. "Thank you for inviting me over. I shall be teaching your wife's classes while she is away."

"I know," Gordon said. "Please, sit down and make yourself comfortable."

Hope sat down on the sofa while Wendy was busy in the kitchen getting tea ready.

"Wendy told me that you are a teacher, too. What and where do you teach?"

"I teach classics and ancient history at Reading School. I was educated at Cambridge, and I have worked here in Reading for two years now."

Wendy came in with mugs of hot steaming tea for them all, a bowl of sugar lumps and a jug of milk.

"Please, help yourselves to sugar and milk," she said. Hope and Gordon did so.

"Tell us where you were before you came to Caversham," Wendy said.

"Well," Hope began, "I was born in Japan where my father was a missionary, but we moved to Calne in Wiltshire when I was six years old. I went to school in Calne and later, I graduated from the London Day Training College and got hired to teach at the Highbury Hill High School for Girls in London. This was in 1915. I taught there during the two world wars, and in 1947, I retired. Then I spent a little over four years in Jersey where my brother ran a guesthouse with his wife, and when they retired, I began looking for something to do in England and was lucky to find this position here. That is the short version of my life story."

"I was born in 1928," said Wendy. "Gordon was born two years before me, and I believe our first memories are from the 1930s. Gordon served during the last year of the Second World War, and we met right after the liberation in 1945. We were both students, so we did not marry until we had both graduated, and then we were both lucky to find work here in Reading, so we moved here in 1951. Gordon is originally from here, but I am from London where I trained as a teacher."

They sat quietly for a few moments, and then Gordon said, "I have heard about the women's struggle to be given the right to vote. Were you a part of that?"

"Yes," said Hope and paused a little, thinking about Emily.

"You look sad," said Wendy. "Does it bring back sad memories?"

"Not at all," Hope replied. "It was an exhilarating time, and it brought about what it was supposed to. I lived with a close friend, Emily, who was also a teacher, and we went to all the meetings and demonstrations we could. We were passionate about women's rights, and that was part of why we became teachers. To teach girls about independence and their freedom to choose. Not just to become a wife and mother with an endless number of children to wear you down... The thought of doing both, as you are doing, Wendy... we just did not seriously think that would ever be a possibility."

"So why did you look sad?" said Wendy. "What happened to Emily?"

"She became ill and died in 1938. She was the closest friend I ever had, and talking about the suffragettes reminded me how much I miss her."

"We are sorry that we brought up some sad memories," said Gordon. "Let's change the subject."

Hope asked them instead how they had planned to cope with raising a child while Wendy worked.

"We are lucky," said Gordon. "We have my mother who will come over every day to take care of the baby and the house while we have to be away. She is on her own now that my father died last year, and she cannot wait to become needed again."

"Well, that certainly sounds convenient," said Hope, but she wondered whether it would work out in the longer run. *The things she had read over the years seemed to indicate that grandmothers and daughters-in-law rarely got along without conflicts. But what did she know?*

"We are saving up to buy a television set," said Wendy. "We will have enough soon, so hopefully, we will be able to see the coronation. Did you know that they are going to televise the whole thing? We can sit here in the comfort of our living room and watch it. If all goes well, we will have some friends over, and you will be invited, too. I just hope it will not happen just as the baby is coming…"

"A television set?" asked Hope. "I have seen them in shops… How exciting. I would love to come over."

"Gordon and I are not all that besotted with the idea of a monarchy," Wendy mused. "But somehow, I cannot help enjoying all the splendour and solemnity, even though I feel that it is a waste of the country's money… do you know what I mean?"

"I guess so," Hope said. "I have not really thought about it, but when I was traveling with Emily in Italy and visited castles, churches and museums, we often spoke critically about the lavishness and luxury which the Catholic Church had amassed through the centuries while people starved. Maybe you notice more when you travel abroad, but I guess the Anglican church and the monarchy are no different from anywhere else."

Gordon added, "Social and economic injustice seems to be everywhere. France and Russia have had bloody revolutions when the people could not bear it anymore, but although France became a republic, nothing really changed for ordinary people once it was over. Russia was so bad that it could not but improve in the beginning, but now, after the war, I have severe doubts about how it will develop. And China, of course, has had a revolution, I guess, but it will be a long time before it can overcome all the damage that Japan and the civil war inflicted upon them… It seems that revolutions easily end up making things worse for the common people, doesn't it?"

Hope felt that she had to protest. "Yes, maybe. But from my point of view, I think we must also look at how things have gotten better. More people get educated and are not so easily taken in by power. Women have gained more influence in society, which I find is a good thing.

Penicillin has been invented, and many diseases that used to kill people can now be cured. There are other terrible diseases, such as polio, for which we do not have a cure yet, but we are so much better off with regard to finding answers there, too. Atlee's government introduced many measures to secure support for the poor, and I feel sure that England does not need a revolution to get on the right track. If only we can avoid more wars..." she trailed off.

Wendy had gotten up. "I do not want to interrupt you, but we must get supper started. Come and see our kitchen," she said to Hope. "Gordon will lay the table while we chat."

There was a roast in the oven, and the potatoes were peeled and ready to put on the cooker with a pinch of salt.

"Let's go to the garden and get some fresh parsley," Wendy said, and Hope followed her into the yard where Wendy was growing many different herbs and vegetables.

"How nice," said Hope. "I must get to work in my own yard and sow some vegetables of my own. Right now, it looks like a junk yard, to be honest. Let me help you pick the parsley, so you won't have to bend over."

"Thank you, Hope. That is very thoughtful of you. It is getting harder, actually," admitted Wendy.

After dinner, Wendy and Hope sat in the sofa and talked, while Gordon cleared away the dishes and prepared a cup of coffee for them.

"I hope you like coffee," he said to Hope.

"Oh yes," said Hope. "I got quite addicted to it in my youth, when Emily and I went on trips to Europe."

Gordon was about to pour milk into Hope's cup, but she stopped him and said, "I like it black with a little sugar, thank you."

"Tell us about your trips to Europe," said Wendy.

"The first time we actually left England was in 1922, when we went on a long holiday to Italy. After the war, Emily had inherited a small sum of money from her late father, and we decided to spend it on a trip to Italy. We stopped a few days in Paris and then went on all the way to Rome. After a few days there, we went on to visit other cities, such as Naples, Florence and Venice. We spent almost a month in the country and saw the most amazing sites. We made some very good friends in Naples and spent a week there. The father of the family was English, but he had settled for good in Naples and married his Italian sweetheart. They sent their eldest son, Antonio, to England for a boarding school education, so Emily and I helped him settle in, and he spent almost all his vacations with us in London. When he went back to Italy in 1930, Emily and I went to Paris together and just managed to catch the last whiff of the roaring twenties there. It was a wonderful time and we met a lot of interesting people, but then, during the thirties, everything began to go wrong. The depression, Hitler and so on. Then Emily died in 1938 and the war began. I took in one of the Jewish girls from the Kindertransport, and she stayed with me all through the war. Anna was her name. She got married when the war was over, and she and her husband went to Palestine to help build the new Jewish homeland. After three years, I finally heard from her, alive and well and the mother of a little boy and a girl."

"So, what happened after the war?" Wendy asked.

"I kept working until 1947, and when the family in Naples wrote and invited me for a holiday, I went. It was wonderful to meet them again and to see a little more of Italy. Then I moved to join my older brother and his wife in Jersey. I helped them run their guest house, and I did some archive work for a British professor, who was doing research on the wartime in Jersey when they were occupied by the Germans. Last winter, my brother and his wife sold the guest house, and the professor I was working for died of pneumonia, so I decided to move on back to England again, and here I am."

"I am quite bowled over by the adventurous life you have had," said Wendy.

"I do not think that it was all that adventurous," replied Hope. "We just did what we could with the means we had. When Emily and I were young, we had dreams of going to faraway places. We wanted to experience much more of the world, but limited means and possibilities meant that we had to work to survive, and wars kept getting in the way. You will probably have a chance to do better in your lives. I do believe that things are going to be much better in the future, you will see."

As she walked home that evening, Hope was feeling quite satisfied. She had liked Wendy and Gordon very much and hoped they would be friends in the future. She might even help out a little when the baby came, she thought.

***

The coronation of the young queen, Elizabeth II, would be held in Westminster Abbey on the second of June. Hope had started teaching Wendy's classes on the first of May, and on May 10th, Wendy had borne a healthy girl. A few days later, she had come home from the hospital, and Hope had come by with flowers and a warm crocheted cover for the perambulator which Wendy and Gordon had bought second-hand. Wendy looked a bit tired and told Hope that the baby woke her up several times every night and needed feeding.

"I never realised how much work a baby creates," she said. "Apart from sleep deprivation, there are the dirty nappies, and they smell until I can wash them. At least feeding is relatively easy as long as I am breastfeeding, but in babies, everything comes out the other end in no time!"

Wendy spoke in a mock-exasperated tone, but she looked very happy at the same time. "At least she sleeps a lot of the time, so I can get housework done in between. She is out in her pram in the yard right now, but she should wake up very soon, so you can see her. She is adorable."

"I am sure she must be the most beautiful baby in all of England," Hope laughed and offered to make them both a cup of tea. Wendy looked gratefully at her, so she went to the kitchen and put the kettle on while she found the tea things and put them on a tray. When she carried it into the living room and put it down, Wendy said, "Thank you, Hope. Some days I just feel so inadequate, and I worry about what it will be like when I go back to work. My mother-in-law keeps trying to teach me how to do everything, but she is rather old-fashioned, and I think she wants to convince me that I am very selfish to want to be a working mother."

Hope put a hand on her arm and said, "I know how strong the pressure has become on young mothers to stay at home and bring up their children while their men earn the money. But in my opinion, you should resist and hang in there. I remember a time when men thought that women should not have any say at all in how things were run. If all women should now accept to be put back in that role as 'weak and silly women', all the progress we made before and during the war would be for nothing, Wendy. Hang on to your independence."

Wendy sighed, "I know, Hope. It is just so hard, and I am not sure I want my daughter to be raised by her grandmother…"

"I do not know much about raising children, but I want to assist you wherever I can, and I will always be there to listen to you."

They were interrupted by wails from the pram outside, and Wendy immediately went out and brought in the tiny girl. She put her on the sofa next to Hope and said, "Please look after her while I get the things."

Hope looked at the tiny wailing child and put her hand on the baby's belly and rocked her a little. The baby calmed down, and when her mother came in and laid out the rubber cover and a towel on the floor, she took the baby from the sofa and spoke softly to her while she put her down to have her nappy changed. As soon as the wet nappy was removed, the baby began to wave her legs in the air and make happy sounds.

"Good," said Wendy. "No rash today." She then washed the baby between the legs and put on some baby powder and a new nappy. On top of that she put a pair of rubber pants and then knitted cotton rompers, which held everything in place. She then dressed the baby in a knitted suit complete with socks, lifted her up and sat down with her.

"Do you mind if I feed her here?"

"No, silly. Of course, I don't."

Wendy pulled out one breast so that the baby could feed.

"What are you going to call her?" asked Hope.

"Gordon wants to call her Charlotte, but I like Diane better. Maybe we will end up giving her both names when we have her baptised, but for now we just call her 'the hump'… Not very nice, I know, but that is how we spoke of her before she was born. I am starting to call her Diane when I am alone with her, but Gordon's mother calls her Charlotte, and she will probably win in the end. Well, who cares anyway."

It was not like Wendy to give up so easily, but she was obviously tired. Hope suggested that she take Diane/Charlotte out for a trip in her pram, so that Wendy could rest a little. Twenty minutes later, she found herself wheeling the pram along the pavement.

Hope made it a good long walk. It was an early summer day with flowers starting to bloom everywhere. The air smelled fresh and flower-scented, and the baby soon fell asleep. Hope took the opportunity to explore the area. She walked all the way down to the river and found a bench to sit on, looking out over the river. She secretly enjoyed being seen by others as a grandma out with her grandchild in the pram, even though it was a borrowed identity. She was tired of being seen as a sad old spinster who had never been able to capture a husband… *If only they knew about the life she had lived and all the love she had known… she would never trade any of that for a more conventional life with a husband and children of her own.*

She thought of Wendy and what would become of her. *Would she give in to the strong pressure to conform and be a housewife, staying at home and taking care of her husband and children, proud of how she kept her house? No, not Wendy. She was such an accomplished young woman with a bright future, if she did not let herself get tied down by housework and children.*

After sitting for a while, Hope got up and wheeled the pram back to the house. The baby was still asleep, so Hope parked the pram in the front garden and went in. Wendy had just woken up and looked much more rested and less worn out.

"Diane is asleep outside," said Hope. "She fell asleep soon after we left, and she slept through the whole trip. You look much better. Did you get a nap?"

"I did nod off for a while," said Wendy. "I feel much better now."

"I sat by the river," said Hope, "and I was thinking about you. You said that being a mother was harder than you had imagined. Are you thinking about giving up your job?"

"Why do you ask? Do you want to have it?"

"Oh no, not at all," answered Hope. "I was worried about you! You see, I wouldn't like to see you give up and become a housewife. That's all. Have you thought about it?"

"Well, I cannot say that I have not. But I am determined to go back to school in August. I will hate to be away from my little girl most of the days, but I am sure I would hate it even more if every day had to be taken up by domestic activities for the rest of my life. Besides, I like to make some money that is my own. And when the hump grows up, I would like to travel and educate myself further somehow."

"I will support you as much as I can," said Hope. "Just let me know. I don't want you to waste that brilliant mind of yours on domestic drudgery."

"Gordon's mother will be a daily warning," said Wendy and laughed.

***

Wendy and Gordon had finally bought the television receiver they had saved for, just in time for the coronation. They had invited Gordon's mother, Hope and two couples whom they saw regularly. The husbands were both teachers, and the wives had jobs as part-time office workers. One of them was pregnant and would be giving up her work to be a full-time mother when the baby came. They came over at a quarter past ten in the morning, and the wives spent the first ten minutes cooing over the baby and taking turns holding her. Meanwhile, the men had settled in front of the small fourteen-inch television screen and were eagerly discussing how the technology worked. When the royal procession began, Gordon's mother put the baby to sleep in the pram outside with a plastic cover to protect against the rain that had begun falling.

The TV coverage of the coronation would last most of the day, so Hope had helped Wendy prepare sandwiches and bake cakes to serve with tea at lunchtime. The two couples had also brought various kinds of food and snacks, and the other two wives helped Wendy in the kitchen. Hope and Gordon's mother were placed in the sofa in front of the screen, while the young people sat on a variety of chairs and on the floor.

The transmission had started with a test transmission, so that people could adjust their aerials to get as clear a picture as possible. A quarter past ten, the BBC announcer had presented the programme after which came the seven-hour coverage of the events.

It began with the queen leaving Buckingham Palace, and it ended after she had returned there. Inside the Westminster Abbey, cameras were set up with discretion so that they showed no close-ups of the young queen. The procession set out in pouring rain, making the crowds of onlookers as well as the people in the procession rather miserable. Heads of state from the countries of the commonwealth rode in the procession, and the huge queen of Tonga, sitting in an open carriage next to the miserable looking Sultan of Zanzibar, smiled and waved all the way through the parade. Richard Dimbleby was commenting on the proceedings. Later in the day, the rain stopped for periods at a time, but while May had been warm and sunny, this day in June was exceptionally chilly for the season. Nevertheless, the planned street parties took place all over England, and people refused to let the weather spoil their enjoyment of the festive day.

Around half past four, the guests at Gordon's and Wendy's house began to say their goodbyes, while Hope and Gordon's mother were cleaning and tidying up in the kitchen. Wendy was feeding the baby who was fretful because of all the disturbance going on around her, so Hope took her in the pram for a walk around the neighbourhood. The rain had stopped, but it was still rather cold, so as soon as sleep had sneaked up on the tired little girl, Hope took her back to Wendy and Gordon.

As she walked home alone, Hope thought about the televised transmission. It had been a tiny screen compared to the movie theatres, but the experience of sitting in one's living room and watching living pictures of something that was simultaneously happening in London was quite special. She wondered what the future would be like for Wendy's generation. So many new things were becoming available, even to people who were not rich, and she hoped that they would make life easier, not least for the women.

***

During the first half of the 1950s, rationing disappeared altogether, and more and more consumer goods became available. Salaries were rising, so that acquiring new household aids came within reach. Vacuum cleaners had replaced the need for hanging up carpets on clothes lines and beating the dust out of them with a rug beater. Refrigerators made it easier to stock food for a few days rather than shopping every single day.

Washing machines with a mangle to press the water out of the wet clothes and a spin drier to get more water out made it possible to do the washing in shorter time and with less hard work. Coal stoves had gradually become replaced by gas fires after the terrible 'Great Smog' in December 1952, which had enveloped London and stopped normal activities for several days.

Wendy had returned to school in September, and Hope went back to library work, only occasionally teaching classes when a teacher was absent. As she had promised, she did all she could to support Wendy. She often came by on Sundays and took Charlotte, as they were now all calling her, for a walk if it was not too cold outside. After Charlotte had been put to bed, she would help Wendy prepare the Sunday supper, which they all had together. Gordon's mother came on all weekdays, but only rarely on Sundays. After dinner, Hope and Wendy would do the dishes, and some evenings Hope might stay to watch the evening's programmes on the television set.

In October, the dreaded dictator of the Soviet Union, Joseph Stalin, died, giving the Eastern European countries a brief hope that the harsh Soviet domination might ease. The following year, Winston Churchill turned eighty but still refused to step down as prime minister, even though Anthony Eden was waiting in the wings and growing increasingly impatient with the old man.

Young women had begun to wear skirts with starched petticoats underneath, the more the better. Older women still wore hats, and shoes with high heels became the fashion. The first narrow slacks appeared but were considered rather provocative. Smoking cigarettes became common among men, while women took longer to develop the habit.

In the early 1950s, there had been several sensational trials against men accused of 'gross indecency' in the shape of homosexual acts, and in 1954, there were more than one thousand men in prison for such offenses. In one highly publicised case, Edward Montagu had contacted the police over a stolen camera and ended up being put in prison himself for a year for being a homosexual. Two of his friends were also imprisoned at the same time. Another famous case was that of Alan Turing who had been instrumental in Britain's winning the war by cracking the enigma code used by the Germans. He was sentenced for his homosexuality and agreed to receive hormonal treatment, and two years later, he committed suicide by biting into an apple covered with cyanide. Cases like these led to the establishment of the Wolfenden commission where three women and twelve men were asked to look into both homosexuality and prostitution in Great Britain. The chairman was John Wolfenden, vice-chancellor of the University of Reading, and

Hope followed the news about the proceedings with interest. The question of women's mutual sexual activities was never discussed, and Hope wondered why male homosexuality was so much more threatening to society than the female variety...

In the years after the Second World War, Britain made efforts to keep its colonies going, but the country was in deep financial trouble after the war. New superpowers were coming onto the world scene, such as the US and the USSR. Nationalism had grown forth all over the world, and one by one, the colonies overthrew their former overlords and shrunk the 'Empire'. Cyprus had been a crown colony since 1925, and Archbishop Makarios had become the political and spiritual leader in 1950. Never a peaceful place, trouble erupted in 1955 with bombings carried out by the Greek *enosis* proponents. Makarios was deported to the Seychelles in 1956, but the unrest continued, and in 1960, Cyprus was given independent status under the commonwealth.

The Suez Canal through which Hope had travelled as a child had become a big political issue when the Egyptian president Gamal Nasser decided to nationalise it in 1956. This led to the 'Suez Crisis' as Britain, France and Israel invaded Egypt, ostensibly to keep the peace but, in reality, to regain control of the Suez Channel. The UN under the Canadian Lester B. Pearson then created a peace-keeping force to keep war from escalating and to ensure access for all ships. A ceasefire resulted, and Britain agreed to withdraw its troops. The canal was closed for a while to clear it of sunken ships, and when it was reopened in April 1957, a UN force was set up to maintain free passage.

In the autumn of 1956, while all this was going on and holding much of the world's attention, trouble brewed in Eastern Europe. Polish unrest brought Wladyslaw Gomulka back into power, and he became First Secretary of the Central Committee. Seeing that concessions could be won from the USSR, Hungarian students also took to the streets in sympathy and to protest against repression and poverty in their own country. Péter Veres, the president of the writer's union, read out a manifesto which contained the demands of the protesters, such as independence from foreign powers, a democratic socialist system, membership of the UN and all the rights of free people. The peaceful demonstrations swelled to 200,000 people in the evening when the first secretary of the Communist Party broadcast a speech in which he denounced the protesters. In response, the crowd demolished a statue of Joseph Stalin and put Hungarian flags in his empty boots. At the same time, a large crowd had gathered in front of the Radio Budapest building, and when they got inside to broadcast their demands, they were shot at by the secret police. What had begun as a peaceful protest had now turned into an uprising, and the next day, Soviet tanks rolled into Budapest and parked in front of the Parliament, but the uprising continued with armed clashes over the next few days. The party secretary and his deputy fled to the Soviet Union, and the government fell. The popular Imre Nagy became prime minister, and when he announced a ceasefire two days later, the Soviet tanks left the city. A period of relative quiet followed while the new government decided how to handle the events, but when Nagy declared that on the first of November, Hungary would withdraw from the Warsaw Pact and become a neutral country, and when the newspapers wrote that a social democratic, multi-party state would be introduced, the Soviet leadership began to discuss how to react. Eventually, on October 31st, they decided to crack down on the uprising, and Soviet tanks and armoured vehicles moved towards Budapest. On November 4th, the Soviet again invaded Hungary, and a protest from the UN Security Council was vetoed by the Soviet Union. Part of the reason why NATO did not intervene was the fear that it might lead to a nuclear war between the USA and the Soviet Union.

Hungary resisted as best it could and appealed in vain for help over the radio, but on November 11th, the last resistance had to give up. Nagy was arrested and so were many thousands of Hungarians. About two hundred thousand people fled the country and were settled in Austrian refugee camps, while many western countries organised events to collect money for the Hungarian refugees. These events were often televised, and large amounts of money were collected to help the refugees. The communist parties in Western Europe lost many of their adherents who would not and could not stomach the bullish behaviour of the Soviets.

England received twenty thousand Hungarian refugees who were warmly welcomed as 'freedom fighters'. During the tense days in October and November, the situation in Hungary was often a topic in their conversation topics over Sunday suppers when Hope visited the Hall family. Gordon, who had been a member of the Communist Party of Great Britain, resigned in protest and instead joined the Labour Party. Wendy and Hope, who had both been sympathetic to left-wing ideas, now condemned the Soviet Union completely. They were both aware of the threat of nuclear war and Hope helped Wendy stock up supplies just in case. Deep down, they both felt a desperation that they could not really do anything to prepare, and they often talked about what was wrong with the world.

"The Americans and the Russians have the potential to destroy each other, and the rest of us will go down with them," Wendy said one day in the summer of 1957 when they were sitting on a bench near a playground watching Charlotte playing in the sandbox.

"I know," replied Hope. "We cannot really do anything about it, can we? Now that Britain and France have become atomic powers, too, Europe will be one of the first places to be targeted. I fear for Charlotte and all the other children who are growing up in this world. What kind of future are they inheriting?"

"I have wanted to join a movement against atomic weapons," said Wendy, "but the peace movements seem to be more or less organised by the Soviet Union. And having seen what happened in Poland and Hungary last year, I do not really trust the motives of the communists."

"I do not trust any of the two, Soviet or America. They are both obsessed with power, and I am afraid that power should not be entrusted to men in politics," said Hope. "When England got the bomb a few years ago and especially now when they have begun to test even stronger bombs at Christmas Island, I have given up on our own politicians, too. All this testing of nuclear bombs cannot be good for our air and water either. Not to mention the amount of money spent... I wish we could just stop all of it and find other, less dangerous ways for countries to compete..."

Wendy laughed with some bitterness, "Yes, couldn't they just play soccer or chess or compete about who could show the most love for their peoples?"

"Utopia," said Hope. "Maybe men are just too 'clever' to be satisfied with that..."

Charlotte had stopped playing in the sand and was now angrily berating a little boy. "Mummy," she cried, "he stamped on the cakes I made for you and Aunt Hope."

Wendy got up to stop what was beginning to look like a fight. Both children were now crying, and the boy's mother had come over, too. Wendy comforted Charlotte and took her back to the bench where Hope was sitting.

"You should not yell at him like that," Wendy said. "It is unbecoming for a nice little girl."

"Don't say that," Hope whispered to Wendy. "She should fight back against boys who are bullies."

"You are right," said Wendy. "I did not think, it just came out of my mouth. Isn't it amazing how often we reflexively repeat what our mothers or teachers used to say to us? I must be more careful, definitely."

Charlotte had stopped crying, and they walked home to clean her up, the world situation momentarily forgotten. They had a glass of cold milk from the new refrigerator and enjoyed its coolness on the hot summer's day. Wendy began sorting out the washing, which would be picked up by the laundry later in the afternoon.

"This is so convenient for us working mothers! Two days and it will come back clean, dry and folded. I wish they had been around when Charlotte was still in diapers."

Hope still did all her washing in a cauldron in the kitchen, but she nodded and said, "It is wonderful with all these new appliances, isn't it? I believe it is liberating for women, who will be able to spend more time outside the house and play more active roles in society."

"Yes," said Wendy, "if men will let them. We still have far too few women who are active in politics and who take up positions of leadership in society. Sometimes I wonder if it will ever change…"

"It seems to go back and forth," said Hope. "But each time we move back like now, we do not move all the way back. And each time we move forward, we seem to get a little closer to real equality. It takes a long time and the changes are incremental; we just have to be so very patient."

"It is so boring to be patient," said Wendy. "I wish there was some action to join."

***

After Britain had successfully tested the H-bomb in 1957, the fear of nuclear war was exacerbated. In November that year, J. B. Priestley had written an article in the New Statesman, which had caught Gordon's attention. It was called 'Britain and the Nuclear Bombs' and in it, Priestley argued for a unilateral decision by Britain to get rid of all its nuclear weapons. Gordon bought the periodical and brought it home to read it again and show it to Wendy, who later lent it to Hope. Priestley was worried about the growing number of so-called ultimate weapons designed to be 'the final deterrent,' which 'no men in their right minds would let loose'. He continued, 'But surely it is the wildest idealism, at the furthest remove from a sober realism, to assume that men will always behave reasonably and in line with their best interests?' Actually, he continued, the atmosphere in which such weapons were invented and built surrounded by secrecy, paid for by a public who has never said they wanted them, gave rise to 'a sinister air of somnambulism' about our major international affairs, which was drifting 'from bad to worse'. Priestley wanted Britain to 'announce as early as possible that she has done with it, that she proposes to reject, in all circumstances, nuclear warfare'.

It was a passionately and sharply written comment on the insanity of Britain, thinking that she could compete on these terms without losing the qualities of life that made her special. Many readers wrote in with comments, and a meeting between Priestley and other peace campaigners was arranged soon after. The result was the formation of the Campaign for Nuclear Disarmament, and Priestley's wife, Jacquetta Hawkes, later formed a special division for women, since she felt that now men had 'got beyond killing each other and are preparing to kill us and our children'.

Like Gordon, Hope and Wendy liked the piece very much, and the two women left Charlotte's grandmother and Gordon at home alone to look after Charlotte in February while the two of them went up to London to join the public meeting at which the Campaign for Nuclear Disarmament would be launched. Among the speakers was the philosopher Bertrand Russell, who had become the president of the campaign. The meeting was held on a Monday in the Methodist Central Hall in Westminster, and after finishing the day's teaching early, Hope and Wendy caught a train for London. When they arrived, the hall was packed, and the large crowd of people was overwhelming. The speeches were rousing, and afterwards, a few hundred participants from the meeting marched along Downing Street to protest. By then, Hope and Wendy had gone to the train station to catch the train back to Reading. Gordon had waited up for Wendy to hear everything about the meeting.

"We signed up both of us," Wendy told him. "The speeches were fine, especially the one by Bertrand Russell, but it was the overall mood that was so exhilarating. Finally, all those of us who think that Britain should stop trying to compete in the race to destroy the world have found a place to go. We can start fighting instead of just being afraid."

Gordon was slightly sceptic. "Do you really think that we can change anything? The world has gone mad, and how do you convince a bunch of lunatics to change?"

"Don't be such a pessimistic defeatist, just because communism disappointed you. Think of Charlotte. Do we want her to grow up in fear? There is a right side in this, and we should be on it, don't you think?"

"I guess so," Gordon replied, "but let us go to bed now and speak more tomorrow. Please be quiet so you do not wake up Charlotte. It took a long time to get her to fall asleep without you."

"Sorry," said Wendy. "I won't make a habit of it."

In the days that followed, they spoke more about the campaign, and Hope also helped convince Gordon that he should take part in the movement. A protest march had been organised for Easter by another

259

group called the Direct-Action Committee, and the CND ended up supporting it. The march would go from Hyde Park to Aldermaston where the British Atomic Weapons Research Establishment was, and Hope decided to go with Gordon and Wendy on the last stretch from Caversham to Aldermaston on the seventh of April. They would bring Charlotte in a pushchair.

The CND had a logo for this march, designed by Gerald Holtom who had used the semaphore signs for N and D to design the black-and-white symbol. When the party of four approached the route of the march, they could hear music and singing as thousands of people came along the road towards them carrying the CND symbol and other protests on signs for everyone to see. Some were carrying banners to show where they were from, including other European countries. It had rained the previous days, and it was miserably cold although the rain had temporarily stopped. Nevertheless, Hope, Wendy and Gordon joined the marchers while pushing Charlotte in the pushchair in front to them. Occasionally, Charlotte wanted to walk by herself, so she got out of the pushchair and trotted along. When her small legs got tired, Gordon carried her so she could have a better view. In the small towns along the route, people had come out to see what was going on, and Hope let her thoughts go back to her days as a suffragette before the First World War. She had not been to any demonstrations since then, and this one had a very different in mood. Then, the cause had been women's right to be part of deciding the country's future, a right which was finally won, though perhaps squandered during the latest war in Europe. This time, the cause was even more important, namely the survival of all living beings in their new world that had come about after the invention of weapons that had the potential to destroy everybody and everything. Hope looked around at the people she was walking among. Most of them much younger than herself, but men and women of all ages and a few children, too, were there, and her heart ached painfully for them. People were singing and shouting *'Ban the Bomb'* or *'One, two, three, four, five – keep the human race alive'* and similar chants. Skiffle bands and brass instrument played American jazz, and several people had written their own new protest songs for the occasion. Their fervour and enthusiasm were infectious despite the cold weather, and even Hope began to feel that maybe ordinary people might make a difference after all.

When they reached the facility at Aldermaston, they were stopped by the barbed wire surrounding the place, and the idea of 'tearing the bloody place down' was defeated. Instead, they stopped and spread out to hold hands outside the fence, while they kept chanting loudly.

The following year, the direction of the march was reversed so that it began at Aldermaston and ended at Trafalgar Square. There were over 4,000 people at the start, but the crowd swelled along the way, and in the end 20,000 people were assembled in Trafalgar Square. Gordon and Wendy participated again, but Hope chose to stay at home with Charlotte and Gordon's mother. Wendy had found a cause she believed passionately in, and that made her feel happier than she had in a long time.

Trip to Israel

Hope was now seventy-two years old and would stop working at the school in April. She was feeling healthy and almost regretted giving up her work, but she had decided that she would finally go to Israel to see Anna and her family in Tel Aviv in June 1959, so she began to read more about the situation there. After the new state of Israel had been declared by Ben Gurion, it had been a fragile state, surrounded by hostile Arab countries which did not want to accept the division of the land proposed by the United Nations. War had broken out almost immediately, and Hope had worried a lot about Anna's safety those first few years. Then in 1950, she had finally received a letter with Israeli stamps. Anna had written briefly that she and David were alive and well, they lived in a kibbutz, and they had a son. She hoped that Hope was well and asked her to send a letter, so that they could reconnect. Hope had reciprocated with a letter, and since then, they had corresponded several times a year. Anna and David had moved to Tel Aviv in 1958 when David had started working for a newspaper, while Anna worked at home as a translator from German and English into Hebrew. They now had four children, two boys and two girls. Both David and Anna had received military training in the kibbutz and fought to defend it several times, but after armistices with Jordan, Lebanon, Syria and Egypt in 1949, the country was opened to Jewish people from all over the world, and the population had doubled in the first three years. The many new citizens, who often came with nothing, were a heavy burden on Israel's finances, and only reparations from Germany and private donations from the USA and other western countries gradually helped to improve the situation.

Hope knew that Israel was a dangerous place under frequent border intrusions from its neighbours, but she decided to go anyway. El Al Israel had started flying from London, so she would take her first airplane trip ever. That, in itself, was daunting, but also a thrill that drew her irresistibly. Gordon and Wendy encouraged her to go and even promised to pay half her flight ticket in return for all the hours she had spent helping them. Hope bought a ticket, and Gordon and Wendy went all the way with her to the airport to say goodbye and see the flying planes up close and show them to Charlotte. Charlotte was not impressed at all but much more interested in the wooden toy plane that had been put up for children to play on. Still, Wendy managed to get her to wave happily as Hope walked out to board the airplane, a Bristol Britannia 100, which had been bought by Israel and was now part of the El Al fleet.

When the airplane lifted off and the landscape below it became smaller and smaller, Hope looked out the window with a mixture of thrill and anxiety. *How could she be up here with just a fragile wall of metal between herself and the air she was flying through?* The land dwindled and then they were flying over water, but soon, clouds were billowing around the plane, and Hope could see nothing outside until they broke through the clouds and there were only blue skies above them. Below, Hope could still see the whitish layer of clouds that looked solid enough to lie upon, and although she knew that was not the case, she could not help imagine that some of them might hold Emily and all the other people she had lost... each living in their own cloud and making profound music or discussing deep philosophical thoughts for all eternity.

Soon they got ready to land in Brussels, where they had to refuel before they continued to Rome. En route to Rome they would be served a meal, and another one between Rome and Tel Aviv, where they would arrive in the late evening. Hope settled back in her seat and decided to take a nap. The flight was smoother than a bus ride, and with the view outside rarely changing much and the drone of the plane lulling her to sleep, she soon closed her eyes and drifted off.

She woke up when a stewardess began serving their noon meal, which tasted wonderful, and she was again gripped by a feeling of wonder at the ordinariness of it all. They were now flying over the Alps, which she could see far below, the tallest tops still covered in snow. *Who had ever thought that one day she would be eating while looking at the Alps from above... like toy mountains far below. It seemed quite unreal.* Suddenly, she felt very happy that she had indeed gone on this trip despite her initial hesitation.

When they landed in Rome, she got off with the other passengers, and they spent an hour in the waiting room to stretch their legs while the airplane was being refuelled and inspected for the last leg of the journey. The woman she had sat beside all the way from London was getting off in Rome, and when they boarded again, Hope found a new passenger sitting next to her. It was an elderly gentleman with a white beard who greeted her politely in Hebrew and then in English, and Hope greeted him in return. He was carrying a small book with what she assumed was Hebrew letters on the front, and he read incessantly while moving his lips all the way until the airplane had reached flying height. Then he packed the book away in his pocket and turned to Hope.

"My name is Jacob Rosenstein, ma'am. Are you visiting Israel for the first time?" he asked in an American accent.

"Yes, I am," said Hope. "My name is Hope Maundrell, and I shall be visiting friends who live in Tel Aviv and who I have not seen in twelve years. Do you live in Israel?"

"Most of the time," said Jacob, "but I go back and forth to the States on business every few years. I came to settle here with my family in 1948 to help build the new nation. What about your friends?"

"Oh, it is a long story," said Hope, "I took in Anna into my home in 1939, when she came to London as a child from Vienna on the Kindertransport, and she lived with me for seven years while she finished school. After the war, she found out that both her parents had passed away, and she started working with Jewish refugees. She met David, and they fell in love and got married. In 1947, she and David left England and somehow got themselves safely to Israel. They lived in a kibbutz for some years before they moved to Tel Aviv, where David is now a journalist. He and Anna have four children, and Anna works as a translator from English and German into Hebrew. For a long time, I wondered what had become of them, but finally, I had a letter from Anna and we have corresponded since. In April, I stopped working and decided that I would finally visit them."

"What a story," said Jacob. "Mine is much more mundane. I grew up in New York as an orthodox Jew and had just joined the military when the Great War ended in 1918. Then after serving in the military, I went into banking with my family. We were a small family bank, so we weathered the crisis in 1929 relatively well, and when Germany began to murder Jews in the late 1930s, I joined the army again and trained as an officer. I fought in North Africa, then in Italy, and when I finally came back to New York and we began to find out what had happened to the Jews in Europe, my family and I were appalled. After Ben Gurion had established the Jewish state, we decided to move there and help to build it. My brother and his family have moved there, too. He is an architect and has helped design some of the newer buildings in Tel Aviv."

"I see," said Hope. "By the way, what were you reading when the plane was ascending?"

"The Torah," said Jacob. "We Jews have prayers for every occasion, and I was reciting the one for a safe journey."

"Oh, I see," said Hope. She did not really know what kind of Jews Anna and David were, but she hoped they would not expect her to blend in too much. "May I ask you a question?" she said to Jacob.

"Sure," said Jacob, "ask me anything, and I will try my best to answer."

"I shall be staying in a Jewish household," said Hope, "and I hardly know anything about the Jewish religion and customs. Are they going to expect me to do the correct things at specific times?"

Jacob smiled and said, "Don't worry. I am sure the people you will be staying with will be just as worried about offending you and also be very willing to explain their religious customs and traditions to you. If you are in doubt, please ask them by all means."

***

Tel Aviv was officially founded in 1909 on the sand dune north of the ancient town of Jaffa. The ambition was to create a modern and hygienic city with wide streets, pavements, open spaces and modern housing with running water and electricity. The ideal was based on Ebenezer Howard's Garden City Movement, which recommended cities built in harmony with nature. In Tel Aviv, this had been sought by laying the streets in a grid with large blocks of low domestic dwellings and with open squares and concentrations of cultural institutions as a civic centre. Tel Aviv was seen as the first Hebrew city in Palestine, and the year in which Hope visited was the city's fiftieth anniversary, 'the golden jubilee'. Despite its modern and glittering façade, the city also had slums to the south where Jaffa over time had become incorporated into Tel Aviv. Since 1950, the city was called Tel Aviv-Yafo, and the slums were inhabited by Jaffa's old population and the many new and poor immigrants. Altogether, the city had a population of around three hundred thousand people. With the establishment of the state of Israel, Tel Aviv had lost its distinction as the only Hebrew city and become an ordinary city but still a large and beautiful one with a proud heritage.

The airplane landed in darkness in Lod Airport, and when they came into the arrival hall, Hope immediately caught sight of Anna waiting for her at the front of a small crowd of people. She was a little broader over the hips than Hope remembered, much more sun-tanned and looked to be thriving. Anna called out to her and after being checked by customs and showing her travel papers, she was let through, and Anna threw her strong arms around her and exclaimed, "Aunty Hope, I am so glad to see you!" Hope held her tight and remembered the shy and skinny young girl she had fetched from the summer camp in Dovercourt Bay together with Sarah twenty years ago. She felt tears coming to her eyes.

"Oh, Anna," she whispered, "I never thought I would see you again…"

Outside, Anna found their chauffeur, one of their friends who had access to a car and had offered to drive for them. They put Hope's trunk in the back and set off towards the city, and after about forty minutes, they arrived at the house where Anna lived with her family. The children were already in bed, but David was waiting up for them and was outside the house to help them inside with their luggage. They thanked the driver, who drove off, and then they went inside into what seemed to be a rather big house. On the doorpost hung what Hope knew was called a 'mezuzah,' and she noticed that both Anna and David briefly rested their hand on it as they entered the house.

"Are you hungry?" asked Anna, but Hope shook her head and asked for a cup of tea instead. David went out and soon came back with mugs of hot, sweet tea for all of them. As soon as they had finished their tea and asked about Hope's trip, Anna took Hope to her room where a freshly made up bed was waiting for her.

"The bathroom is the first door on your left," explained Anna, "and David and I sleep upstairs, so please don't hesitate to wake us up if you need any help. Otherwise, we will talk tomorrow. Sleep tight, Aunt Hope."

"Good night, Anna," said Hope and took out her nightgown from her trunk and went to the bathroom to brush her teeth. Back in her room, she changed into her nightgown and crept to bed, falling asleep immediately.

***

The next morning when Hope woke up, she wondered for a few seconds where she was, but then it all came back, and she realised that she was now in Israel, of all places. She went to the bathroom first, and then she returned to her room to get dressed for the day. She could hear children's voices in the kitchen, speaking a language she expected must be Hebrew. When she was dressed and had combed her grey hair, she ventured out of her room and into the living room, where Anna heard her and came to take her to the breakfast table in the kitchen. She was seated, and Anna brought her a mug of tea and then introduced her children.

"Aunt Hope, this is Akiva, our oldest—he is off to school in a minute."

"Good morning, Aunt Hope," said Akiva in English.

"Good morning, Akiva. Can you speak English?"

"Yes," replied Akiva, "we all can, but we speak Hebrew in school and among ourselves."

Anna indicated the three other children. "Esther is six and has just started school. Akiva will take her with him. Then there is Hannah, who is four and will be picked up for kindergarten by bus soon, and Moshe here is only two, so we shall have to take him to the nursery nearby at 9 o'clock. David left for work an hour ago and will be back tonight. Today is Wednesday, and I shall take a few hours to show you around Tel Aviv and we can talk!"

She put a glass of freshly squeezed orange juice in front of Hope and some bread, cheese and jam. Hope thanked her and began to eat. The bread was freshly baked, and Hope asked Anna if she had baked it this morning.

"We bake fresh bread every day except on Shabbat, and we try to make most of our food by ourselves. The oranges and the jam we get from a kibbutz just south of the city, the butter is also made in Israel, and if you would like some eggs, I can get them from our own hens. We shall probably give up having hens, but only when the children grow a little older."

"It is the most delicious breakfast I have had in a long time," said Hope, "but I wonder how you have time for all that when you also have your work."

"It is all a matter of routine," said Anna. "I prepare the dough every evening before I go to bed, and in the morning, I put it in the oven. While it bakes, I feed the hens, gather the eggs, squeeze the oranges so everything is ready when David and the children wake up. When they are all out of the house, except Moshe, I clean everything away, and every Friday, we all help clean the house and prepare the Shabbat food. When I have taken Moshe to the nursery, I have time for my work. And sometimes I work in the evenings as well when I have a deadline."

"That sounds admirably efficient," said Hope.

"Please enjoy your breakfast while I get the children off," said Anna. "I will make you some coffee in a little while."

Hope was left in the kitchen with Moshe, who was looking at her in alarm from his high chair.

"Don't worry, Moshe," said Hope. "I will look after you." She found a few toys on the floor and gave them to him to play with, and she succeeded in getting a smile from him. Soon, Anna was back and prepared them both some hot coffee, and then she sat down with Hope to drink it.

"Is there anywhere in particular you would like to go today?" she asked.

"Everything is new to me, so I would just like to stroll around town, if you do not mind," said Hope. "I am not as young and strong as I used to be, but I would like to learn more about what your life is like and what living in Israel entails. I get the impression from what I have read that it can be quite dangerous now and then. But mostly I would like to know about your life and how you have been doing since we were last together."

"Fine," said Anna. "So let me clear the things away while I explain, and then we will walk to the nursery and leave Moshe there. After that, we can walk to the Dizengoff Street and sit at one of the cafés and talk. You must also tell me about what has happened in your life, Aunty Hope."

Anna got up and began to clear the breakfast things away while she talked.

"David and I got into Israel about nine months after we left England. It was not easy because the British were blockading the coast, so we lived for a while in a camp in Cyprus. But finally, we were allowed entry and David fought with the Irgun for a few months until we became a state in 1948. We had both become members of a kibbutz where we received military training, and we both helped fight the Arabs until the ceasefire. Then we returned to the kibbutz and helped turn the desert into fertile soil. I became pregnant with Akiva in 1948, and David began to write articles, which he got printed in some newspapers. In 1951, Esther arrived, and in 1955, we moved to Tel Aviv with Akiva and Esther, so he could write about all the things that were going on with the Suez Canal. I was always good with languages, and I got a freelance job translating official papers from Hebrew into German or English or vice versa. When there was nothing else to do, I also translated some English poetry and short stories into Hebrew, and now I am getting more requests than I can handle. Hannah was born in 1955 and Moshe in 1956, so I did not accept as much work for a few years, but it is picking up again. When they both get old enough to be in school, I am planning to start a translation bureau and hire more translators…"

Anna trailed off.

"I think you are magnificent, and I think your bureau will be a success. It makes my heart glad to hear that you have both survived so well. Especially you, who have experienced so many hardships in your life."

"Well," said Anna, "you have no small part in my survival, you know."

She grabbed Moshe out of his high chair and took him upstairs to get him changed and dressed for the nursery. Moshe had begun to complain in a mixture of Hebrew and English, but Anna soothed him by talking to him in Hebrew and carried him upstairs. Twenty minutes later, they were ready to go out with Moshe and deliver him to his private nursery three doors down the street.

When they left the nursery, Anna told Hope that when they lived in the kibbutz, the children had stayed in a separate 'Children's House' and parents only spent a few hours with them every day. "Both Akiva and Esther started their life that way, and I think it was fine for them. But when I was expecting Hannah and we got the chance to move to the city, we decided to leave the kibbutz and live a more individual life in the city. It was quite hard to leave the kibbutz and all our friends, but for David and me, it was also liberating to live on our own."

"The kibbutz sounds rather like communism to me," said Hope.

"I would say 'socialist'," said Anna. "It really is not about politics or revolution, but only about working together and living in harmony. Of course, there were external enemies who would attack us several times, but all in all, we managed to defend ourselves reasonably well."

"I wonder if humanity will ever be able to live in peace," sighed Hope.

"I don't think so," said Anna. "There will always be struggle everywhere humans live. We will always covet what our neighbours have, even if it is just a productive and peaceful existence, and therefore, we must always be prepared to defend such an existence, or it will be taken away from us."

Hope could see how the people of Israel had to feel that way. They had been a dispersed and persecuted minority, and now that they finally had a nation of their own, they had to keep it that way at all costs.

They had reached the Dizengoff Street.

"It was named after Tel Aviv's first mayor, Meir Dizengoff, in 1934 when he was still alive. Come," said Anna, "I will show you where our first department store will open in September, and then we shall walk along to sit in a café and watch all the people pass by."

Hope was quite impressed by the many fine shops along Dizengoff Street, but she felt no inclination to buy anything. The coffee house that Anna took her to afterwards actually impressed her more. The Café Kassit had opened in 1946 and was very European in style. It reminded her of the bohemian cafés she had visited in Paris with Emily in 1930, noisy and thronged with mostly younger people engaged in lively discussions or sitting alone engrossed in a book. Several languages were spoken at the various tables. She and Anna each ordered a cup of coffee and sat down outside where they could watch the passers-by.

"I think this is the closest you get to European style," said Anna.

"I can see and hear that," said Hope. "I suppose most of the people here speak Hebrew, but I can hear other languages, too, which I cannot place."

"Great efforts have been made to make Hebrew the official language here," said Anna. "I was told that there was a time when the city officials would only deal with letters in Hebrew. If you had written to them in any other language, they would return your letter with a polite note asking you to submit it in Hebrew instead. The German language was very unpopular, which was hard for the German refugees who had moved here in the early 1930s. For David and me it was easier, because we had both studied Hebrew before we left England, and we really wanted to speak it, so after a couple of years, it became natural for us to speak Hebrew at home, too."

"You have three languages that you can speak and write fluently. I am impressed," said Hope. "I know only English fluently, and the French I once read and spoke with ease has really become quite rusty."

"It is because so many people all over the world have had to learn English, because you had so many colonies," said Anna. "You never needed any other language. In Israel, there are many people who can speak three or four languages or even more. We are a small country made up of people from many countries, and everybody speaks at least one language besides Hebrew." She laughed, "I think it is more uncommon to meet people who know only one language, actually."

"I guess you are right," said Hope. "If your mother tongue is English, there is really no need to know other languages. People born in Britain or America, who leave their home country, arrogantly expect everyone else to speak at least some English…"

"Would you like to stroll along the street and look at some of the shops?" asked Anna. "I also have a bit of shopping to do for our supper today."

"I would like that very much," said Hope. "If I can find some small presents for my friends, that would be very nice too."

"We will look at the street vendors to see if you can find something there. Many artisans sell their goods here, so it is the best place for finding souvenirs."

Hope ended up buying a cuddly toy cow for Charlotte with the word KOSHER written on its stomach and with all four legs splayed outwards in the likeness of a teddy bear. Then they bought some vegetables and spices from the supermarket in Ben Yehuda Street before going to buy meat at the butcher's.

When they got back home, Hope sat in a reclining chair on the veranda and took a little nap in the shade. It was a hot day, and she soon sought shelter inside the house and sought out Anna, who was sitting at the kitchen table working. She looked up when Hope came in and asked her if she had rested a little.

"Certainly," replied Hope. "I actually took a little nap on the veranda under the pergola. Everything is so peaceful, and your garden is really nice."

"We do not really have the energy for gardening," said Anna, "but the sycamore and the acacia were here when we moved in, and David planted the eucalyptus when Hannah was born. We have tried planting a lawn, but it is hard to keep it looking nice here. We have the potted plants on the veranda which need watering every day; they make the air smell nice, don't you think?"

"Yes," said Hope. "What is winter like here?"

"It usually rains some of the time," said Anna, "and it can get quite cool. We even had some snow nine years ago, but that was a rare event. We have no spring and autumn like we had in England. I sometimes miss that, you know. But let's go down to the beach and have a look at the Mediterranean before we go and pick up Moshe."

While they were walking towards the beach, Anna told Hope that there would be an election later that year.

"We all expect Ben Gurion to continue as our prime minister for some years. Did you know that he is about your age?"

"Is he really," said Hope. "I guess I thought he was a bit younger. He seems so energetic."

"I think he was born a year before you," Anna said. "I admire him so much for founding Israel and fighting so hard to maintain it in face of all difficulties."

"I can see that he must be a very special person," said Hope.

Now they could see the ocean with the promenade, which Anna called the Tayelet and the sandy coast in front.

"It is really beautiful," said Hope. "Do you take the children here to swim and play?"

"Well, yes, now and then," said Anna, "but not too often, because the Yarkon river empties into the sea and the water gets more and more dirty from industrial waste, and sewers from the city also empty directly into the sea. I do not think the sanitary conditions are quite healthy. Tel Aviv-Yafo is the largest city in Israel, and only ten years ago, the beaches were closed for a time because of the unhealthy conditions. I worry that it has not really gotten much better, and David says that the country will need to do more soon, both to clean up our sea and make sure that we not destroy our fresh water resources from the rivers."

"Oh, I see," said Hope. "Everything looks so nice and green that I keep forgetting that most of Israel is actually desert, and water must be scarce."

"Indeed," said Anna, "and our population is growing very fast with all the immigrants from the rest of the world. Of course, that is a good thing, because we need the people, but it also means that our resources are stretched somewhat."

They walked along the promenade for a little while and then turned when the time had come to pick up Moshe and get home before the rest of the children arrived.

***

The next few days passed in pleasant relaxation, and Hope helped out wherever she could. On Friday, David and the children came back early, and Anna put them all to work cleaning the house and grounds. After they finished, they all bathed and dressed in their best clothes. Hope did the same. Just before the sun set, they all gathered by the dinner table, and David said a short prayer in Hebrew before Anna lit the two candles on the table. Everybody circled their hands three times before their face and recited yet another prayer. Then they sat down and began to eat the delicious Shabbat dinner that Anna had prepared, and the adults drank wine. The children were talking in Hebrew, while David and Anna stuck mostly to English for Hope's sake.

"We are not very observant Jews," said David, "but I have always liked the Shabbat since I was a child, and in the kibbutz, we learned to like it even more. Besides, it is something we want the children to carry on with when they grow up."

Anna continued, "Tomorrow morning, David will walk to the synagogue with Akiva, but I will stay here with the other three to play games and sing. Then we eat lunch and relax in the afternoon, take a nap and go for a walk or visit with friends until the sun goes down, and then we eat the third meal of the Shabbat, say a prayer and that is it. Twenty-five hours of rest and restitution, I cannot help but think that it is both mentally and physically healthy to have one day every week with special rituals and peace and gratitude in your heart."

"It is not unlike what we used to have on Sundays when I was a child. There were not as many rules as you seem to have, but I remember my eldest sister telling me about Sundays in the mission. The family would read from the Bible and go to church. The children had Sunday school and were expected not to be too noisy the rest of the day. In the evenings, there would be more reading from the bible… from what I remember,

Sundays could be pretty boring for children. Going to church was actually the best part of it."

"Well, now you get to experience a Jewish Shabbat," said Anna, "but of course, you are free to do whatever you like, since you are not Jewish."

"No, no," said Hope. "I am here to learn, so I will do what you do as best I can."

In the morning, they all had a light breakfast before David and Akiva left for the synagogue. Anna got the children ready, and they all gathered in the living room to sing. Esther and Hannah already knew the songs, and Moshe clapped his little hands, mostly in time to the music. Then Anna got out a board game called 'Ludo' and Hannah and Esther chose a colour each, leaving yellow and green for Hope and Anna.

"Now, as long as we play Ludo, everyone must speak English," said Anna. "Is that all right?" Esther and Hannah both promised that they would speak English only, and Anna promised them a story afterwards if they did well. Moshe sat in his high chair and followed what they did. He wanted to grab the pretty tokens, but Anna gave him some toys to play with, so he would not ruin the game for the other children.

"Mom, will you move my tokens for me, so I do not get them wrong," Hannah said.

"I will help you get them right," said Hope quickly and smiled at Hannah.

Then the game started, and Esther was the first to get a token home. The others soon followed, and in the end, the game was won by Hannah, who was very proud.

Just when they had finished the game and Hope had packed it away, David and Akiva returned from the synagogue.

The lunch meal had been prepared the day before, because cooking is one of the things you cannot do on the Shabbat. It was a leisurely meal and after it was ended, the children had a long nap, and so did Anna and David. Hope sat down to read, and in the end, she, too, nodded off for a few minutes.

After everybody had finished napping, Hope kept Anna's promise of reading a story for all the children if they remembered to speak English during the earlier game of Ludo. She had brought them a gift, namely A. A. Milne's 'Winnie the Pooh', which was her own favourite children's book: 'Here is Edward Bear, coming downstairs now, bump, bump, bump, on the back of his head, behind Christopher Robin.' Hope showed the children the picture in the book of Christopher Robin dragging his teddy bear downstairs by holding on to one of his legs.

"Bump, bump, bump," said Hannah with delight, and Moshe echoed her, "Bum, bum, bum." Hope's reading was excellent and all the children, including Moshe, were listening to the tale. Meanwhile, Anna had come down from her nap and also sat down to listen. She remembered the story; it was one of the first stories Hope had read to her in England while she was still struggling with the English language, and later, she had read it by herself.

Hope read the first three chapters of the book and then gave it to Anna, so she could read the rest when Hope had returned to England.

They all got ready for an afternoon walk with Moshe in a pushchair, Akiva pushing him. The two girls with their light brown curly hair wore identical summer dresses which Anna had made for them from the same cloth that she had used for her own skirt. Hannah was holding her mother's hand and Anna had put her other arm through Hopes. Esther was walking with David's hand in hers next to Akiva. They ended up by the sea before they turned back, and on the way, they greeted several neighbours and friends and introduced them to Hope.

In the evening, they ate a light meal, and then the Shabbat ended with a cup of wine and the lighting of the braided *havdalah* candle with two wicks while David intoned the blessings, '*Baruch atah Adonai…*' and in between, Anna and the children all chorused their 'amen'. Then the candle was extinguished in a bit of wine poured on a plate, and everybody wished each other a good week by saying '*shavua' tov*'.

***

After the children had been sent to bed, Anna asked Hope whether she would like to come with her and a friend on a trip to Old Jaffa the next day and see something of the ancient Israel. Her friend had moved here from Denmark two years ago, and since David would be home early from work on Monday and could look after the children, they would be able to stay out late. Hope agreed enthusiastically, and Anna told her that her friend Deena was still learning Hebrew, but she spoke excellent English. "How far is it?" asked Hope.

"Just a short bus ride," answered Anna, "but it will seem a world apart from Tel Aviv. It is so ancient that some claim it was named after Noah's youngest son, Yafet.

"Our friends are called Lars and Deena, and they have recently moved here to Tel Aviv. They have no children yet, so Deena is free and will take a pause from weaving. You met her husband, Lars, who drove us from the airport the day you arrived, and Deena is coming by

273

tomorrow to pick us up and meet you. They are both learning Hebrew, but they speak very good English as well."

Hope met Deena on Sunday morning and found her easy to talk to. She was about Wendy's age, and it turned out that she was a professional weaver and made carpets and wall decorations, which she sold through Scandinavian dealers. Lars, her husband, was a journalist like David.

When they had taken Moshe to the day-care centre, they caught a bus for Jaffa. On the way, Hope asked Deena about Denmark. She had never been there and wanted to know what it was like.

"Beautiful in spring and summer, but rather cold in winter," said Deena. "It is flat or hilly, with no real mountains, which is very good for agriculture. Both Lars and I spent some years as children in Sweden, because Denmark was occupied by Nazi Germany. In October 1943, the Germans started to round up the Jews in Denmark, so we had to get away. Some Danish fishermen took us in their boats and made sure we reached the safety of Sweden, which was a neutral country."

"Then you came back to Denmark when the war was over?" Hope asked.

"Yes," said Deena, "and then after we had finished our education, we both decided to spend some weeks in a kibbutz growing oranges, and after we came back to Denmark, we got married and we worked for a few years in Copenhagen before we decided to come to Israel in 1957. We felt that we wanted to live among other Jews in our daily life, and also that we might be able to accomplish more here than we ever would in Denmark and so we decided to emigrate."

"I see," said Hope. "I think that was a brave decision. But do you not miss your families back in Denmark?"

"Occasionally," admitted Deena, "but they come to visit at least once a year, or we go back to see them. Who knows, my younger sister may move down here, too, and when we have children, they will grow up as *sabra*, strong native-born Israelis who will defend their homeland."

Hope had heard the word *sabra* before and recognised the distinction between the tough pioneers who had been here to create the state of Israel and fight the war that ensued and those who had suffered in Europe without being able to defend themselves. She understood that many Jews were determined never to be victims again… and she wondered how many lives might still be lost before that goal was achieved.

The bus let them off by the clock tower near the harbour. Hope could immediately see that it was indeed worlds (or maybe rather ages) apart from Tel Aviv. Everything was more old and dirtier than in Tel Aviv but also more real, somehow. Anna pointed to the harbour and said that it had been a natural harbour in ancient times where the cedars of Lebanon had been brought in for David and Solomon to build the first temple in Jerusalem.

In 1799, the French under Napoleon had ransacked the city and killed many of its inhabitants and massacred thousands of Moslem soldiers who had surrendered to him. During the First World War, Jaffa and the rest of Palestine came under British rule, and tensions between Jews and Arabs began to escalate in the 1920s. That was one of the main reasons why some Jews had decided to establish Tel Aviv. In the late 1930s, there were bloody Arab riots against the British, and the British forces demolished a large number of buildings. After the war ended in 1945, Jaffa had a mixed population of Arabs, Jews and Greek Orthodox Christians, and when Israel was established in 1948, many of the Arab inhabitants had fled.

"I have been told that it was a very troubled time," said Anna, "but eventually, the two cities were unified as Tel Aviv-Yafo. Now, if we somehow get separated, let us find each other again here by this clock tower before 5 o'clock."

Both Deena and Anna looked rather doubtfully at her and each took one of her arms.

"We will not get separated," said Hope. "I will hold on to you!"

"First, let us go to the flea market," said Anna. "We call it 'Shuk HaPish Pushim'. Did you know that, Deena?"

"Yes," said Deena, "it must have been among the first one hundred words I learned…"

They crossed the street and went up one of the narrow streets and noticed the remnants of the old city walls, which had never been rebuilt after being destroyed in an earthquake in 1836. They turned right at the Russian Street and saw the Jaffa Mosque across from the great fountain called Tabitha's well, intended to refresh travellers on their way to Jerusalem. The mosque was closed, so they went on further upwards and soon got lost in the narrow winding alleyways that housed the flea market. They found great variety of goods, clothes, lamps, rugs and various bric-a-brac for sale, some of it possibly real antiques, but they did not have the expertise to tell. They mostly looked without buying unless they found something they really liked. Deena haggled a bit over a nice brass lamp but soon gave up. Hope found a beautiful metal tray and asked Anna to ask the shopkeeper for the price. It was not too much for her budget and she decided to buy it when Anna had haggled the price down to about half what the trader had originally asked.

They stopped at a Jewish bakery and bought some delicious-looking cakes, and then they found a nice outdoor café, where they could sit down and have some coffee. They had all brought a bottle of water each to keep from dehydrating in the heat.

"It is so different from Tel Aviv," said Hope.

"Yes, indeed," said Anna. "I am glad we live in Tel Aviv, but I am also glad that such an old and 'lived-in' city is so close by. Here one is really reminded of how ancient the Jewish history is and how much it has been one of turmoil and pain."

"Still, we have survived so far and kept many of our traditions intact," added Deena, "and I think we will continue to do so."

"Amen!" said Hope. She liked what she had seen so far of Jewish customs and traditions, and while she felt deeply sad and troubled by the holocaust the German Nazis had perpetrated, it made her glad to see how the surviving Jews had come together with such a strong determination to create a new homeland. She fervently wished them a peaceful future while at the same time thinking of how much the odds were against their success.

That evening, after they had returned to Tel Aviv, Lars had come over to keep them all company for supper. The children were happy to see their mother back home, and they all had an enjoyable supper together. After the children had been put to bed, the adults talked about the upcoming election in November. The number of parties running for places in the Knesset seemed completely staggering to Hope, who was used to only two parties to choose from on election days, so she asked about it. David explained that although almost everyone could win representation in the Knesset and make sure their voices could be heard, but governments had to be formed by the largest party in coalition with other parties.

"Right now, Ben Gurion's party *Mapai* leads a large coalition of parties, and I think it will be more or less the same after the election. Israel has come together as a nation consisting of people from all over the world, and there are many special interests who want their own political party. Some are more religious than others, some more socialist, others more conservative, and all are very stubborn in their view on how Israel should move forward. New parties come up while others disappear, so it can be very confusing for newcomers.

"When Israel was proclaimed in 1948, a war broke out with the Arabs and many of them fled Israel and never returned. Instead, we received a great number of Jewish immigrants settling. Ever since, Israel's biggest problems have been how to make the economy grow to take care of all these new people of different backgrounds and at the same time, how to keep our defences strong against our neighbouring countries by creating a national and religious identity backed by a strong defence force."

"I think you are all doing very well," said Hope. "The war was traumatic for all of us, but especially for the Jews. I am glad I came here to see Anna and David and got to see how well Israel is doing. I think I understand a little more of what is happening than I did before. But now you must excuse me, it has been quite an exhausting day for an old woman, and I shall withdraw." She bade everybody goodnight and went to bed.

The next couple of days were tranquil, and soon, the day of Hope's return was upon them. Deena had offered to drive her to the airport, so Hope said goodbye to all the children and David the evening before. Anna went with her and Deena to the airport, and while Deena waited outside, Anna went in with Hope. They both had tears in their eyes when they said goodbye, and they promised to write letters to each other as often as they could.

***

Back in Caversham, Hope invited Wendy and Gordon with Charlotte for tea on Sunday afternoon. She would tell them all about her trip and show them the pictures she had gotten back from the photo shop. It was the first time she had brought a camera on a trip, and she was rather surprised that the pictures had turned out as well as they had.

It was a hot summer's day, so Hope had set up her table in the yard with the new garden chairs around it. She put the tea things on a tray and took it outside before Wendy and her family arrived.

"Hi, Auntie Hope," said Charlotte, and Wendy and Gordon followed by wishing her welcome home.

"Haven't you just got a nice sun tan," commented Wendy. "I get quite envious. Today is the first day since you went away that it has not rained."

"We should be glad that we get so much rain," said Hope. "My friends told me that water shortage is one of their country's big problems."

"Well," Gordon said, "they can certainly have some of ours. We get entirely too much of it, I think."

"Come out and sit in the yard," Hope said. "I have prepared some sandwiches and cake, and the tea will be ready in a minute." She went to the kitchen and came out a few minutes later with the teapot and milk on the metal tray she had bought in Israel.

Wendy noticed it at once. "What a beautiful tray! Did you get that in Israel?"

"Yes, I bought it on a trip to the Jaffa Flea Market, and Anna helped me bargain it down to half the price. I bought a little thing for you, too, Charlotte, perhaps a little too childish for you, but at least it is from Israel." She handed Charlotte the package, which she had put in her knitting basket, and Charlotte began to tear off the paper. Hope poured tea for everybody and served sugar and milk, which she stirred with a teaspoon. Charlotte showed her mother and father the new cow toy and read the word on its stomach, kosher.

"What is 'kosher', Mummy? she asked, and Hope answered her, "Kosher actually means 'pure' or 'clean', and it is used about food that has been prepared in the ritual way that Jews must follow. There are a lot of rules about food and daily life that one must follow as a proper Jew."

"Why?" asked Charlotte.

"Let us talk about that later," said Gordon. "Now let us hear about Aunt Hope's trip. How did you like going on the airplane?"

"Yes, weren't you frightened?" asked Wendy, who had never been on an airplane either.

"It was quite a thrill to leave the earth behind when we ascended, dizzying and hard to believe that we were really flying through the air. But once we levelled out, there was only the blue sky, and it felt rather like riding a bus. I even fell asleep part of the way. We had several stopovers before we reached Tel Aviv, and it was dark when we landed, so I couldn't see much. My friends picked me up at the airport and we went to their house. They live in a very nice two-storied villa with their four children—let me show you a picture of it."

She showed them a picture of Anna and her family all standing in front of the house. "This is Anna and her husband, David," she said. "Anna is holding the baby, Moshe, and the children in front of her are from the left Akiva, Esther and Hannah. Esther is the same age as you, Charlotte."

"It must be cool to have sisters and brothers," said Charlotte.

Wendy laughed a little and said, "You would have to share everything with them, and there would be much less for you, honey."

Hope told them about Tel Aviv and Jaffa and the difference between them, and she showed them pictures of Jaffa's narrow streets and of the lovely coast and views of the Mediterranean Sea. She told them about the Shabbat she had participated in and the rules they had had to observed. Charlotte, who was listening intently, again asked a question again.

"Are the children allowed to play on that day you mentioned, Auntie?"

"Oh, yes," Hope answered. "They can play all they want. It is only work that is not allowed, so the parents play or go for walks with their children."

"Is school work and studying allowed?"

"No," replied Hope. "It is supposed to be a break from all the things you do on ordinary days."

"I think I want to go there," said Charlotte wistfully.

"It looks like a wonderful city," said Wendy. "I hope we shall have a chance to travel abroad in the future. We are actually thinking of buying a car this autumn and get driver's licenses for each of us. Who knows, we might even buy a tent and go camping. More and more people do that, don't they?"

"I am getting too old to sleep on the ground," Hope said, "but I am sure it is a great way for younger people like you to spend their holidays. And much cheaper than staying in hotels and pensions."

"We would be able to go to official camp sites, where there are toilets and showers and even small shops where one can buy oil for one's primus and other things," said Wendy.

"That sounds nice," Hope smiled. "You should do that."

Part Eight
The 1960s

Affluence

In 1960, Gordon and Wendy bought their first car, a used Morris in a bright blue colour. It could comfortably sit a family of four, so Hope was often included on their trips to the countryside that summer. Wendy and Gordon were gradually getting used to driving and had decided to take their first camping trip around England the following year. They had bought a folding table with room for four canvas stools inside, and they found a trunk that held a complete set of Melmac service for four people with cutlery. Finally, they had a small primus stove to heat water for tea or meals. With this, they went exploring the countryside in all directions.

Gordon and Wendy still participated in the anti-nuclear marches from Aldermaston to London, and in 1960, there were more than 60,000 protesters gathered in London. More and more former colonies gained independence from the United Kingdom, and in a reflection of that fact, *The Times of London* stopped using the term 'Imperial and Foreign News,' changing instead to 'Overseas News'. The 1960s seemed a relatively peaceful time in Caversham, but in London, many things were changing. For a while, 'Swinging London' became the capital of chic, dominated by teenagers and tourists shopping in Carnaby Street and the broad thoroughfares nearby. Rock 'n Roll music had gained attention already in the 1950s, but in the sixties, it became the music of the teenagers. In 1961, John F. Kennedy became the president of the United States, the first Catholic to ever hold that position, and he seemed young and charismatic with his beautiful wife, Jacqueline, and their two small children. Even when the Soviets built a wall through Berlin in 1961 to keep the East Germans from escaping into the Western sector of the city, and again in 1962, when the cold war almost turned hot and brought the world to the brink of a nuclear war over Cuba, Kennedy's popularity grew all over the Western world.

Hope and Wendy were as worried and frightened as everyone else during the Cuban missile crisis, and although Wendy was trying to be reassuring both to her students in school and at home with Charlotte, she could not quite hide her fear. To Hope, she poured it all out when she came by almost every afternoon during the week and a half until the crisis was resolved and the Russian ships carrying missiles to Cuba were reported to have turned back.

The winter between 1962 and 1963 seemed to be the coldest ever in anyone's memory. Huge amounts of snow fell, and lakes and rivers froze over. Schools closed, and power lines came down in many places. In March, the snow began to thaw and turn into melt water, which brought its own problems, and things did not really become normal until May.

The awareness that the world was now capable of destroying itself completely several times over and in a very short time had been sobering. If all the nuclear weapons were fired in a brief moment of panic, no life would be left on earth… Hope thought of the apocalypse she had learned about as a child… that would, at least, perhaps, have an all-knowing God to oversee it all. *The nuclear apocalypse would be caused by sheer human stupidity, vanity and—what should one call it?* She struggled for a word to describe the absurdity and lunacy of it all, but there was no word strong enough.

They were almost giddy with relief when the Cuban crisis was over. Both Kennedy and Khrushchev gained in popularity for their ability to solve the crisis, but at the same time, seeds of anger were sown, especially among the young. They had accepted the fact that a nuclear war might well happen in their lifetime, and they had been taught to seek the nearest cover to protect themselves, but in the face of the near and present danger of the possible reality of it, many recognised that crawling under a table could not save them.

Hope lived a quiet life, reading books and listening to the radio. Occasionally, she would come by Gordon's and Wendy's house and watch television with them or simply sit with Charlotte if her parents were going out. Gordon's mother had died the year after Hope had visited Tel Aviv, so Hope had gradually taken the place of the trusty old grandmother who could always be depended on to babysit. In 1963, Charlotte was ten years old, so the role of babysitter had mostly become one of just being there for reassurance.

On Friday November 22, 1963, Hope was there alone with Charlotte and was listening to the news on the radio. The six o'clock news came and went, and then they had a light supper. Afterwards, Hope began to clear away the supper things so that she could sit down with Charlotte and help her with her homework if needed. The radio was still on, and just as Hope got up to turn it off, a news flash broke into the programming.

"News has just come in that President Kennedy has been shot…"

They both sat down stunned and listened while they were told that the American president had been visiting Dallas in Texas and riding in a motorcade, and then someone had shot him.

"How could they?" asked Charlotte. "Who would do such a thing?"

Hope put her arms around Charlotte's shoulders and did not answer for a while. Then the teacher in her reasserted itself, and she began.

"America is very different from England, you know. Presidents have been assassinated before and probably will be in the future. It is a young nation where weapons are easily accessible to anyone and where social and racial problems are abundant. Their presidents are generally very well protected by the secret service, and I do not know what went so terribly wrong today."

"Can we keep the radio on?" asked Charlotte. "I would like to hear if there are any more news about Mr Kennedy."

"We can keep listening for a little while, but then you must go to bed. You need your sleep, dear."

Soon after, the radio confirmed that the young American president was dead and the vice-president, Lyndon Johnson, had been sworn in as the new president. The usual programming had been stopped and mournful music was broadcast instead. Charlotte had reluctantly gone to bed, and Hope sat alone and thought about all the changes that were happening so rapidly in the world. She felt more than a little detached, an observer who would no longer influence anything. *Bad things were definitely happening like tonight's events in America, but good things were happening, too. Gut-wrenching, desperate poverty seemed to be a thing of the past in Britain, where everyday living had become so much easier and affordable. The young people were asserting themselves and no longer seemed to be tamed and harnessed by religion and old customs. They were beginning to think for themselves… no, they had probably always done so, but now they were speaking out as well, weren't they? The music that seemed so important to them was a little like the jazz she and Emily had discovered in Paris in 1930, wasn't it? Some of it wasn't all that bad like the American singer, Ray Charles, for instance—or even some of Elvis Presley's songs. But this shooting in Dallas, what did it portend?*

She heard Gordon and Wendy by the door, and as they came into the living room, she could see that Wendy was visibly upset. She went over to her and hugged her. "You have already heard," she said.

"Yes," answered Wendy. "They shot Kennedy. It is a terrible thing."

"Charlotte and I heard it on the radio, so we sat up a little longer before I put her to bed. Let me get us a cup of tea," said Hope and went to the kitchen.

When they all sat with a mug of strong tea with lots of sugar and milk, Gordon said that their party had broken up when the news spread a little after seven o'clock.

"First, we all gathered in front of the television set or in the kitchen, where the radio was on. After it was announced that he had passed away, nobody seemed in the mood to continue, and little by little, everyone made their excuses and left."

"It was such a shock," said Wendy, "and his poor wife and the two small children. It doesn't bear thinking about."

"Just now that things seemed to go well after the scare last year," said Hope.

Soon, she got her things together, and Gordon walked her to her house, where they said goodbye.

***

Early in 1964, the trials of the men who had been caught after the great train robbery in 1963 began. Only a small part of the 2.6 million pounds sterling was recovered, and the men found guilty got long prison sentences. When the BBC started a new broadcasting channel, Hope finally bought herself a small television set for her living room. She now had both her daily newspaper, the radio and the TV to keep her occupied and informed. Wendy and Charlotte dropped by at least once a week and Hope enjoyed surprising Charlotte by being well versed in the newest music and fashions.

In October, the Labour Party defeated the conservatives, and Harold Wilson became the new prime minister. The death penalty was finally abolished like in most European countries after the Second World War. In January 1965, Sir Winston Churchill died at the age of ninety and was given a state funeral. Hope could not help thinking about her siblings. Sarah and William had been older than Churchill, but most of her siblings had been close to Churchill in age, and they had all died years ago. In fact, Hope herself was only twelve years younger than Churchill, but still, his death made her think of her own as she watched the funeral on TV. It was a magnificent funeral with representatives from 110 countries paying him a last salute by attending, and crowds had lined up despite the cold to wait for hours to catch a glimpse of his casket covered in the Union Jack.

In the early 1960s, young women's skirts had been creeping up above the knees, and in 1965, Mary Quant began selling very short skirts in her shop on King's Street in London. She named them miniskirts, and they soon caught on. Women liked the freedom of movement, and men liked seeing the shapely legs of young women in the streets. Schoolgirls in uniforms hiked up their shirts as much as they could get away with, and Charlotte came to Hope to win some sympathy that she was not getting at home. Hope allowed her to listen to the newest music on pirate radio, and although she did not think that miniskirts were pretty, she recognised that they were part of a youth rebellion that she approved of and thought was sorely needed to shake up English traditional values. Women were getting less satisfied with the roles they were expected to conform to, and so were the young men for that matter. They were growing their hair longer now and did not care when others teased them for being girlish or fags. Hope was a little surprised to find such sympathy in herself, but she could not help feeling that the wild-looking and anti-establishment youths had every right to seek their own alternative identity and new ideas to live by after half a century of insane wars and upheavals. At least the young men with their long hair and their mini-skirted girlfriends were mostly preaching peace and love. They reminded her of the interwar years that had given rise to free thinkers and bohemians. She had experienced some of that when she and Emily had visited Paris in 1930 and met the free spirits who had attempted to live their lives without bourgeois traditions and restrictions. They had been crushed in the end by the financial depression and then the terrible and dehumanising war. *Maybe their time was finally coming back, and she certainly would not be standing in their way.*

***

In 1967, colours had been introduced on British TV, and Wendy and Gordon had bought one of the new television sets that could receive colour programmes. By the end of the year, only the news was in black and white. All the technical and material progress was impressive, and it seemed that new wonders were put on the market every month. More and more people could afford to follow the newest trends, or so it appeared.

***

As the 1960s neared their end, Hope was feeling more and more tired. In the winters, her body ached in the mornings as she got out of bed, and she needed a lot of light to see clearly, so one day in the spring of 1967, she went to an ophthalmologist to have her eyes checked. She had been using spectacles for several years, so maybe her lenses needed adjusting. But the doctor told her that she was suffering from a clouding of the lenses called cataracts and that she would need eye surgery, or she might end up going blind. They set a date for the surgery on the eye that needed it the most, while the other eye might need surgery later. Wendy drove her to the hospital and waited while the procedure was done. It was unpleasant, but not painful, and when it was over, they sat for a while until Hope felt sufficiently recovered to walk to the car with Wendy supporting her arm. Her eye was covered by an eye patch, which she could remove after a few hours, and she had been given eye drops to use for two weeks.

The surgery turned out to have been very successful, so Hope went a month later to have the other eye done. After that, she felt much more confident in her daily life, and she could knit and sew without trouble. To her surprise, she noticed that a skirt she had bought a few years ago thinking that it was a plain dark blue was actually chequered in various shades of blue.

***

In the late summer of 1967, Hope decided to celebrate her eightieth birthday with a few friends and old colleagues from school. Wendy helped her arrange everything, and she sent out invitations. She even sent letters to her friends in Italy and Israel and told them that she would be eighty and would hold a small party, even though she did not expect any of them to come all the way to England. However, she received a long congratulatory letter from Antonio and his family. She was more worried about the welfare of her Israeli friends after the Six-Day War in June, and she was relieved when she received their letter, telling her that they were all fine but were sorry that they were not able to travel.

A surprise visitor turned up the day before the party, namely Emma. She had moved to London in the early 1960s and found work as an illustrator for women's magazines after her relationship with Felicia had come to an end. They had corresponded over the years but less after Emma had moved to London and built up a successful career. She had recently gotten her British citizenship, and when she suddenly knocked on Hope's door the day before the party, Hope was overjoyed.

"I am sorry to surprise you," grinned Emma, but Hope did not believe her for a minute. She was not sorry at all.

"You might have given an old woman a heart attack," Hope shot back and invited her in. "Sit down and let me make us a cup of tea."

Emma had brought some cakes from London, so they had them with their tea. They sat and talked for several hours, catching up on each other's lives. Emma loved living in London where she had made lots of new friends.

"My family came to accept that I was living with Felicia, but it was never talked about, and her family shut us out completely. In the end, we decided that we were making each other unhappy, so we split up and I decided to move to London, as you know. The first year was hard, but then my illustrations began to sell really well, and now I feel like a fish in the water."

"Have you found a new partner?" asked Hope cautiously.

Emma smiled. "I have found many," she said, "but not anyone in particular. You would probably call me promiscuous, but that seems acceptable in the circles where I move."

Hope had to admit to herself that she was somewhat shocked to hear this. She thought about it a moment before she answered. "As long as you are happy with your life, I will not call you anything. After all, I am going to be eighty tomorrow, and many things have changed in the world. I think changes are for the good, even if I do not understand all of it. You will be here tomorrow for my little party, won't you?"

"Of course," said Emma. "I am staying in Reading for a couple of days to do some business, but tomorrow I have set aside for your birthday."

An hour later, Wendy and Charlotte came by to make sure everything was all right for the following day. They were introduced to Emma, and Hope noticed that Charlotte seemed almost star-struck by this elegant Italian woman who now lived in London. Wendy was a bit more reserved, but after a while, they seemed to get along as they helped each other move the furniture around so that Hope's living room could seat all the ten guests that had been invited. With Emma and Hope, they would be twelve.

"I will come over at one o'clock to get the last things ready. I shall bring the extra things we need in the car, so you just get a good night's sleep tonight, Hope."

Emma, too, offered to come early to help, and Wendy thanked her and offered to take her back to the hotel she was staying at. However, Emma had come in her own car and did not need Wendy's offer. Around five o'clock, they all said goodbye and left.

Alone in her house, Hope thought about Emily. *What would their life had been like if Emily had lived? Out of her eighty years, Emily had been her friend and partner for about one third, but it still felt as if those years had been her real reason for living and the only time she had been really alive. No, she must not think like that.*

Hope felt suddenly ashamed at her lack of appreciation for the many good things that had happened in her life. *Taking in Anna had been a blessing for her. The realisation that there were others who needed her love and care for a while had certainly helped her keep her mind off her loss of Emily. And after the war…she cherished her years with Arthur and Amy in Jersey, her chance to revisit Naples and Antonio's family, her tenuous bonding with Emma… And after she had moved to Caversham, she had been lucky enough to meet with Wendy and Gordon, to live nearby them and share part of their life with them and Charlotte. All the students she had taught over the years who occasionally made contact…all of this had made her life so rich and full.*

Hope watched TV for a little while in her night dress before she went to bed.

***

The next day as her guests arrived, Hope noted briefly that they were all younger than her, but she enjoyed her little party. Wendy had arranged everything very well, and Charlotte, who was now fifteen years old, brought her boyfriend and the two were in charge of the music on the condition that they should keep it reasonably low. The lunch was arranged as a buffet in the kitchen, and the guests were encouraged to help themselves. They would then take their plates and glasses and find a place to sit in the living room or outside in the little garden. Wendy had brought some extra chairs so that all could be seated. Gordon and the three other men who attended the party, Henry, Robert and George, chose to sit in the garden most of the time. They were joined by Emma and occasionally, Charlotte and her boyfriend Tommy. Hope sat in her comfortable armchair in the living room, and on the sofa sat Henry's wife, Brittany, George's wife, Ethel and Robert's new girlfriend, Linda. Apart from Linda, Hope knew them all from the school and from frequent get-togethers at Wendy's place. Linda was new because Robert had recently been divorced, and so far, he had brought a new girlfriend every time they had been together.

Emma seemed to enjoy herself among the men, but she seemed especially interested in Charlotte's view of things and what she liked and disliked. Later, when they had all finished lunch, they moved around while Wendy and Emma cleared the things away and began washing the dishes. Emma had brought coffee and an Italian coffeepot where she brewed strong coffee for them all, and around half five, the three couples took their leave. Charlotte and Tommy gathered the records they had been playing and also left with Gordon who promised to come back later with the car for the rest of their things. Wendy and Emma put the living room furniture back in their original places, washed the cups and left everything as it had been before. Hope asked them to sit down for a little while, and she and Emma had another cup of the Italian brew. Wendy made herself a cup of tea, claiming that the coffee made her heart beat too fast.

"Thank you both for making this party possible," said Hope. "You have been magnificent, both of you."

"I am glad I could be here," said Emma. "You helped me during one of the most difficult times in my life."

Wendy added, "You have been an incredible support to me, too, and I am glad we could do this for you."

"What a lovely daughter you have," said Emma to Wendy. "I must admit that I used this opportunity to find out more about how young people think in order to target them better in the new illustrations I have been asked to bid for in a magazine for young people. If she wants a summer job, I would like to offer her one."

"That sounds great," said Wendy. "I will talk to her about it. I am not sure how good she is at drawing, but she is doing a lot of creative writing."

Gordon knocked on the door to pick up Wendy and the chairs and other stuff they had brought for the party. Emma got up too and helped put the things in the car. Then she came in to give Hope a big hug before she left, and she promised to come again soon.

***

By the end of the 1960s, not only a wealth of new consumer goods but also the many new social services that had been created made the country feel like the best of all worlds. There seemed to be no limits to what humans could do. When Russia had sent a manned flight in orbit around the earth in 1961, the Americans had followed that same year by sending Alan Shepard into orbit. President Kennedy had then announced that America would put a man on the moon before the end of the decade. Also, in medicine, great progress had been made when Christian Barnard had carried out the first heart transplant in 1967. These achievements promoted even wilder dreams, and a number of young people sought the fulfilment of those dreams in music, art and psychedelic drugs like LSD. But there seemed to be a less attractive side to the material progress. All over the world there were demonstrations against the senseless American war in Vietnam, which came right into people's living rooms through their television screens. In March in London, one such demonstration turned violent and several policemen were injured, and two hundred people were arrested.

On the fourth of April 1968, the non-violent civil rights activist, Martin Luther King Jr, was shot dead as he stood on the balcony of a motel in Memphis, Tennessee. His murderer was caught two months later in London and turned over to the United States. But that was not the end of senseless murders of famous figures in the United States. The next followed in June when John F. Kennedy's younger brother, Robert, who was looking very likely to become the next democratic candidate for president, was shot in a hotel kitchen in California.

Many young men and women, especially university students, struck out in anger and began to protest against their professors all over the world. In many places, the protests were met with violence by the authorities and the violence escalated. Somehow, that year, a lust for change had ignited a turning point for students as far apart as Japan, Mexico, Europe and America. In most cases, it began with a reaction against the rigid and old-fashioned structures in the universities, fuelled by the feeling that something was wrong with the world in general. Their protests spread to the streets and spilled over into political protests. Television helped spread the feeling of solidarity among the young internationally, and when students in Paris proclaimed that 'under the cobble stones lay the beach' young people everywhere grasped the symbolic sense of freedom and happiness lying just below them, ready to be liberated. Their feelings were magnified in their own languages and contexts, accompanied by music, and it spread inexorably. Although the specific authoritarian structures in different countries were of different hues, the idea that it was possible to revolt united the young people all over.

What kind of a world was it that they were expected to take over and perpetuate? Was it a fair world for all? Why did there have to be so much tension between east and west? Why did America send young people to die for a corrupt Southeast Asian regime? Why had the older generations of people made such a mess of everything, and why did they not listen to the young? Something had to be rotten in the very structure of the state establishments, so the fight against 'the establishment' became central, regardless of whether it was democratic or autocratic in its expression. Authorities had to be challenged and replaced, but nobody really agreed on what they should be replaced with. Naturally, 'the establishment' had to fight back at what they saw as anarchy and they put in police armed with teargas and water cannons and outfitted with shields and other protective gear. The students were throwing stones dug up from pavements and putting up barricades with whatever material was at hand, but it was an unequal fight, and occasionally, a young student was badly hurt or killed.

***

Hope and Wendy followed these developments closely. Wendy was worried about Charlotte's small rebellion against her parents and about her future education when she would leave home in a few years. They often argued when Hope seemed to take Charlotte's side, but Hope kept believing that the revolt of the young people would soon find a level with both sides settling down in a new equilibrium, at least in Europe. Wendy seemed more worried about what would happen if the young really rejected the parental authority and if teachers were forced to discuss with their students what they should teach. Hope could not help thinking of the panic many men had felt when women demanded a place in politics in her youth.

"I am sure they also thought that the world would go under if they allowed women to have political opinions then, but it did not, and everyone was better off when the men agreed to share their power."

Wendy could not disagree with that but argued that at least both parties had been adults.

"That is not what the men at that time thought," said Hope. "They honestly thought that women were weak, less intelligent, unable to think logically and so forth. We think that young people are childish, naïve and foolish, but how can we be so sure when we never allow them to talk about it or listen to them? I think we should take them seriously instead of just trying to shut them up. They might have new insights after all."

"But look at them," Wendy protested. "They do not dress decently, the boys have long, unkempt hair, and the girls are barely dressed. They do not wear shoes and apparently never wash their feet. They are barely civilised! How can one take them seriously, tell me that?"

"Oh, come on Wendy," said Hope. "Cleanliness and short hair were not a virtue a couple of hundred years ago, and as far as I know, even Jesus grew his hair and wore his feet bare and probably very dirty. Fashion changes, and how people dress has more to do with what is available and the kind of weather they live in. Going barefoot in summer when it is hot is actually very sensible, and when winter comes, I am quite sure that they will all start wearing socks and shoes."

Wendy had to admit that Hope made partly sense, so she changed her tack.

"Charlotte's newest idea is that she wants travel to Woburn where there will be a rock festival this summer. She wants to go with a group of friends to hear somebody called Jimi Hendrix play. They want to stay overnight in a tent. Gordon and I think she is too young to go. What do you think?"

"Woburn is not all that far away, and I would suggest that you or Gordon could drive her up there and pick her up the same day. Even if it is a two-day event, it seems that this American guitarist, Jimi Hendrix, is the main reason why she wants to go, isn't it? So how about making a compromise with her? I agree that she is too young to spend the night in a tent with her friends, but you could drive her there and take her home after the concert, couldn't you?"

"Well, she might accept that, but as far as I have been able to find out, he will come on stage as the very last performer on Saturday, so it might become very late before we can go back... Still, the next day is Sunday, so it might work. I will suggest it to Gordon and see what he says. But how can you be so permissive, Hope? I would have expected that someone of your age would be stricter, actually."

"I do not know, Wendy. Maybe because of my age, rather than in spite of it. I have experienced so much folly among adult people, so many people hurt because others thought they knew how to run the world. The young people today gather around rock music and ideals, they protest against war and advocate love, they wear colourful clothes which to me seems to be the opposite of military uniforms... I think they should have a chance. That is all. Nothing may come of it, but I just like them so much better than the fascists supporting Mussolini, the Nazis or the American and Soviet madmen who compete about who can first destroy the world. I would much rather see Charlotte being besotted by heavy rock music and the friendship of her peers than any other movement..."

Wendy thought for a while before she answered.

"But the militant students are throwing rocks at the police. You must admit that they are going too far, don't you agree?"

"I abhor violence, but I am not sure if the students are not simply reacting to the overwhelming and better armed police forces who are called in when they demonstrate. Anyway, I think we have to distinguish between the angry university students and the teenagers who care only about the music and their idols. There are some similarities in their behaviour and the music they listen to, but the music crowds are not violent, at least not yet. You must see that, Wendy."

"Hope, I love your wisdom and the way you think. You seem to be so well informed about everything. You have always been able to let me see the nuances of things more clearly and helped me expand my own views. You are such a precious friend and mentor. I will try to support Charlotte better, even if she can be incredibly annoying at times…"

"I wouldn't know about that," said Hope. "I have never had a mother or any daughters, just a very loving older sister, who was like a mother to me. I have read about mothers and daughters who cannot get along, but maybe it is inevitable that teenage daughters feel restricted by their mothers when they get old enough to find out what they want in life. They have only their mothers as a reference point to define themselves against, and so they rebel against that. They are probably bolder and more outspoken than previous generations, but I am pretty sure it is just a passing phase."

"I certainly hope so," sighed Wendy.

The Sunday after the Woburn festival, Wendy came over in the morning to tell Hope how it had been. "I drove her over there and left her with strict instructions about where to come out to find the car. Gordon drove up there around eleven o'clock in the evening and waited a little over an hour in the car, until the music finally stopped and the crowds of young people came out. It was rather dark, and it took them almost half an hour before they finally found each other. Charlotte brought three friends and asked if Gordon could drive them, too, so he spent another hour dropping them off in the neighbourhood. I heard them come in around four this morning, and they are still sleeping. Poor Gordon, he got the worst end of the stick."

"Did you hear how it had gone?" asked Hope.

"I got up for a few minutes when I heard them," Wendy said. "Charlotte had slept in the car, and when I asked her if she had enjoyed herself, she just said that it had been 'out of this world' and then she went off to bed. Gordon told me that he had ended up driving three teenagers home, and he was knackered, so we both went to bed. I promised to wake them both up around noon, so I thought that I might as well pop over to your house and put the kettle on to give you a brief report."

They sat for a while before Wendy had to go and wake up her sleeping family.

***

The following summer, they read about a music festival in America at Woodstock where 350,000 people had turned up and which seemed to have come off very well. In England, the Beatles played their last concert together from the roof of their production company, Apple

Records. After that, both Paul McCartney and John Lennon married, Lennon for the second time.

But as always, there were black spots that year as well. Charles Manson and his followers murdered five innocent people of whom one had been the very pregnant Sharon Tate, an actress married to the director Roman Polanski. Ted Kennedy, younger brother of John and Robert, got involved in a car accident when he drove his car off a bridge on the island of Chappaquiddick. He got out of the car and saved himself, but his passenger, who was a young girl, did not get out and was found later drowned in the car. This incident ruined the last chance of yet another Kennedy brother running for president. However, the promise of Jack Kennedy to put a man on the moon before the end of the decade was fulfilled when Neil Armstrong and Buzz Aldrin became the first humans to step from a spaceship and onto the surface of the moon.

1969 was also the year 'the troubles' between Catholics and Protestants began in Northern Ireland and Britain deployed troops to restore law and order. In America, Richard Nixon had been elected president, and he promised that the war in Vietnam would end soon. But in November, the story began to break about the My Lai massacre the year before, when over a hundred defenceless villagers had been killed in a shooting frenzy by American soldiers. As the world realised that the US government had tried to cover up the incident, resistance against the war grew stronger than ever.

In Caversham, Hope was picked up in the car by Gordon to celebrate New Years' Eve at their house. The 1960s had ended and a new decade would start.

Part Nine
Old Age

Hope woke up one morning a few days after the new decade had begun. She felt confused and thought, *I need my tea. It will clear my head.* She sat up and remained sitting on her bedside until she felt less dizzy. Then she got up and walked unsteadily into her kitchen and managed to put the kettle on and light the gas. She brought out her teapot and put in the tea leaves. Then she turned off the gas, but when she tried to lift the kettle to pour from it, she dropped it on the floor. The hot water spilled out from it, and shocked, she tried to take a few steps back away from the searing hot water, and then she slipped and fell to the floor. She lost consciousness for a few moments, but the pain from the burn she had got on her legs woke her up. Instinctively, she tried to stand, but to no avail, so she lay back and thought, *Is this it? Am I going to die now?*

Her next-door neighbour, who had heard the noise from the fallen kettle and Hope's cry of pain, came over and knocked on the door. When she got no answer, she went in and found Hope lying unconscious on the floor. She put a pillow under her head and covered her with a blanket before she went to the living room to find Hope's telephone. Then she called first an ambulance and then Wendy, who ran over and arrived breathless a few minutes before the ambulance and accompanied her friend to the hospital. Hope woke up in the ambulance but was only semi-conscious and apparently in some pain. Wendy spoke to her and held her hand before Hope slipped into unconsciousness again.

At the hospital, Hope was given painkillers and a thorough examination. The doctor could not explain her initial dizziness or how she had lost her grip on the hot kettle, but he said she might have suffered a small transient stroke to her brain. He assured her that she had not broken anything in her fall, but she had bad burns on her legs and feet, and she was bruised and might have suffered a minor concussion, so they would keep her a couple of weeks to treat her burn and observe her.

When Wendy and Charlotte came to visit her later that day, Wendy broached the idea of finding a nursing home for Hope.

"You should not be living all by yourself now; it is too dangerous. Let me look around for you at some of the possibilities."

Hope, who was feeling somewhat better now except for the still painful burns, said, "Don't put me away too soon, dearest. I think I can still manage on my own a while yet. You can look around at the possibilities, so we can discuss it, but I think I would miss my house and garden and all my friends and neighbours."

"I will look around just in case," said Wendy. "Is there anything I should bring you from your house when we come in tomorrow? I brought you a few of your toiletries and the book you were reading, but is there anything else you need?"

"I don't think so, but if you could bring me my daily newspaper now and then, I should be very happy."

After two weeks in the hospital, Hope was ready to go home. Her burns were healing gradually, and she would have to have a nurse come in every day for a while to check on her and to change her bandages. Her bruises were healing well, too, and she had taken several short walks in the hospital garden on sunny days. When Wendy drove her home, her neighbours had put up a banner saying 'Welcome home' and told her that they had set up a roster so that there would be someone looking in on her every day for the next two weeks. They would also take turns bringing her supper, so that she would not need to cook for herself.

Hope was grateful and touched at this evidence of the tight-knit community she had become a part of. She looked at Wendy and wondered if she was behind the whole thing, but Wendy seemed as surprised and happy as she was.

***

1970 saw the burgeoning of the women's movement. Wendy gave Hope Germaine Greer's new book, 'The Female Eunuch' for Christmas, and Hope duly read it although she could not quite share Wendy's enthusiasm for it. Nevertheless, she was enthusiastic to see women beginning to protest against male domination of everything. Voting rights had seemed such a fantastic step forward, but only a few women had been able or willing to take up the challenges of formal equality. Finally, something seemed to be happening.

As she entered the last decade of her life, Hope had withdrawn more into herself. The fuss over supersonic flight did not really touch her, but the space programme of the United States engaged her attention, and she imagined the future possibilities for mankind finding new worlds in space. If she had been born seventy years later and in the USA, she might have been an astronaut flying into space… It was a favourite fantasy of hers, and she read the books by Arthur C. Clarke and Isaac

Asimov with great pleasure. The protests against the Vietnam War had grown even larger and more violent, but Hope had stopped following the news as intensely as she used to. She had the TV on a lot, but she could no longer really think of the reports as real. She might follow what was being said, but she would forget it a moment later.

By the summer of 1972, Wendy broached the subject of a nursing home again. "Gordon and I are looking for a cottage in a village near Caversham, now that Charlotte has moved to London. With two cars, we shall still be able to keep working, but we would really like to live in the countryside when we grow older. We are planning to start looking for a place this summer."

"That sounds like a wonderful idea," said Hope. "I hope I can visit you there."

"Of course, you can," said Wendy. "You may even be able to have a room of your own for when you come. But before that, I would like to see you safely settled in a nursing home with people around you all the time to care for you. You are, after all, eighty-five now, and if you should fall again or anything else, I would like to know that you shall be taken care of."

"You are right," said Hope unexpectedly. "My eyesight is not what it was, and I am often dizzy. My body is full of aches and pains, especially in the winter time. I guess I am becoming forgetful, too. I think the time has come for me to find a nursing home to spend my last days in. Will you help me?"

"Certainly," said Wendy with relief. "I wanted to do so when you had your fall, but you convinced me that you would be all right alone then, and the neighbours promised to help. Shall I look around for a nice residential nursing home for you?"

"Yes, please, but not more expensive than I can afford on my pension and insurance."

Two months later in October, Wendy had found two residential care homes and came by to take Hope there for a visit. It was early October and rather cool, but the yellow and brown leaves fitted Hope's mood exactly. *I, too, am in the late autumn of my life*, she thought. *I am still clinging to my branch, but I hope I will be blown down gracefully by a gentle breeze when my time comes.*

***

The car had stopped in front of a large two-storied red brick building. "Here we are," said Wendy. "I have looked at two possibilities, and this is the first. They have sixty residents and a very good reputation for great care in any way possible. They have a very nice garden, too. Your room will be on the ground floor, since the upper floors are for those who need more care and are too weak to go out."

They went inside where they were met by a Mrs Hudson who showed them a nice room and the common living room, which she would share with the other ten people in her corridor. The room had its own toilet, and there were two bathrooms on that floor.

"If you decide to take our offer, we shall have a longer talk about your preferences. For now, I will bring you a cup of tea in the living room, so you can talk it over with your daughter." She left.

"She thinks you are my daughter," Hope said, surprised.

"Well, I would let her think so… it is almost true, isn't it? In spirit, I am your daughter, I think."

"I wish I had had a daughter like you," said Hope, "but I have never had any children…"

Mrs Hudson brought the tea on a nice silver tray and sat down and began to tell about all the activities they offered their residents, but Hope had already made up her mind. She did not really like this place, nor the woman sitting in front of her. There was nothing specific she could put her finger on. It was just a feeling that she did not fit in there, that she would never feel comfortable in this house.

They thanked Mrs Hudson for the tea and for showing them around, and then they got up and left. As soon as they sat in Wendy's car again, Wendy said, "I could feel that you didn't like it, right?"

Hope nodded. "I have nothing specific against it, but it felt wrong. Maybe it was the smell, maybe it was the sound of us walking in the corridor. I really do not know, but I did not feel that I could ever be comfortable there."

"Let's go and see the other one," said Wendy. "It is a smaller place with fewer residents, but it is also slightly more expensive."

They drove up in front of what looked like a yellow brick bungalow, but upon closer inspection revealed that buildings had been added to the side and the back. They were greeted at the door by a young girl, who took them into the living room and brought them tea while they waited for Mrs Henderson, who owned the place. After ten minutes, Mrs Henderson joined them and apologised for having kept them waiting.

"Welcome to our little place here. We call it St Luke's Residential Home, but we are not a particularly religious place. We have a gathering every Sunday after breakfast when we sing and have a nun or a priest give a talk for those who want to attend. But it is quite voluntary. On weekdays, we have a variety of activities that you can join if you like to. Let me show you the room we have available for you."

Mrs Henderson was a little younger than Wendy, somewhat on the heavy side with brown short hair and a friendly face. As they walked through an inner corridor to the side building where Hope's room would be, Mrs Henderson told them that she and her husband had built the house in 1961 after working a few years in the sector. "We wanted to offer a small place with no more than twenty residents, so that we could take proper care of everybody and give our guests a feeling of home. We have fifteen residents now but may add five more when we have finished the other side building. We have six gentlemen and eight ladies right now, so we have a room available for you, Miss Maundrell, if you should wish to move in this month."

Hope looked at the living room with its red velvet covered sofas and chairs, and she liked it. Then she and Wendy followed Mrs Henderson along the corridor to the side building, which was of a newer date. They turned a corner and entered another front room from which five different doors led into the rooms. All the doors except one had nice wooden signs with the inhabitants' names painted on them within a wreath of different flowers. Mrs Henderson opened the door without a sign and said, "This would be your room."

The room had light streaming in through two large windows, one of which was actually a glass door leading out to a miniature front porch and a large garden. It was a reasonably sized room with a hospital bed in one corner and otherwise empty. The floor was made of wood, but Mrs Henderson said, "You are welcome to put in a rug or two, but we don't like to cover the whole floor as it is easier to keep clean this way."

The walls were painted yellow, and again, Mrs Henderson said, "You can bring your furniture and hang your pictures on the wall as you like. We have a young man who can help you with everything of that sort. Mr Evans is his name, and he also keeps our garden for us."

She showed Hope the tiny kitchenette where she could boil water for tea or coffee and keep a few things. The bathroom seemed nice and surprisingly roomy. There was a shower, but Mrs Henderson said that they also had a room with a bathtub, where a nurses' assistant could help them take a nice hot bath when they wished.

Wendy tried the door to the garden and went out on the porch. It was a cool day, and when Hope joined her there, she said, "Come spring, I will help you plant some flowers and bushes out here."

Mrs Henderson quickly added from the door opening: "Mr Evans is planning to put up some partitions to the sides to give the residents more privacy and to provide some shelter from the wind."

"I like it here," said Hope. "I would like to move into this room if I may."

"Of course, you may," said Mrs Henderson. "When do you want to move in?"

"As soon as possible," Hope said, "but you had better decide on the exact day and time with Wendy, and she will also help make all the financial arrangements for me."

Wendy went with Mrs Henderson into her office to fill in the papers needed. Hope stayed in the living room until it became time for her to sign the papers. She felt suddenly extremely tired and almost tearful. *I have no energy left to start living in a new place and making new acquaintances. I wish I could just die and get it over with...*

Then she chided herself for her self-pity, and just then, two old ladies and an old man came into the room and greeted her. They had red cheeks and wind-blown hair, so Hope concluded that they must have been out walking.

"I am Hope Maundrell," she said. "I shall be moving in here very soon, so I guess we shall be seeing more of each other from now on."

The old man came over and held out his hand. "Welcome, Miss Maundrell. I am Tom Wesley, but please call me Tom. We are all on a first-name basis here."

"Then you must all call me Hope."

The two women introduced themselves as Lydia and Emily and welcomed Hope. Tom left them to go back to his room, but Lydia and Emily sat down to talk. Lydia was the widow of a merchant and had lived in the residential home for a year. Emily was unmarried and had been a teacher like Hope, and they agreed to have a longer talk about their respective lives and experiences after Hope had moved in. Hope felt a lot better after meeting Emily and began looking forward to getting to know her.

Then Wendy came back from the office to fetch Hope to sign some papers, so Hope said goodbye to the two women and went with Wendy back to Mrs Henderson's office. She signed the necessary papers and Wendy asked her if she would be ready to move in in two days' time when she and Gordon would be free to help her. Hope agreed, and they took their leave of Mrs Henderson, who handed them a drawing of the room with exact measurements so that they could decide what furniture Hope should take with her.

***

On the day that Hope moved in, the home held a small welcome party for her at teatime. Gordon, Wendy and Mr Evans had all helped her to get her furniture placed in the room: the comfortable chair next to her bed, a bookcase with her favourite books, a sofa and two chairs around a sofa-table, her TV-set and radio, her knitting basket, her tea kettle and some cups and tea spoons. In the bathroom, her toiletries and towels had been placed, and finally, the pictures she had selected for the walls had been hung. On top of the bookcase, she placed her precious photograph of Emily and herself as young women in Paris. On the walls hung a photograph of her sisters, Sarah and Eleanor, with Antonio standing between them. Anna's and David's wedding picture hung next to them, and below were smaller photographs of Wendy and Gordon with Charlotte, a colour photo of Charlotte from her graduation and a few others. She had more pictures in her albums, which she put in the upper drawer of her chest while other drawers held her underwear and stockings. The room had a built-in cupboard with shelves to one side and a place for hanging dresses to the other.

After a couple of hours, everything was in place, and Mr Evans excused himself to go and work in the garden. Gordon took off for work while Hope and Wendy made tea and sat chatting for a little while.

"I think I will really like it here," said Hope. "Thank you for helping me find such a nice place."

"Not at all," said Wendy. "We will come and see you every Sunday, and when you get your telephone installed, please call right away to let us know that it works. Then we can chat whenever we want to."

The bell for luncheon sounded, and Wendy got up to go. "Take care," she said. "I really hope you will like it here."

"Don't fuss about it," said Hope. "I will be fine."

They walked together to the common lunchroom, and Wendy hugged Hope goodbye and left. Hope went over to the table and introduced herself. "Is there anywhere in particular I should sit?" she asked, and Lydia and Emily, whom she had met the other day, beckoned her over to their table where Tom also sat. There was one more chair at the table, and soon, the fifth person appeared. He was very old with white hair and a beard, and he wore a conspicuous hearing aid.

"I am Jack," he said loudly to Hope. "Pleased to meet you. You must be Hope, aren't you? And hello to the rest of you. How are you today?"

He did not wait for an answer before he sat down.

"Hello, Jack," said Lydia in a loud voice. "How did you spend your morning?"

Jack adjusted his hearing aid on his chest and muttered, "Don't yell at me, woman." Then in a normal voice he said, "I read the newspaper and nodded off. Tomorrow, Denmark will have a referendum on whether to join the Common Market with us or not. Let's hope the poor bastards will do the right thing."

Hope cautiously asked him what he thought would be the right thing. "Speak up, woman," he said, and Hope repeated her question in a louder voice and tried to enunciate more clearly.

"They should vote yes," he said. "It's the only sensible answer for a small country directly attached to Germany. With the Americans to the west and the Soviets to the east, Europe must be united to keep the peace. Now that de Gaulle is no longer here, we finally have a chance to do just that."

"But Norway voted no," said Hope. "Don't you think that Denmark will stick with its Scandinavian neighbours?"

"Not if they have any sense," said Jack.

Hope found Jack too boisterous for her liking but was ready to excuse his bad manners by his hearing handicap. She looked around at the people at her table and wondered about them. She had liked Emily from the beginning but reserved her opinion about Lydia and Tom. As lunch came to an end, Mrs Henderson asked that they all come to tea at four thirty so that they could celebrate their new inhabitant, Hope, with a nice piece of cake and a song. She told the other inhabitants that Hope had been a teacher in London and here in Caversham.

After lunch, Emily invited Hope for a walk in the neighbourhood. They went and got their coats and walking shoes and went outside.

"It is funny," said Hope. "I used to have a very good friend named Emily just like you. She was a teacher, too."

"I think Emily was a very popular name in our generation," said Emily. "I must have known at least ten women with that name. What happened to your friend?"

"She died just before the war with Germany broke out," said Hope.

"Oh, I am sorry to hear that."

"Were you a teacher during the war?" Hope asked.

"Yes," said Emily. "I was born in 1890 and finished my teacher's training just after the Great War. I taught primary school in Liverpool and lived a quiet life until the next war came and the blitz began. During the war when most of the children were evacuated and the school, which was very near the harbour, was closed, I went to Scotland and taught school there in a small village where I had an uncle. Their only teacher had gone to join the army, so I took over from him and stayed there until 1945. Then I returned to England and found a teaching job here in Caversham, where I also had some family."

"My school moved its whole operation to Huntingdon in Cambridgeshire where we stayed until late 1943. I had a young Jewish girl from Vienna, Anna, staying with me during the war. Both her parents got killed, and after the war, she moved to Israel with her husband. I visited them some years ago in Tel Aviv where they live now with their four children."

"How exiting," said Emily, "and what a wonderful thing to do. Are you Jewish, too?"

"Not at all," replied Hope and smiled. "My parents were Anglican missionaries in Japan. It is a long story, which I will save for another time. Now tell me a bit more about St Luke's and the people we live with."

"Well," Emily began, "as you have already noticed, there are five of us who live in one wing. There are two other wings just like it with five people in each. A fourth is being built, so eventually, there will be twenty of us old age pensioners. Our wing has you and me, and then there is Lydia, Tom and Jack. Jack is ninety years old and as you have noticed at lunch, pretty hard of hearing. He does not speak much about his past, but we all think that he must have been a sailor or an officer in the military because of the gruff way he speaks. He follows the news very closely and tries to tell us what we should think about them. He is very opinionated."

"I gathered as much," Hope commented.

"Then there is Tom, who is eighty-eight years old, I think. He was married once and has five children who occasionally visit him. He was a cabinetmaker and is very mild-mannered and gentleman-like in his behaviour. He and Jack do not get along and rarely speak to each other. The last one is Lydia. She is the youngest one of us, I think. She refuses to say how old she is, but I guess she is in her late 70s. She has been a well-to-do housewife and she has three daughters who almost never visit. Poor Lydia! I have no children, so at least I do not have to go through that kind of disappointment. Do you have children, Hope?"

"No," said Hope, "not any of my own. But Anna was like a daughter to me, and before Emily died, we had an Italian boy, Antonio, who lived with us in his holidays from boarding school. His father was English and wanted his oldest son to go to a British boarding school, so my family and I helped with that."

"I see," said Emily, although she did not quite see. By then, they had turned back and were approaching St Luke's again. "I must hear more about all that, but we will have lots of time to talk later. Now we had better get back and have a nap before tea."

Hope did not usually nap in the daytime, but when she was back in her room, she lay down on her bed to rest a little and before she knew it, she was asleep. She woke up an hour later and felt quite refreshed as she washed her face and combed her hair. There was a knock on her door as Mrs Henderson came to take her to the dining room for tea.

"Have you settled in already?" she asked Hope.

"Yes, thank you. I went for a walk with Emily and then I napped for almost an hour."

"Well, that is nice," said Mrs Henderson as they entered the dining room. She accompanied Hope to her seat and then clapped her hands to get everybody's attention.

"Let me introduce our new member of the St Luke's family, Miss Eva Hope Maundrell. She is very welcome here, and I hope you will all help her and make her feel welcome. Would you like to say a few words, Hope?"

Hope was a little surprised to be asked, but she stood up and said, "Please call me Hope, everybody. I am a former school teacher from London, but I have lived here in Caversham since 1953, and I look forward to getting to know you all."

She sat down, and some applauded. Mrs Henderson suggested that they sing a song before they started on the tea, and she sat down in front of the piano and started playing. They sang '*Happy days are here again; the skies above are clear again...*' and everybody pitched in as best they could. The jazzy melody cheered up everybody, and after that, they got served a sumptuous tea with finely cut sandwiches, scones with clotted cream and finally, a sugar-decorated sponge cake with a layer of vanilla cream.

***

The days went by in a quiet rhythm, and on most Sundays, Wendy would visit, sometimes with Gordon. Charlotte came whenever she was back in Caversham, but she was living in London now, so it was not often. Jack died that winter, and a new inhabitant took his place. Hope and Emily grew closer and often visited each other's rooms, where they spent long hours talking about their past experiences or watching television together. The news was full of 'the troubles' in Ireland and 'Bloody Sunday' in January was followed by several violent bombings in London by the Provisional Irish Republican Army. Neither Hope, nor Emily had ever been to Ireland, and they found it hard to fully understand the feelings, which fuelled the conflict. Was it primarily a religious conflict between Protestants and Catholics, or was it more an endless anti-colonial fight? Both of them could see that Catholics had reasons to feel badly treated by the Ulster Protestants who kept them from jobs and privileges, and it all went back to the fact that the British had moved into the northern parts of Ireland in the 16th century and acquired land and prospered, while the original Gaelic population had been left behind socially and culturally. To Hope and Emily both, it seemed silly to continue to uphold a divided island just off Britain's coast, when the greater part of that island had won its independence in 1921 and become a country in its own right.

Israel was at war again, and as usual, Hope worried for the safety of her Israeli friends. When she got a letter from Anna telling her that their oldest son Akiva had lost his life in the war, she could hardly bear it. She looked at the photo of the bright and clever little boy she had met in 1959 in Tel Aviv, and she wept bitter tears. *What a terrible waste!* Mostly she was sad for Anna who had to be heart-broken over this loss. *Does it never end?* she thought. *Will this world always be so cruel and merciless? Why, oh why?* When Emily sought to comfort her by referring to man's inability to fathom God's plans, she almost exploded.

"Do not speak to me of God! I do not believe he exists. And if he does, he is a sadistic monster!"

Emily fell silent at this outburst, and they tacitly agreed never to speak of God again.

America was also in the news as the world watched Richard Nixon's pathetic attempts to reassure his people that he was 'not a crook.' As it turned out, he was just that, and when impeachment procedures were started in 1974, he stepped down, and his vice-president, Gerald Ford, became president. The Americans had withdrawn their troops, but the war between north and south continued with American support of the South Vietnamese government. Sympathy was with the North Vietnamese troops, and the protesters yelled *Ho, Ho, Ho Chi Min!* as they walked hand in hand down the streets. The North-Vietnamese forces had gradually moved south, and the fighting ended in 1975 when the last Americans in Saigon were evacuated from the roof of the American embassy. Hope and Emily watched the television coverage, and Emily said, "Why did they even go over there and get involved?"

"Well, they felt they had to fight world communism, didn't they? It is all part of the Cold War and the 'domino theory'—the Americans are just terribly afraid of communists. Wasn't it the Americans who coined the phrase, 'Better dead than red'?"

Emily laughed. "I learned that one as 'Better red than dead' in the late 1950s. That was what we said in the anti-nuclear movement."

"You are right," said Hope. "I was part of that, too. I was in the first Aldermaston march with my good friend Wendy and her husband. Were you there, too?"

"No, I never marched," said Emily, "but I admired those who did. Not that it did much good—the world still has enough nuclear weapons to destroy itself several times over."

"That is true," admitted Hope, "but if good people do nothing, there is no hope at all, I suppose."

They sat quietly for a while and reflected on that. Finally, Hope said, "We may not be able to do anything much anymore at our age. I am glad we have televisions nowadays because they have become like windows to the world."

"Yes," said Emily, "but we are just spectators now, aren't we? It is not really our world anymore. The line between fiction and reality has become very thin. The only thing that feels real now is this place, and I am getting more interested in what we are having for dinner than who wins what war…"

"True enough," said Hope. "What are we having, by the way?"

"Welsh rabbit, I think," said Emily, and they got up from their chairs and went to the common living room to go through the day's newspapers until dinner time.

***

1976 presented the hottest and driest summer on record in Britain. All through the summer months there was no rain, and it was sweltering. Hope and Emily spent most of their days in the shade in the garden together with the other residents or lying lethargically on their beds. The staff brought cold water or tea with ice cubes and encouraged everybody to drink as much as they could. Electric ceiling fans were installed in the common areas, and that helped a little, but several inhabitants got ill from the heat and were taken to the hospital, and some never came back. Finally, in the last days of August, thunderstorms broke and were followed by rain. The rain kept on falling through September and October and temperatures went down. Hope had felt all right during most of the hot months, but Emily suffered a great deal. Their daily walks resumed in September but became shorter and shorter. In February 1977, Emily became ill and stayed in bed. Hope visited her room every day, but Emily did not get better. She died in March, and Hope felt very sad and lonely afterwards. *This is the second time I lose an Emily,* she thought. *I cannot bear more losses…*

When Wendy came alone to see her that Sunday and brought her flowers and chocolate to celebrate her ninetieth birthday, Hope was morose and depressed. She thanked Wendy for her presents, and Wendy tried to cheer her up with stories of Charlotte and Gordon, but all Hope could say was, "I am tired, Wendy. I don't really want to live anymore."

"But spring is coming soon," said Wendy. "You will feel better when we have green leaves and flowers in the gardens. The skies will be blue again; please do not despair, Hope."

Hope tried to smile for her old friend. "Don't worry, Wendy. I will be fine again. I just miss Emily to talk to. I know I have been blessed to have known so many wonderful people, including you and your family. I will feel better tomorrow, I promise."

When summer came, Hope was feeling much more positive and happier every day. She had become forgetful and needed more help from the staff. Much of the time she spent lost in her memories, and when Wendy came to visit her, she often called her Emily or Sarah. One evening in February 1979, she went to sleep, and when morning came, she was found dead in her bed. She appeared to have died peacefully in her sleep.

Her funeral was very small. Wendy and Gordon arranged it, Charlotte came from London together with Emma, who brought a wreath from Antonio and her family, and Anna sent a telegram from Tel Aviv. A few of the staff from St Luke's were there, too. Hope had outlived all her contemporaries, and she had not wanted a religious funeral, so she had been cremated and her urn had been set down in the Garden of Remembrance. There were no sad tears among the mourners, and when the brief ceremony was over, Wendy invited Charlotte and Emma for dinner before they would return to London.

Hope had lived her life, and now it was over. It had been a long life, she had loved and lost, she had survived two world wars, and all through that, she had been uniquely her, like every one of us is, both unique and ordinary.

THE END